ON GUARD

ON GUARD

KELS & DENISE STONE

BETWEEN THE SHEETS
PUBLISHING

Published by Between the Sheets Publishing

betweenthesheetspub.com

Copyright © 2025 Between the Sheets Publishing LLC

Paperback ISBN: 978-1-964675-13-8

EBook ISBN: 978-1-964675-04-6

On Guard

Editing & Proofreading:

Caroline Acebo at Brass House LLC

Caroline Knecht

Christine Yates

Cover Design: Chloe Friedlein

Being good doesn't always mean following the rules.

Chapter 1
Reese

Are They More Than Co-Stars? Sparks Fly Between Reese Sinclair & Jaxon Elio After *Love and Loathing* Filming Wraps!

"Smooth and thick, one little lick will do the trick!" I recite the nonsensical campaign slogan. My advertising smile is pristine as I balance on the unsteady edge of a diving board. It's only a few feet above a vat of yogurt—a vat that is making the entire set of the 'Gurt commercial smell like a tangy nightmare.

"That's the one, Reese! Let's prepare for the jump!" the director, Roland, hollers from his fortress of lights and equipment. The crew scurries around me, their walkie-talkies crackling with urgency as they reposition lights and adjust markers.

I glance below one more time at the creamy substance swirling lazily. It could so easily suck me in, envelop me, suffocate…

Maybe this is a bad idea. There's still time to revise the script. I'm sure the director would make an exception.

No—I can't be difficult.

"Ready, sir," I announce, squaring my shoulders and lifting my chin.

"Excellent! Let's see some Reese Sinclair magic, darling!"

I force myself to take three deep breaths. Inhale for four, hold for seven, exhale for eight.

You are Reese Sinclair. You can dive into anything and emerge looking like you've been kissed by a rainbow.

Be radiant. Be flawless. Be yogurt-proof.

Be perfect, Reese.

Perfect.

Bending at the knees, I leap feet-first off the diving board in five-inch heels. My '50s-style skirt billows around me like a pastel parachute. With a disturbingly wet splat, I land in the thick liquid, maintaining absolute control over my skirt like I'm Marilyn Monroe atop a subway grate.

"Your creamiest desires come alive with every bite," I purr, with a hint of my southern charm. I maintain perfect posture in the lukewarm yogurt bath, mentally cataloging every detail that went wrong—the way my left foot landed first, sending an awkward ripple through the surface, and the tiny splash of yogurt that hit my cheek, probably messing up my makeup.

"That's it! You're sailing through this!" Roland's enthusiasm bounces off the studio walls.

"Roland, I know we're on a schedule, but"—I make eye contact with each crew member, acknowledging their exhaustion —"I'd really appreciate one more take. That one wasn't quite there." I gesture at my yogurt-drenched outfit with a self-deprecating laugh. "Promise it's the last time you'll have to dunk me today."

He considers it. "Alright, people! Final take! Let's make it count!"

Under the hot studio lights, a wardrobe assistant efficiently swaps out my soaked skirt and shoes for fresh ones, dabbing at my blouse. The props team levels out the pool of goop. We roll again. This time, everything clicks—the timing, the product placement, the unnecessarily sexual tagline.

"Good girl, Reese! Exactly what we needed!"

The praise lands wrong, making me bristle. Nearly twenty years in this industry, and I'm still fighting the same battles— being the perpetual good girl, America's golden sweetheart.

"Thank you all so much for your patience today." I smile and gesture at the yogurt soaking me. "Who needs a spa day when you've got probiotics by the gallon?"

The crew laughs politely. A production assistant steadies my arm as I carefully step out of the slippery bath.

"Thank you, hun," I say to the PA just as Heather, my agent, materializes beside me, neat as a pin in her silver bob and signature tailored suit.

"Take this and let's move," she says, handing me a mint, already striding toward my trailer. I follow her, ignoring the squelch of yogurt between my toes.

Heather's an industry titan. She's managed some of the biggest stars through the years and has been shepherding me through the industry since I was a spunky, pigtailed eleven-year-old on *Clubhouse*. These days, she's narrowed down her client base to work with only her favorite people.

Translation: her real moneymakers.

Double translation: me.

"Do you think I said *creamiest* weird? You know when you say a word too many times it starts sounding made-up?" I ask, catching Heather's dismissive look but continuing. "*CREAM*-ee-est. Cream-*EE*-est," I mutter under my breath, stepping over the taped-down cables running through the set.

"Reese, it was flawless. *You're* flawless. But if you'd like to take fewer yogurt baths, we need to stop being so selective with the scripts."

She's not happy with me. I have a three-month pile of

rejected projects that probably weighs as much as a sculpture from City Park back home in New Orleans.

"The roles aren't challenging enough," I remind her, kicking off my heels and ascending the stairs to my makeup trailer. From my stainless-steel mini-fridge, I grab an iced tea for me and a Diet Coke for Heather. "They're…"

The words hang in the air. In the world of carefully scripted kisses and airbrushed love, I'm as successful as they come. But with just one more year until the big 3-0, I worry my days of starring in romantic comedies are numbered.

Aniston fought the same battle, trapped in the rom-com box because heaven forbid we allow pretty women to be complicated. At least she broke free in her thirties, proving she could do more than merely make audiences comfortable.

For a woman in Hollywood, getting older is practically a death sentence. If I can't demonstrate that I'm an actress with range, I might as well sign up for water aerobics and 4:00 p.m. dinners now. I refuse to fade into the background playing mothers and quirky sidekicks to some twenty-year-old's great romance.

The next movie I choose is my chance to land a messy, complex role. I need a character who has more on her mind than finding Mr. Right—a film where I get to feel in control, come into my power, and be fearless.

I want more.

I *need* more.

"They're your bread and butter, Reese," Heather states, settling in at the tiny table in the middle of the trailer and popping open the tab on her Diet Coke. "Those scripts are what you excel at. Quantum Media Group is begging for you to sign on to a new film. The signing fee alone could pay for a new summer home for us both."

"Heather," I plead, fidgeting with the label on my bottle of tea. "One summer home is plenty!"

"Maybe for you, darling." Her expression remains granite-solid. "Besides, we should focus on your second *Vogue* cover this weekend. Have you prepared for your interview?"

The vapid interview questions already echo in my mind:

Who was a better kisser, Chalamet or Powell? Be honest! Chalamet, though a lady would never admit that.

What's your secret to staying so thin? Forcing myself to resist my favorite carbs.

Is Reese Sinclair dating anyone new? Sorry, I only fake-date my costars.

"My plan was to sell *Love and Loathing*." My newest film is about a clumsy but gorgeous real estate agent who keeps getting flustered around her client, whose steely gaze and perfectly tailored suits make her forget how to operate basic elevator buttons. "And Geraldine can prep me with some other good gems that will keep people entertained." My publicist is a genius when it comes to question-dodging.

"Ger can't help you lie through the *What's next for you?* question, sweetheart. But maybe you can keep the conversation bubbling about your relationship with Jaxon."

"*Fake* relationship," I remind her. Selling my kind of movies usually means selling a lie that I'm dating my latest costar. As if standing on my own is too much for the public to bear.

"The fans don't need to know that."

"Are you sure no other scripts have come your way? An indie film? A wayward drama? I'd work for free for the right project!" I slide across from her, slumping forward on the table.

Heather studies me, pursing her lips as if reluctant to share something. "Lawrence just dropped out of *Robyn Hood.* But, Reese—"

My spine straightens. "Status?"

"Still happening," she says, arching her perfectly manicured eyebrow at me. "Their casting agent inquired about your previous audition, but—"

"Book it."

Earlier this spring, I auditioned for a gender-bent Robin Hood role in which Robyn transforms from a cunning thief into a fierce warrior determined to save her town from a greedy king. An R-rated film with violence and cursing. No romance. No manufactured chemistry with the latest heartthrob—just raw storytelling about lawlessness and corruption.

I'd never felt more alive during an audition. Yet they initially chose an actress with prior action-movie experience. Someone who hadn't spent years trapped in the sugar-plum prison I'd meticulously built for myself.

This is my chance to gain control over my image.

"Reese, we already talked about this. Felix Langford is directing. And you know how I feel about him." Heather plays with the tab on her aluminum can.

Sure, he has a reputation for treating women like set pieces to be gawked at, yet he remains one of the most esteemed action directors of our time.

"I do, but people change. He did agree to do his first female-led movie, so maybe he's growing."

"Growing? More like the studio's chasing trends, throwing around terms like *female empowerment*. We both know Langford's idea of empowerment is showing half-naked women doing roundhouse kicks. Your talent deserves better."

"No, my talent deserves to be stretched and challenged. Doing a Langford movie will open so many more doors for me."

"There will be other roles like this one."

With Heather in her sixties, I don't want to explain that I'm afraid of aging out of my niche. I have to start taking charge of my life. She may be my agent, but I still get the final say here.

"I can handle him," I promise. "Maybe we can learn something from each other."

"There's a charming rom-com about an environmentalist with a cat—"

"I want *Robyn Hood*," I state firmly, finally unscrewing my tea and taking a swig.

Nonnegotiable.

Heather's forehead creases. She wants to argue. "Filming begins mid-August, with a scheduled three-day table read a few weeks prior. The production team is specifically looking for an actress capable of performing her own stunts. The physical training required for this role—"

"Will be handled."

All great actresses go through metamorphosis for their characters. I am destined to be a great actress.

"It films in Redwood National Park. Two-hour flight from LA, you'll be back and forth for months."

"I can do that."

"Are you sure, Reese? We've built a reliable reputation here. This role may change the trajectory of your career."

Anxiety coils around me. Part of me wants to acquiesce and say forget about it. But the other part of me, the one that's tired of being in a box, wants to push myself.

I'm capable of so much more, regardless of the director.

"I need this." I reach across the table and rub the back of Heather's hand with my thumb. She's been like a second mother to me all these years; I know she only wants the best for me.

She exhales, drops our grip, and immediately springs into action, pulling out her phone. Without looking at the keyboard, she types out a message. "We'll need to prepare a press release. Geraldine and I have a ton of work to do!"

I barely register her words, my mind already racing through the transformation ahead.

The training.

The preparation.

This is my moment.

A knock comes from the trailer door. "Ready for the spoon scene, Miss Sinclair!"

I can endure one last yogurt-soaked humiliation because now I see it as a mere stepping stone on my way to becoming more than the actress I've been told I can be.

8   Kels & Denise Stone

Chapter 2
Dante

BETWEEN ENDLESS ROUNDS of drinks and the blur of faces, I've lost track of all my hours and minutes. Laughter cascades across the Mediterranean as sun-kissed bodies launch themselves off my yacht's gleaming deck. The August sun blazes down on the French Riviera. It's been a summer of pure decadence. Of lapping up what pleasures and beauty the world has to offer. Of forgetting I should be in my mask and plastron right now.

From my perch in the salon, I watch my company mill about. The goddess on my lap—Alessandra? Anastasia?—runs a finger over the tattoos on my neck as she chatters with the group around me. Her barely-there bikini leaves little to the imagination.

Another pretty distraction that won't last past sunrise.

My favorite kind.

My gaze flashes to the muted TV hanging over the bar. Someone had the genius idea to flick on the Tokyo Olympics. I'm inexorably drawn to the screen, where the first men's Saber team match is unfolding. The same event I took gold in four years ago.

I'm too sober for this.

"Be a dear and fetch me a drink, would you?" I tap on Alessandra's thigh and reach for my unbleached cigarette papers and imported French tobacco—a vice, one I would never turn to if I were in competition, but fuck it. What more do I have to lose?

The chipped nail polish on my fingers looks like blood. I roll the cigarette, my fingers moving over the paper with the same precision that makes me deadly on the fencing strip.

Made, I correct. *Made* me deadly.

I light my cigarette with a vintage Zippo, inhaling deeply to allow the smoke to burn and plume within my lungs.

My eyes flit back to the screen. There they are—my U.S. Fencing teammates, standing on the sidelines and on the piste.

Competing without me.

The camera flashes to him. Quentin Brisbois.

I white-knuckle the armrest, feeling the phantom hilt of the saber in my hand before I'm transported back to Budapest, where everything went to hell in the most righteous way possible.

The Fencing World Cup. A week after my twenty-sixth birthday.

The beginning of the end.

I'd solidified my spot for the Olympics months earlier. This match was supposed to be a breeze. A stop on my road to defending gold.

I was running through my pre-match routine when I saw Quentin Brisbois swaggering over to me. He'd been the thorn in my side at every competition. Always trying to get in my head before matches with his mind games and insufferable sneer. His blade work is solid enough, but his real talent is being a first-class pain in the ass.

He cornered me by the equipment check, away from prying ears. "Saw you with Linus earlier. Heard you two are quite close."

"He's my teammate, Quentin. Can you get fucking lost? I'm getting in the zone."

Quentin's smile turned predatory. "Can't help but think how…*intimate* some teammates can be. Personally, I never took a dip in my teammates' pool. But maybe you and Linus don't mind breaking that particular taboo."

My blood ran cold. That night with Linus flashed through my mind—post-semifinals victory, adrenaline running high, stolen moments in the locker room. His first kiss with a man, desperate and searching.

For me, it was another night of fun, but for him? It was everything—his identity, his career, his family relationships—all balanced on the edge of a blade.

I saw the terror in his face afterward, his hands shaking as he made me swear secrecy. I planned to guard his secret as carefully as I protected my flank in competition. Not because I was involved, but because Linus trusted me with something so fragile.

"Watch your fucking mouth, Quentin, or I'll shut it for you," I said.

The World Cup arena blurred around me.

"Such compromising positions, *mon petit champion.*" Quentin's voice dripped poison. "Imagine the photos I could share. What would happen if his father found out—he's quite the traditionalist, from what I hear. How would sweet Linus handle being disowned before the Olympics in a few short months?"

Photographs? That would be fucking impossible. Unless someone broke into our locker room. Quentin had done petty shit before, but this would be a new low.

Growing up a Hastings meant mastering the art of defense against threats and jealous tongues. I've deflected countless attacks at galas, charity events, anywhere the elite gathered to whisper.

But this wasn't another social bout.

This was fencing. My sanctuary. Where I'd transformed from the dyslexic, fucked-up rich kid into someone worthy of respect. My teammates came to me for technique tips, studied my footwork, watched with reverence as I commanded the piste.

They saw me as their champion, and like hell I'd let this snake poison what we'd built.

"If you didn't hear me before, I'm going to shut your mouth for you. Get fucking lost."

"*Mais non*, Dante. I've already sent photos to my friend at *Sports Illustrated*. One word from me and they go public. Wouldn't want the U.S. team to lose an up-and-coming fencer like Linus to such a *scandale*, would they?"

The threat was enough.

The crowd faded to white noise. My vision narrowed like it does before a crucial match, everything crystallizing into perfect focus. Protective instincts surged like an inferno.

Quentin pulled back, getting a good look at the fire burning in my eyes, but my fist was already flying. It connected with his nose in brutal slow motion—a sharp crunch, a shockwave up my arm, and the bloom of crimson on his pristine white uniform.

After I punched him, I grabbed Quentin by his collar, yanking him close as blood ran down his chin. Fear replaced his smugness.

"That's what gets your rocks off, huh? Ruining someone's life for sport? Say you'll never breathe a word about Linus again."

"I won't! I swear it! I don't have photos, I was bluffing." His voice cracked, his panic evident. "I won't say anything."

I knew he was telling the truth. Quentin was a coward at heart. But the damage was already done.

My coach, Lev, screamed in Russian. Before the crowd could gasp, security materialized, dragging me out of the arena.

The fallout came fast.

The United States Fencing Association committee has a zero-tolerance policy for violence, and SafeSport doesn't take context into account. They wouldn't care about Quentin's words or his threats. All they saw was me—fist raised, temper flared, reputation shattered.

Suspended.

For one full year. Pending disciplinary review.

Banned from every U.S. Fencing event until next May. Not allowed to compete, attend, view, or be near fencing.

And to top it off, I have to spend the year doing community service.

I was stupid, reckless, arrogant. I know better. In fencing, there's no room for hesitation. You react. Instinct takes over. That's what always made me one of the greats, the ability to move first and think later.

But this time, acting before thinking cost me everything.

If I'd waited. If I'd let it go. If I'd handled it the way I should have, I might be standing in that stadium with my team, wearing red, white, and blue, competing against the best in the world.

The memory of Quentin's sneer dissolving into shock. Knowing I'd protected Linus from that bastard's threats, I can't bring myself to fully regret it.

Even if I'm here.

My life on pause.

It's all so vivid I forget where I am. Forget I'm not supposed to care anymore.

I drag my cigarette until the taste of the filter fills my mouth and will those memories back into the recesses of my mind where they belong.

"Here's your drink, Dante." The beautiful woman who was here earlier returns with a perfectly crafted Manhattan. "Shouldn't you be up there with the rest of them?" She gestures toward the TV.

Everyone turns to face me.

They all read the headline: *Dante Hastings Suspended from*

United States Fencing Association and the U.S. Olympic Fencing Team. Yet they're starved to know the real reason behind my punch, not the fluffed news coverage.

I toy with the idea of lighting another cigarette as I formulate my response, ignoring the way my chest tightens at their scrutiny.

Finally, I flash her my most charming smirk. "Why settle for a gold medal when I can have a yacht full of golden goddesses?"

The group erupts in laughter, though the reality is I've spent the last two months numbing my existence at the bottom of bottles and meaningless hookups. My fingers drum against the Olympic rings I have tattooed on my upper thigh.

It's enough to satisfy her curiosity, and she makes a move to reclaim her spot on my lap. I stand in one fluid motion, my six-foot-two frame towering over her.

I need to get away from the television.

"Jerry," I call out to my bartender, "can you be a good man and turn that off? And while you're at it, crank up the music."

The music shifts to Euro house. The kind of sound that drowns out thought and makes you forget that anything exists. The kind that makes you forget you're watching your team compete without you.

Perfect.

"Why don't we take this out onto the deck?" I wrap my ring-embellished fingers around my drink and gently place my free hand on the small of the woman's back.

The sun seeps into my bones as I adjust my sunglasses. My bare chest glistens with a sheen of sunscreen.

"Dante, my love!" Amara Bellamy's melodic voice floats across the deck like expensive perfume. She's sprawled on a chaise, her skin glowing in the sunlight. At her side, Mei Wei and Tiago Fernandez are soaking up the sun. The three of them are part of my entourage from Princeton, all kids from families like mine—too much money in their hands and a ravenous taste for fun.

"Mari!" I call out her pet name, gliding over to her.

"You simply must dish about your upcoming adventure," Amara purrs.

"Wouldn't want to spoil the mystique."

"Oh, please," Amara laughs. She's one of Hollywood's most acclaimed directors, with two Oscar wins this year for her latest groundbreaking, character-driven film. "I'm on my self-imposed exile from the machine, pursuing my artistic awakening or whatever. The least you can do is keep me entertained with gossip while I'm pretending to enjoy my hiatus."

"My agent pulled me into *Robyn Hood*. They needed someone who actually knows their way around a sword, both as a consultant and for the role of the sheriff." I lean back. Todd used his connections, and he helped me land a job that finally puts my Princeton theater degree to use. "A corrupt lawman with a penchant for swordplay? It's practically typecasting. Besides, it'll keep me sharp for my triumphant return to the piste." Before anyone can dwell on that last part, I add smoothly, "And naturally, you'll all have prime seats at the July premiere."

The Manhattan in my hand can't quite mask the bitter truth—I'm filling time. A year of suspension stretches before me like an endless void.

But Dante Hastings doesn't wallow.

He reinvents.

Princeton's theater scene taught me that spectacle masks pain beautifully. Hollywood will adore me—I'm their catnip.

A Hastings pulled away from sport for a big-screen debut.

"Is it true that you'll be on set with Reese Sinclair?"

"Jennifer Lawrence was their first choice, but she's off doing some pretentious Nolan thing." I wave my hand dismissively. "Sinclair's the consolation prize."

"She's absolutely divine!" Mei gushes. "We were at

Wilhelmina's charity thing last month—a dreadfully boring affair—but Reese was just delightful. A true darling."

"Are you planning to turn America's good girl bad?" Susan Martin from the *Stone Times* interjects, her martini untouched beside her notebook.

The reporter's here because I want her to be—better to feed the press stories about my indulgent escapades than let them focus on the reality of my grim situation. This way, I control the narrative.

"Hardly." I brush her off. "Reese Sinclair is not my type of woman—far too sugarcoated for my liking." Sure, as a teenager, I had a poster of her taped up on my bedroom wall, but who didn't at that age? Nowadays, I prefer a taste of someone more sour and full-bodied. "Besides, remember, I'm a changed man this year." I raise my glass in mock solemnity. "I have to be good."

"But, Dante!" One of the models Tiago invited last night frowns.

What the press doesn't know can't hurt me.

I lean over to her. "What happens behind cabin doors, though?"

"No one needs to know." She giggles, and I grin, letting the façade of innocence settle in place.

"Find it hard to believe Reese is slumming it in a Langford action film." Susan taps her pen against her notebook. "It's so pedestrian."

"America's sweetheart probably needs a taste of something stronger than vanilla rom-coms," I drawl.

Mari looks at me over her Chanel sunglasses. "Dante, you absolute devil. Some of us actually admire her work."

"Maybe I'll give her a cultural exchange. My world of champagne and scandal for her world of sweet tea and southern charm."

"Sources say she's still mourning her fling with Jaxon Elio," Susan says.

"I saw an early showing of *Love and Loathing*, and they were marvelous together," Mei chimes in. "But if those rumors are true, you could show her that nothing cures heartbreak like a fling with a bad boy."

"I told you, not my type," I lie.

Susan tucks her notebook away and loosens her shoulders. "Well, I hear that filming is happening around Redwood National Park later this month through late November."

"It's an undisclosed location," I tsk.

"Can't you fill me in a little? I'm dying for a good scoop."

"You are always so well-researched, Susan," is all I say, confirming her suspicions. "Though all of this stays between us. Off the record, of course."

I laugh softly, masking the unfamiliar tension in my gut at the thought of the Los Angeles table read next week.

Acting feels like a half-forgotten language—something I haven't touched since Princeton theater, and now here I am, opposite big stars like Reese Sinclair.

No sweat.

I'll walk in there, let my natural charm do its work, and show them exactly why they made the right call.

"This is why we keep you around, darling! You're our dealer of delicious scandal and fun."

Mei's words hit like cheap vodka. Bitter and hollow. At times, it feels as if they toast to my failures like they're collecting fine art, but no one has asked how it feels to watch your Olympic dreams shatter.

It's why I don't get too close to any of them.

Don't let them see all of me.

My entourage of trust-fund babies and professional party-crashers. Everything's been handed to them on monogrammed silver—their names etched in privilege.

But me? Every medal, every victory was carved from raw talent and brutal determination. I had to prove I was more than another rich boy playing with swords.

I push the thoughts away.

"I never get this enthusiasm for my movies," Mari pouts.

"Cast Reese Sinclair, and I'll wear Harry Winston to opening night." Mei shoots her an air kiss.

"After it wraps, you must introduce us, Dante. I'd kill to work with her."

"Add it to your tab of favors, darling. Along with borrowing my yacht for the rest of the summer." I wink.

"Yes, yes." Mari dismisses me.

The rest of the conversation swells like the waves against the hull. But I can't listen to it for much longer. "Another round for my beautiful people?"

Catching my reflection on the polished bar surface stops me short. The man staring back at me isn't the one who stood atop that Olympic podium. My eyes hold shadows that no amount of Mediterranean sun can chase away. I adjust my tousled hair and drain my glass.

One year.

Just one year of playing the reformed fencing bad boy before I can return to the piste where I truly belong—where the roar of the crowd means something real.

My whole life's been a performance of one kind or another.

At least this time, I get to choose the role.

Chapter 3
Dante

AUGUST 12TH

OLYMPIC HERO'S DOWNWARD SPIRAL: Dante Hastings Spotted Living Fast Life in Monaco While Former Team Claims Gold Without Him

THE UNFORGIVING LA heat burns mercilessly, indifferent to my pounding hangover.

Last night served as my farewell to summer—a decadent blur of top-shelf liquor, pristine lines of white powder on sleek black marble, and models whose endless legs defied gravity. All of it a desperate attempt to numb reality.

The U.S. Fencing team claimed Olympic gold. Without me. As if I hadn't shed blood on those strips for years, hadn't transformed that team into something remarkable. I single-handedly elevated fencing into a sport worth watching, yet they act like every medal and victory I brought them meant nothing.

Now I must wait four more years to reclaim my title—a title that should have secured me a second gold this year.

Four years to prove I remain unrivaled.

Four years fighting against obscurity.

My legacy dissolves like cocaine in champagne, ephemeral and fading.

To compound the injury, my baby brother, Ezra, claimed two medals in swimming this year. I should be proud—I *am* proud.

But this bitter, resentful person isn't me.

I'm Dante fucking Hastings.

The studio lot signs shift and blur, refusing to hold still. No piste, no saber, no beautiful violence of competition. I take a deep drag of my cigarette, spot Studio F through the haze, and force myself to move.

Three days of table reads and in-person meetings with the stunt and props teams await me. As the stunt coordinator consultant on this project, I've been collaborating with Marcus, the head stunt choreographer, working through the film's sequences over email. It's my first time working on a film, but the process has been surprisingly straightforward. The props team regularly sends me sword specifications for my professional feedback.

Today, I have a four-hour meeting with them immediately following the first-act table read. The script my agent, Todd, mailed me sits untouched in my suitcase, as pristine as the day it arrived. Why cloud my mind with it when we'll be reading it today anyway?

I haven't read a script since college. Surely I've overcome the fact that sometimes when I read, the words tend to swim together.

Dyslexia can't be permanent, can it?

Whatever. I've managed fine without much assistance for twenty-six years.

When I reach the door, I check my Patek. I'm fashionably late, but these Hollywood types probably expect that. I crush out my cigarette, pop a mint, and take a deep breath.

I push through the studio doors and into the table read room.

A mahogany table dominates the space, surrounded by leather chairs and expectant faces.

"Morning," I say crisply to no one in particular.

Felix Langford, the action movie mogul, lounges at the head of the table like he's sitting on a throne. His wire-frame glasses and shaggy gray hair dip forward. "Well, well, if it isn't Mr. Hastings finally gracing us with his presence."

"Charmed." I grab a coffee and a crimson apple from the snack table. The familiar preperformance stiffness settles into my shoulders—until everything stops.

Because there she is.

Reese Sinclair.

One look, and I'm not an Olympian, not a Hastings—simply struck speechless.

Lost in her script, she's ethereal. Golden curls caught in a velvet headband, impossibly long lashes casting shadows as she works. Even her fingers are elegant, wrapping around a strand of that famous Sinclair mane. The haircut that both of my sisters—and thousands of other girls—ripped straight from magazines to show their hairdressers, hoping to capture a fraction of its effortless perfection.

She's pure grace.

A strand of pearls adorns her slender neck. She has perfect cheekbones, a soft jawline, and a pink cardigan falling just so off one shoulder. The glimpse of a silk strap beneath feels like a deliberate temptation.

As a teenager, I spent hours staring at her poster on my wall before falling asleep, dreaming about what her signature peach lip gloss tasted like. She wets her lips, and my cock hardens in my trousers.

Fuck.

"Mr. Hastings," Felix seethes. Reese looks up, and our eyes meet. Something shifts in her expression—curiosity perhaps, or recognition. Then her face hardens into perfect disdain, as if I've committed some unforgivable social transgression. "Are you planning to read your lines from there or join the rest of us?"

"Searching for a seat," I say, glancing away for a second. But when my gaze returns, Reese is already back in her notes. Completely ignoring me. There's some kid next to her—Simon something, my supposed second-in-command in this thing.

I head over, trying not to look too eager, though the spring in my step threatens to betray me.

I've done the whole celebrity scene—met the who's who, mingled with all the big names, collected numbers from Met Gala royalty, and saved them under fake names in my phone.

But seeing Reese Sinclair in person makes me reconsider my assumption that this sugarcoated darling isn't my type.

"This seat taken?" I ask Simon perfunctorily, sliding next to him before the kid can answer. Her scent hits me immediately— cedar and magnolias, but darker, earthier. I turn to her and say, "Good morning, Reese, I'm—"

"Dante Hastings." The way she says it—crisp, rehearsed— makes my own name sound foreign to my ears.

Interesting.

"Indeed." The room's ambient noise fades as I lean closer. Close enough to drown in her perfume, yet far enough to main- tain plausible deniability. "I have to wonder," I say, refusing to let our brief introduction die such an ordinary death, "if we've crossed paths before. Perhaps at one of those tedious LA parties where everyone pretends not to notice each other?"

"Excuse me?" The air around her turns cold, but I catch that telltale tension in her shoulders. She's aware of me and resisting that fact.

"Well, you know who I am."

"I'm a professional, Mr. Hastings. I know everyone I'm working with."

"Of course," I concede, watching as she returns to her script annotations, her pen moving across the margins in decisive strokes. Where is America's darling starlet? Where's that musical southern drawl she carefully conceals in interviews? "You got any notes you can share with me, help get me up to speed?"

"Where's your script?"

"Didn't think I'd need to bring the one I've been poring over endlessly," I bluff.

She flicks her fingers, still absorbed in her page. A PA appears with a script as if she summoned them from thin air.

I murmur thanks. My shirt collar tightens like a noose. What's with the indifference?

The script before me might as well be written in Sanskrit. I stretch out beneath the table with calculated indolence, but she remains immune.

Doesn't spare me a glance. Doesn't flinch.

Well then.

I reach for my apple and roll it between my fingers, pretending to read my lines but tracking the way she tucks a strand of gold behind her ear, exposing that unfairly perfect jawline. I bite into the fruit, letting out a loud crunch that's impossible to ignore.

Her eyes catch mine, lightning-quick and scorching. Dismissive, but there's finally a glimpse of heat beneath the ice. I place the half-bitten apple between us—a dare, an offering, a trap.

"Terrible manners of me. Should've offered to share."

"No, thank you." A flush blooms on her throat. There it is.

"Have you worked with Felix before?" I ask, though I've memorized her IMDb page.

She glares at me again, and isn't it fucking perfect? Especially when it's less of a glare and more of the kind of look that would send lesser men running. Not me.

"If you'd bothered to show up for introductions this morning…"

I grin. Christ, she's magnificent.

"My sincerest apologies. Though I've found that timing, like everything else in life, is an art form. The best moments tend to be unscripted."

"Some of us actually value professionalism over performance." She flips through her script, marking pages with pink Post-its.

"An Olympic gold tends to speak for itself in the professional department, wouldn't you say?" The moment it leaves my lips, I recognize the desperation in it. Like a teenager showing off his varsity jacket. Pathetic, really. I haven't needed to prove myself to anyone in years.

Her lips curve into something caught between a smile and a weapon. "Fascinating," she says. "Is that why Tokyo had to make do without your…particular brand of professionalism this year?"

The air rushes out of my lungs. For a dangerous second, I want to confess everything. The fight. The SafeSport decision. The USFA's pending disciplinary review. The shattered dreams that still wake me at all hours of the night. "I—"

"Precisely," she says in a clipped tone, a clear instruction to back off. "Now, Mr. Hastings, since we've all been waiting on your arrival, perhaps we could redirect that famous focus of yours to something productive?"

Her words should deter me, but instead I want to press for another reaction.

"Alright!" Felix shouts. "If you two are finished, shall we begin?"

"Ready, Felix." Reese brightens and turns her gaze to Felix, her hand twitching up like an eager student before she catches herself and lowers it.

"Let's dive in," a young man beside Felix, probably a head writer, announces.

The table read starts from the beginning of the script and moves devastatingly slowly. Reese is the biggest star on set.

Next to her sits Omar Reeve, playing Foxborough's king, and then Robyn's sidekick, Elizabeth Brando, who's only ever been an extra in television dramas. They all breeze confidently through their lines while I find myself increasingly conscious of my limited acting experience.

Theater at Princeton feels distant now—those small roles squeezed between fencing competitions. The reality of film production looms large, and my hangover isn't helping.

They hired me for my blade work, of course. The acting is merely an extension of the Hastings brand—another performance, another stage.

I settle my gaze back on Reese. She's amazing, like watching the sunrise—knowing you should look away, but you can't.

Simon nudges me. "You're up next. Act one, scene three."

I flip to the scene where the sheriff of Foxborough makes his grand entrance. Todd, who read the script before signing me on, said the role would be perfect for me. It would give me extra media coverage that being a mere stunt coordinator wouldn't.

"Hey, Sheriff," Reese says, and I falter.

"Dante?" Simon whispers beside me.

"Your line is," Reese prompts through gritted teeth, "'The common folk show such spirit.'"

Fuck. I look down at my script. The familiar panic rises as letters dance and blur, a childhood nightmare revisited. My brain scrambles for purchase but finds none.

I stammer, "The common folk show such spirit. But slowly...surely?" Heat creeps up my back. "No, surely you understand, taxes are the crown's...crows?" Damn it. I know the words, but as soon as I open my mouth, my tongue stumbles. "No, the crown's divine...divide? No—divine right."

The heavy silence in the room speaks volumes. I laugh, too sharp, too quick. "My copy is all smudged."

"Sure it is. Have everything memorized for the shoot or don't bother showing up," Felix spits, like Coach Lev does when I tell him I wasn't drinking the night before training. "Let's move on. We have the fight scene—sheriff wounded but alive. Robyn escapes to the forest with Merrick."

I grasp at fragments, improvising poorly. "Find that thief. Tell Foxborough her head's worth gold."

"Fox-burr-o," Reese corrects, leaning close enough that her breath ghosts my ear. God, she's giving valedictorian energy.

"Robyn, let's go," Elizabeth, playing Merrick, shouts.

"Sheriff, I won't let you down," Simon says.

"Now the monologue."

Reese clears her throat. "They've underestimated me my whole life. While our king indulges in opulent feasts behind his fortified walls, our children languish in destitution. No more." Her fist meets the table. "They forget, true power lives in the people. And we will have our justice, whatever the cost."

"Good," Felix says, "but let's make the dialogue more accessible. Peasant women wouldn't use such fancy words. Keep it authentic." Reese's knuckles whiten around her pen as she marks through her lines. "And add some tears. You know, to soften up Robyn's edges and make her someone worth rooting for."

Reese's mechanical obedience while defiance smolders behind her eyes makes my blood sing with recognition. This has been happening throughout the entire table read. Reese will say her line, and Felix will have notes.

But this time, instead of replying, *Of course, Felix, how high do you want me to jump*, she says, "I'll work on incorporating those elements, but maybe instead of crying—"

"Trust me," Felix interrupts with a wave of his hand, "it'll play better."

Sexist prick.

"You're right," she says, clipped and perfect.

"Okay, next scene with the king," Felix says.

Omar starts, and Reese slumps back into her seat, reorganizing her pens and colored markers in front of her. A perfectly manicured pink finger curls around the ends of her hair. She catches me watching and raises an eyebrow.

"Have you lost your page again?" she whispers.

"Your performance. I'm a bit lost for words."

"Yeah…lost for words," she says sarcastically. I'm so fucking embarrassed that she saw me stumbling over myself, but I won't let her see.

I throw on my charm, changing the subject. "You know," I say, "last I checked, thieves aren't exactly known for their waterworks. Just saying."

Without looking at me, and with the room distracted by the king and his men plotting to take more taxes from the town, she says, "We're in the hands of one of the most successful action directors in the industry." Interestingly, she's neither disagreeing nor agreeing with me. "Now please pipe down; you're going to get us in trouble."

"Rule follower, huh?"

She glares at me again. So fucking gorgeous.

"Pay attention, Mr. Hastings."

"Please," I flash the smile that's gotten me out of trouble more times than I can count, "call me Dante."

She regards me one final time before turning away.

Maybe it's the competitive instinct, but I can't seem to let her go.

In Saber, the point goes to whoever attacks first.

Always press the advantage.

This just became a game, and now I need to figure out what riddle she's spinning. And I've never been able to resist turning the tables on an overconfident opponent.

After the table read wraps, I head to my meeting with the stunt team. As we file out, the head PA stops us. "One more thing—cabin assignments will be emailed shortly. Supporting cast and crew will share cabins with two others."

The thought of Reese as a potential roommate makes the corners of my mouth twitch.

"Shooting starts the Monday after next. We'll film Monday to Saturday, Sundays off. Check your email for weekly schedules. Fight scenes are on Thursdays and Fridays—longer days, so plan accordingly." The head PA scans the room. "Questions?"

No one raises a hand. Before I head over to the stunt team meeting, I should corner the production team about my cabin situation. And Friday shoots? They'll have to work around my training schedule and whatever charity circuit Lev has planned for me. I start to make my way over, but Reese breezes past, all dangerous curves wrapped in denim with her perfume lingering in the air.

On second thought, I'll let Todd handle the scheduling details. And the stunt team can wait a few more minutes.

I match her stride. She's shorter than I thought; her head barely reaches my shoulder. Must be about five-four, though her PR team lists her as five-six online.

"The pronunciation thing earlier? Brutal." I drone playfully. "Are you always so merciless with your scene partners, or should I feel special?"

She turns, a sweet smile crossing her face. "I only sharpen my claws for the ones who can't be bothered to learn their lines." My blood sings at her bite. "Though most gentlemen have the decency to fake it better than you did."

"Straight for the kill." I laugh. "Fair enough. But watching you take me apart? That was something else."

"Have you read page fourteen, section KD-33 of your contract?" She pauses, and I track the careful shape of each word on her lips. "No need to admit you haven't. There's a strict no-fraternization clause, so why don't you be a dear and keep your energy focused on your lines instead of attempting to hide the fact that you don't care for this project?"

I know the section. Todd made me recite it to him over the

phone. These clauses appear in contracts when someone looks like Reese—beautiful in a dangerous way that makes men forget themselves.

I find myself wanting to impress her, to make up for my earlier shortcomings.

Perhaps showering her with praise will get her to warm up to me. "Maybe you'd prefer me admitting that your take on Robyn is revolutionary. It's refreshing, new. I mean, compared to your other great roles, what you brought back there? It was impressive."

"I take my craft seriously, and I don't plan on letting anything get in the way of this movie's success," she says, side-stepping me.

"It shows, and if you ever want to take your sword fighting to the next level, I'd be more than happy to help. I'm working with the head of stunts and leading a team through some fight choreography each morning before shooting."

"Thank you, Mr. Hastings, but Felix procured a qualified trainer for me. Nick Valentine has trained all of the best male action heroes of our time. I don't need any additional lessons."

"Well, I'll be here should you change your mind. I do have a gold medal," I remind her, noting how she unconsciously mirrors my posture—a dance of symmetry neither of us acknowledges.

"Yes, you've already mentioned. But it's curious how you keep leaving out the details of your fall from grace."

"Careful, Reese, you keep bringing up my career this much, and I might think you're interested," I say, leaning in closer.

"Definitely not," she snaps, looking flustered. "What I'm trying to say is that people work hard on films; they dedicate their lives to thankless tasks to make magic happen—"

"Undoubtedly."

"They work years for these opportunities. They don't land them because of who they are or who their family may be."

Her implication hangs there, tedious and predictable. The

Hastings name is all anyone sees when they look at me. My father with his tech empire, Viggle, my mother coaching champions, my siblings stockpiling accolades for the family trophy room.

Everyone assumes my success came without any struggle or effort.

Yes, I have money. Yes, I know the right people. I won't pretend otherwise. But there's something reductive about assuming privilege eliminates all obstacles. The world sees the Hastings name, not the pressure that comes with it—the constant expectation to be exceptional.

Society runs on connections and capital—that's just reality. I've learned to navigate it, but that doesn't mean I haven't earned my place. Doors may have opened for me, but I still had to walk through them and prove I belonged there.

"And you didn't get cast as Robyn Hood because of who you are?"

"I've been in this industry since I was a child. I know what hard work means." Her voice is steel. "Meticulous, calculated, exhausting work. Just last month I did an entire PR circuit for my latest film, started an intense workout regimen for this role, and shot a national commercial where I had to execute a perfectly timed dive into a pool of yogurt."

I remember the commercial. The way she emerged from a sea of dairy like Venus rising from seafoam, except it was vanilla yogurt, and she was selling processed food to the masses. "Right. The 'Gurt ad." My laugh comes out hollow. "Quite the cultural touchstone."

"I've done what needed to be done, and I will continue to excel at whatever challenge is placed before me," she says, and something in her determination makes me want to reach across the space between us. Instead, I watch her shoulders square, her posture as perfect as a prima ballerina. "I have earned every single role through dedication and sacrifice. And I will ensure this film receives the critical acclaim it deserves, with or without your contributions."

The little crease around her eyes as she narrows her gaze at me sends blood below my belt. There she goes with the glaring again.

"And all I'm suggesting is we might understand each other better than you think." I hold her gaze, watching her pupils dilate in the afternoon light. "And I'd like to prove it. Over lunch, perhaps? We could discuss…technique."

"I don't mix business with pleasure."

"Who said anything about pleasure?" I counter. "I'd call it tactical planning. Two fighters comparing notes. I have plenty of knowledge to share with you, and you seem like the kind of person who likes to get intimate with their characters."

"Right. Thank you for that impossible-to-refuse offer, Mr. Hastings. But I have a packed schedule with costumes for the rest of the day."

She turns on her heel, walking away. Those damn blue jeans are a masterclass in temptation.

"I'll see you tomorrow, Reese. Save me a seat, why don't you?" I turn in the opposite direction, having to walk off the semi.

She's nothing like I expected.

And for the first time since Tokyo slipped through my fingers, since the fencing world watched me fall, I find myself wanting to prove something—to her, to myself.

Not just that I can remember my lines or handle my saber, but that underneath the carefully crafted image of Dante Hastings, there's someone worth knowing.

Someone who could match her fire with his own.

I'll show her I'm more than her first impression of me, however accurate it may be. I'll prove I can be as dedicated to this craft as she is, even if it means confronting every demon that's been chasing me since my suspension.

I'm more than my gold medal.
I have to be.

FRANKIE

wheres my autograph?!?!

DANTE

Another admirer playing hard to get.

FRANKIE

DANTE I STG if u dont get this done im gonna cry and then moms gonna get involved and then u'll REALLY be sorry…

DANTE

The thrill of the chase, little sister. Some things can't be rushed.

Besides, it seems America's sweetheart isn't a fan of mine.

BROOKLYN

Her birthday is on June 3.

So she's a Gemini, Dante!!! She must've been matching your energy

DANTE

If only.

BROOKLYN

Though, since you're a Taurus, you may not be compatible

It says here your match will be interesting but tricky! You're super different but it can work if you could meet in the middle!

DANTE

Well, she wasn't interested in meeting me anywhere.

FRANKIE

OMG STOP BEING DRAMATIC FOR LIKE 2
SECONDS PLEASE IM LITERALLY
DYING HERE

DANTE

I'll grow on her.

BROOKLYN

What happened? What did you do?

FRANKIE

BETTER QUESTION WOULD BE WHAT DIDNT
HE DO???

get that autograph and my premiere tickets

or Im telling mom about Monaco and showing
her ALL my crying selfies!!!!!!!!!!!!

DANTE

Why is it always my fault?

BROOKLYN

Your reputation precedes you.

DANTE

She read up on me. You know how the press
has been. Got miss goody two shoes' panties
in a twist.

BROOKLYN

You could tell her the truth about what
happened at the World Cup.

DANTE

Definitely not. Don't worry, you'll both get your
autographs and meet and greets. That's why
I'm your favorite brother, right?

FRANKIE

who told u that? loooool

BROOKLYN

Why not let some of her good rub off on you for a chance?

DANTE

Stop your fretting, children. I'll be putting the sin in Sinclair in no time.

Chapter 4
Reese

"I HATE when we don't talk!" Cleo's raspy voice floats through the phone. I can picture my best friend lounging on her trailer's leather couch, dark waves framing her striking face.

"I've missed you," I groan, sitting at my vanity at home in LA. "How's murder-solving in the wilderness?"

"Yosemite has me paranoid. I've been bingeing true crime podcasts, and now I'm convinced every tree is hiding a serial killer." I smile at her dramatics. "How was the table read?"

"Felix decided Robyn can't say words like 'opulent' because it's not realistic to the women of the fictional medieval times. Then he revised the script by giving Robyn this tragic romance backstory. When I pointed out that it undermines her motivation to help her village, he smiled and said audiences need to see her heart."

"These old-school assholes need to stop treating their leading ladies like damsels in distress."

"You're telling me."

"Remember, babe—you're the star of the movie. Don't let him steamroll you."

"But he's the director," I say, massaging my temples. "I'm

trying not to rock the boat. It's my first action movie, and I'm his first female lead."

"You're not rocking the boat by speaking up for a character you're passionate about!"

"Cleo, if I don't nail this, no one will take me seriously as an actress, and I'll be pushing thirty as a forgotten pretty girl with no work, no prospects, and I'll be—"

"Well, now you're just quoting *Pride and Prejudice*."

I laugh with a snort, then wince. "Please don't make me laugh—my abs are already killing me from training. I'm discovering muscles I didn't even know existed."

"Tell me more. Has your trainer given your ass BBL status yet?"

"Not yet, but Nick is…interesting. Yesterday, in the middle of shadowboxing, he told me to 'man up.'"

Slumping deeper into my chair, I take another sip of my nutritionist's mandatory kale juice. The afternoon sun filters through my mama's lace curtains, a touch of New Orleans. I focus on the Post-it notes lining my vanity mirror: *Be perfect. Be flawless.*

I repeat the words in my head like a mantra, willing them to settle into my bones, to push out the self-doubt that creeps in with every one of Felix's exasperated sighs.

Cleo groans. "He didn't."

"It's fine, part of the new gig, I guess. The most important thing is that I'm getting stronger, even if the basic exercises are starting to feel like torture. At least we're moving to prop weapons next week. Any advice?"

Cleo and I have come a long way since our Bright Light Network days. Back then, we were two tween girls playing sisters in *The Sweet Life of Kiara and Bella*, sharing scenes and sneaking snacks between takes. I was the adorable, clumsy one, while Cleo was the tough-talking rebel, already showing glimpses of the powerhouse actress she'd become.

These days, Cleo plays a complex, gritty detective on TV, and I'm still cast as the sweet, clumsy character in one role or another.

"Hold your weapon as if you've got your fingers wrapped around a big, vulnerable—"

"Cleo!" I screech, feeling my cheeks flush bright red.

"What?" she says innocently. "I was just going to say cock!"

My best friend's brazen humor never fails to send me into fits of laughter. "What did I say about making me laugh?"

"Alright, Reese's Pieces, I'll behave," she sighs dramatically. "But I don't think you need to stress over the weapons. You juggled flaming batons in that talent show during season two."

"I was fourteen."

"And you still didn't set anyone on fire. That's a win."

"You're right. Plus, for the first act, Robyn's supposed to be learning anyway, so my awkwardness will make it realistic."

Hopefully.

Cleo pauses. "Did you tell anyone about your fear of water? Have you thought about using the double they offered?"

My neck tenses.

I saw the raft scene when I got the script. Robyn and her crew steal from the king's boats, get caught, and fight off guards. I lose my sword and have to jump into the water to retrieve a new one. I've had nightmares about it for weeks.

I inhale a deep breath.

"No, but I have a plan," I lie. "The casting director specifically requested an actress who can do their own stunts. I'm not going to have them bend the rules to accommodate me. Besides, real leading ladies don't use stunt doubles."

"Grit is great, but one scene doesn't make or break the movie. You can't overcome decades of fear in a month."

"Says the queen of the perfect chokehold escape."

"That took me three seasons to learn. In your case, following

Johansson's workout plan won't help you get over your fear of water."

"Maybe it will. Lawrence would've done the stunt herself. Any other serious actress would have committed to the role fully. I'm not going to be the exception."

"Does committing to the role fully include the celibacy part?" Cleo teases.

"It's for inner warrior focus! Ancient samurai did it!"

"*Suuure*. Speaking of focus," Cleo sings, "I read there's a certain someone on set who could make things interesting."

"Dante Hastings?" I scoff.

"Wow, you sure did say his name fast."

"No," I protest. "You brought him up."

"I could've been talking about any cast member. But please, continue."

I scowl. I should drop the conversation right here, but I need to vent about this. "He was so unprofessional. Showed up late, didn't know his lines, and spent the entire table read trying to chat me up."

"Scandalous!" Cleo gasps dramatically. "What did he say?"

"I don't know, I wasn't listening," I fib again.

It's completely unfair how he towered over everyone with that insufferably relaxed attitude, like he owned the room. And that stupid chipped black nail polish should look sloppy. It should be a red flag. And yet, it isn't.

But I refuse to be affected. I absolutely refuse.

"Yet here you are thinking about it," Cleo continues.

"It's only because he sat next to me," I explain. "I did my research on him. The Olympian. The Sheriff. The Alleged Master Swordsman."

The way he placed that half-bitten, shiny red apple next to me. *Terrible manners of me. Should've offered to share.* I sat there, staring at it like he was the wicked witch in Snow White, tempting me with poison fruit.

And honestly, in a near lapse of self-control, I thought about taking a bite.

"Master swordsman, huh?"

"Yes, and now he's somehow part of the stunt consultation team. Which doesn't make sense considering his fencing involves those tiny toothpicks. Those aren't exactly real swords."

"Since when do you know anything about fencing?"

"I don't," I admit. "Okay, I watched one video."

And it was…hot. Fitted white uniforms. The sweat after the masks are pulled off. The groans. The speed.

Stop thinking about it!

Cleo groans. "Girl, you can just admit that he caught your eye. Everyone watched him and his teammates at the Olympics four years ago. And listen, I never had a hand kink before, but those fencer's hands—"

"Oh my heavens, don't even remind me. At the table read, he wore these silver rings that kept catching the light and distracting me."

Knowing my luck, he'll park himself next to me tomorrow too. I need to arrive early and sit between two people, create a barricade.

"Rings, you say? Takes a certain kind of man to pull that off."

"I just don't understand how he got the role of the sheriff," I continue. "He's the only one who's not in the industry out of the entire cast."

"His dad owns Viggle, honey. You know how it goes."

Another nepo baby gets a part in a film. But this isn't a minor role. "The sheriff is supposed to appear villainous and antagonistic, not be portrayed by someone with a reputation and an eight-pack."

I might need to write a strongly worded letter to casting.

"Did he take off his shirt so you could count all eight?"

"Not the point," I sigh. "Can't you see how this is a disaster waiting to happen? I mean, he punched someone at one of his matches. He obviously has a temper and no interest in obeying the rules."

But as I list his faults, my traitorous brain keeps throwing out unhelpful observations. Like how his tattoos on all that muscle basically suck the oxygen out of the room. He's like some unfairly attractive vacuum cleaner.

I hate it. I hate him!

"You seem to know an awful lot about someone you claim not to care about. Isn't this how all your movies start?"

"I pay attention to everyone I work with," I say primly, ignoring how my cheeks heat up.

"Don't resist too much, or you'll star in your very own romantic comedy."

"There will be no romance." The last time I mixed work and romance, it exploded in my face.

"I never said anything about getting romantic. It could be erotica. Late nights sneaking into each other's cabins—"

"Hush," I say too sharply. "Remember Ricky?"

Cleo's tone softens. "That was different. You were just a kid."

My fingers curl into fists. Ricky Tribbiani and I were costars in a teen summer blockbuster. He was twenty-three, and I was seventeen. My first and only real Hollywood relationship.

When the movie blew up and I got nominated for a Teen Choice Award, I thought it would be my moment to shine. Instead, it became a nightmare I'll never forget.

The night I won my award, he drunkenly climbed onto the stage during my acceptance speech for Choice Summer Movie Actress and kissed me without consent. Instead of focusing on my achievement, the media turned it into a spectacle about him. My voice was silenced while his actions dominated the narrative.

"A man who'd prey on a teenager, then try to capitalize off her growing career? That's on him, not you."

"Yes, but it doesn't mean I'm going to welcome another man into my life and risk having him define my career." I want Reese Sinclair to be known for her abilities. No matter how many awards I've won, without an Oscar I'll always be a popcorn actress, loved by audiences but not edgy enough for critics. "But thank you for looking out for me, Cleo."

"You're welcome, sugar. Now, back to this totally-not-distracting stunt coordinator who we aren't going to invite into your life but can still admire from afar…"

I groan. "Can we not?"

"Have you seen those yacht photos from this summer? Because, girl—"

"I am NOT looking at salacious photos of my colleague! That would be completely unprofessional and—"

"Sending them now!"

"Don't bother, I won't look—"

"Too late."

"I'm hanging up now," I announce.

"Actually, before you let me go, I probably won't have service for a few weeks, but if you need me, send a carrier pigeon or something. Love you!"

"Love you," I say.

After the call ends, the unread message blinks temptingly. One peek wouldn't hurt.

No.

I do not need to spend time looking at cliché bad boys on yachts. But as my thumb hovers over the delete button, another photo loads and—oh.

Oh.

I swallow hard. Well, there's nothing cliché about this.

Is that a thigh tattoo?

I pinch the screen, bringing it closer, my pulse quickening.

Dante lounges on the yacht deck, sun-drenched and effort-less. His linen shorts ride up enough to reveal sharp lines of black ink against his thigh. He's all lazy sprawl and long limbs. Over six feet of infuriating perfection. Wind ruffles the dark curls that tease the nape of his neck. A half-unbuttoned shirt frames abs that look painted on. I try to count how many abs there are but can't make them out in the blurry photo. The skin on the backs of my arms pebbles.

My phone pings, and I swipe away from the photos so fast I drop the device.

Professional, Reese.

Be professional!

Chapter 5
Reese

Augustus 16th

HOLLYWOOD'S LATEST GENDER-SWAP GIMMICK: Felix Langford's *Robyn Hood* Trains Pretty Face to Swing Swords in Studio's Desperate Bid for Relevance

THE BIG PINE Lodge thrums with movement. Outside, towering redwoods cast long August shadows across the old summer campgrounds. The set crew converted this building into a makeshift training gym. Mirrors line the walls above a patchwork of exercise mats.

My muscles burn as I lunge forward, attempting a direct thrust. The wooden waster sword feels impossibly heavy in my grip.

While we are filming, I'll use a lightweight steel sword, but for training I have to use these heavy wooden waster swords. They're designed to build strength, though right now, all they're doing is making my arms scream.

After six weeks of practicing sword forms in empty air,

holding an actual weapon feels jarring. I've done the work—grueling cardio and strength training in LA, hours of visualization exercises, mostly just me chanting Michelle Obama arms with every bicep curl—but I'm still not strong enough for this. The waster sword is far heavier than the two-pound dumbbells Nick had me using to tone my arms.

My breath comes in ragged pants behind the too-tight headgear Nick insists I wear "for liability reasons." He watches me with thinly veiled impatience.

In the mirror, my sweat-darkened tank top, flyaway hair, and bulky protective gear make me look like a kid playing dress-up in a world of professionals.

"Focus on your stance, dude," Nick says, checking his phone for what must be the fifth time in ten minutes. "Try it again."

I reset and attempt the attack again. *Arm not extended enough.* And again. *Balance is off.* And again. *Lunged too early.*

I've challenged myself countless times in my career. Yet here I am, completely unable to execute basic fight choreography.

The worst part? *He's* here.

Dante Hastings.

Across the room, he moves with ease and precision. His waster sword cuts through air with controlled power. Every movement purposeful.

Stop looking! He's nothing but a distraction—an infuriatingly skilled distraction who's clearly never struggled through training.

In my strongly worded email to casting—which went unanswered—I specifically noted that the classic sheriff should be played by an unpleasant everyman. Not someone whose hamstrings have their own hamstrings.

I suppress an eyeroll. The isolated training without the crew has been absurd, but, in the director's words, we have to protect our lead. Tomorrow I'll face my first real combat scenes with the full cast, going straight into filming. I must nail it perfectly on the first take.

I grit my teeth and try the direct thrust attack one more time, but Nick sidesteps effortlessly. My fingers tighten around the sword's hilt as frustration builds.

"Come on, princess, this isn't Pilates!" Nick calls out. "Stop being so delicate about it. You got this. Your body just needs to learn this the hard way—no shortcuts."

I abandon the direct thrust and work through basic offensive and defensive techniques. Horizontal cut. Defensive parry. My arms tremble as doubt creeps in.

In mere hours, I need to embody Robyn—fierce, untouchable—for promo shots, then film an emotional scene with my character's dying father. My lines are solid, my motivations clear. If only I could master this sword work that Nick never properly prepared me for.

Nick sighs. "Little more effort, rookie." The nickname he's used since day one, despite my repeated corrections. "Put those pretty arms to work."

"Maybe I need to practice saying my lines with the movements," I manage between breaths. "Since that's what I'll be doing on camera on Thursday, during our first fight scene."

"I don't think that's what's missing."

I try anyway, raising my sword. "They've underestimated me—" The words catch as I perform the horizontal cut, stumbling forward. "My whole—" Another failed parry. "My whole life."

Why can't my brain and body connect? I can cry on command, fake trip with practiced grace, nail emotional beats perfectly—but the moment I have to deliver lines while wielding this waster I should have been training with all along? My body refuses to cooperate.

"Less talking, more practicing." Nick suggests, lowering his waster sword.

"But I have to master saying my lines *and* the choreography," I argue, struggling to keep annoyance from overtaking my voice.

Nick frowns. "Look, sweetie, maybe you should leave some mental room to focus on those delicate little feet of yours."

Mental room? What does that even mean?

"Argh!" I groan, my blade jolting to the side as Nick effortlessly parries my offense.

Across the room, the male actors continue their drills uninterrupted. Dante executes another flawless sequence. No one walks on eggshells around him; no one treats him like he might break at any moment. No one is calling him princess, sweetie, or rookie.

Must be nice.

"Have you given more thought to the stunt double?" Nick suggests for the hundredth time.

My stomach knots. My own trainer has lost faith in me.

"I can do it!" Heat rises in my chest, intense and persistent. I can't breathe with this protective gear weighing me down, restricting my movement, making me feel awkward and sluggish.

"We're not going to reach Felix's standards at this pace."

Something inside me breaks.

I tear off the headgear, pulling it over my head so forcefully my braid comes loose. Then I strip away the chest padding and wrist guards.

"Put that back on—" Nick starts.

But I've already made my move.

I advance, forcing Nick into a defensive position.

"I can't—" I pant between strikes, my sword movements becoming more desperate with each swing. "Breathe in that—" Another slash. "Ridiculous thing!" I regain my balance after stumbling. "I can't move!" My frustration mounts. "And these —" I growl, striking harder. "Lines—" Faster, making him retreat. "I can't deliver my lines properly!"

Nick's expression shifts to panic.

Let's see who's the amateur now.

"Reese, enough—we need a break."

I swing again, my frustration reaching its peak. Our wooden swords connect with a sharp crack. Block, defend, thrust. My body responds instinctively now, fueled by weeks of accumulated self-doubt and criticism.

"Either train me properly—" My arms ache, but for once I'm not second-guessing my every move. The waster isn't just a prop anymore; it's an extension of myself. "Or get out—" I groan. "Of my way."

Nick winces as my next strike connects solidly with his forearm. "Ow! Easy!"

His eyes flash as something in him snaps. Gone is the condescending trainer. His stance changes. No more holding back. He meets my next attack with genuine resistance, and for the first time, we engage in a real fight.

Finally!

To my amazement, my strikes follow perfect form. Lead with the blade, extend, lunge forward. My weapon arm throbs, but I push through the pain. A surprised laugh escapes me. I'm doing it. I'm actually—

My concentration breaks. A movement in the mirror—Dante is observing, his expression inscrutable.

Nick's sword slips past my guard.

White-hot pain explodes across my jaw as wood connects with skin.

I crash onto the mat, the impact forcing air from my lungs and sending stars dancing across my vision. Through the haze of pain, something unexpected stirs beneath my ribs.

Something electric.

Excitement?

Adrenaline?

Through blurred vision, I see Nick's face hovering above me, panic etched into every feature. "Oh god, I'm so sorry. Are you okay? Can you see me?"

Despite the throbbing in my jaw, my lips curl into a crooked smile.

Then—

"What the fuck?" The voice cuts through the gym like thunder.

Dante.

He crosses the training floor in four long strides, his broad shoulders blocking the fluorescent lights overhead.

"It was an accident. She stepped into it," Nick explains, holding up three fingers. "How many fingers am I holding up?"

"Three," I mumble, trying to push myself upright. My arms wobble beneath me, and my fingers slide uselessly against the sweat-slick mat. My waster lies out of reach.

A hand enters my field of vision.

It's his.

"Let me help you up," he offers, hand extended but waiting for my permission.

"I'm okay," I insist, though the words come out thicker than intended. My pulse pounds as Dante turns his attention back to Nick.

"An overhead strike? On a beginner?" Dante's voice is controlled but tight with anger. I watch the muscles in his forearms tense as he steps closer to Nick. "What were you thinking?"

"She's tougher than she looks," Nick says, glancing at me. "Right?"

I give him a thumbs-up and reach for my weapon.

Dante's boot presses down on the wooden blade before I can grab it. I look up, meeting his stern gaze through strands of damp hair. His expression doesn't change, but something in his eyes shifts—so subtle I almost miss it. He turns back to Nick.

"You should never let her engage without gear."

"I was just defending myself," Nick protests, taking a defensive step back. "What was I supposed to do?"

"You don't hit back," Dante says flatly.

The gym falls silent, everyone's eyes on us.

"Basic rule of instruction—you don't strike an untrained student. You let them learn control first."

"I'm licensed," Nick counters, crossing his arms.

I exhale through gritted teeth. So much testosterone for so early in the morning.

Thank goodness my bodyguard, Ramsey, is doing his regular perimeter check, or I'd have yet another man arguing over me.

Through their escalating voices, I struggle to find something stable to pull myself up with. My hand connects with what I think is a wall, but warm pressure envelops my fingers. As my focus returns, I realize I'm gripping Dante's forearm as he helps me stand. The solid strength of him momentarily disorients me. I pull my hand away, irritated with myself for noticing anything beyond my throbbing jaw.

"Hey!" I snap, wincing as pain shoots through my face. "This is unprofessional. I'm fine." Neither man acknowledges me.

Dante steps forward, his presence commanding the space between practice mats and mirrored walls. "Licensed or not, I'm a professional fighter. I am the stunt coordinator consultant on this production." I flinch at his authoritative tone. "I know how to train beginners without injuring them."

"Well," Nick sneers, "you weren't professional enough to qualify for the Olympics this year, were you?"

A flash of genuine hurt crosses Dante's face before it hardens into anger. This is escalating quickly.

"There will be no fighting on my movie set," I announce, mustering as much authority as I can.

Dante turns, lowering his voice so only I can hear. "I wasn't going to fight him." I instinctively step back. "You should never get hurt like this during basic training," he continues, his eyes darkening with something I'm not entirely comfortable with.

"It was an accident," Nick mutters, looking away.

"I'm honestly fine," I insist, though my rapid breathing might not be entirely from the adrenaline.

Or maybe it is. It's difficult to distinguish between genuine concern and the rush that comes after being struck by someone twice your size.

Dante turns back to Nick. "Get her some ice, Mr. License."

Nick glances at my jaw, which must be visibly swelling by now. "I'll get you some ice. Let's take ten." He walks off, leaving me alone with Dante.

I huff so loudly there could be steam coming out of my nose. *Don't they get it?*

"If you don't mind, I'd like to get back to work." I bend down to pick up my waster, but my head throbs so much I nearly topple over. I grit my teeth, swallowing a wave of dizziness. *No weakness.*

Dante's foot doesn't move. My mouth goes dry. I'm so close to his solid legs, I can see the outline of his quad strength through his sweats. "Absolutely not."

"Excuse me?" I glance up at him. "Get your foot off my training sword."

He stands still.

Why is he staring at me so intensely? Why do I care? Why can't I seem to stop staring back even though there's a roomful of people watching us? This is *so* not the kind of drama I want following me on set.

"Please," I add, hating how pleading I sound.

"You should take me up on my offer and let me show you a thing or two."

"I'm working with a professional," I reply.

He scoffs, and a laugh escapes that seems to loosen the tightness in his shoulders, making the muscles in his neck flex. "A professional would never let this—" He reaches for my jaw, and I freeze. *What is he doing?* My heart hammers so loud I'm sure he can hear it. But then, as if he suddenly realizes that he's about to touch me, his hand drops away, swiping through his hair instead. "—happen to you. Or any of the students they train. Ever."

"It's my fault," I say, feeling dazed, though whether it's from the hit or from Dante, I can't tell. "I shouldn't have pulled my gear off and started attacking him."

"Most definitely not your fault."

My body betrays me at the softness in his voice, making my breath shallow.

It must be the workout adrenaline. Definitely not the faint trace of smoke that seems to follow him everywhere he goes.

Goodness gracious, Reese!

"I've just—I've been training nonstop." The words pile up in my throat, too heavy to hold back. "And I'm not making any progress. It's not coming easy to me."

"Don't be hard on yourself. Your form is impressive for a beginner. Decent balance. Obviously determined. Sometimes that matters more than being a natural." I'm taken aback by the sincerity in his tone. Before I can react, his mouth curves into a smirk that is both infuriating and gorgeous. "Look, I know you want to go at this on your own, but I train here, around eight, by myself. I'm happy to help you work on that sword grip."

Cleo's words echo in my mind. *Fingers wrapped around a big, vulnerable—*

No.

Absolutely not.

He swooped in here trying to be some kind of savior. Sure, it was impressive. But I'm certain he'd love nothing more than for me to *thank* him. The implication is heavy. And I hate how much some untamed and ridiculous part of me wants to take him up on his offer—with his talk of sword grip and training alone.

Just when I think he's being genuine, he ruins it.

"I appreciate your offer, but I can take care of myself," I say reluctantly, not forgetting my manners though he's driving me up a wall.

"Suit yourself, fighter." He shrugs, his gaze never leaving mine.

"Fighter?"

"With a mark like that, I'd say you've earned it."

I nearly blush, or maybe I don't. I can't tell. Another trainee calls out Dante's name, and he looks back, craning his neck so I can see the tattoo. *What is it?* Intricate, highly detailed artwork that has my stomach going tight again. I spin away, desperate to break the spell.

How dare he make me feel things?

With his stupid perfect hair, his stupid perfect smirk, and his stupid perfect…everything.

This is a betrayal to feminism of the highest order.

"We should both get back to work," I say when he looks back at me—does he know I was staring?

"My cabin's the one closest to the lake."

"Okay?"

"Now you know where to find me," he says over his shoulder as he walks away. "I'm at your beck and call."

I retrieve the sword from the ground and hurry away from him and whatever strange tension was radiating between us.

Focus.

I head for the mirror, propping my weapon carefully against the nearby wall.

My hair has escaped its French braids, strands of blonde clinging wildly to my sweat-soaked neck. I imagine cutting it all off, how liberating it might feel, and the thought lingers rather than vanishes. There is a bruise already forming on my jaw. It's an angry purple mark.

I study it, deliberately not shifting my gaze to the figure lingering behind me in the mirror.

The woman in my reflection isn't simply pretty—she's

commanding her space, she's tough, she makes tough choices. Maybe those choices aren't well-thought-out, like ripping off her gear and whacking her trainer with a wooden sword. But she's never done that before. Progress.

That's what matters.

Not whatever that was with Dante.

Of course, my eyes shift to his reflection as he directs the other stunt performers. I can't forget how I spent hours watching his matches on YouTube last weekend, how he seemed to dominate every match he was in.

But seeing it in person…

Focus on your bruise. Your hair. Anything else.

It's no use. I can see why he was hired now. Not for his line delivery, but for the way he moves.

He's in the middle of a complex fight sequence, the bandit ambush scene, facing off against four attackers at once. *Mesmerizing*. Each strike and defending block flow into the next like liquid mercury.

I swear a droplet of drool is hanging from the side of my mouth.

Why is the sweat on the back of his compression shirt so…attractive?

No. It's gross.

Ew, men.

He moves again, muscles shifting as a stuntman lunges. Dante pivots seamlessly, blocking the attack while simultaneously disarming another. He shoots me a glance—none of that winking or smirking, but something heated before he looks away.

It's like watching a deadly dance.

I need to get to that level.

Maybe his helping me wouldn't be the worst thing in the world?

The pros are undeniable. His athletic background speaks for

itself. He's mastered his craft in a way that could elevate my performance beyond what any training with Nick could achieve.

But the cons…I've dealt with enough guys like him in Hollywood to recognize the warning signs. The constant flirting, that playboy reputation, the way he seems to treat everything like a game.

Can I trust someone who appears this unserious to take my training—to take me—seriously? Even if his dedication to his sport suggests otherwise, getting involved with him in any capacity feels like asking for complications I can't afford.

I'll master this blade, this role, this transformation. And if my heart tries to lead me astray? Well, that's just one more opponent to defeat.

Chapter 6
Reese

August 19th

BREAKING: A-List Star Reese Sinclair Rejects Lead Role in a Cozy Holiday Romance—Sources Say "Grumpy Veterinarian Meets Single Dad Reindeer Ranch Owner" Plot "Too Predictable"

THE METAL BREASTPLATE digs into my ribs with each breath, and I'm seriously questioning why Felix thought this Xena Warrior Princess look was appropriate.

Sculpted metal boobs? *Check.*

Exposed midriff? *Check.*

Leather miniskirt that rides up every two seconds? *Double check.*

I didn't sign up for this. Who in the wardrobe department thought this was superior to the jumpsuit costume I tried on during my fittings in LA?

"Would you focus?" I snap at Dante, who's busy flashing his playboy smile at the nearby crew. Per Felix's instructions, they're resetting Robyn's village for the third scene of act one—where Robyn stands up to the sheriff for the first time. "It's your line after I pick up the weapon."

He turns his devastating grin toward me, looking criminally good in his sheriff's getup—a weathered leather vest that hugs his broad shoulders, kohl-lined eyes that promise trouble. My stomach does an inconvenient flip.

"I think I need another glance at that script," he says.

"It's one line, Mr. Hastings," I frown. "You don't need to look at the script."

"Wait, that's not your sword." He stares at the weapon in my hands, then slowly shifts his golden eyes back to me, deliberately lingering on my lips for just a moment too long.

"No," I groan, fighting the urge to step back, to put space between us, "the line is, 'Oh, how delightful, the common folk—'"

"I saw your form during training," he cuts in, as if I hadn't even spoken. "And when Marcus and I were talking to the props team this morning, I told him—"

"You talked to the head stunt coordinator about me?" My bruised jaw throbs. Thank heavens for industrial-strength concealer.

"Part of my job," he reminds me. *Of course it is, Reese.* "The distribution on this sword is all wrong for your weight and—"

"There's nothing wrong with my weight," I snap. Though the lightweight steel blade I expected to use today is a lot heavier than the waster I used for practice.

"Trust me. You're perfect exactly as you are." He pauses. "But each weapon needs to suit its wielder. That one's fighting you because it wasn't made for someone so…" Another pause; his pupils expand. "Elegant."

I can't tell if he's mocking me or something else entirely.

Focus on the set, Reese.

The cameras. The scene.

Anything but him.

"Let me see that sword," he insists.

"No," I say, hiding it behind my back. "This is the weapon props gave me. I can do my choreography with it." There's nothing wrong with my sword. There's nothing wrong with my technique. I can do this. I don't need to be fussed over. I don't need to be saved.

"Take it from the top," Felix's bark interrupts us. "Dante and Reese. Try to remember your damn lines. And, doll?" He turns to me. "For the love of god, strive to look like you know what you're doing with that fucking sword."

My shoulders instinctively curl inward before I catch myself and force them back. The weight of everyone's stares presses against my skin as I reset.

"Oh, of course, Felix!" I chirp, bouncing on my toes. "I'll do my very best to get it right this time!"

I still can't land my lines with the choreography. It's as if my body and brain are in open rebellion against me. During the first three days of shooting, I hit every one of my dialogue cues, but something about this sword renders me speechless.

This time, I'll get it right. I have to.

Felix sighs at my response. Dozens of crew members scurry about, adjusting lights, checking equipment, and fussing over every detail. It's a far cry from the rom-com sets I'm used to, where the biggest concern was whether my blush looked right. Here, everything is bigger, louder, more intense. The barrage of criticism isn't helping either.

Is this what it means to be pushed to my limit? To grow?

Or am I simply out of my depth?

Maybe I'm nothing but an impostor in heavy armor, fumbling both my lines and my footing.

Still, I square my shoulders. Serious actresses don't crumble. They command the screen.

From behind the grimy window of Robyn's home, I watch

the sheriff's men terrorize our village set—their boots kick up dust on the weathered cobblestones. The props master spent hours arranging those knocked-over market stalls.

My heart races as I wait for my cue, trying to channel Robyn's righteous anger. I spot Jeremy Vaughn, who plays our priest, taking his practiced fall as Dante looms over him. That's my moment.

"Action, still rolling!" calls the assistant director.

I burst through the door.

"Hey," I shout, charging forward toward the sword lying in the dirt. I reach for the weapon, but the grip still feels awkward. *Wait, that wasn't my whole line.* "Sheriff."

"CUT!"

Felix's megaphone pierces through the air, and I flinch.

"For the tenth time," he groans, "the line is 'Hey, Sheriff,' not 'Hey,' pause, 'Sheriff.' This isn't working." He paces through the crowd for a breath, then snaps his fingers. "Also, it'll be better if you say it with some of the feminine vulnerability you're known for?"

My cheeks burn.

Robyn is attacking the sheriff. Why should she be vulnerable right now?

"I can try it that way, but it may take away from Robyn's momentum."

He exchanges glances with one of the studio executives hovering nearby, his jaw working as if chewing on words he can't say in front of witnesses. "Look, I get the whole female empowerment angle. I do, trust me—I have a daughter, okay? But maybe having you deliver the line naturally, instead of forcing a tough-lady persona, will help you nail it."

Well, that's one way to tell me my acting is atrocious.

"Sure, let's try it that way." I can't let him make me feel small.

The costume department descends on me again. I struggle

with the chest plate, fingers clawing at the pinching metal. "Ouch, these leather straps are driving me mad," I hiss, my words barely audible over the set noise.

"Not your best wardrobe." Dante's voice slides in from behind, hot breath tickling my ear. My stomach lurches as he materializes beside me, too close for comfort.

I backpedal. "I didn't mean anything bad by it, I—"

"My sisters would kill me if they saw this scene." He cuts me off with a casual shrug, leaning against a nearby set piece.

"Your sisters?" I spin toward him. "I didn't know about them." The words tumble out before I can stop them, revealing I'd memorized—I mean, happened to read about—the three brothers he's mentioned in countless interviews.

"They're huge fans of yours." His eyes spark with amusement. "Been begging me for your autograph since I got on set."

"Oh." *Eloquent, Reese*. I'm absolutely crushing this conversation. I cross my arms, skepticism dripping from my voice. "Is that why you're such a sudden feminist now?" I immediately want to dissolve into the floor.

"Fuck yeah," he fires back without hesitation, "but in no way am I claiming to be a perfect ally. I know fighters, though, and whatever suggestions Felix has aren't true for a warrior like you."

"I—" The words catch in my throat as Dante moves with lightning speed. Suddenly, he's in front of me again, his blade glinting under the set lights.

He drops his voice to a commanding whisper. "Since you won't let me inspect the weight of your sword, try holding it with two hands. Keep your shoulders squared and your knees bent."

I wind my fingers over the hilt. "Like this?"

"Weapon hand near the guard, the other on the pommel when you pick it up." His lips curl into a seductive, megawatt smile, and—against all odds—something inside me loosens.

I walk back to my starting position, feeling the heat of his gaze on the back of my neck.

"Rolling!" Felix shouts.

We run through the scene again. When I charge forward, I snatch up the weapon. I pray the movement looks more graceful than it feels as I follow Dante's suggestion and hold it with both hands.

"Hey, Sheriff!" I shout.

Dante hesitates for a heartbeat until I give him a subtle signal, my eyes widening. His own flash with recognition as he delivers the line.

"Oh, how delightful," he drawls, circling me like a predator. "The common folk show such spirit. But surely you understand, taxes are the crown's divine right."

I go to strike, but the sword betrays me and falls out of both my hands with a cramp. The blade clatters to the ground, the metallic ring echoing across the silent set.

"Cut!" Felix stalks toward me, the crew parting before him like sheep fleeing from a hungry wolf. "This is pathetic. You won't infuse sex appeal into the role; you can't manage your weapon." His voice slices through the air. "Your agent promised me an actress who could handle both the physical and emotional demands of this role."

"The stumbling matches Robyn's character at this point in the story," I blurt out, my voice trembling with desperation. The excuse tastes like ash in my mouth as Felix's eyes narrow.

"Oh darling," he drones, "you're supposed to act uncertain, not embody it." He wheels toward the crew, his voice deliberately loud enough for everyone to hear. "The studio specifically wanted someone who could do their own stunts for this role—no doubles, no CGI tricks. We're paying triple-A action movie rates for someone who claimed they could handle fight choreography. Instead, we got…" He gestures vaguely at me, leaving the insult unspoken.

"What we got," he continues, yanking off his glasses, "is a pretty face who can't deliver a single line without stumbling. Sure, you'll look great on the poster, but at what cost?" He massages his temples. "Each reshoot day burns through a quarter million dollars, and the investors are breathing down my neck."

My eyes drop to my boots, the lump in my throat threatening to choke me.

His mouth twists into a sneer as he turns his back to me. "The whole marketing campaign is built around you doing your own stunts—the behind-the-scenes footage, the promotional interviews, everything. Your contract specifically states no stunt doubles. And we're a month away from the big raft sequence, which requires perfect execution."

The collective groans of the crew hit me like physical blows. This can't be happening.

"I can do this," I insist. My accent betrays me, rounding with each word, as it always does when I'm nervous. "I've trained for months. Something feels off with this sword. It's heavier than what I've been practicing with."

"Marcus!" Felix calls out above the uncomfortable murmurs. "Get over here."

The head stunt coordinator emerges from behind the trunk of a nearby redwood. "What's the issue?"

"Props must have had a mixup. This isn't her weapon," Dante explains, biceps flexing as he picks up my fallen blade. My cheeks burn as I catch myself staring at his arms, remembering how he'd pulled me aside earlier to warn me about the weight being off. If only I'd listened instead of being too proud to admit I was struggling.

Marcus examines the hilt, deep creases forming between his eyes. "You're right, it's not what we approved for this scene." The validation in his voice only makes me feel worse about dismissing Dante's concerns.

"Exactly," Dante mutters. "We need her designated sword,

the one balanced specifically for these early scenes where Robyn's still learning." He turns to me. "Your sequence requires specific balance points. The weapon you should be using is intended to be lighter than the waster you've been practicing with." The gentleness in his explanation, especially after Felix's public dressing-down, makes my heart race for entirely different reasons.

Marcus nods, agreeing with Dante and turns to the crew. "Props! Armory! We need the B-14 sword setup, now!"

"Why the hell wasn't the right sword on set?" Felix's face reddens. "Get her the correct weapon. And someone find out who messed up the equipment rotation so I can fire them. We're not paying millions to shoot with the wrong props."

The props master stammers something about inventory mix-ups, but Felix is already moving.

"With my regular sword, I know I can nail this," I call after him.

"Here's what we'll do, sweetie." His rancid coffee breath singes my nostrils as he walks back toward me. "We'll reorganize the shoot. All dialogue scenes and basic choreography first. I'm giving you a month to master the advanced sequences before the raft scene—that's your make-or-break moment. If you can't handle it by then, we bring in a double, contract or no contract. Clear?"

I nod, relief and panic mixing in my chest. "Crystal clear. I'll be ready."

The condescension in his tone makes my skin crawl, but I keep my face carefully blank. His lips curl into a satisfied smirk before he turns to the EP and instantly switches personas.

"Victor! This staffing situation is exactly what I was telling you about." He gestures at the sword with exaggerated frustration. "Let's discuss this over coffee. Fifteen-minute break, everyone!"

One month to master this new sword, strengthen my body, perfect these lines, and prepare for the raft scene.

I'll need to double my training, maybe even triple it.

And I'll have to convince myself that putting my head underwater isn't as terrifying as it feels.

As the crew disperses, I catch sympathetic glances from the sound team and realize there's still a boom mic hovering above me. *Ugh.* I want to vanish. But before I can escape, I find Dante watching me.

"That guy is a fucking asshole," he says.

Of course he heard everything. Having been dressed down like a child in front of a real fighter compounds my humiliation.

"It's fine," I lie. "Thank you for intervening with the sword." The words taste bitter. I feel stupid and helpless, as if I've let him fight my battles. He pointed out the equipment issue earlier, and all I could do was criticize him about his lines.

His gaze turns all business now. "Just looking out for your safety."

"Really?" The question slips out, more vulnerable than I intended.

"The safety of the crew is my job. And I know how much you value professionalism. Besides," he continues, "I've seen too many people get hurt trying to prove themselves with the wrong equipment. Your choreography is solid, Reese. Let's keep it that way."

"Thanks for—" I pause, my tongue twisting itself into a knot.

"All good." He shrugs, a strand of hair falling into his eyes, and he blows it out of the way with a cocky flick, like he's James Dean.

I take a deep breath. "I'm sorry for being hard on you about your lines. Clearly I'm in no position to judge, since I can't seem to string together a coherent sentence today." I sigh, rubbing my forehead.

"I want this to work. It's not just another role to me. It's important. And—" I stop myself before I blurt out something horrifically earnest, like how terrified I am of failing and being stuck in rom-com purgatory forever.

Instead, I clear my throat and force a more dignified approach. "What I meant to say is, I'm sorry for being impatient with you."

"I get it. I know what it's like to struggle with something that should be simple." His fingers tap against his sword hilt, a nervous gesture I hadn't noticed before. "I have dyslexia. I can wield a sword, but if you make me read 'ether'—I mean, 'either,' it always trips me up."

"Either versus ether," I repeat, nodding with understanding.

"Yeah. My brain says 'either,' my mouth says 'ether,' and now I'm going to be fucking up that word for a week." He chuckles, a little sheepish, a little endearing. The kind of laugh that makes me want to learn every word he struggles with—

Nope.

"That must be frustrating," I offer, my tone gentler than it's ever been with him.

"Sometimes the simplest lines…" He bites the inside of his cheek, tilting his head. "What I'm saying is, everyone needs the right tools, whether it's a properly balanced sword or…"

He trails off, rubbing the back of his neck. "Anyway. I'll figure it out. You focus on nailing your scenes, with the correct equipment."

What is wrong with me? I've spent the entire three days at the table read and this week rolling my eyes at him, convinced I had him pegged as the irritating playboy who coasts by on good looks, a family name, and never-earned talent.

But I was wrong.

Not *completely* wrong—he's still frustratingly flirtatious when he should be focusing—but wrong enough that shame burns in my chest.

While I've been up here on my moral high ground, he's been silently dealing with challenges I never bothered to consider.

The rest of the day drags on. Despite the better sword, I still can't manage to say my lines while performing my choreography, earning many of Felix's signature *I am deeply disappointed in you* stares. His one-month ultimatum looms over me like a storm cloud.

I need to start taking things into my own hands.

Chapter 7
Reese

IT'S NOW OR NEVER.

I traverse the path between the cabins to the one closest to the lake. My boots crunch on the gravel. My metal bra digs into my ribs with every step, the chain mail belt clinking like demon toddlers banging pots across the quiet lake.

I should've changed out of this costume. But it's already late, I'm fresh off set, and if I stop walking now, I'll overthink it and talk myself out of it.

I rehearse what I'll say: *I need your help.* My lips move silently, practicing.

Simple. Professional. Not desperate at all.

I approach what should be Dante's cabin. Laughter spills from the window, along with the sound of bass. Of course he's having a party.

This is a bad idea. I fidget with my leather skirt.

I could back out, ask Heather for another trainer, but that would cost the studio money.

Money Felix has been complaining about nonstop.

Plus, requesting another trainer screams "disagreeable diva."

I have to do this.

It's either ask Dante for help or fail tomorrow. What if he rejects me? I was kind of mean to him. He seems like the type to enjoy that sort of thing, though. I bite my lip, weighing options.

You're out of options, Reese. I huff, inching up his cabin steps. When I reach his porch, I peek through the window.

The place looks like he personally flew in a designer from *Architectural Digest*.

How did he get his own cabin? There are shearling rugs and a large couch. A Vitamix blender on the counter and a fully stocked bar cart?

The only thing I packed was my workout gear and a kettle for tea. What more could a person need? We're only here for three months.

I raise my fist and knock twice. No answer. I ball up my fist tighter and slam it hard, but the door swings open and my fist connects with warm, bare skin. I stumble backward and find myself staring at Dante's very firm, very naked chest, which is shimmering like a disco ball. The faint scent of smoke wraps around me like a spell.

Goodness gracious. I can't help but stare, momentarily frozen.

Someone calls, "Dante, darling!" from inside, where willowy figures dressed in cashmere are lounging. "Is the delivery finally here?"

Ignoring them, he glances between my fist pressed against his sternum and my revealing costume. We're standing too close for two people wearing so little, and his body heat is making it difficult to remember why I came.

I yank my fist away, cradling it.

Beyond his shoulder, Marcus and Simon laugh by the bar. Is that our head writer raising a glass like tomorrow's 5:00 a.m. call time doesn't exist?

Loneliness slithers down my neck, cold and familiar. A PA hastily hides her drink, eyes widening with recognition. *Great.*

The staff always avoids me on set, yet here in Dante's cabin, they look comfortable—at ease in ways they never are around me.

"To what do I owe the pleasure of Hollywood's next action star showing up at my door?" He surveys me, eyebrow arched. "Does production know you're out past curfew?"

Yeah, I was right. Coming here was a mistake.

I should flee to my own cabin, but I can't. My feet remain rooted, betraying me. I need this. I need him.

I clear my throat. "Does production know you're hosting a party during filming, Mr. Hastings?"

"*Touché*." His mouth quirks. "Though we both know the crew turns an eye to certain indiscretions."

Do they? I didn't know that.

"Some of us care about the rules," I say, lacking conviction even to my own ears.

"How's the bruise healing? Makeup did a good job hiding it." His gaze licks over every inch of my face as if he's savoring me.

"Nothing I can't manage," I clip.

He steps back, giving me the space I desperately need to remain focused. "What really brought you here, fighter? Something tells me it wasn't to check on my line memorization."

"I need you to train me," I say, meeting his gaze.

He crosses his arms, muscles flexing. "Thought you weren't interested in my help, Miss By-The-Book."

"I wasn't, and this is probably a horrible idea." I swallow. "But you're obviously incredible with a sword. The way you move—" I pause, getting a handle on myself. "You had my back when no one else did. That counts. And I need to impress Felix, which means I need—" I gesture toward him.

"Me."

I grimace at his mischievous grin. "Unlike you, I'm struggling to nail the choreography and lines at the same time."

"What about Nick Valentine?"

"Nick follows Felix's orders to focus on my appearance instead of giving me the help I actually need," I say, shifting my weight. "I've never struggled like this before—my lines vanish when I move. The sword's throwing me off."

He steps closer, his tall frame filling the doorway. "On the piste, I can only focus on my saber and my opponent. Reciting all of your lines while fencing would be impossible."

Relief washes over me. "So you understand."

"I've never actually trained anyone," he admits, running a hand through his tousled hair.

"Then why offer in the first place?"

"Thought you'd appreciate my work ethic."

"Never mind, this was desperate," I sigh and turn to leave.

"Wait," he says, stepping onto the porch. "Not desperate—dedicated." His sincerity catches me off guard. "I haven't trained anyone officially, but I mentor teammates constantly. Felix brought me on for authenticity. Helping you is part of my job."

I spin back, my hope returning. "You'll actually train me?"

He moves closer. "Of course. Now, be honest—do you always show up at strangers' doors demanding help?"

"Only as Xena the Warrior Princess," I quip, hands clanging against my chain mail skirt.

His laugh—head tilted back, eyes bright—sends goose bumps up my arms. That sound shouldn't affect me so deeply.

"She jokes! You might have a future in comedy. I thought you were all schedules and drills."

I glance up at him, straining my neck. He towers over me—imposing yet somehow reassuring. I wonder if he means what he says or if I'm just his next target. From what I've seen, it's the latter.

"Ha ha," I mock. "Let's focus. I won't expect free training."

"Do tell."

"I can help with your dyslexia," I offer. "My best friend has it too. Cleo says it's cruelly ironic they named it dyslexia, considering it affects people who struggle with spelling."

"It's Greek. *Dys* meaning 'difficult,' *lexis* meaning 'words.' Ironic, indeed." He smiles, angling toward me, waiting for reciprocation. I don't oblige.

I nod briskly. "I helped her with recordings and phonics-based techniques. It bridges written and spoken words. I can make recordings for you."

Surprise flickers across his face. "I used that method in college."

"At Princeton, right?" I realize my mistake instantly, eyes widening.

"Don't wear out that Wikipedia page." He smirks.

I cringe. "If we have a deal, let's start training."

"Tonight? During my carefully curated soirée?"

"Felix wants reshoots tomorrow. If I mess up again…" Anxiety silences me.

His golden eyes trace over me again, considering. "Fine. Ten minutes. Studio."

"Great, thank you, I'll go change—"

"Keep the costume." His grin turns wicked, sending heat racing down my spine. "I'm starting to like it, *Hollywood*."

I step closer until we're inches apart, my head tilted back to meet his gaze. "Never call me that."

"You're right," he concedes. "'Fighter' suits you better."

I retreat before he sees how his words affect me, trying to ignore the tempting urge to trace the trail of glitter on his chest.

This knot in my stomach isn't attraction. It can't be. I walk away. I've been here before—watched my career nearly collapse because I confused fiction with reality. I don't fall for costars. Not again. Not with everything at stake.

Chapter 8
Dante

Through the on-set training gym window, there she is, already lost in her stretching routine.

She leans forward, her arms arcing gracefully, extending to the side in a seated hamstring stretch. A sliver of skin flashes at her waist, teasing me before she pulls herself deeper into the stretch.

Fuuuck.

My cock hardens at the perfect sight.

Decidedly unprofessional. What would Reese think?

My phone vibrates insistently, notifications from the cabin party crowd demanding attention. I silence it.

Teaching Reese Sinclair to fence is exactly what I need.

It's the perfect credential to present at my disciplinary review. *Look, I've changed so much that America's darling actually hangs out with me.*

And maybe she intrigues me. There's an intensity to her that those polished interviews miss completely. I want to discover what other surprises she's keeping under wraps.

"Different look," I say, pushing through the door, allowing

myself one lingering glance at how her oversized workout sweats make her somehow magnetic.

"I was not going to keep wearing that costume."

"This is better," I admit, holding up my hand. "I brought you a proper blade."

She arches one perfect eyebrow. "Thought those were under lock and key."

"I can be very persuasive when motivated," I say, letting the steel sword dance between my fingers before extending it to her. I can't resist showing off a little. Old habits. "And I may have a key to the armory."

Our hands brush as she takes the sword, sending an unexpected spark of awareness through my fingers. Her pupils dilate. No matter how much she tries to remain professional, her small tells give her away—the quick, nervous sweep of her tongue over her bottom lip, the way she blinks a fraction too fast before glancing down.

"Of course you do."

I grin, not concealing how eager I am to be here. I have nothing to hide from her that I don't already keep hidden from everyone else.

We circle each other on the exercise mats. "Let's start with the scene you need to nail for tomorrow," I say, cracking my knuckles. "Show me where you're getting stuck."

"You saw me on set today. Every time I try to use this thing, it's like I've forgotten how to think, let alone look like a real thief."

"Show me," I repeat.

She doesn't hesitate, launching into her monologue.

"They've underestimated me my whole life. While—the king —our king—" She takes an unsteady step forward, the sword wobbling in an awkward arc. Then she moves the blade through the air in front of her, hesitant. She bites her lip, her brow furrowed, too in her head. "See what I mean? This is impossible."

"Not impossible. Go through the entire scene from the top. Don't stop even if you fumble."

Her gaze sharpens, like she's deciding whether to listen or not. But then she drops the sword at my feet and strides across the room. Frustration flickers across her face as she tucks her hair behind her ear.

She begins her advance, but her footwork is wrong—leading with the back foot instead of the front. Her recovery to pick up the blade shows poor form—back curved, no power from her legs.

The misbehaved part of me itches to show her exactly how it's done, slide behind her, press close, and guide those tense muscles through every motion. But I hold back, keep my hands in my pockets. She needs to move through this on her own, even if watching her struggle is delicious torture.

"Hey, Sheriff." She points the sword at me and stumbles with the choreography, hacking stiffly at the imaginary soldiers surrounding us.

Her stance is all wrong, her core disengaged.

"They've underestimated me my whole life. While our king eats his feasts—" She's supposed to be moving, fighting off the sheriff's soldiers.

Instead, she's planted like a statue.

What the fuck has Nick been doing? Probably too busy ogling her.

My jaw clenches.

I can't watch this anymore.

"Enough." I step closer. "Your stance is killing me. That's your foundation. Without it, you'll never maintain that blade while delivering those eloquent speeches of yours."

"This is the best I can do," she sighs, her southern lilt emerging in her frustration.

"May I?" I gesture toward her, already anticipating how the perfectionist in her will bristle at correction. Surprisingly, she nods.

I'm about to touch Reese Sinclair. I bite my cheek and inhale deeply.

Then I'm standing behind her, my hands hovering above her hips. My body responds to the proximity. My blood rushes in strange patterns beneath my skin. I use my foot to nudge her feet apart. She yields without resistance.

"*Rasstav'nogi*," I command.

"Huh?" She turns, her lips pursed in confusion.

"Sorry—fucking habit from my fencing coach. He trains us in Russian half the time," I explain, regaining my composure. "Spread your legs wider, weight back," I instruct, keeping my voice low near the top of her head. "Relax. You're too tense." I brush my fingers along the back of her neck, and a shiver rolls down her spine.

A soft exhale escapes her lips before she swivels around, brown eyes flaring.

"I wouldn't be tense if you weren't hovering over me like some…" She searches for the right word.

"Like?"

"Like some, I don't know, know-it-all!"

"I've been called worse." The corner of my mouth quirks up as she bristles. "Usually by much scarier people than America's sweetheart."

"Somehow that doesn't surprise me."

"You know your accent slips when you're frustrated," I note. "It's charming."

"It does not." She scowls. "Let's try again. Please."

The transformation is fascinating—one moment she's all controlled poise, the next she's barely contained.

"Fine, but you're not going to like my advice." She waits for me to continue. I don't break her stare. "You're fighting yourself.

I see how hard you're trying, but that's what's holding you back. Trust your instincts. Square your shoulders. Loosen your arms and put a soft bend in your knees."

"I am doing all of that, I promise. But trying to remember the lines, the footwork, where the camera is going to be, and making sure I don't block my face, on top of your—" She cuts herself off, flustered.

"Okay." I want to make her see what I see. "Let's simplify. Just the movement first."

She exhales sharply and centers herself.

"When you move, engage your core first, your obliques, then your back." I give her lats a playful pinch. "Here."

She groans again, not a pretty one, but something bordering on a vexed cry. Maybe I should stop fucking around. "I've never struggled this much with a role before." She collapses onto the mats.

I sink down next to her. There's that determined look in her eyes, the same one from set and the table read.

"I know what it's like when everyone else makes it look effortless and you're grinding twice as hard." Then, because I can't help myself—and because she's too damn serious for her own good—I lay on the thickest cowboy drawl I can manage. *"But sugar, you gotta get back on your horse and ride. Cowgirls don't cry."*

She blinks, a genuine smile tugging at her lips despite her obvious attempt to maintain distance. "Did you just quote *Heartland Heritage* to me?"

I shrug. "When I said my sisters were big fans, I should've admitted that I was too. For a year straight, they couldn't stop saying that line." Neither could I.

"I'm flattered," she says carefully, her professional mask slipping back into place. "I'd be happy to sign something for them like you mentioned. Just not during training."

"Noted." She stares at the ground, and I don't want her to

close up. A second passes, and another, until I say, "My favorite of yours was *Strings of Time*, actually."

"Are you messing with me right now?" She squints at me, like she's waiting for the punchline. "You're seriously telling me you liked a romance where a physicist discovers time travel, tries to stop the apocalypse, and somehow finds time to fall for a time refugee?"

"Would you rather I lie?"

She cracks a little with a laugh, shaking her head. "Not a lot of people have seen that one, but I loved playing Aria. It was the first time I wasn't cast as the ditzy girl."

"That scene where you're talking about being the oldest, carrying all that weight but wanting to make a name for yourself?" I lean in. "Hits close to home. Middle child here—always trying to prove myself against my siblings." I catch myself getting too honest.

Her brow lifts. "I'm impressed you remember so much of it."

"My sisters were all rooting for her and Julian to get together, but I thought the romance kind of undercut her story. She didn't need him to save her—realistically, she would've figured out that time machine mess on her own." I smirk. "Just like you're going to figure out how to do this choreography."

"That's kind of you."

"Not trying to flatter you. If I were, I'd tell you I had your poster up in my room, the one where you're lying in all those magnolias."

"Are you serious?" Her pupils dilate.

I shrug. "What can I say? You're my generation's it girl."

"Not the worst thing I've been told by a fan." She emphasizes the word *fan* with that frost I'm getting used to, but there's a warmth underneath. "I once had a man tell me he got a life-size doll made of me."

"That would be very interesting." I hold back the cringe.

"Don't get any ideas." When she gives me her real smile—

not the Hollywood one—I want nothing more than to see it again.

"How did you prepare for your role as Aria?"

"I was twenty years old and had no clue what I was doing. It was all awkward line readings and praying I wouldn't trip over my own feet. I did learn the Charleston, though, for when we traveled back to the twenties and had to dance. It was really fun."

Dance.

"Sounds like you weren't trying so hard at being perfect. Unlike now."

"This is different. I have to nail tomorrow's scene. And then there's the one next week, with the bandits, and the one after that with the king, and—" She catches herself. "A leading lady doesn't get out of her head during a scene. She stays focused."

A leading lady? It catches me by surprise. She's one of the most famous actresses of our time. "Come on, how many movies have you been in?"

"None like this," she whispers, and then I see it.

There's a need here. A desire to assert herself on this set.

Damn. Her vulnerability gets under my skin, seeing someone else wearing a mask like that. Because I know exactly what it's like, keeping up appearances while something wilder claws to get out. It makes me want to show her just how good it feels when you finally stop fighting it.

For a split second, the moment burns too hot, too fast, and I want to do what I do best, to show her how much I see her, to enjoy whatever the tightrope of tension is between us, but I keep the reins on myself.

This is important to her.

I'm going to do my best to get her to where she wants to go, because where else am I going to do that this year?

"Right then, time to shake things up." I say, standing. "You'll never nail this if you keep overthinking everything. We gotta adapt, improvise, and own it."

Before she can protest, I pull my phone from my pocket and scroll through my playlist until I find what I'm looking for. French electropop fills the room, and I turn up the volume to full blast, slide the phone onto the bench, and stand up, shaking out my legs and arms. Bass thrums through the mats beneath our feet as I roll my shoulders, letting the infectious rhythm take over.

"What exactly are you doing?"

"You need to get out of your skin," I say, extending my hands palm-up in invitation. When she hesitates, I wiggle my fingers playfully. "Come on, Reese. Dance with me."

Her look could freeze hell. "Absolutely not."

"Your form is too rigid." I move closer without quite touching her. "Let go a little." Before she can retreat, I capture her hands in mine and pull her up.

"The whole point is to have control," she argues, but her fingers curl into mine despite her protests.

"Sometimes control comes from surrender." I guide her into a gentle spin, keeping my touch light.

"This is ridiculous!" She stumbles, colliding with my chest. I fight the urge to pull her closer. "I'm supposed to be learning choreography!"

"And I'm helping you." I place a hand on her waist to steady her, the thin fabric of her shirt doing nothing to mask the heat radiating off her. "My coach, Lev, scariest Russian bastard you'll ever meet, made us take ballet and ballroom when we got sloppy in training. Seemed ridiculous, but it worked."

Reese looks skeptical, but she starts to sway, her body unconsciously leaning into mine. "*Tantsuy so mnoy*," I murmur, my lips barely brushing her ear. "Come on, dance with me."

"I don't know about this." She hesitates but doesn't pull away.

I let the music guide us. It pulses through the speaker on my phone as I lead her across the floor. I tower over her rigid frame and hum along to the song with an easy smile.

"Relax. This isn't the Charleston." Her face remains carefully neutral. "Like this—it's like advancing and retreating with your sword." She follows my lead, still too formal, still thinking too hard. My hand finds her waist, steadying her before gliding to the small of her back and guiding her through a turn. "Swordplay is its own kind of dance," I tell her. "Let it flow through you. Light. Fluid."

"This isn't helping."

"Let me worry about that," I say, twirling her out of my arms and giving in to my wilder impulses. I drop to the floor with theatrical flair, belting the wrong lyrics out as I go. She stares at me with equal parts exasperation and fascination.

Then it happens. A laugh bursts out of her, and slowly, deliciously, she starts moving to the music. All unconscious sensuality.

"There we go. You're loosening up," I say, standing back up. "Now. Say your lines."

"I feel ridiculous," she mutters. Her fingers brush against mine as she moves—definitely not an accident, though we'll both pretend it is for the sake of her carefully constructed boundaries.

"Humor me."

And she does.

Not only does she humor me, but she nails every single line, the words rolling off her tongue. There's this new fire in her voice I haven't heard before—the rhythm's unlocked something feral and real inside her. When she finishes, those brown eyes go wide, like she can't quite believe what just happened.

"Keep moving," I encourage. She's all hips and strong arms, moving with a sway that's impossible to ignore. When she catches me staring—oh, and I'm definitely staring—I don't look away.

I grab her sword, bringing it over. "Keep listening to the music and watch me in the mirror," I say, retrieving my own blade. I stand beside her, getting into position. "Ready to dance, fighter?"

"What do you want me to do?" She laughs.

"Repeat after me."

We flow through her sequence, and fuck, it's mesmerizing. Every step of hers lands exactly where it needs to. My chest tightens with a rush of pride because I knew she had this in her, she just needed the right push to unleash it.

"Again," I call out, "but this time, I want to hear those lines. Loud and clear!"

Her words cut through the music.

"Yes, Reese! That's exactly it!"

Her face lights up with pure victory as she twists around. We're both on a high. There's a flash in her eyes, a split second where she realizes we're crossing lines we can't uncross.

And yeah, maybe I'm looking at her like she's everything I want wrapped up in one stunning package. Maybe that's exactly what's got her spooked.

Can't bring myself to care, though. Not when she's in front of me like this, her whole being illuminated beautifully.

As a fencer, I'm trained to pick up the most subtle shifts in movement. It's a sixth sense, honed over a decade. Walking with Reese at midnight is no different.

Our breaths have synced, as well as our strides. She notices but remains quiet.

The forest feels alive around us, darker than city nights, even with crew lights throwing shadows on the path. Everything's sharper out here, pine needles crunching underfoot, August air biting like early San Francisco training mornings, the wild darkness calling to my restless soul.

Her cabin appears too soon.

"Thank you for walking me back tonight." The first porch step creaks as she steps on it. "You don't need to go out of your way next time."

"You never know what's hiding in these woods, Reese." I finally hand over her bag that I'd been carrying during our stroll.

"Well, good night."

I should leave, find something to shake this feeling. Probably indulge in one of the late-night distractions waiting at my cabin. But my feet feel like vines have wrapped around them, attaching me to the earth.

She pauses, fingers trailing along the weathered wooden railings. "Wait," she says, and my pulse kicks up. "I need your number." She digs in her bag and holds out her phone. It's in a simple case, white, no frills or extras.

"For training purposes only, of course," I say, reaching for it.

"To confirm our training schedule and the scene recordings I promised." Her eyes don't meet mine.

I input each digit deliberately. "Purely professional."

"Exactly."

"I had fun tonight," I admit and return her phone.

When she looks up, there's a quirk to her lips, her curated mask slipping. "Yeah? Me too. Thanks for helping me…you know. Get out of my head a bit. I have to admit, I didn't have much faith in you, but you're not a bad teacher."

"Oh, don't flatter me," I laugh. "You're pretty good at having fun, even if I didn't have much faith in *you*."

"Hopefully it'll help me succeed tomorrow, Mr. Hastings."

"You don't have to do that, you know." The words escape before I can stop them.

"Do what?" She shrugs, playing coy. My eyes flicker down to her wrist, lingering on a freckle I noticed tonight. The way she swayed her hips earlier, how the scent of her thick blonde hair lingered, how it brushed against my biceps every time she turned…it's all there, clear in my mind.

I take a breath and decide that if I want to break down these walls, my usual charm won't work. I'll have to be direct. "Since you love rules so much and we'll be training together…how about we make some? Starting with dropping the professional act. At least with me."

"What act?"

"I see right through all your sugarcoating."

"To what?"

"Something that burns."

On cue, she finds the end of her hair and spins it between her pointer and thumb. That nervous tic again. "Fine. Then here's my rule: no distractions."

"Distractions happen naturally," I say, thinking of midnight swims and impromptu adventures. "The trick is learning to dance with them."

She rolls her eyes, jutting her hip out. "Just…keep it professional. No flirting, no jokes, no distracting comments."

"*Kak skazhesh', milaya.*" My Russian is barely proficient, but it's enough to make her brows furrow.

"What does that mean?"

"Where's the fun in telling?" I grin, enjoying how she fights her curiosity.

"Not fair."

"Life rarely is."

She steps back, all playfulness fading. "I'm serious. The nonfraternization clause might be a joke to most people, but it matters to me. I've worked too hard to be seen as another actress sleeping with her costar. I understand the benefit of our new… engagement. But that's all it is. A *temporary* engagement."

"Well, you're in luck, because I take my training partners very seriously," I say. "Everything else…that's life's way of making things interesting."

Something in my voice must convince her. "Good. Set tomorrow, then training after?"

"Can't tomorrow. Heading to San Francisco after the morning shoot. My coach wants to see me, something I can't miss. Saturday?"

"Premiere. Back Sunday."

"Sunday then."

"Fine. After that, we can train most nights. *If* shooting wraps on time."

The space between us shrinks with each word. Every instinct screams at me to move, to chase this spark wherever it leads, but for once I hold myself in check.

I force myself back. "Night, fighter."

The air crackles. Her eyes lock with mine, and I think maybe…

She breaks first, clearing her throat. "Right. Good night."

The entire walk to my cabin, I fight the urge to look over my shoulder. Some habits die hard. But then again, the best pleasures in life are worth waiting for.

Chapter 9
Dante

French Fencing Star Quentin Brisbois Signs
Multimillion-Dollar Stryde Sneaker Deal

My training gym has always felt like home. Today, I barely feel welcome. It's my first session with Coach since he returned from the Olympics.

I lunge forward, sluggish. Too many late nights, too many drinks—we both know it.

"Still favoring that left leg," Lev grunts, jabbing his saber toward my foot. The blade catches light like a warning.

Shit.

Lev Petrov, a Russian-American Olympic Saber coach, has trained me since Princeton. He's the U.S. Men's Saber national coach and my second father—tougher than my real dad and far more intimidating. His love expresses itself through brutal honesty and punishing workouts.

"*Bozhe moy*, you think I don't see? Hungover, reeking of

cigarettes. *Burnaya noch'?* You party all night yet expect to fence like a champion?"

I white-knuckle my saber, swallowing the urge to lash out. Old me would've stormed off. Instead, I breathe, letting the familiar weight of the blade ground me.

This training is crucial. Since my suspension, I haven't trained with my team. Lev's been coaching everyone else, leaving me solo—it's the longest I've gone without a real opponent. I'm rusty.

I've kept up drills in my San Francisco apartment's training room—state-of-the-art dummy, mirrors, space to lunge—and worked with the *Robyn Hood* crew, but nothing replaces facing someone who breathes, moves, and thinks.

It's about more than bad form.

It's everything since the suspension. Lev saw past the rich party boy and made me something real. My impulsiveness—that need to be seen, to react, to fight—got me suspended.

I plant my feet wider, focusing on my burning thighs as I reset. Gotta prove I'm worth his time.

"Another gold medal turned you into a drama queen, Coach," I say, masking the sting of his disappointment. "I'm fencing fine."

His laugh cuts deep. "Fine? *Nyet.* You're a ghost. Too slow. Where's my champion who made this blade dance?"

Four months, and the champion is gone.

The rich kid who fucked it all up.

The disappointment.

The unlovable one.

The saber feels wrong in my hand—heavy, foreign. I adjust my grip, searching for that sweet spot where it became part of me. My throat tightens.

Inhale.

Three hundred forty-two days until the new season. Three hundred forty-two chances to prove I'm still relevant.

"Yeah, fine. That means shut up and keep going, right?"

"*Da.* What else you have that's more important?"

Nothing. Without fencing, I'm nobody. The movie set, parties, agitating Reese—all distractions. Only with a blade do I matter. Only here does my family see me as belonging among the Hastings.

Outside the piste? Different story. The Princeton crew only shows up for the Dom Pérignon. My contacts want Party Dante, not me.

My teammates ghosted me—afraid of USFA or SafeSport finding them with a suspended player. Only Linus sent a *hang in there* text.

The fencing world turned its back. Nobody's risking their career by associating with me. Where do I fit when they're all living our old life—training, competing, being champions?

I try to bury it all, but my chest constricts.

Lev's eyes narrow with pity. Worse. "*Khorosho,*" he says, raising his blade. "Advance-lunge drills. Show me your fire can do more than burn you."

I nod and set my stance. The world fades as I grip my saber, my mind finally quieting.

It's just me and my blade.

I lunge—step too short. Miss by inches.

"Fuck," I mutter, resetting.

"*Opyat,*" Coach barks. Again.

I repeat until my quads scream.

"Too slow. It's the drinking. People expect you back stronger next season. Can't defend your title like this."

"I'm not drinking that much," I lie. Maybe that stops today. Smoking's my only other vice now—no partying, no drugs, no bodies.

Lev's eyebrows shoot up. "*Vresh' kak siziy merin,*" he says. *You're lying like a gray gelding.*

Whatever the fuck that means.

He lowers his blade, crossing his arms. "How many years I watch you grow in this gym? *Khuligan.*"

"Your point?"

"My point?" Lev growls, accent thickening. "You're always chasing cameras, media, interviews. Your teammates? All timid, focused. But you need attention. An obsession, Dante. A dangerous one."

"I'm the most handsome guy on the team. Can't blame the media for wanting my picture."

"*Krasota ne vechna.* But skill? Passion? These things last." He studies me. "Why did you start fencing?"

I sigh. "You know why."

"Tell me. I suddenly forgot, like you've forgotten basic forms. *Moya pamyat' uzhe ne ta.*"

I snort at his games. "It was my punishment."

"*Gluposti*, Dante. Not why you keep fencing. You could quit after school, *da*? But you don't. Why? Because fencing is in your blood. Natural, like breathing. You love it, even when it hurts."

He's right, and I loathe him for his relentless wisdom.

He never grasped why I must embody this alter ego—the rebel, the showman. The one who effortlessly extracts smiles from strangers.

In a dynasty of overachievers—siblings flaunting their trophies, medals, and endless accolades—being merely "good" is worthless.

Alec conquers mountains. Brooklyn dominates figure skating. Cameron claimed the Premier League after a lifetime of soccer devotion. The younger ones follow suit: Ezra practically evolved gills in our Marin County compound pool. Francesca rocketed from go-karts straight to professional racing.

Childhood rendered me invisible. A phantom. Before fencing, I existed as nothing but a shadow.

Then I discovered power in attention.

It began subtly: pilfering alcohol from my parents' cabinet, ditching classes to crash exclusive parties. Each reckless decision, each calculated risk, delivered an intoxicating high nothing else could match.

People finally noticed me. They whispered my name.

At fourteen, they expelled me for chronic truancy. That same year, I commandeered my father's car for a joyride. Police apprehended me within fifteen minutes.

My mother's anguish guaranteed Dad's intervention. They'd exhausted every remedy—counselors, wilderness camps, nearly house arrest. Useless. While my siblings collected championships, I wore the mantle of family disgrace.

Following my joyride, I was shipped off to a boarding school that was renowned for reforming delinquent rich kids. Mandatory athletics offered two choices: fencing or water polo. No fucking way was I going to swallow all that chlorine.

During that first fencing practice, everything aligned. The perpetual noise in my mind silenced. I understood the blade. I mastered it. Instinctively.

Academics? Still an exercise in futility.

But fencing? Undeniable brilliance.

By fifteen, I dominated Nationals. At seventeen, Princeton offered a full scholarship to represent their Division 1 team. By twenty-two, an Olympic gold hung from my neck.

Fencing transcended sport. It became my salvation. The discipline, the precision—it forged purpose. Direction.

People carved my name into memory.

My reputation shadowed me everywhere. Rather than shed it, I amplified it. I inked my skin. I wore jewelry, started caring about how I looked in my clothes, and used my image as a weapon. I pushed cars to their limits, bought my yacht. I fucked, partied, and fenced like a god. I became fencing's notorious bad boy in a landscape of privileged, country-club competitors.

Yes, I shared their wealth, but I cultivated difference. I ensured everyone recognized it.

The strategy triumphed. The world validated my existence. Magazine covers, lucrative endorsements, insatiable fans. Everyone craved my friendship, my affection, my rivalry. For the first time, I wasn't someone's brother or the family failure—I was Dante fucking Hastings.

"It was the first thing I excelled at," I settle on. "But more than that, it made me feel whole."

Lev nods, a glimmer of understanding in his eyes. "And now? Without it, you feel lost, *da*?"

Yes. I swallow hard. "What if USFA doesn't let me back on the piste come next year?"

"More *gluposti*," he scoffs, but his tone is gentle. "You will fence again." He pauses, his eyes softening before he glances at the clock.

I lower my saber, wiping sweat off my brow. "What's the deal, Coach? You trying to get away from me?"

"No," he grunts, shaking his head. "I'm waiting for your charity work."

"This lecture wasn't enough?"

His bushy brows draw together, his face darkening. "*Nu chto…*fight like dogs with SafeSport and USFA to get you only one year suspension with community service. You will do what I tell you, *kapishe*?"

"What's the plan?" I sigh, already dreading whatever he has in store.

"I start youth program here for kids without rich parents to put them in sport and hopefully get scholarships. The ones with talent but no direction. I have one who needs role model." He fixes me with a stern look. "And speaking of direction, how is work going as stunt coordinator on movie?"

"They haven't fired me yet," I say carefully, avoiding any mention of Reese. Last thing I need is a lecture about professionalism from Coach's mustached face. I'd much prefer to hear those scoldings from Reese's soft lips instead.

"Good, good. Then you can handle this too. If you work hard there, you work hard here." He doesn't seem amused as he continues, "This girl I found, Dante. *Shestnadtsat let*. Reminds me of you when you first came here. She needs someone to show her the way. You could be that someone."

The words hit me like a roundhouse kick to the chest. A sixteen-year-old mini-me? *Fuck that.* I'm barely keeping my own shit together, and Lev wants me playing mentor?

"Come on, your girl needs a real coach, not some hothead who got suspended for starting fights."

"We both know why you did that, Dante. Even if you don't want to say truth or let me or Linus stand up for you." I groan at the reminder. What was the point of coming clean about the fight when I meant that hit? "You have much to offer, *blin*. Think about it. Sometimes, teaching others helps us remember why we love something in the first place. And this girl could benefit from someone who understands her."

"This is one of your worst ideas," I say.

"You underestimate yourself." He pauses. "Plus, you have no choice."

I set down my saber, running a hand through my hair as I consider my options. Not that I have many. It's either play nice with Coach's pet project or kiss my career goodbye.

But maybe this isn't the worst thing.

Training some kid will clean up my image, turning me from *hothead who got suspended* into *reformed bad boy who gives back to his community*. That's what the committee wanted, isn't it? Fuck, it might impress Reese, show her I'm not the trouble-maker she thinks I am.

"And how often are we talking?"

"You will work with Em every Friday at the end of our training," he says. "She practices with the other kids in the program Monday and Wednesday, but the others go too easy, and I want her to see one of my real stars."

"So the logical thought was to stick me with the trainwreck who's been suspended?" A girl's voice joins us in the room.

I turn and—Christ, Em is exactly what I was afraid of. Sixteen, half her head buzzed, thick black eyeliner like war paint. I used to armor myself the same way, all spikes and studs and fuck-you attitude, daring anyone to get close enough to see past it.

"What's wrong? Did Hot Topic run out of safety pins?" I say with the same old defensive rhythm I perfected at family dinners of six hotheaded kids growing up.

"Go fuck yourself," she snarls, hands clenching into fists. "At least I'm not some has-been who got kicked out of fencing for being a violent asshole. Did they take away your participation trophy when they suspended you?"

"You have some bite to you, kid."

"I'm not a kid—"

"*Ty sovsem obnaglel!*" Coach barks, his accent thickening with frustration.

"What's he saying?" she demands.

I smirk. Not so clever now. "He says I'm a natural talent, and you should be honored."

Coach's weathered face darkens. "*Vrosh i dazhe ne krasneysh!* I said no such thing, you little troublemaker. I said you are being rude and childish." He turns to Em. "This one, he thinks he's clever. Always has. Don't trust his translations."

"Great, so I get stuck with a liar for a sparring partner? I told you, I don't need another training day." Em crosses her arms, rebellion written in every line of her body. It's the same way I used to stand, challenging the world to prove me wrong.

"You two are giving me headache already. Em, this is Dante Hastings, my most talented student. Also most difficult. Like you!"

"And this is my charity case?"

"I'm not a fucking charity case," Em snaps. "And besides,

that's rich coming from the guy I saw in those photos. Doing lines on a yacht with Instagram models? Real role model material."

The words catch me off guard, heat rising to my face as I catch Coach's disapproving look. Great. *Just great.* I force a tight smile.

"*Zatknis,* both of you!" Coach thunders, making Em jump. "Em, get equipment. Dante, stop being *pridurok*. You will work together, or I make you both do footwork drills until your legs fall off."

Em stomps off to grab her gym bag, which has a few too many holes, muttering under her breath. In her angry stride and clenched fists, I see my younger self.

"This is a bad idea. She's too much like—"

"Like you were?" Coach interrupts with a snort. "*Da,* this is exactly why. You understand her fire, her pain. And maybe if you make her champion, show her discipline like I showed you, USFA will see you are more than an angry boy with sword."

I want to argue, but I can't.

"Fine," I concede. "But don't blame me if this blows up in our faces."

Coach smiles, that infuriating, knowing grin of his. "Sometimes the best things start with a little explosion, some big boom, *da*?"

As my private jet leaves San Francisco, the city lights shrink like scattered gems.

Em is trouble. Unlike Reese's by-the-book precision, Em's chaotic streak feels too familiar.

Our first practice devolved into insults until Coach threatened us with sock-stuffed mouths.

Her technique is sloppy, but beneath the attitude lies a spark of genuine talent.

I don't know why Coach paired us, but if working with her helps reverse my USFA suspension, I'll endure it.

Even if it means dodging her wild attacks for months.

I signal to Archer, our silver-haired flight attendant who clearly wishes to be elsewhere. He's our family's assistant, Carlyle's, latest attempt to keep me focused after I charmed my way through three previous attendants.

They were more amenable to distraction.

Now I'm stuck with Archer, whose scowl could curdle milk. He delivers my Manhattan and retreats, leaving me with my thoughts and the night sky.

I check my phone for a distraction, but an unsaved number catches my eye instead.

UNKNOWN

Mr. Hastings, this is Reese Sinclair, following up as per our previous arrangement.

Attached you'll find your scene recordings for next week's scenes.

sherriffonguardweektwo.m4a

I save the contact under a name I know will stab at her ego: Little Fighter.

Settling back, I slip on my headphones and brace for impact.

"Hello, Mr. Hastings." Her voice cuts like a diamond through glass. "Now, I know you probably don't have your script in front of you, but I want you to take notes. So I'll wait while you get it. Go on, ticktock."

The audio goes silent. I down a burning sip of whiskey, savoring both the heat and her calculated patience.

Classic Reese.

"If your physical copy is too stained with drink rings or

flecked with cigarette ash, I sent one to your email. Go on, open it." I click into her file. "Reading while listening will help, so next time, have your script nearby. Now, for this to work, you need to repeat after me. And don't just parrot the words—pay attention to the emotions. The sheriff is arrogant, power-hungry, and he thinks he's untouchable. Shouldn't be too hard for you to channel."

I chuckle, gulping more whiskey as I surrender to my one-on-one with Reese Sinclair. I picture her sitting ramrod straight, methodically checking off her arsenal of jabs as she dissects each line.

It's oddly endearing.

The flight to the redwoods vanishes as I let Reese's voice consume me—half drill sergeant, half theater critic. Each barbed insult strikes with surgical precision, and damn if I don't hang on every syllable.

Maybe I'm developing a thing for verbal abuse.

Or maybe it's just her.

"Thank you for last night's training session," she says. "After you wrapped, Felix told me that I'm not moving like a robot anymore. Try not to let that inflate your already impressive ego."

I chuckle as she clears her throat. "Now, Mr. Hastings, I have some homework for you, though I have to admit it's purely selfish. I am an actor, after all, and I have a fighter I can take advantage of—" She pauses. "For research purposes, I mean. I expect actual answers to the following questions: What keeps you going when you're ready to collapse? What's your pre-competition routine? And…" There's another pause, which makes me lean forward. "Since you play our rebellious sheriff so convincingly, tell me about your last brush with authority. I imagine you won't have to dig too deep.

"As I said, this is strictly for character development, of course," she adds. "Training me and mastering the script is still your priority." Her tone shifts, taking on the edge that makes me want to push her buttons. "If at our next practice time allows, I wouldn't mind if you showed me the leg sweep counter you demonstrated to your cohort of cronies this morning. Sunday, 8:00 p.m. sharp. Don't be late."

A beat of silence. "And Mr. Hastings? If you're listening to this on Monday, you need to take this more seriously." The recording ends with an exasperated sigh. Her irritation is starting to feel like foreplay.

I type out a text to her, but it doesn't quite sit right. I try again. Fuck. My fingers hover over the keys as I knock back more whiskey, attempting to steady my nerves.

This is ridiculous.

I've got socialites and starlets practically begging for my attention, my phone constantly lighting up with flirtatious messages. So why am I sitting here like some lovesick teenager, overthinking every word?

DANTE

Your voice has quite the effect on me, Professor Sinclair. Even when you're critiquing me, I can't help but want to hear more.

LITTLE FIGHTER

Focus on the content, not the delivery, Mr. Hastings.

DANTE

I've always been a model student, you know.

LITTLE FIGHTER

I don't believe that for a second.

DANTE

Okay, you caught me. But maybe I needed the right instructor to keep me in line. And you've already scolded me enough to make me do my homework.

No response.

DANTE

For battling exhaustion? The best cure is a mix of intense training and more intense enjoyment of life. No release valve, and you burn out fast.

Though I imagine your version of relaxing involves reorganizing your script annotations.

LITTLE FIGHTER

Organization can be its own form of release.

DANTE

Intriguing...

She doesn't take the bait, so I keep going.

DANTE

As for my pre-competition routine: painting my nails and visualizing victory.

If you'd like, you can follow me around for a day, get the full experience. We can end our next training session with a real lesson in unwinding.

LITTLE FIGHTER

You still haven't answered my question about your last encounter with authority.

DANTE

That story requires an in-person telling. Along with the leg sweep you're curious about.

LITTLE FIGHTER

Good night, Mr. Hastings.

DANTE

Break a leg at tomorrow's premiere.

The message shows delivered. Three dots appear, then vanish. *Gone, just like that.* I drum my fingers against the leather seat, fighting the urge to send another message.

Something witty, something that would make her roll her eyes but smile anyway. But I resist.

The drive from the airstrip stretches endlessly, my phone a dead weight in my hand. Her cabin stands dark when I pass it. Windows black, no sign of life. She's probably already in LA, practicing those perfect sound bites for tomorrow's red-carpet interviews.

By the time I'm showered and in bed, there's still no response. Not even one of her signature comebacks. Crickets chirp outside while this persistent ache in my chest refuses to subside.

It's too quiet.

Before I can stop myself, I'm scrolling to find her voice memo again. *Pathetic, really.* But I click play anyway.

"Hello, Mr. Hastings."

I close my eyes, letting myself imagine the quirk of her lips, the way she probably shook her head while recording this.

Fuck, I'm in so much trouble.

This isn't like picking up some socialite at a charity gala or flirting with flight attendants to pass the time.

This is Reese. Brilliant, infuriating Reese Sinclair, who sees right through my carefully crafted bullshit and makes me want to let her. And that's fucking dangerous.

Chapter 10
Reese

AUGUST **22**ND

Reese Sinclair and Jaxon Elio Spark More Dating Rumors at the *Love and Loathing* Premiere

HEATHER

> We need to talk about Felix. People are catching on to the fact that he's turning this into some B-movie cash grab.

REESE

> Aren't you the one who always tells me not to listen to whisperings?

HEATHER

> Yes, but listen to me. After all these script changes and what happened with that trainer, at least let me bring in additional security, and we'll get Sarah as an intimacy coordinator!

REESE

> There aren't any intimate scenes. You're overreacting.

HEATHER

Overreacting? That bruise on your arm from
yesterday's shoot was absolutely horrific!
Think about the national Diamond Essence
campaign we're going to be filming in
October.

REESE

I promise I won't be bruised up come October.

HEATHER

You're missing the point. Felix is pushing you
too hard, and it's not allowed. I can sue him for
endangering my talent.

REESE

Heather, it was an accident during the fight
scene. I'm fine.

HEATHER

I won't let some patronizing patriarchal
director derail your big move into a new genre.
This is about protecting your career. I've got
three other scripts hot on my desk right now —
all action roles, all powerful female characters.
We put an opt-out clause in this contract for a
reason.

Please, Reese.

REESE

I appreciate you looking out for me, but I can
handle Felix. This is the role I want, and I'm
not walking away. Trust me on this one.

In twenty-five days, I'll either prove myself worthy of playing Robyn Hood or confirm Felix's doubts about casting me.

The scene that terrifies me most looms ahead: diving head-first off a moving raft into freezing water to retrieve my sword after being disarmed while battling the king's army. Two days of shooting. Extremely limited windows for the full moon that's needed for the shot. There can't be any mistakes.

An entire production crew is counting on me.

People's time and efforts. The budget.

I put my phone back into my bag and take off my sweatshirt, standing in the pajamas I woke up in. I kick off my shoes next. The lake stretches before me in the early morning light, deceptively peaceful. Sunlight dances across its surface, creating a masterpiece of golden ripples that would take any normal person's breath away. But it takes mine away for a different reason. My chest tightens looking at it.

I pull myself off the rocky ledge and walk toward the lake, digging my toes into the damp earth at the water's edge. My heart pounds.

Heather's doubts echo in my mind, her well-meaning concerns making me feel like that same naive actress who needed her hand held through every decision. But I'm not that girl anymore. Maybe I should've woken up Ramsey to watch over me, but I want to do this alone.

I'm Robyn Hood—or at least, I'm supposed to be.

Her character should embody a revolutionary force, fighting for justice and building a family out of society's rejects. She's a warrior who sacrifices everything to help people who can't help themselves. But Felix's gutless vision has stripped away her essence. The searing commentary on gender barriers and systemic corruption? Completely erased.

Now it's me running through forests in outfits that keep getting tighter, trying not to lose my fake eyelashes during slow-motion fight scenes.

At yesterday's premiere of *Love and Loathing*, the reporters' whispers were draining. *Is she doing her own stunts for* Robyn Hood? *Is she still hooking up with Jaxon Elio?* And then the questions. *Who are you wearing? How did you manage to fit into that dress? Are you planning to start a family soon? How long did hair and makeup take? Is it intimidating to work with such a powerful male director in your new role?*

No one takes romance films seriously, as if falling in love makes you weak or shallow. The industry dismisses them with contempt, as if exploring the depths of human connection is somehow lesser than violence and spectacle.

There's nothing wrong with romance films. I loved being in them. But I've only been offered big roles in picture-perfect fairy tales with neat and tidy happily-ever-afters. Stories where trust is never tested, where love conquers all without cost. Producers don't want to see me portray the devastating reality of how relationships can wound us. The tears, the heartache, the longing that makes love stories truly potent.

Maybe after *Robyn Hood* succeeds that will change.

A heavy sigh escapes me.

I'm drowning in expectations, and not the metaphorical kind.

Something urgent coils in my stomach.

My feet move before my brain catches up.

One step. Then another.

The lake water splashes up as I charge in, each droplet a tiny icy dagger against my skin. The smell of wet earth and algae fills my nostrils.

Seventeen years, Reese.

Seventeen years of letting this fear win. *Not today.*

I survived Friday's fight scene. Ran through the forest while Felix barked directions. This is just water. One quick dip under. Tomorrow, I'll hold for a second. The next day, two. Baby steps.

Soon I'll be diving for Robyn's sword, showing them all what I'm made of.

Water laps at my knees, creeping up to my waist. The cold seeps into my bones.

My breath comes faster. Shorter.

My pulse drums in my ears.

My muscles seize. The memory hits, that heavy cover sliding inexorably forward, water rushing in, my small fists pounding uselessly against solid plastic. Time stretches like taffy, each heartbeat an eternity.

"Simply a memory," I tell myself, my tongue thick and clumsy in my mouth.

The lake feels just as suffocating. My vision starts to tunnel, the edges of the world going dark and fuzzy. A metallic taste fills my mouth.

The whirring gets louder again, the clanging of the pool cover filling my ears, and I whirl around, a child's scream caught in my throat.

Still nothing.

Only trees, their shapes warping and swaying, though there's no wind. My legs tremble violently, my knees threatening to give out beneath me.

"One…two…" I sound small, disconnected, like that little girl. Like I'm already being swallowed by murky depths.

I pinch my nose, bend my knees, and try to swallow a breath before descending into the lake water. The cold bites at my skin, creeping up my body like icy fingers.

In an instant I'm back there, trapped under the dark cover, pounding my tiny fists against it, screaming for Daddy as water fills my lungs.

I lurch upright, a strangled "HELP!" tearing from my throat.

My heart hammers against my ribs like it's trying to escape. The world tilts. Trees blur into a green smear through my tear-filled eyes. Through the haze, a figure sprints toward me.

Daddy?

"Help!" The word escapes on a child's terrified sob. "Help me!" Each breath comes in desperate gasps. Not enough air. My lungs feel like they're filling with concrete. The roar of blood in my ears drowns out everything but my own panic.

"Reese!"

It's Dante.

Strong arms wrap around me, pulling me up and out of the water.

"It's okay, Reese." His voice cuts through the static in my head. "You're okay. I've got you."

He sets me on the rocky shore, yanking off his running jacket and wrapping it around my shoulders. His eyes dart around until they land on my water bottle by my tote.

"I—I can't breathe!" I sob, my fingers clutching at his arm. "I'm having a heart attack."

"It's not a heart attack." He moves, shaking the bottle hard, listening for something. Then he uncaps it and dumps the water out. "Stay present. Stay with me."

He reaches for me, gently prying open my clenched fist. Something cold presses into my palm—ice.

"How does that feel? Cold, right?"

"Yes," I manage, taking a deep breath. The ice stings my skin, sharp and biting.

I stare at it in my palm. One of his herculean hands draws slow circles along my back, and my breathing naturally falls into sync with the rhythm. Inhale for four, hold for seven, exhale for eight.

Four. Seven. Eight.

"There you go," he says. "Keep focusing on the ice."

The chill burns away the panic, bit by bit. With each drop of melting water that trickles between my fingers, the memory of the pool fades into a dull background hum. The world comes back into focus. First the whisper of wind through leaves, then the rough texture of pebbles pressing into my legs, and finally, most distractingly, Dante's hand on my lower back.

It's comforting.

"How?" My words catch in my throat as I look at him properly. He's soaked to the bone, dark brown hair plastered to his forehead, white T-shirt clinging to his chest. Why did it have to be him to find me? I can't think with him so close. His gaze bounces from my eyes to my lips to my fingers, which are rubbing along the zipper of his jacket. "What are you doing here?"

"I was out for a run and heard you scream."

Scream? I didn't scream, did I?

I lean away from him as my traitorous body shouts to sink into his warmth. The circles on my back stop, and I wish I hadn't said anything.

"I haven't felt like that since I was a kid. I thought I was going to die." The explanation feels weak.

"You had a panic attack."

"I—how did you know what to do?"

"My oldest sister gets them real bad," he says. "Figure skating comes with a lot of pressure. Not that Brooklyn would ever admit it. Her therapist taught her this thing with ice. Now whenever she hits the rink, the first thing she does is touch the ice. Grounds her, you know?"

I blink at him, unsure what to say. This side of him is so different from the smug playboy mask he usually wears. I've caught glimpses, but I want to see what else he's hiding.

"You look like you don't believe me."

"No," I say, "I do. I didn't expect that. Sounds like you're close to your sister."

He looks boyish as his head tilts to one side. "I am. Brooklyn's a rock, always rounding us up like it's her job. But while I was giving my parents a headache, my oldest sister was always there."

His words lodge between my sternum, and my mind wanders to what it would feel like to nudge my head into his chest and be held for a while.

"This stays between us, okay? No one can know."

"Take it to the grave," he says, crossing his heart. "But what were you doing out here in the first place?"

"I'm afraid of water," I whisper, the admission making my throat tight. "Not water itself, but diving under it."

"Southern girl like you never went tubing on the river?" He asks like he genuinely wants to know, not like it's a setup for some line he wants to use on me.

"I almost drowned as a kid." I study the pebbles at my feet, aware of his steady gaze on me. "I was twelve. Our pool had this automatic cover. One night, I was swimming alone when it started closing. I got trapped underneath." My lungs burn at the memory. "The saltwater —Daddy had it converted from chlorine that summer—it burned like fire in my eyes, my nose, my throat. Everything was a blur of dark blue and panic. I was screaming and pounding on the cover, but it kept whirring shut above me, this mechanical monster stealing my sky." I pause, taking a shaky breath, the phantom taste of saltwater flooding my mouth, metallic and sharp. "If he hadn't heard me…"

Dante's expression remains steady.

Every instinct honed from years in this industry screams at me to stand up, say thank you, and return to my cabin. To maintain professional distance.

But I don't.

"So you were going to try and tackle that head-on. Alone? At the ass-crack of dawn? That's pretty fucking badass, fighter."

He manages to pull a small laugh out of me. "There's a scene coming up."

"The raft scene? When Robyn dives in for her sword?"

"Yeah," I manage, surprised he remembers. "Been reading the script after all?"

"Professor Sinclair told me I can't come to class unprepared anymore."

Ignore him!

I wrap my arms around myself, suppressing a shiver. "You heard Felix last week when he mentioned bringing in a double, but…" I trail off, hating how vulnerable I sound.

"You're obviously too stubborn for that?"

"I need to do this myself," I say, and he nods like he understands.

"Maybe next time you try to conquer your fears, you could start slower? Like dunking your head underwater in the bath?"

"What do you mean, my plan to walk into a freezing lake in my pajamas wasn't brilliant?"

"It is an interesting choice of swimwear," he teases.

We let the silence linger between us, neither of us rushing to go. It's not uncomfortable like it usually would be with a fellow actor, chattering about himself or showing pure indifference.

Instead, Dante studies me with an intensity that makes my cheeks burn, like sunlight on cold skin. His eyes track every micro-expression, every shift of my posture, and I sink deeper into whatever this is between us.

I'm comfortable.

And that makes it dangerous. I already have my circle: Cleo, Heather, Ramsey, and my loving parents.

That's all I need.

I can't like him. I just can't. It's not the no-fraternization clause. It's not even Ricky, though maybe some small part of it is.

It's the fact that I have everything to lose, and I can't afford to throw this dream away on some silly schoolgirl infatuation with a boy who looks like he'd be a good time.

"You're under a lot of stress, aren't you?" he asks.

"It's nothing I can't handle."

"There's a stretch of coast up here I used to visit with my family. You should go. Definitely nothing pool-like about it. It's different from the Gulf, but peaceful in its own way."

"Sounds nice," I admit, "but it's impossible to leave set. Between my bodyguard and the paparazzi…" I twist my fingers into the ends of my hair, slowly exhaling. "I can't really get up and go places. Not alone. Not without it becoming a thing." I hate how pretentious it sounds, but it's true. I can't step outside to get my mail without someone getting a shot of me.

"Even though we're nearly seven hundred miles from LA?"

"These reporters, they find out everything." He nods, eyebrows crinkling in thought. "Well, I should get back and dry off," I say and shrug off his jacket to return it to him.

"Keep it."

I look down at the striped cotton pajamas clinging to my skin, suddenly aware of how much more vulnerable this feels than any costume I wear on set. There, I have layers of makeup and fabric to hide behind.

Here, it's just me.

I pull his jacket tighter around myself.

He stands, helping me up. His palms are rough with calluses, and he holds mine a beat longer than necessary.

"Maybe we should skip our training session today," he suggests.

"No," I blurt. "There's no need to fuss over this. We'll train as we planned."

"Alright, well, let's get you back home before you catch a chill." He picks up my stuff, folding my sweatshirt carefully over his arm and carrying my sneakers, and joins me at my side as we walk back.

"Thank you, Dante," I say quietly. His name feels sweet on my tongue.

"You know, I was just starting to like 'Mr. Hastings.'"

Chapter 11
Reese

YESTERDAY'S TRAINING session left me with sore muscles and an even sorer ego—though the latter might have more to do with my embarrassing near-drowning incident. I'm sprawled on my cabin bed, feeling like a human-shaped collection of sweat and conflicting emotions.

The thing is, Dante saved my life *and* discovered my deeply mortifying diving phobia that could blow up my entire role in this movie. That's the kind of leverage that requires at least a text message.

Not that I'm overthinking this or anything.

I'm being professional, making sure he keeps my water-related trauma under wraps. Surely that level of vulnerability earns him a spot on the list of people I *very* occasionally text?

Before I debate much longer, I pull up our message thread.

REESE

Thanks for keeping the lake incident under wraps. I appreciate your discretion on set.

DANTE

A promise is a promise.

REESE

Who knew getting thrown around a gym could
be a great way to forget a lifelong fear of
diving underwater?

DANTE

I'm a man of many talents. Keeping secrets
and throwing you around are just two of them.

REESE

slow clap Your humility is truly inspiring.

DANTE

One of my better qualities, I've been told.

REESE

About that bath suggestion…I might actually
take your sage advice.

Tonight's the night.

DANTE

Want daily accountability checks via text?
Wouldn't want you slacking, Miss Type A.

REESE

You're already doing more than enough.

DANTE

I live to serve.

Just remember who prescribed this luxury
when you're soaking in bliss.

REESE

Speaking of prescriptions, might I suggest one
for you? Something to address that cigarette
smell you keep bringing to practice?

It's very…distracting.

DANTE

The cigarettes are distracting?

Or is it something else?

REESE

Good night, Dante.

MY PHONE BUZZES AGAIN as I sit in the makeup chair on set. I nearly drop it, fumbling to angle the screen away from prying eyes.

I'm not delusional. This flutter in my chest is clearly a symptom of isolation-induced desperation. Cleo's gone off-grid for this new season she's shooting, and I'm so starved for human interaction I'd probably get butterflies from a spam call.

Plus, Dante and I are basically partners in crime now—we share a secret, for heaven's sake! That makes these predawn text exchanges totally normal, right?

DANTE

It's Wednesday, which means you're in luck.

REESE

Luck?

DANTE

I got my fresh shipment of Berg since you keep "accidentally" taking the water bottles from my bag. Got you your own case. Though I suspect the theft was never about hydration.

REESE

And rob you of your daily chance to lecture me? I wouldn't dare deprive you of such joy.

DANTE

Keep stealing them. I'm keeping a tab of favors you owe me.

REESE

A tab? How very methodical of you.

DANTE

Keep the compliments coming though. They
might improve your form in training.

REESE

Tempting, but Felix is torturing us with
reshooting the same scene from this
afternoon. Again.

Send thoughts and prayers.

DANTE

What's in it for me?

REESE

One bonus minute of Friday's voice recording.

Yes, that means extra homework. Try to
contain your excitement.

DANTE

I solemnly pray for your deliverance from
Felix's tyranny.

Divine spirits of Hollywood, grant her the
perfect take.

Oh mighty cinema gods, please free Reese
from Felix's 47th take of her walking through a
door with more emotion.

REESE

You're ridiculous lol

DANTE

That was three very heartfelt prayers. I believe
the going rate is one minute per prayer? I
don't make the rules.

REESE

Here are your scene recordings for the week. I made sure to speak extra clearly and added timestamps in case you need to pause and replay any tricky dialogue.

DANTE

It's Friday already?

REESE

Time flies when you're working hard and memorizing all of your lines…

And don't even think about using the weekend as an excuse to slack. I know where you train.

DANTE

Already planning our next rendezvous? I'm touched.

REESE

Our strictly professional training sessions are hardly a rendezvous. Though your ego seems to be getting quite the workout.

DANTE

Speaking of workouts. These homework assignments are starting to feel less like fight prep and more like 20 Questions. Not that I'm complaining.

REESE

Your top three regrets are vital character research.

DANTE

Careful with all this research, you might actually start to like me.

REESE

Don't get carried away.

A SMILE TUGS at my lips as I place my phone on my nightstand, snuggling deeper into my bed. It's been a long week. What started this Monday as purely professional exchanges about training schedules has morphed into something dangerously close to banter. Ever since that day at the lake, our daily check-ins have become as much a part of my routine as my morning cup of tea—which is exactly the kind of realization that should send me running for the hills. And yet here I am, actually looking forward to his messages.

Dang it.

Chapter 12
Reese

"Good morning, sunshine." Dante's voice slices through my closed front door.

Dawn creeps through the windows of my cabin, painting stripes of pale blue light across the wooden floor. The camp is unnaturally quiet at 6:00 a.m., most of the crew having cleared out Saturday night, leaving behind only the whisper of wind through the pines and the distant call of early birds.

I crack the door open and find him leaning against the doorframe like he owns the place, a metal mug steaming in his hand.

"Shouldn't you be terrorizing some other actress at this hour?"

We've slipped into an easy rhythm this week. He shows up to our sessions each night with an extra protein bar and extra Berg water. After training, he insists on walking me home. He holds open the rec center door, carries my bag when it's too heavy, and always asks before touching any part of my body to adjust form. We text, small conversations here and there.

He's been studying my recordings, repeating tricky words from his script, and answering all my sword-fighting questions—like how fencers scream to influence right-of-way decisions and the strange pre-bout rituals some have, including Dante painting his nails black.

"You're my favorite to terrorize."

His weight shifts, a lazy, unhurried movement that shouldn't affect me. Shouldn't send a sharp awareness skittering through my chest. But it does. My gaze snags lower. His sweatpants are riding low. Too low.

Absolutely, unequivocally *distracting*.

I snap my attention to the giant redwood behind him. I need to look literally anywhere but at him.

When I don't speak for far too long, he says, "Besides, I'm here strictly on business."

"How did you know I'd be awake?"

"Lucky guess."

"Okay…well, do you need to, uh…" The thought dissolves as his fingers brush absently over the delicate chain around his neck, drawing my attention to the tattoos climbing up his throat.

"Are you not feeling well?"

"Why would you say that?" I pull back with surprise.

"You're all flushed."

"I'm not! I'm just tired," I lie, and the smirk on his face tells me he knows I'm lying too. "Do you need to cancel our training today?"

"No, I wouldn't dream of it. But we are doing something different today, and as your instructor, you're going to have to trust me."

Trust.

"I don't know."

"Well, I'm not asking. I'm telling you." I hate how my body responds to his authority, the same authority that's improved my swordplay more in ten days than two months of training with Nick. "I mean, as long as you agree…" He pauses, extending the mug like a peace offering. "Here, have a sip of this first."

The cup of tea I brewed a few minutes ago sits forgotten on the kitchenette counter.

"What is this?" I eye the mug. "Because if it's coffee, I don't—"

He cuts me off. "I know. *Vanity Fair* mentioned you like English breakfast tea with honey. I guessed on the sweeter side, since you admitted to sneaking sugar in your mom's sun tea."

A shiver runs down my spine, one that has nothing to do with the morning chill. "Some might call it creepy to research someone so thoroughly." Red flag number twenty-three waves bright in my mind, but I take the mug anyway.

"But *you* find it endearing because you love research." The knowing look in his golden eyes makes my stomach flip, and I hate that he's right—both about the research and about how I feel about his attention to detail.

The first sip spreads across my tongue. It's perfectly steeped, the honey melted just right. Damn him.

"Thank you, Mr. Hastings," I manage, eyeing my script like a lifeline. "As much as I'd love to see whatever you have planned, I'm planning to spend the morning reviewing Felix's notes and triple-checking my lines for next week."

"Let me guess, Felix added more tears?" It's a rhetorical question, because he knows the answer is yes. Every day, Felix is either wanting more cleavage or more waterworks.

"Once he gets into the editing process, he'll see that my suggestions are superior." At least, I hope so.

"Sure." He says it half-heartedly. "And until then, we're going for a drive."

"I told you, I can't leave the camp." The words come out automatically. "And my lines—"

"Won't go anywhere. Come on, Reese. When has playing it safe ever served you? Or Robyn, for that matter?"

"That's different," I manage, but my resolve is already cracking. "Robyn has a cause. She has—"

"Nothing to lose? Neither do you." He takes another step closer, and the doorway shrinks. "Think about it. What if Robyn had stayed in the village? What if she'd never picked up a sword, never challenged the king's men?" His eyes lock onto mine. "Some risks are worth taking, Reese. And I promise you, this one is. It's just like how we danced that first night of training. You need to get out of your head."

I do, but I shouldn't leave. Not with him.

But this is about the role, I tell myself firmly, ignoring the way my skin tingles when he smiles.

Just the role.

To become a better Robyn.

Nothing more.

I raise an eyebrow at him. "No underlying intentions?"

"From me?" He gasps dramatically. "It's my job to make sure you perform your best, and you've been so diligent in providing me weekly homework assignments that today I thought it's time I give *you* a lesson."

I shouldn't go. Not when I'm thinking about what other *lessons* he could give me.

"Give me five minutes to change," I hear myself say, even as my inner voice screams something about career suicide. But there's no denying that his unconventional methods have results, do they?

"Yes, ma'am." He turns away instantly, a gesture so respectful it aches. I dress in a sweatshirt, jeans, a cap, and sunglasses, adding lip gloss before I can question why.

When I emerge, his back is still turned. Something flutters beneath my ribs.

"I should give this back to you," I say, holding out his jacket carefully to maintain the air gap between us.

"Keep it," he replies, eyes dancing. And I reluctantly hang it back up on the coat rack by my door.

We leave my cabin and cross the parking lot, gravel

crunching under his heavy boots. The security teams are at the camp entrance, monitoring every exit. My pulse quickens. Dante leads me to his blacked-out Range Rover.

"After you." He opens my door, offering his hand to help me up.

My mama would swoon over his southern-boy manners. Though I've carefully avoided mentioning Dante in any of my weekly calls with my parents.

His hand lightly touches my back, and I rocket into the car.

He slides behind the wheel. "Buckle up," he says, not starting the engine until he hears the click.

"How exactly are we dodging my bodyguard, Ramsey? Let alone the rest of security."

He leans over, his bare arm hovering inches above my thigh. I fixate on the hair at the nape of his neck, wanting to run my fingers through it.

He yanks my seat lever, and I drop backward, gasping as he stares above me.

"There," he says plainly, like he isn't the reason my heart is beating in my throat and at the base of my stomach.

"This is your master plan? Really?"

"One more thing." He pulls off his hoodie in one fell swoop.

"If someone catches me hiding in your car…" The threat hangs unfinished.

"They won't." His playful tone shifts to something more serious. "I've got you. Now cover up." Without warning, he drapes his hoodie over me.

Every muscle in my body tenses and then melts because I'm engulfed in him. His warmth lingers in the fabric, wrapping around me. I squeeze my eyes shut, inhaling.

For a split second, I imagine what his weight would be like pressing me into this seat, what it would be like if his fingers wrapped around my thighs instead of that lever. My pulse matches the purr of the engine as I lie under my trainer's jacket, escaping from set. Without Ramsey's protective shadow, something wild and forbidden unfurls in my chest.

We drive for a while as I lie there, completely still. But beneath the soft gray cotton of his hoodie, I'm smiling—because deep down, I'm having fun.

"You can sit up now, Thelma," he says.

I do, fixing the seat upright while keeping his hoodie draped over my lap.

"Now *that* is a movie I'd love to be in the remake of." I roll down the window, letting the crisp forest air whip through my hair.

"Rebellion looks good on you," he says, shooting me a wink.

We wind our way through towering redwoods, the sunlight filtering through the canopy in scattered beams as French techno music fills the car. The trees gradually thin until suddenly the coastline appears—a stunning expanse of blue ocean meeting the horizon. That's when a cheerful yellow stand catches my eye. Hand-painted red letters read, *Mama Jones' Biscuits.*

Biscuits? Out here?

All the effort I spent maintaining my collected attitude falters in the face of proper carbohydrates.

"Pull over," I demand, already reaching for my seatbelt. "Now."

"Since when do you give the orders?"

"Since there's butter and honey involved. Stop the darn car before I grab the wheel myself."

He swerves off the road, tires crunching gravel. I adjust my baseball cap and sunglasses, already halfway to the stand when he calls out, "Running away again? And here I thought we were making progress."

The double meaning in his voice makes me smile, but I don't turn back.

Once I reach the stand, my heart doubles in size. Fresh-baked buttermilk biscuits, rows of homemade jams, and the kind of authentic, small-town charm that's impossible to find in LA. The aroma of butter-brushed tops and honey brings back memories of Sunday mornings in New Orleans.

"Hello, darlin'." The elderly lady at the stand gives me a beaming smile that reminds me of home.

"Biscuits?" I exclaim. "Real southern biscuits? Here?"

The elderly woman gestures toward a small cabin nestled up the road, her southern drawl wrapping around me like an electric blanket. "Been bringing a piece of home to these California roads for over a decade now."

"You're heaven sent."

"And you," Dante murmurs, so close his breath stirs my hair, "are a mystery. The great Re—" He catches himself, and my heart skips a beat at how quickly he corrects course, protecting my identity here. "*Rebel* pulled apart by the sight of biscuits."

"Biscuits are my second favorite carb, next to beignets," I tell him, then I turn to the lovely lady at the stand. "He's not southern. Doesn't understand the sacred art of biscuit-making or the magic pastries and powder you can find at Cafe Du Monde."

"Oh, honey." The woman's eyes crinkle knowingly. "It seems to me he understands plenty about what makes you tick. We operate on the honor system here, take what you need, pay what you can."

She waddles off, leaving us alone.

"Let me guess," he says, reaching past me with deliberate slowness, "a traditionalist like you probably never strays from her comfort zone." His fingers hover near the strawberry jam.

I snatch the apricot instead. "Some of us know what we want without needing to sample everything on the menu."

"Interesting. Is that why you've been avoiding the advanced parry training? Sticking to your fundamental sequence when the world has so many new, sweet rewards?"

I roll my eyes and regain focus, filling up my paper bag with biscuits and jars of jam.

When I go to reach for the wallet I tucked into my jeans before leaving, he stops me.

"Here, allow me."

"I got it, Mr. Hastings, but thank you." I fold two crisp hundred-dollar bills, shoving them in the jar.

He adds three hundred more. "Consider it an investment in your training."

"Your investment strategies need work." I counter with five more bills. "Just like your teaching methods."

"Always so much bite from you," he says.

"Wait until you see what I do with these biscuits."

Chapter 13
Reese

THE BISCUITS WERE PERFECT, the view is unreal, and I hate how much I'm enjoying this.

Or at least that's what I tell myself as we settle against the windshield on the hood of Dante's Range Rover. He found a small overlook that's secluded and out of the way down a gravelly road. No other cars, let alone people, in sight. The Pacific crashes below us. The morning air is crisp, and despite my reluctance to admit it, it is nice to be away from set for just a few hours. Even if all I can focus on is the way his foot taps against the metal hood and how he keeps stealing glances at me.

There's a tiny biscuit crumb on the side of his mouth, and I can't stop thinking about wiping it away. *Don't look at it.*

He packs up the leftover biscuits and tosses them in the car. When he hops back onto the hood with way too much ease, he says, "I think I'm overdue on a homework assignment, Professor Sinclair."

The crumb is gone. Damn wind.

"You are," I smile.

"Okay, so I owe you three big regrets. Right? First one…" His eyes trace a seagull flying above. "Most definitely when I took my dad's car for a joyride when I was fourteen. Peak rebel stage, but seeing my mom cry after my dad picked me up from jail, not my finest moment."

I blink at him, actually stunned. Fourteen?

"What, you didn't expect me to take your questions seriously?" His elbow brushes mine, and for a second I want the wind to blow me right off this hood, away from him, because he's too close. "I'm hoping for straight A's this semester."

"I thought you were going to say you regret one of your bicep tattoos or crashing one of DiCaprio's many Hamptons parties," I say, my voice teasing but careful.

"My regrets are far more interesting."

"How did you know how to drive? Why would you take the car?"

"My sister Frankie," he says. "She was some kind of karting prodigy, started competing when she was eight. Taught all of us how to drive like professionals even before some of us could see over the dashboard. Technically illegal, but that was kind of the point." He shrugs, a hint of his old recklessness showing through. "As for why…I wanted to see what it felt like, you know? Driving a Phantom. I had no boundaries back then, no sense of consequences. If something looked interesting, I did it.

"After that little incident…" His voice trails off, and he shifts in his seat, avoiding my gaze. "They shipped me off to boarding school." There's an edge to his voice I haven't heard before, a crack in his usual confident façade. "Found fencing there. First thing I was actually good at." He lets out a bitter laugh that makes my heart twist unexpectedly. "While my siblings were…" His hand waves dismissively in the air between us. "Well, everything came easier to them. Earlier."

"They sent just you?" I ask softly. My actress instincts kick in, wanting to understand every detail, but I force myself to stay quiet, giving him space to answer. "What about your siblings?"

"They never needed a leash," he says with a sharp laugh

that doesn't quite reach his eyes. "But hey, boarding school wasn't complete torture. Got to take that poster of you with me." He pauses, something raw flickering across his face before he masks it. "And you know what? When you grow up in a house that feels like a circus, sometimes solitary confinement is exactly what you need. All that…silence. Space to breathe."

When I was younger, I used to play characters with lonely childhoods, kids who were desperate to be noticed, to be loved. Sure, they acted out—skipping homework, giving their parents the silent treatment—but it was nothing compared to what Dante did.

I can't imagine.

My parents showered me with the kind of love that felt like honey, constant and sweet. I wonder what path I might have taken if I'd followed in his footsteps. Looking back now, I can count on one hand the number of actors I started with who are still in the business. The rest disappeared like morning fog, leaving behind only faded headshots and half-remembered names.

I study him carefully, the way his shoulders tense as he tries to seem casual. "Must have been lonely."

"Don't look at me like that and psychoanalyze me," he says, running a hand through his hair. "I was a little shit who needed discipline. Still am, just with better clothes."

The self-deprecation hits a nerve. I've spent my whole career playing roles, reading people, but Dante's different. Every layer I peel back reveals something more complex.

"I'm not trying to—" I pause, choosing my words carefully. "It's different. Being an only child, I never had to compete for attention. I guess it was also that my dad was a dentist and my mama was a teacher."

His expression softens, barely. "Love isn't a finite resource, you know. Though don't tell my siblings, but Brooklyn and

Frankie are still my favorites." The charm is back, but now I can see it for what it is—armor.

But I wear mine too. Under our carefully crafted personas—his charm, my poise—we're both trying to protect ourselves.

I find myself leaning forward, my voice softening. "You know, I may not have siblings, but I understand isolation. When I started on *Clubhouse*, everything changed. Homeschooling, constant travel, my parents gradually stepping back from set visits." I pause. "In this industry, real connections are rare. Besides Cleo, my best friend since forever…" I let out a small laugh. "Most of my twenties were spent alone in five-star hotels or luxury rentals near set. Sounds glamorous, right? But it was just me, takeout containers, and endless script revisions."

"Is that why you're such a perfectionist? No one watching your back?"

"No," I say firmly. "I came out of the womb color-coding my toys."

"Baby Sinclair." He smirks. "Organizing her blocks by size and aesthetic appeal."

"Oh, hush," I say, but I'm fighting a smile.

"Now my second biggest regret," he says. "Wait, should you be taking notes for your *character* study?"

"I have it all up here." I tap my head, not wanting to admit that I don't think I'll ever forget a thing about him.

"Right," he chuckles. "You've read about my second biggest regret. Everyone has."

"Getting suspended," I say tentatively. This was the main reason I wanted to ask him about his regrets. He told me there was more to the story, and now, more than ever, I desperately need to know what that *more* is.

"I was meant to be there. Gold medal favorite, both individual and team. But at the World Cup, this guy threatened to out one of my teammates, and his family's not exactly accepting." He pauses, and I see him weighing how much to reveal, probably calculating the risk like he does with everything. "I was his first. With a guy, I mean. It was one of those things that happen in the heat of the moment after a match."

There are plenty of rumors online about Dante being bi, but this confirms it.

"So what happened?"

"I lost it," he continues. "Stupid, really. I'm used to threats before matches. That's sport—in fact, that's being a Hastings most of the time. But this dick was threatening to destroy some-one's life? Take away their only constant?"

He says his family's name like it's a responsibility, the same way Heather talks about my reputation. Like it's something to uphold, something that defines me.

"They suspended you for defending your teammate?" I ask, tilting my head. "That's—"

"The United States Fencing Association takes misconduct seriously. No attending matches, no participating in matches, no fencing for one whole year."

"But you'll get to fence again, right?" I can't imagine being forced to step away from acting.

"I have to petition the disciplinary committee next spring and prove to them I've been on good behavior. Got off easy though, if I'm honest. Being one of the top fencers helped, and Coach pulled strings until they reduced it to a year and some commu-nity service bullshit."

"Community service? How very bad boy of you," I tease, hoping it will loosen his jaw, which is clenched so tightly he may break a molar.

"Coach has me teaching this kid, Em, on Fridays. She's insufferable, all teenage angst and rolled eyes, hates the disci-pline of it all."

"This Em sounds like someone else I'm getting to know."

"Hardly," he huffs. "It's so strange. I never thought I'd be a trainer or a coach. I'm not exactly the role model type."

"You don't say."

He bumps my shoulder, and my skin is alight in goose bumps when he continues, "My mom's a coach. She played on the Houston Comets, winning three championships. Now she pretends it's her grand calling or whatever, but I think she's trying to convince herself she's found meaning after the glory days."

He speaks so openly, no jokes or façade. It's refreshing.

"Coaches are like directors, you know? They create legacies. A lot of people don't know their names, but they decide if the film or their athletes turn out good or not. Once they're ready to hang up their hat, they get to pass on their knowledge. It's not all bad."

He looks away. "Yeah, well, following her footsteps into coaching? That's too conventional for my taste. Maybe I'll inherit my father's work ethic, though with my dyslexia I doubt I have another Viggle empire in me."

"I think you can do anything you want. Be kind and patient with Em, like you have been with me, and she'll warm up to you in no time."

"Thank you, Reese."

I sense he wants to change the subject. "So, are you and your teammate…?"

"Ancient history. A fleeting thing, like usual. What happened with Quentin wasn't about that; it was about choices. Everyone deserves to write their own story."

"That's admirable. You know, I've never…" I try to find the word. *Interested? Captivated by? Maybe mildly obsessed with?* "Uh, *shared biscuits* with anyone who's openly…" I trail off.

"Interested in women *and* men?"

When I nod, he shifts closer, pulling at his gray hoodie.

"I don't like labels. To me, people are people, and enjoying them is part of life. It's another part of who I am. Like fencing or"—his eyes lock onto mine with predatory focus—"having an overprotective streak. Does it bother you?"

"No! Absolutely not," I confess. Heat floods my cheeks as I recover my composure. "I mean, where I grew up, people didn't talk about these things." My fingers trace nervous patterns on the sun-warmed hood, buying time. "Actually…" I hesitate, then offer my own vulnerability like a peace offering. "My best friend Cleo was my first kiss."

"Yeah?"

"I was fifteen," I admit. "The studio was pushing for on-screen romance plots. I didn't want my first kiss to be with some twenty-something actor pretending to be sixteen. So, Cleo and I made a pact—something real, just for us. Not for the cameras."

"Smart girl. Having your firsts stolen from you isn't right."

"That's Hollywood for you; they steal all your firsts." I gather my courage. "My first love was no different."

He narrows his eyes. "Was it that guy, Ricky something?"

I nod. "Ricky Tribbiani. My first real boyfriend."

"There's a but, isn't there?"

"We were the media's it couple. Then I got an award for the movie we shot together, and he didn't…" I curl my fingers against the metal. "Stole away my first moment winning an award. Had to make it about himself." I cut myself off, the old wound still raw.

"Fuck him." The words come out as a growl.

"The worst part?" I whisper, watching a seabird wheel overhead, free and untamed. "When he broke up with me, he said he was only dating me to advance his career. Just another stepping stone. How ridiculous is that? I should've known better."

"Bullshit," he bites out. "You didn't deserve that. And you were a fucking child—he should've known better than to fucking use you."

"It's not only him." I wrap my arms around myself, fighting a shiver that has nothing to do with the breeze. "Decades in this industry teaches you that too many men see young actresses as means to an end. That's why all my boundaries matter to me, from the no-fraternization clause to keeping myself focused on my career."

"So all those rumors about you and Jaxon Elio?"

"Like you said, there's more to the story." I echo his earlier words.

When those golden eyes turn to me, his smile turns wicked, promising trouble. "Your turn. I want three regrets."

"I'm the one giving homework here."

"Come on, humor me. You want me to get a perfect score, don't you? All three regrets? So I'll give you my last one if you give me three in return."

"Nothing exciting," I admit, suddenly fascinated by my hands, aware of how tame my rebellions must seem to someone like him. "Talking in class in fourth grade?"

"That's it?" His knee brushes mine, and neither of us moves away. "Come on, there has to be more."

I bite back my smile, but his energy draws it out of me. "Well, in fifth grade, I carved 'Mrs. Tracy is amazing' into a picnic table because some kids were being mean to her."

His laugh wraps around me like a caress. "You vandalized school property to defend a teacher's honor? Actually kind of perfect."

"Don't mock me!" I snort-laugh, loud. My hand flies up to cover my nose like I can take it back.

A slow grin spreads across his face. "Adorable."

"It was not."

"Oh, it absolutely was." His voice is all amusement, but he doesn't push, only tucks the moment away like it's something to keep.

I peek at him through my fingers. "Everyone thought I had a crush on my teacher."

"I had my own Mrs. Tracy. Ms. Austin, my art teacher before

boarding school. Ancient as a dinosaur, but man, the way she talked about art had me completely starry-eyed. She'd tell these stories about partying with Fonda, and she claimed she dated Bowie. Total nonsense, but I ate it up." He chuckles at the memory. "Thought I was so grown up and sophisticated getting to hear all her tales, you know?"

"So why didn't you become Mr. Austin?" I tease.

"Wasn't long before I realized my love for her was teenage hormones," he teases. "Second one, Reese."

I ponder. "Not letting myself off my own leash. I was so focused on being perfect, on being a good role model, that I never got to live. Never got to do anything. No outlandish stories followed me around, and I'm grateful for that—the media is ruthless. But maybe being known as unproblematic isn't something that fits me anymore, especially since I'm turning thirty next year."

"Sounds like we're both in a bit of an identity crisis."

The weight of his words settles in my chest. He sees whatever small fire I keep hidden there. The sun is high above us. An hour here has slipped into three.

Dante pulls out tobacco and papers. "Mind if I smoke? Or do you find the smell distracting?"

I know.

Smoking is bad for me.

Secondhand smoke is bad for me.

Dante is bad for me.

But I find myself saying, "It's fine."

"It's a bad habit, I know." I observe his practiced motions, cataloging each movement like I would for a role. He seals the paper with a flick of his tongue that I absolutely do not fixate on.

"Then why do it?"

"Helps take the edge off," he says with that devil-may-care smile, lighting up his cigarette. The smoke curls away from me as he exhales. "Sometimes you need something to ground you when everything else is moving too fast."

"Do you smoke while you're competing?" I ask, watching the way his fingers dance with the lighter.

He barks out a laugh. "God no, my coach would skin me alive."

"I find it hard to believe anyone could make you do anything you don't want to."

"Wait until you meet my coach," he says. "He'd beat me with my own saber if he caught me slacking." The way he grins suggests it's not entirely a joke.

His lips curl around the end of the cigarette, Adam's apple bobbing as he inhales.

I was part of the D.A.R.E. campaign right after *Clubhouse*. Smoking anything was an absolute no, but why does he make something so deadly look tempting?

The sight ignites something molten and rebellious in my chest, making me want to shatter every careful boundary I've built.

"Let me try," I breathe, reaching for the cigarette with deliberate defiance.

"Absolutely not."

"Since when do you get to decide what I do?" I lean in, thrilled by my own boldness, and get close enough to catch the spicy scent of his cologne mixed with smoke.

"I am not going to be the one to corrupt you."

"Maybe I want to be corrupted," I challenge, letting my good-girl mask slip further. "Consider it another thing to add to my character research."

"Reese." He says my name like a prayer and a warning combined. "No."

The denial stirs something in me.

I pull off my baseball cap with deliberate slowness, letting my hair cascade down in waves. The motion reminds me of a thousand romance scenes I've filmed, but this time there are no cameras, no directors calling cut.

Just Dante Hastings and his adamant need to say no to me.

I turn on *the* Reese Sinclair.

I remove my sunglasses, hooking them into the collar of my sweatshirt. There's a hunger in his eyes. I lift my chin to meet his gaze, and my lips curve into a smile that was drilled into me during intimacy training. This smile is all heat and promise. This is the one that gets that million-dollar kiss for the cameras.

"Dante…" I mewl. My fingers trail along the hood between us. "Please?"

He freezes, the cigarette trembling, forgotten between his fingers. "Are you—Christ, are you serious right now?"

"What?" I whisper, gravitating closer until I can count each of his dark eyelashes. Every rational thought about maintaining professional boundaries evaporates like the smoke I'm desperate to taste.

"That…" His voice comes out rough, despairing, as he gestures vaguely at my face with his free hand. I can see him fighting for control, and something wild inside me wants to make him lose it completely. "That whole act."

"Is it working?" The words come out breathy, challenging.

"Not even close," he lies.

My body hovers above his, blocking the sun from his face. A sharp movement shifts beneath his sweats, and the sight of it sends a rush of heat through me. His composure is cracking for once.

I trace my finger along his chest, watching as his breath catches, ragged and uneven. "Come on, let this be the third thing I regret."

I wet my lips slowly, and his jaw clenches as he bites his lip.

"Fuck, Reese," he breathes. "How does anyone say no to you?"

I shrug, eyeing the cigarette between his fingers. I swear the birds above could hear the pounding of my heart, but I stay in character, liking the way she feels.

Powerful. Sexy. All things I forgot I could be.

He breaks, taking a long drag from his cigarette. And then one of his large, calloused hands lands gently on my jaw, guiding me closer. There's a tenderness in the way he touches me, as if I could break with the slightest pressure.

The little game I decided to play shatters under his touch. Where did the acting end and this need for him begin? I want this, want him, more than I care to admit, with a hunger that excites and frightens me.

"Open up," he says.

I close my eyes, my lips parting.

Dante's nose brushes mine; my lips tingle at his proximity.

He's going to kiss me.

He exhales, warmth caressing my lips, the smoke curling around us. It's not a kiss, but he's giving me exactly what I asked for. And I like it more than I should.

"Breathe in," he whispers hoarsely.

I do as he says, inhaling bitter smoke, but it burns, and I break away coughing. "Heavens, that's awful," I gasp, eyes watering, even if I'm already craving more—of the smoke, of his touch, of the way everything feels real.

"Told you," he teases, but his thumb tenderly brushes away a tear.

"You should quit, immediately." I laugh.

He wets a finger with his lips and presses it against the ember without breaking our gaze. The sizzle slices through the quiet afternoon air, and my pulse races. It's the hottest thing I've ever seen.

"I'll think about it."

Chapter 14
Dante

Love Scene or Real Thing? Star's Beach Escapades Raise Eyebrows

By Susan Martin

America's sweetheart Reese Sinclair (29) is reportedly pursuing decorated Olympian Dante Hastings (26), the youngest scion to the Hastings athletic empire, causing tabloids to dramatically label this her "cougar era."

The pair's intimate beach encounter in Northern California during production of Robyn Hood *has fueled speculation. No stranger to headline-grabbing romances, Sinclair's pattern of selecting spotlight-adjacent men continues, reminiscent of her notorious Teen Choice Awards kiss incident.*

Meanwhile, Hastings is crafting his redemption arc. The fencing champion, whose shocking suspension earlier this year rocked the sports world, is now channeling his legendary intensity into Hollywood as both stunt coordinator and supporting actor in the Felix Langford-directed film.

As critics question Sinclair's unexpected pivot to action films following her split from Jaxon Elio—some suggesting a mid-life

crisis—Hastings appears to be successfully reinventing his public persona.

BROOKLYN

DANTE HASTINGS!!!!!! Explain this article.
Immediately.

FRANKIE

omgggggg our brothers in loveeeeee. finally
sum1 2 take him off our hands lololol

DANTE

It was a day at the beach. We're friends.

FRANKIE

suuuuure bestie. ur never just friends w any1…
remember dad's pickleball instructor last
summer lmaoooo

DANTE

Can we be serious for a minute? I think I
screwed up.

BROOKLYN

You're responsible for this?

DANTE

You know Susan was on my yacht this
summer. I think I may have confirmed our
location.

How on earth would someone be able to track
us down in the redwoods?

BROOKLYN

She's Reese Sinclair, you absolute walnut! She
can't even buy coffee without 50 cameras in
her face!

FRANKIE

brooooo u done messed uppppp

BROOKLYN

This is bad. She's been dealing with stalkers since she was literally 12! Some psycho paparazzi literally ran her car off the road last year!

DANTE

You're the one who sounds like a stalker now.

FRANKIE

brookie's right (4 once lol) thats pretty uncool bro

DANTE

I completely forgot that even happened. Alright?

BROOKLYN

If you actually care about her, you better start being MUCH more careful. I mean it, D.

FRANKIE

omgggg u DO care about her!!!

I can't believe I did this. The thought of betraying Reese's trust, of becoming just another vulture using her for headlines, makes rage burn through me. I need to put it somewhere, anywhere.

Susan. She's the reason I'm in this mess. I pull up her contact.

DANTE

What the ACTUAL fuck Susan? Off the record means OFF THE RECORD. Or did you conveniently forget that part?

SUSAN

New phone who dis?

My laugh comes out like broken glass, sharp and bitter.

DANTE

Cut the bullshit. I gave you a summer of drugs
and hookups on my yacht. This is how you
thank me? Violating your own fucking
journalistic integrity?

SUSAN

Welcome to the real world. Your little romance
with America's sweetheart? That's GOLD. I did
you a favor. You got your redemption story.
Everyone wins.

DANTE

Fuck you and your "favors."

SUSAN

Don't be so belligerent, darling. I'm hardly the
only reporter on Reese Sinclair's tail. How else
do you think I knew about the shooting
location earlier this month?

The thought that there could be more of this didn't even occur to me. This is what Reese meant when she told me about living her life in the spotlight. I've experienced my own fame, but this…this is a fucking monster I can't manage.

SUSAN

She's a superstar. I simply got to break the
story first and make a pretty penny by selling
that photograph. Don't believe me? See for
yourself.

I open the link Susan sent to find dozens of articles from different news sources reporting on the beach sighting. The same photo is attached to each article. Me helping her into my car, her eyes tilted up at me, my hand resting on the small of her back. It must have been taken when we were leaving.

Fuck. I try to call Susan, but it goes to voicemail. I call again and again until I hear, *The number you have dialed is not in service. Please check the number and try again.*

Blocked. Seriously?

My sister's warnings ricochet through my skull like bullets. God, that stupid fucking name-drop about Reese this summer.

The bragging. The boasting. I can't help but feel responsible.

Anger builds in my body, the way it did before my fist landed in Quentin's annoying sneer back at the World Cup.

I pace around the cabin. I need to run through my lines for my scene today, but I can't focus. My mind keeps running back to the day on the yacht.

You're always so well-researched, Susan.

Off the record, of course.

I barely told her a thing. Barely said yes, and she still fucking got on our tail because I somewhat confirmed *Robyn Hood* would be shooting in Redwood National Park, which stretches hundreds of miles.

Those asshats at the *Stone Times* constantly terrorize people. My ears start to ring, and I stop pacing. Can't get angry. Can't risk everything again. What am I going to do? Let myself snap again and risk losing everything a second time?

Need to calm the fuck down.

Calm down.

Maybe if I tell Reese about Susan now, she'll understand? She'd get that I talked to Susan before I met her. Before I saw under the mask she wears just as tightly as I wear mine.

The thought rings hollow in my mind.

There's no way Reese would understand me talking to the press about her.

And I don't blame her. She'll see me as another Ricky trying to use her for fame, and she'll end whatever it is that's going on between us.

And it can't end.

We just got started.

But as that thought comes to mind, so does another, more bitter one.

Am I using her?

If something like this had come out over the summer, I would have been fucking elated. An article with my name, finally untethered from my suspension. The USFA committee's gonna see this, think their problem child's reformed. My DMs are already flooded. They think I'm back in form, back in play. America's sweetheart's new arm candy.

What better redemption story?

And yeah, there's some perverse satisfaction in seeing my name beside Reese Sinclair's instead of Jaxon's—or anyone else's, for that fucking matter.

I thought I knew what I wanted, but this victory feels like a hollow point.

I stare at the article. The photo of us is grainy, imperfect, but Reese's smile is genuine. God, when she pulled her Reese Sinclair charm. *Fuck*. The same magic that had teenage me drilling lunges in front of her poster. Up close, she's nuclear. The calculated batting of her lashes, that practiced smile. She could have whispered anything, and I'd have followed her into the Pacific.

Yeah, I want her.

But it's deeper than flesh.

With her, the titles fall away. Not Olympic champion Hastings. Not the redemption-seeking hothead. Not the heir to generations of expectations.

Just Dante, stripped bare.

I can't let her find out.

REESE'S SCENE is shooting in an open clearing about a ten-minute walk from our cabins. They've upped security, got all these big fuckers standing around camp. Another consequence of my actions.

I have to talk to her, see if she knows it was me who invaded her privacy.

I'm such an idiot. Guilt sinks deeper into my chest.

When I reach the set, Robyn and Merrick are trekking through the open field, searching for women to join their makeshift army against the king. Reese is focused on her lines, giving no indication that she's mad.

I pull out my notebook and try to give myself a reason to be there other than spiraling.

Frantic for a distraction, I crouch and scribble onto the page, *Marcus—reshoot bandage scene, weapon placement*. The notes are real. A real enough excuse to come see her.

"Cut!" Felix shouts. "Sound's fucked. Take ten. This goddamn cash grab," he snarls at the techs. "Should've shot in Malta. Real action, real story—" He storms off.

Reese's head tilts to the side as she sees me. She waves at Elizabeth and walks toward me.

"Hey, what are you doing here? Aren't you supposed to be shooting at the jailhouse set?"

I should tell her. Susan's name sits like ash on my tongue, but Reese looks at me like everything is normal. Like I didn't screw this up before it began.

Interesting.

"It's in an hour," I say, handing her my notebook. "Looks like Felix is a real peach today."

"He's refusing to reshoot this scene with my notes," she huffs. "Says we don't have time, but somehow he can account for an hour of me in slo-mo shots. I'm going to lose my nerve."

"I can't figure out why he agreed to do this movie."

"He loves female empowerment, *duh*," she says dramatically. "And the big fat director's fee from the studio. But there's only two more months of this." She sighs before glancing down at my notebook in her hand. "What do you have here?"

"Notes on your scene. You know, for your choreography."

"Oh." She eyes me like she knows I'm hiding something. "We sneak off set for a day, and suddenly you're all notebook and pen?"

"I can take them back." I reach for my notebook, but she steps away, holding it out of reach.

"No. I want them. Just next time, maybe type them up." Her eyebrows crinkle as she skims the page. "Though the messy handwriting does fit the medieval vibe."

"Don't worry, next time I'll use a quill. Heart-dotted I's and everything."

"That's the extra effort I like to see." She toys with her hair, studying my chicken scratch. "You know, your spelling's not really all that bad—maybe my homework is helping."

"It is. Plus, autocorrect is a lifesaver."

She laughs easily. It's so easy with her. Fuck.

Focus.

Maybe she hasn't seen the article yet. I inspect her face, getting caught on the way she bites her lip.

"Gosh, yes, this footwork analysis! I've been researching techniques, thinking about those defensive positions you showed me. Robyn's always three steps ahead, just like real combat."

"Smart."

"Excellent work, Mr. Hastings. Also…" She leans in close. "I think the little break worked. It helped me get into character better. I felt myself channeling Robyn."

"You don't say."

"You were right. About getting out of my skin. I need to be more bold, more magnetic—"

"Like me?"

She pauses. "Honestly, yeah. Exactly like you!"

"Let's document this praise."

"Hush!" She waves her hand at me, then grins, stretching her arms over her head. "Actually, speaking of our outing." My breath stills. "Did you see the article about us this morning?"

"Yeah, and—"

She cuts me off. "I'm so sorry about that."

"Sorry?" I ask carefully.

"It's impossible for me to go anywhere without the media catching on. Even though our set location was meant to be undisclosed, they found out. I still have no idea how. But I definitely didn't want you to get roped into my tabloid nonsense."

"You're not upset?"

"Why would I be? It's not like you sold them the pictures." My jaw twitches. But she keeps going. "My publicist is handling it. Especially all the commentary about our age—that's the most ridiculous part of it. Three years between us, and they're acting like I'm robbing the cradle. I turned twenty-nine, and suddenly I'm vintage goods. 'Still stunning,' they say, like they're shocked I haven't crumbled to dust."

"What the fuck? You're—" But the words don't exist for what she is.

"Oh, it's not just this world. My Aunt Mabel married younger back home, and you'd think she'd committed treason. Meanwhile, Omar is dating someone half his age, and they're calling it romance." She shrugs, feigning lightness. "Different rules here. Men age like wine, women like milk, right?"

"That's fucking stupid."

"Well, regardless, I had fun yesterday." Her voice is small, like she can't believe she's admitting it.

"Me too."

"And I was thinking…" She tilts her head, studying me. "Maybe soon we could arrange another lesson off-grounds. Strictly professional, of course. For character research. Since it helped me so much. Robyn's quite the bad girl, so it's only right to follow in her footsteps." She's talking too fast, like she's thought about this extensively.

"You want *bad girl* lessons?"

"I simply…well, this is going to sound odd, but I want to study you, like I have been with my homework." Cowardice and embarrassment press against my chest. "Though Heather was furious about the beach—mostly because I left Ramsey behind. He wasn't thrilled with me either, but he'd never say it. Next time we'll have to bring him with us, otherwise, I'll give her a heart attack. Can't put her star talent in danger."

I force a laugh, but my mouth is dry. "Is sneaking off again a good idea?"

I should back out.

Be responsible.

Be good.

I should remind her that every second we spend together is another risk, another headline. But then she tilts her head, eyes bright with mischief, and I know whatever argument I'm making in my head is feeble.

"Are you going to deny me more hands-on instruction?" she teases, flipping on her charm.

I can't tell her about Susan. It really isn't that bad, and because Reese Sinclair wants to let me orbit her atmosphere again.

I can keep this a secret. Reese doesn't seem upset. Guess it's not harming her, and that's my priority.

I'll keep her safe. Keep our time together out of the media to the best of my ability. I can protect her from my world. Because sometimes protection means carrying the burden alone. And I've always been good at carrying weight—what's one more secret to break my back?

"Reese, we're going to need you in your chair to adjust the hair here; we're losing some volume," a makeup artist calls over, eyeing us both.

She steps back, holding up my notebook like a shield, and the distance feels like the judgment I deserve. "Of course. Just getting some notes from the stunt team. I'll be there in a jiffy."

"What do you say, up for another adventure? If we can find something away from the tabloids, of course."

I have no clue who this Reese in front of me is, but I want to find out.

I hesitate. The right answer is no. The right answer is distance.

But when have I ever done the right thing?

"I'm sure I can find something for us to do next weekend," I hear myself say.

Being good is fucking overrated.

LITTLE FIGHTER

I finally did the thing!

DANTE

Conquered that stunt sequence we rehearsed today?

LITTLE FIGHTER

Not exactly.

I managed to submerge myself in water without having a complete meltdown.

DANTE

Funny, I recall someone claiming they'd been doing that all week.

Have you been feeding me little white lies?

LITTLE FIGHTER

I may have slightly exaggerated my progress with the diving. The bathtub was very intimidating, okay?

DANTE

Looks like I'll have to start doing nightly
check-in calls instead of texts.

Keep you accountable and such.

LITTLE FIGHTER

Even during night shoots?

DANTE

Especially then. I'm nothing if not thorough.

LITTLE FIGHTER

Such dedication to my hydrotherapy.

DANTE

I contain multitudes.

LITTLE FIGHTER

Care to reveal any of those multitudes
regarding our weekend plans?

DANTE

Planning your escape route already?

LITTLE FIGHTER

As if.

DANTE

Perfect.

Remember, evidence must be provided daily
from now on. Otherwise, I might have to
personally supervise your diving lessons.

Chapter 15
Reese

THE CHECK-IN CALL comes as promised. My phone balances precariously on the edge of the tub, his voice threading through the humid air.

"Is the bath ready?"

"Yes." I sigh and readjust my shower cap.

"Good." He pauses. "Listen to me, Reese Sinclair—you can do this. You *will* do this." His words vibrate through the phone speaker and straight into my bones. "You got this."

I exhale, staring at the water. "I really don't think I do."

Twelve days until the raft scene. I need to get over this. But I don't want to. Still, with him on the phone, my hesitation weakens a little.

"Don't keep me waiting."

"Okay, hold on." I struggle with my robe. "I have to get this off."

"This is torture."

"You're being a good coach." I chuckle. Once I'm ready, I sink into the bath, letting the heat lick up my body. "Okay, I'm in."

"Now let's get you there," he says in that authoritative tone. "Want me to count you down?"

"Yes." I lower until the water laps at my collarbone. "Just… keep talking, okay?"

"I'm here, Reese. Now, take a deep breath. Feel the warmth of the water. How comforting it is. You're in control, Reese. Always in control."

I usually hate when men tell me what to do, but with Dante, I don't want him to stop.

I inhale slowly as his addictive French techno playlist hums through my cabin. I picture him here with me—his solid presence calming the nerves bubbling up inside of me. If they can help me master sword training, perhaps they can help me overcome my fear of water too.

What else do I have to lose?

"Ready?"

"No, but I'll do it anyway."

"Brave girl," he purrs. "One…two…three…"

I stop hesitating and slide beneath the surface, bracing my hands on the side of the tub. Partially because I have to, and partially because if I stay above water any longer, I may tell him to come over and join me in this bath.

The water singes my skin, but cold panic scratches at the edges of my ribs. His voice becomes muffled, otherworldly, counting steadily through the speaker at full volume. Each number feels like an eternity, but I focus on the memory of him touching my back after that day in the lake. His steady presence. The circles on my back.

"Eleven…twelve…thirteen…that's it, Reese, stay with me…"

I squeeze my eyes shut, clinging to the sound of Dante's voice.

"Twenty-two…twenty-three…twenty-four…twenty-five…"

I burst up, gasping, blinking water from my lashes, feeling

both vulnerable and capable.

"Twenty-five seconds," he harrumphs in satisfaction. "That's longer than yesterday. I'm proud of you."

"Still not good enough," I pant, gripping the edges of the tub.

"Hey, progress is progress. Want to try again?"

"I think that's enough near-drowning for one night," I say. "Though I appreciate the personal coaching service."

"Speaking of tonight…" His tone shifts, becoming playful, seductive. "We're going to a little gathering. Very exclusive. Very discreet. Very private. It'll give you the perfect opportunity to method act; it's a no-identity thing."

I pause, heat curling in my stomach, and not only from the bath. Tonight? I'd been waiting all week to hear what he had planned for us, assuming it would be something low-stakes, something I could prepare for.

Instead, he's springing *this* on me? "I thought we were going to do something tomorrow. During the day."

"What made you assume that?"

"Well, we went to the beach on a Sunday," I say, like it's obvious.

"And tonight we're going to a party."

I sink deeper into the water. A night out with Dante?

"Dante…" I hedge, unsure if I'm trying to warn him or myself.

"Come on, you deserve to celebrate. Twenty-five seconds is practically Olympic level. I'm certain Ezra would tell you himself."

"I doubt your accomplished merman younger brother would think anything of the sort." I've had to refresh my memory on all the Hastings siblings, but thankfully Wikipedia has a family chart for me to stalk.

"Maybe. But I'll be your lifeguard either way."

I laugh despite myself. "You're ridiculous."

"Does that mean you're coming tonight?"

"No. But my day is open tomorrow," I say, finality in my tone. "Now, I need to actually relax in this bath."

"Well, if you wanted to relax, you'd invite me over."

I don't know if it's the fact that I'm naked on the phone with him or that I've lost my mind, but I find myself saying, "And what *exactly* would you do to help me relax?"

"I'd ease away the tension from your demanding day on set. I'd help you unwind completely, make you forget everything but…" His measured pause holds a wealth of meaning. "Fuck, Reese…the things I'd give you."

The bath heats up like a tea kettle. My core throbs at the sardonic laugh he lets out. I nearly have to grab my free hand to stop it from dipping beneath the water's surface.

His voice, so perfectly crafted, so him, could make a nun regret her chastity vows.

"Anything?" The word sticks in my throat. The steam rises around me, creating my own world. A world in which he is here.

I imagine his hands, his large, veiny hands, running up my inner thighs while his lips whisper his devotion to me. My breath hitches.

"Whatever you want, it's yours. Want me to give you some ideas?"

Yes! I nearly scream. *Please keep talking. Please keep telling me exactly what you'd like to do.*

Instead I say, "Good night, Mr. Hastings."

"Wait—before you hang up. I realize I never told you my last regret."

"That makes you a bad student," I whisper, blushing. "Let's have it."

"My third regret is that I didn't meet you sooner."

The line goes flat. He seriously hung up after divulging that. I splash water on my face.

My mind swims with images of his perfectly messy brown hair falling just so across his forehead, begging me to run my fingers through it. Those impossible cheekbones leading to a jaw so sharp. And those eyes—golden and intense, framed by criminally thick lashes, burning like honey in sunlight whenever they lock onto mine.

My self-control snaps like a glowstick, silent at first, then a little too bright to ignore.

One hand finds my breast, the other runs down between my thighs until it reaches the spot that's been begging for him. His praise fills my mind.

Reese, you're doing so good.

Move your legs apart.

Straighten your back.

Breathe, fighter.

These are dangerous thoughts. But the neediness pooling in my core tells me it's already too late—I'm in deep trouble when it comes to Dante Hastings.

The things I'd give you.

I circle my clit, moving from wandering to desperate.

What he wore to training today was pure torture—the loose tank did nothing to hide the broad stretch of his shoulders, the ink snaking down his arms like an invitation. And those shorts. Too fitted, too unfair, clinging to every muscle like he'd gotten them personally tailored to ruin me.

I caught myself staring more than once, heat crawling up my neck as my gaze dipped to where it shouldn't go. Not that I could help it. Not when there is something there…a very large something that jerked in his sweats when we sat on the hood of his Range Rover.

My fingers work faster; a moan slips out of me.

Would it be so bad to sample him just once?

Water sloshes with my quickening movements, my free hand gripping the tub's edge, knuckles white. French techno pulses through the bathroom. My breath grows ragged, syncing to its beat.

"Please, Dante. More," I whisper, picturing his demanding hands guiding me, coaxing me to the edge. It's enough. My legs shake, sending small waves splashing against the porcelain.

When was the last time I let myself lose control like that?

Afterward, I sink back against the cool tile, letting the water settle around me as reality seeps back in.

It's frustrating, because I know this game—his low, sincere tone, the perfectly timed sweet nothings. I'm probably another chapter in Dante Hastings's playbook. Yet that thought doesn't stop the effect he has on me.

I hurry out of the bath, carefully removing my shower cap and running a brush through my waves. My eyes drift to the sticky notes framing my mirror—*Be a leading lady. Trust your instincts.* Mixed between them are Dante's handwritten choreography notes. *Stay grounded* and *Lead with intention.* Reading them makes my cheeks flush with a mixture of pride and lingering embarrassment from what unfolded in the bath.

After patting on my nighttime serums, I head to the living room. There's a knock at the door.

Oh no, it can't be him.

Oh no, what if he knows what I did?

My third regret is that I didn't meet you sooner. Dante's words fill my thoughts.

Inhale for four, hold for seven, exhale for eight. I open the door.

"Now what are you doing here?" I say flirtatiously, trying to mask my nervous anticipation—only to find a PA standing in the doorway with a large box.

"Hello, Miss Sinclair."

"Hi, Casey."

Without meeting my gaze, they hand me the box. "Mr. Hastings asked me to drop this off as I was on my way to my cabin."

"Oh," I stutter. "It must be, uh, more stunt notes. He likes to package them this way." I laugh, trying to act natural, though nothing about this feels natural. The old Reese would never accept a mysterious package from her costar.

"Right. Well, good night."

I shut the door, my heart racing, and take the box to my bedroom, pulling the curtains closed like I'm hiding evidence. I lift the lid and peel back layers of delicate tissue paper with trembling fingers.

Inside, the most gorgeous red gown I've ever seen pools like liquid fire—nothing like the pastels and florals that fill my closet. I run my fingers over the fabric, heavy and soft against my skin.

The dress is nothing like my usual red-carpet choices, the ethereal Elie Saab gowns, delicate Chanel pieces, or the romantic Carolina Herrera designs I'm known for. This one whispers of danger and desire. It's beautiful, seductive—something my version of Robyn would wear without hesitation. Beneath it lie a pair of heels and a matching red mask, elegant and mysterious, like something from a masquerade ball.

I grab it out and hold it up to the mirror. Then I pull out my phone and open our text thread.

REESE

I'm certain I said no to the party.

DANTE

What do you think of the dress?

REESE

You can't use the PAs for your personal errands.

DANTE

Personal errands? Hardly. I'm helping our production's leading star with her method acting. Besides, Casey and I go way back—he owed me a favor.

My stomach tightens at what he might mean by *way back*.

Dante's got a way with everyone—I see it on set. The crew, the cast, they're always all over him, and that bothers me more than it should. No, this tightness in my chest must be because he's asking me to sneak out again.

As if reading my mind, he texts:

DANTE

My friends know how to keep secrets. The thing tonight is very hush-hush. No cameras, no gossip. Just good music and better company.

REESE

I really can't have another tabloid scandal.

DANTE

Promise.

The dress looks to be exactly my size. *Of course it is.*

This is a dress for someone who isn't afraid to be bad. A slit up the leg, backless and daring in every way. Does Dante see me as someone who could pull this off?

Do I?

I pace the length of my bedroom, the mask dangling from my fingers. Would it be so terrible to try out being a woman who would wear something like this for one night? Just an hour or two, hidden behind silk and secrets. The mask would protect me. No one would know it's Reese Sinclair underneath.

Besides, after what I did in the bath thinking about him… well, doesn't that mean I've gotten it out of my system? That I won't put myself in any compromising positions at whatever party he's inviting me to?

Or maybe—and this thought makes my cheeks burn—it means I'll want to make all those bathtime imaginings come to life.

Heavens, I don't know anymore.

Before I can overthink it, I pull up my phone.

REESE

Ramsey has to come.

DANTE

Don't worry, he can lurk in the corner like he always does during our training sessions.

REESE

Fine.

DANTE

I'll be there in twenty minutes. Be ready, Reese.

A real night out—not a publicity stunt, not a carefully orchestrated photo op. Me, a mask, and the promise of something dangerous.

I drop the dress onto my bed next to the mask and notice something black peeking out beneath the tissue paper in the box. I pull it out.

Lingerie.

Not one of the sweet, innocent pieces wardrobe usually hands me—no baby pinks or delicate lace here. This is Agent Provocateur, all black and structured lines. The corset feels decadent in my hands, its boning firm yet flexible. There are sheer stockings with delicate seams up the back and a garter belt that makes my cheeks flush just looking at it.

I catch myself in the mirror again, holding the corset against my body, and my reflection startles me. Heat creeps up my neck as I imagine wearing it. No man has ever bought me lingerie before.

Sure, I've worn plenty for movies—always sweet, always safe, always carefully chosen so as not to tarnish my image.

But this is different.

This is meant to be seen.

To seduce.

The silk whispers against my skin as I trace the intricate

patterns, and I realize I'm holding my breath. There's a force in these pieces—a dangerous, thrilling kind I've never let myself explore. The kind that makes good girls bite their lips and bad girls smirk.

This is pure Dante Hastings—bold, unapologetic, daring me to step out of my comfort zone.

Looking in the mirror, I see someone who's capable of being those things too.

I think about all those fierce women in movies I love—Blunt kicking butt in *Edge of Tomorrow*, Theron owning every scene in *Atomic Blonde*, Yeoh moving like poetry in *Crouching Tiger, Hidden Dragon*.

They make being strong and desired look darn good.

My hands shake a little as I put on each piece of lingerie. Every lacy bit feels like giving the middle finger to my good-girl image. The red dress hugs every curve I usually hide.

The mask feels heavy as I tie it on. Just like that, I'm not Reese Sinclair anymore. I'm whoever I want to be tonight.

My phone buzzes.

He's here.

One last glance in the mirror, and I barely recognize myself. The mask helps, sure, but it's my eyes that stop me—they're blazing with something I always keep locked away. My heart's racing against the corset as I head for the door, each click of these heels taking me farther from the old me.

No turning back now.

Tonight, I'm not asking for permission to be bad.

I'm taking it.

Chapter 16
Dante

Reese grips the edge of the boat rail, as if she'll topple over with one sudden movement. Ramsey looms beside her. After much protest, the Volto mask I got him hangs ridiculously on his face. Around us, the beautiful and the damned drink champagne behind their masks, safe in their anonymity.

Crater Lake sleeps, or pretends to. Tonight, it belongs to people who bend reality with black cards and backroom deals. But this party isn't about money—it's about knowing which doors to knock on, which palms to grease. The cave's location passes through whispers in penthouses, traded like currency. Wizard Island looms ahead like a dark promise. Our boat cuts through black water, prow slicing past pines.

Music pulses somewhere beyond the dock, while water runs down cave walls like tears of light. Each droplet catches the lanterns' glow.

My eyes flit to the gorgeous gown hugging every curve of her body. Did she dare put on the lingerie? My fingers itch to find out.

"You didn't tell me there was going to be water," she groans.

"Almost over, sweetheart." The endearment feels dangerous

in my mouth as I wrap my arm around her shoulder. She doesn't bristle at my touching her. A win.

"I hate you," she lies.

"Too bad you're stuck with me for the next couple hours. Unless you'd like to swim back to shore." She shakes her head profusely, like I asked her to eat a worm. "You did get up to twenty-five seconds tonight."

"You seriously are the worst," she lies again.

"The only other suggestion I have for you would be to ask Rams to swim you back," I say and face Ramsey, who glares at me. "What do you think, buddy? Think you can handle something out of *The Scorpion and the Frog*?" No response. I turn back to Reese. "I think he's warming up to me."

She gives me a scolding look—the one that makes me feel seventeen again, stripped of everything I've built. The one that makes me feel a little bad about being bad. Yet she's still here, solid and real beside me.

"I don't think so."

My hard chuckle fills up my chest. This bit of bite from her is worth it, because I'm taking Reese fucking Sinclair to the most exclusive party of the year, and no one will know but me. Tonight, I'll show her what freedom tastes like, what it means to belong to no one but yourself.

"If I'd told you there was a boat involved, you would've never agreed to come. And I couldn't risk that." I lean close enough to breathe her in, testing both our limits. "Trust me. And now that I've distracted you long enough, give me your arm." The boat clanks against the dock as the captain secures us to the wooden planks. "We're here."

Around us, there are dozens of glamorous guests bustling off of their tiny boats, walking down the dock toward the cave.

Reese shifts closer, all wide-eyed as she takes in the masked strangers. "This isn't exactly what I'd call intimate."

"Numbers were never my strong suit."

Her nails dig crescents into my bicep as I help her off the boat and onto the dock. "Drop me in the water, and I'll destroy you during training," she says through gritted teeth.

"Looking forward to it."

The boat lists under Ramsey's weight as he attempts to take Reese's other arm. "Maybe you should let me—"

"I got her, big guy." The words come out harder than intended. Or maybe exactly as intended.

She quiets Ramsey with a look. He retreats, radiating disapproval.

"Here, since heels and planks don't mix." In one fluid motion, I step off the boat and sweep her into my arms. Her body curves into mine like muscle memory. Ramsey's glare burns between my shoulder blades.

She flicks her brown eyes to mine. "You orchestrated this whole thing to carry me, didn't you?"

"A boat, a Balenciaga, a genuine Venetian mask, all to carry you down ten meters of dock?" I adjust my grip, drawing her closer to my chest, letting Ramsey see. "Sounds like me."

She laughs against my collar, a private sound. *Mine.*

The ceiling's crystalline formations catch the light just so. Murano orbs house colonies of bioluminescent creatures. The guests—all properly vetted, of course—drift through the space in their inherited masks and bespoke silks. Near the back, where the cave opens into a natural alcove, a bartender crafts cocktails using spirits older than most small nations.

The fog machine's haze mingles with cigarette and weed smoke, layering the air with memories of places that would make Reese flinch.

When I set her down, her pulse jumps visible at her throat. Behind her mask, her eyes dart around, taking everything in.

"What is this place?"

"Impressed?" I try to sound casual.

"You want me to be impressed that you're disturbing sacred

ground?" Her hip juts to the side as she crosses her arms across herself.

"The organizers preserve this place, protect it. Nothing illegal happens here—at least, not to the environment. We leave it better than we found it." I give her a wink. This isn't rebellion, it's sanctuary.

"And you come to places like this often?"

"When the opportunity arises."

I need her to see it.

There's something untamed in both of us. Her fire forged into steel, mine left to burn. I want to watch her discipline crack, at least for a night. Let her taste what she's denied herself.

After years of keeping everyone at a clinical distance, showing her this side of me—the one people usually see first, before they piece together the mess underneath, before the drinks blur their judgment—feels like stepping off a ledge.

And fuck, I want to fall.

"Then I want to see it. See you." She flinches. "For my research, of course."

"What other reason is there?"

There's so much unsaid, and every inch of me screams in desire. I've never been with someone like her before, never hung out with someone so casually. I want to kiss her. I want to undress her and devour her right in front of everyone.

But that's the old Dante.

Patience. The best things in life are worth waiting for.

Her fingers twitch at her side. Is she thinking the same things I am? Then a sequined woman careens toward us like a meteor of glitter. Her face locks onto Reese's, and my protective instincts spark up. My pulse races, my body her shield.

Headlines scroll through my mind: *America's Darling Caught in the Undertow of the Underground Scene.*

My scene.

"I love you!" The stranger laughs and embraces Reese as

time suspends. Fuck, I promised her this wouldn't happen. Reese's careful composure fractures. Then the stranger turns to me. "I love you too." And she drifts off, rubbing the leaves of an innocent potted plant against her face.

I exhale, and so does Reese.

"Oh heavens, I thought—"

"Your cover was blown?" *Me too*, I don't add. "Don't worry, she seems to be experiencing some chemical-induced enlightenment."

"Right, uh." Reese shifts, her fingers worrying a strand of hair, her eyes wide with discovery. "I don't—I don't want to do that."

"You don't have to," I say. "Say the word, and we're gone."

I've had my fair share of nights dissolved into altered consciousness, but being here with Reese fills me with unease, like I have to stay alert, to stay focused.

To make sure she's safe.

"No, I trust you. I can't see anyone's face; I doubt they'll see mine. This is a lot."

Maybe it's too much too fast?

"I knew you were a good girl, but you're from New Orleans. You never go down to Mardi Gras?'"

"My parents never let me go downtown when the parades were happening. We did the sanitized version—St. Charles early in the morning, church bells, Mom's store-bought king cake." Her hand moves to her pearl necklace. "But I was also out of town a lot. Left at eleven to shoot *Clubhouse*."

So much of her childhood was taken away. "When they clipped your wings."

"I'm not some caged bird." But her voice wavers. "Just…inexperienced."

I lean close enough to catch her perfume. Cedar. Magnolias. All Reese. "Don't worry. Tonight we'll break every rule you never knew you wanted to break. Safely."

I want to show her everything. The violence of surrender, the sweetness of defiance, but I want to do it right.

Tonight, she's in my world, and I want to ensure it doesn't swallow her.

"This is hardly a place for fairground rides."

"Better. It's a place for pure fucking transcendence."

Tonight isn't exclusive—it's forbidden. And that makes all the difference.

"Show me," she says. Her smile turns feral, unscripted. This is what I've been chasing—not the high, but this moment of watching someone step off the edge of themselves. "I said I wanted to get into character, and that's what I'm going to be doing. And I feel like Robyn would go for a drink in this situation."

"Follow me."

We head to the bar. I order and grab the drinks, but not before grabbing the bartender's wrist.

"Clean?" I ask.

"Clean."

They better be. I know drugs all too well, and the last thing we need is laced decadence. I nod, releasing him as Ramsey gives me an approving glance from across the room.

"Everything okay?" Reese asks.

"Yes. I just want to make sure you're safe."

Her face tilts down, but I see the shadow of a smile on her lips. She takes the drink, inhales, and sips, eyes widening. "My goodness—what is this?" Her face sours as her southern drawl slips out.

"Easy there," I warn. "Absinthe. The good stuff. Strong enough to make you see stars, but not strong enough for you to turn all van Gogh and cut an ear off."

She takes another sip. "Tastes like licorice and hellfire had a love child." Her eyes flash with something dangerous. "I think I want more."

"One's enough. Training tomorrow, remember?"

"I can handle it," she shoots back, swaying closer. "Isn't that what tonight's all about?"

Yes, it is, darling.

Before I can answer, she grabs another drink from the bartender and tilts the cup back in one smooth motion. "That's enough."

"You're not allowed to be bossy in the gym *and* out of it." She pauses, and I recognize that look—it's the same calculated recklessness she gets in training before attempting something bold. Her shoulders drop, tension melting. "Why don't I give the commands tonight?"

My cock hardens at the words. She moves closer, tongue darting across her lower lip, and desire hits me like a physical blow. She lets her fingers dance in the silver chain along my neck.

Her hand drops lower, pausing at a pearl button on my shirt, unfastening it with a tortuous slowness.

Fuck.

"You're so buttoned-up, Mr. Hastings. We're meant to be letting loose."

"Fucking hell, Reese." My pulse thunders beneath my starched collar, her fingers electrifying my chest. Absinthe's sweet sharpness lingers on her breath.

Rising to her tiptoes, swaying, she whispers hot against my ear, "Let's see if you move as well here as you do with your sword." Her words slur at their edges.

The bass drops. Tonight, Reese finally lets go. Inhibitions dissolving with each beat.

She throws her head back in wild abandon, joy erupting from her throat like it's her first taste of freedom. That smile could topple dynasties. She spins through the kaleidoscope of bodies, stumbling yet catching herself with a giggle.

Otherworldly. Untouchable.

I can't look away.

A masked couple tries pulling me into their orbit. I growl them off, irritated. Normally, I'd be hunting my next meaningless distraction. But this isn't another night, another willing body.

This is Reese Sinclair crashing into my world, her cheeks flushed with one drink too many.

She grips my hand with startling force. "Don't leave me," she hiccups.

Her red dress teases me with each sway. When she traces her clavicle, I forget to breathe. I spin her into my arms to steady her wobble, and the heat of her back against my chest nearly shatters me.

She reaches for another drink, fingers unsteady.

"Easy, Reese," I warn as she sways dangerously, my hand instinctively finding the small of her back.

"Join me," she challenges, eyes flashing with mischief. "Aren't you made for this kind of fun?"

"I'm watching you," I counter, my voice rougher than intended.

She invades my space, her lips barely brushing my ear. That innocent contact ignites a current down my spine, scorching everything in its wake. "Why? Afraid I'll see the real you?"

Something honest splinters right behind my ribs. Part of me wants to dull this feeling with a pill, a shot, anything to keep myself floating in this perfect moment without having to face what it means.

"You're drunk," I say firmly, but there's hesitation in my voice.

"I know," she says proudly. "Isn't it nice? Everything's… softer." She gestures vaguely. "Do you ever feel that way? Like the edges aren't so sharp anymore?"

"That's what people look for here," I admit. But from my

own experience, you rarely find what you're looking for at the bottom of a glass. I steady her as she tilts too far.

"Maybe I'm not looking for anything," she says quietly, her voice cutting through the noise.

"Maybe you're just tired of being looked at?"

"You need to get out of your skin," she teases, throwing my words back at me with devastating precision. "Dance with me."

"I shouldn't," I say, though my body follows hers. "You're not…not in a state to—"

"To what?" she interrupts, suddenly lucid. "To make decisions? To feel something? I'm just drunk enough to be honest, Dante. Are you brave enough for that?"

I'm torn between instincts—to protect her from harm and to revel in her wildness. The selfish part of me hungers to watch her break free, to show her life beyond the pages of a script. Every nerve demands I lose myself completely in her chaos.

But for the first time in my reckless life, I want to savor something—savor her.

"Let me tell you a secret," Reese whispers as we step into her cabin. She's very tipsy. Not the kind of drunk that'll knock her out the minute her head hits the pillow. But the kind where she wants to keep the party going, all night if she could. Even on the boat ride, the drive back to the jet, she didn't care. Just kept dancing.

She chose this, but I can't help feeling responsible.

"What is it?"

She kicks off her heels, turns to me, and giggles with a hiccup that's so sweet it stings. "I'm wearing your gift."

My spine stiffens, jaw tightening. All night I've itched to discover if she chose to put it on, and now she tells me.

"Let's get you to bed," I say, ignoring her despite how badly

I want to find out what all those black lines and lace look like on her.

Her fingers trace over my arm again. "Bold of you to figure out my size. But I like that about you. How you know things about me."

I inhale. *Don't pay attention, Dante. She won't remember any of this in the morning.* I pull away from her, though every cell in my body screams at me not to, and I find a bottle of water in the fridge.

"Here, drink up. You need to hydrate after all that partying, wild child."

She ignores my offering and steps closer. Palms on my chest. The smell of absinthe still on her breath. "What I *need* is for you to kiss me, Dante." My name leaves her lips like a confession. "Please."

I press crescents into my palms, needing something to ground me. This is worse than any craving, worse than withdrawal. She's right here, willing and wanting, but this isn't how we're going to do this. I've waited weeks for her to warm up to me; I can wait a little longer to melt into her.

"You're drunk," I say, barely holding on.

"So?" she teases. "You're telling me *the* Dante Hastings never kissed a person who was a little tipsy before?"

"Not if they aren't sober enough to consent."

"I'm sober, and I consent," she insists through another hiccup. She pulls her hand away before winding it into mine. I stiffen at the contact. Holding hands isn't something I do. Unless there's a practical reason, like helping someone over a fence or through a crowd. But she's drawing our joined hands up, tracing my fingers along her jawline, her gaze heavy-lidded as she watches my reaction.

Her skin is soft, flushed from the alcohol, or maybe that's just her. Her pulse thrums where our wrists cross.

"You're nowhere close to the definition of sober," I scold.

She glares at me, her nose scrunching and lips pouting. It can't be healthy that I get this fucking turned on by her being frustrated with me.

"I can prove it," she says, glancing around the cabin. To her right, a pile of scripts and pens sits atop the entryway credenza. Reese's eyes flit back to me mischievously before she reaches over and grabs a pen. "Would a drunk person be able to sign their own name perfectly? I don't think so."

"I'm certain you can autograph in your sleep," I chuckle at her terrible argument.

Ignoring me, Reese nudges the cuff of my sleeve without letting go of my hand, revealing my wrist. She finds a patch of clear skin between my tattoos and presses the pen's tip into me.

"Who should I make it out to?" she asks with a smirk.

Fucking hell. Is this seriously happening? Is Reese Sinclair about to write her name on my skin? I almost can't speak. "Your biggest fan."

She steadies her grip, the sharp point of the pen digging into me. My blood races, the flesh hot as if the black ink is branding me. A bead of sweat rolls down my neck and into the collar of my shirt. I'm so fucking hard I might actually explode.

No. Absolutely not. Don't come. Don't you dare come in your trousers while she's signing her name onto your skin.

There will be nothing more pathetic than that. Fuck.

Once Reese finishes her handiwork, I manage a deep breath. She holds up her neat script for me to see. *To my biggest fan, xo Reese Sinclair.*

My mouth dries.

"How's that for having all of my faculties in order?" she quips.

"Reese," I beg.

"You like how that looks, don't you?"

"I do."

"Well, I like these rings you wear," she murmurs in her

honeyed voice. "I like them so very much." She grabs my hand, gaze fixed on my pointer finger as she inspects the silver band. When her plush lips press against the metal, a jolt shoots straight down my spine to my already hard cock. The intimacy of it makes my throat tight. Her eyes connect with mine, and she pulls away. "Sorry, I'm getting carried away."

"Trust me, there's nothing more I want to do than get carried away with you right now. Pin you against this wall and kiss every smart thing you've ever said to me off your damn lips," I say through a hoarse throat. "You have no idea how little I want to be a gentleman toward you right now."

"I want that too."

"Not like this," I say, lowering my voice. "You want to know what it's like to be with me? Then I want you to feel everything I do to you." Reese moves like smoke before me, all heavy-lidded eyes and parted lips. "That means waiting. For *both* of us. Can you do that?" I exhale hard through my teeth. "You have no idea how easy you are to need, Reese."

She deserves a clear head and clean memories.

"Can you help me get more comfortable?" She spins in front of me, and her fingers fumble with the dress. "If that doesn't violate your *gentlemanliness*?"

"It does not."

I hold my breath and brush her hair off her back. The zipper slides down with agonizing slowness. I force my touch to remain clinical—professional, as sober Reese would want it to be—even as the sight of her exposed skin makes the need in my blood burn.

"Your touch feels so nice," she exhales with a moan.

I'm going to die in this delicious hell she's put me in.

Once the dress is unzipped, I force myself to turn around and give her some privacy. But in a breath, Reese appears in front of me.

And, fuck, there she is. In my gift, which has transformed

into pure torture. Her curves, the untamed waves of hair, the smudged lipstick. I clench my fists, my cock trapped in my trousers. Now this…I don't know if I have enough self-control left.

"I didn't get a chance to thank you for your gift," she says with a slow twirl of her hair and that same lip bite from her little seduction act at the beach. "I don't want you to think I have terrible manners, Dante."

Jesus fucking Christ.

She lets a bra strap slip, and the flash of her bare shoulder is enough to shatter my control. I force myself to turn away, even as every muscle screams in protest.

My heart pounds in every artery. Loud and impossible to ignore. Since I met her, she's been with me, this fixed point in my consciousness. Nights fixed with a smile that triggers some dopamine response I can't rationalize. As tempting as every perfect curve of hers is, I want that Reese. The woman who snorts when she laughs and gets giddy over fight choreography.

"When I finally have you, Reese"—she blinks rapidly—"and I *will* have you, I need to know, without a doubt, that you want me as much as I want you. Now, let me take care of you." I force myself to step away and grab a robe, draping it over her shoulders. The sheets whisper as she sinks into her bed.

I head to the bathroom, gathering up makeup wipes and a hairbrush, and I find sticky notes covering the mirror like confessions. *Trust your instincts. Be the leading lady.*

This is my Reese.

Back at her bedside, I kneel. "Close your eyes." She does, making these small sounds that hit me straight in the chest as I gently remove her mascara. I move on to her hair, the famous Sinclair mane.

I grip the brush carefully and work slowly through her thick, golden hair. My body burns with an unspoken need. Then the brush catches, and she groans as I gently work out the knot hiding at the nape of her neck. She leans into my touch, her head heavy in my palm.

I'm in so much trouble.

She's like nicotine. Like air. Like the first time I held my saber.

"There," I whisper, brushing the strands behind her ears.

Her eyes open, slow and soft, meeting mine. "I miss that smell of yours. All the smoke."

"I gave it up," I reply.

She drifts off to sleep without knowing I'd give up more than cigarettes if she asked. Since she started occupying all my empty spaces, I haven't needed that vice.

For an hour, I linger, haunted by her cabin. Her world, filled with scripts, sword fighting books, and photos of both her polished celebrity and the laughing girl I'm falling for.

When I'm sure she's asleep, I slip out. The cool air hits my skin like a rebuke.

Ramsey's eyes find me instantly. Silent, ever-watchful.

"She's sleeping," I say, my words falling short.

His gaze narrows, the warning clear: *Don't fuck this up.* I nod, but he sees right through me.

Message received.

Walking away feels like ripping out a part of myself. She's under my skin now, in my blood. And damn it, I want her to stay there.

Chapter 17
Dante

"I SHOULD LEAVE. You're obviously distracted." Em gestures toward the bench, where my phone vibrates face up. "Must be killing you, missing that tournament to babysit."

While my teammates are at the World Cup in Bulgaria, I'm stuck here. The *Fédération Internationale d'Escrime* tournament points that help with Olympic qualifications are slipping away.

I ignore Em; she's trying to get out of drills. This is our fourth session together, and it's always the same. She shows up late, bristles at every correction, and leaves early. I've tried different approaches: strict technique, free sparring, even letting her attack while I defend.

Nothing seems to stick. And now here we are again, her frustration building like a pressure cooker.

"You're not bending your back leg anymore," I say, tapping my blade against the floor. "Again."

"How much longer?" The borrowed, ill-fitting uniform—scavenged from a former student since she'd refused Coach's offer to buy her proper gear—hangs loose and awkward on her frame. It's dark with sweat despite the early hour. I feel a twinge of sympathy watching her struggle with the hand-me-down equipment.

"*Povtoreniye, mat' ucheniya,*" I say, quoting Coach's favorite Russian proverb. "Repetition is the mother of learning. So we're going to do this until you can do it in your sleep." I demonstrate but notice my own stance has grown slack, professional standards eroding in this fluorescent-lit purgatory. "This isn't aimless stabbing. It's precision. Art."

"Art, stabbing, whatever." Her fingers trail along a curved saber with unexpected reverence. "I want to fight."

"This isn't street fighting," I say, watching her shift weight between her feet. "It's about control. Discipline." I pause. "I used to think like you."

"Right. Because you know all about real fights, preppy boy."

She has no idea how much the fight means to me. How I crave it, every hit and point and chance to break free, to let loose, to lose control and have all that fire and energy centered onto something.

Even though the temper never fades and the touch of skin-to-skin contact is sometimes better than sword-to-sword, fencing is my lifeline. Old memories surface, unwanted but familiar.

"The anger you're carrying? I recognize it," I say.

"Sure you do. A trust fund baby with a movie star girlfriend."

All week I've been trying to figure out what to do with Reese. Since the party last Saturday, she's clicked back into her professionalism. My concern that I showed her too much of myself swells in my chest.

"Get your nose out of my personal life and focus on your form. Why are you here if you won't take it seriously?"

Em rips off her mask, her saber hitting the ground with theatrical force. "Coach Lev said he could help me get out of this fucking state if I was good enough. Colleges love this fancy shit, apparently."

"He's right. I've seen plenty get full rides. But you won't be applying for another year," I remind her. "You got your sights set on something?"

"Columbia or Princeton."

"Your grades good enough?"

She rolls her eyes. "Were yours? Oh wait—sorry, you had the big family name to help you get in."

I realize it then. The bus is her daily transport, not the chauffeured rides I took for granted. Parents remain conspicuously absent from her stories. This place isn't a choice, it's her only option.

Coach said she joined the fencing club to have an excuse to hit something. But I've seen the way she moves. *If* I can get through to her and help her get a scholarship somewhere, it'll be another thing to add to my list of accomplishments for the disciplinary committee.

"You've got real skill," I admit. "Way beyond most kids your age."

"Whatever," she sighs, stretching her arms above her head. The movement yanks the wrist of her jacket down, and a flash catches my eye. A watch—a couple grand on her wrist. Last practice, it was new headphones. I know she doesn't have a job. There's only one way she's getting this stuff.

She's stealing.

We all have our vices. Makes sense why Coach paired us together.

"You know, I hated fencing at first. When I was your age, I loved getting in trouble. Had nothing to work toward. Sound familiar?" I pause, aware of the weight of what I'm about to say. "The hard truth about the difference between you and me is that my parents could afford private-school solutions."

"You want me to feel bad that your parents sent you off to some fancy private school?"

"They tried everything else first," I say, remembering the

endless parade of counselors and specialists, each promising answers. "But yeah, eventually. Boarding school became the solution after I got arrested..." I exhale slowly. "The school made me pick a sport. Fencing provided me structure. A way to channel all of this—"

"You got arrested?" Her eyes light up like she's met a celebrity.

"Saber found me when nothing else could. It's the rawest form of fencing—pure velocity and aggression compressed into technique. Your entire body becomes a target. Every slash, every movement has to mean something. When you're carrying that much inside you, Saber teaches you to transform it. Not to extinguish the fire, but to give it purpose."

"Sounds inspirational, but all we're doing here are drills."

"And if you stopped being lazy with your lunges, we'd be able to move on to the piste."

"And if I don't want to do stupid lunges? What are you going to do? Kick me out of the program? Pawn me off on someone else?" Her eyes dart between me and her discarded mask. "Like everyone else fucking does."

Her words linger in the stale gym air. *Everyone else fucking does.*

It's true. I could walk away. Ask Coach to give me a new kid to train. One that's less of a pain in my ass. Let Em think she's right about everyone bailing.

Yet there's a crack in her that hits close to home. I've bailed on enough obligations to recognize it. Commitments and expectations that felt like they were suffocating me. Running away from shit has always been my go-to, my escape route.

But maybe the real power move is staying. Maybe it's standing your ground when everything in you screams to get the hell out.

I could be another statistic in Em's careful catalog of abandonments, or I could be the exception that makes her question her own math.

Not everyone leaves.

Some people stay.

Reese's advice rings in my ears. *Be kind and patient.* That's exactly what Em needs.

"Pick up your mask," I say, walking onto the piste. Without hesitation, she joins me. "You want to stop doing drills? Show me what you got."

For the next hour, we fence. Em's blade rips through the air, her feet dancing across the strip with deadly precision. Our sabers crash together—parry four, riposte, remise. Through my mask, I track her every move, waiting for the tell.

Winning used to mean becoming another champagne-soaked legend, upholding the work I put into making this sport the best it could be. But what if the committee doesn't clear me to keep fencing after my disciplinary review?

What happens then?

A reality without fencing is terrifying.

For the past month, I've been training Em and Reese, becoming something like a compass for them—just like Mom is for her players.

It twists in my gut, the thought of watching others claim what used to be mine. The media reduces coaches to footnotes, if they remember them at all. Do you learn to romanticize the aftermath of glory? The shift from star to spectator feels like a slow death. A glimpse into my future—another has-been fading to static.

Fencing barely registers in the cultural consciousness, though I built a brand, made them notice. But however much I hate to admit it, the sport will keep spinning, with or without me.

While I'm distracted, Em's there, faster than she has any right to be, front foot pivoting while her back leg drives like a piston. Her saber curves under mine in some wild move that would make Lev cringe. The tip slams into my lamé.

Touch.

"Holy shit," she pants, holding the perfect extension. "Did I just…?"

I pull off my mask, genuinely startled. "Unorthodox but brilliant. Where did you learn that?"

"I didn't. It felt right. Like my body knew."

My phone's harsh alarm cuts through the moment. Time's up.

As Em packs up, something metallic falls from her bag—a handful of security tags.

"It's not what it looks like," she barks, scooping up the stolen items, her eyes darting to me.

I pretend to fumble with my gear. "You want to get into those colleges?"

"I do."

She's talented in a way that makes my chest tight, maybe better than I was at her age. But talent isn't everything, and I see too much of my younger self in her restlessness. "How about this? You clean up your act, and I'll write you a recommendation letter to Princeton, straight from an alumnus and the best fencer that D1 team ever had."

"Are you serious?"

I understand what Coach must have seen in me back then. Not just potential, but someone who needed an anchor. Maybe I could be that for her, someone who sees past the defenses to what lies beneath.

"Yes. But that also means you're going to need to start entering tournaments."

"And I've done enough lunges to do that now?"

"There's no such thing as enough lunges. But the Southern California division holds monthly tournaments with U16 categories. I'll enter you for October's competition—if you stop slacking off."

She pauses at the door, adjusting her bag. "Fine."

"Same time next week?"

Em turns back to me, something like a smile breaking through. "Thanks. You know…you're not as much of an asshole as I thought."

I laugh softly, the sound filling the empty gym. "High praise. I'll take it."

Her "whatever" carries less edge than usual. When she's gone, I check my phone again.

No messages from Reese. Em was right. I am pathetically checking this thing.

DANTE

No homework tonight?

LITTLE FIGHTER

Been a little busy today.

We'll be shooting late again. Can I get it to you tomorrow?

DANTE

Some would think you're avoiding me after last weekend.

So many cancelled training sessions…

LITTLE FIGHTER

Take it up with Felix.

DANTE

Sad. I won't have anything to listen to on my flight home.

LITTLE FIGHTER

You could listen to your own voice. You love the sound of that.

DANTE

I recall last Saturday, you loved it too.

LITTLE FIGHTER

Doesn't sound like me.

DANTE

Want me to refresh your memory?

LITTLE FIGHTER

My, aren't we feeling bold today?

DANTE

You should know by now I like to keep things interesting.

LITTLE FIGHTER

How was Em's practice?

DANTE

Deflecting? Fine.

Entering her into a competition. She's getting there.

LITTLE FIGHTER

Well, you do know exactly how to bring out the best in your students.

DANTE

We're still on for our Sunday outing, right?

LITTLE FIGHTER

I guess you'll have to wait and see.

My fingers hover over the keys, muscles tight with restraint as need courses through me. The words *I miss you* appear on the screen before I violently delete them, curses falling from my clenched jaw.

Every cell in me rebels against this careful distance we maintain. She'll never give in. She's too polished.

My hands flex as I remember the silk of her hair, her voice from Saturday still echoing, *Please, Dante. Kiss me.*

Her scent of cedar and magnolia lingers, weaving through my dreams, leaving me tangled in my bedsheets, aching.

I should find someone else, someone temporary, but every option feels hollow. It's been weeks since I've touched anyone else, since I've wanted to. The memory of past dalliances feels like watching a stranger's life through dirty glass. My body craves only her.

All I see is golden hair catching sunlight, that devastating pink-lipped smile, the way her sweat clings to me after we train, driving me mad.

The way she makes denial feel like the sweetest torture. The tension coils tighter as I reread our messages, each word a perfect little wound. And God help me, I'm addicted to the way it hurts. *What the fuck has she done to me?*

My hands itch for a cigarette, but that vice is done. I turn to the next best thing and open the group chat with my Princeton crowd, desperate for distraction.

DANTE

What's happening later?

TIAGO

Getty mansion's going off. The usual suspects. Pure MDMA.

My form's already gone to shit from all this time off, the last thing I need is chemical assistance derailing me further.

MEI

Legion of Honor Auction. Ancient Greek artifacts up for bid. Last year some tech bro dropped 8 figures on a private island just to fuck with his ex's head. Fun drama.

TIAGO

Your call.

DANTE

Let's play aristocrats tonight.

A classic scene: rich people pretending to care about dead civilizations while eyeing each other's collarbones. Perfect place to fuck the memory of her right out of my system.

Chapter 18
Dante

I LIE ALONE in my bed.

Six hundred and fifty thousand dollars spent at that auction on a gift for her, and still I haven't touched her lips with mine.

The want is becoming violent. All-consuming.

Fuck.

Chapter 19
Reese

Reese Sinclair and Dante Hastings Caught Training After Hours

By Susan Martin

"WHERE EXACTLY ARE WE GOING?" I adjust my baseball cap and sunglasses as I follow Dante down a set of dimly lit stairs behind a pet store in Portland called Squeaky. My heart pounds with each step. If this is anything like the party at Wizard Island last weekend, I'll be underdressed in my blue jeans and hoodie.

"If I told you, it would ruin the surprise," he says with an infuriating smirk that makes me want to either slap him or kiss him. Ramsey's bulk casts a shadow as he follows behind. "Trust me."

"You do know all the most interesting places, don't you?"

Dante looks back at me, and there's a twinge of something in his face before he says, "That's why people keep me around."

He doesn't elaborate before he extends his hand, and I take it, feeling like I'm crossing some invisible line. I'm already here.

And honestly, I need the distraction. The raft scene is in four days, and my stress level is peaking and spoiling every chance we get to relax.

From all the time we've been spending together, it's been harder to remember why I should keep resisting him. The movie, my reputation—they all seem meaningless when he looks at me. I may have made an emergency trip back to LA for certain battery-operated necessities. And if the cabin's utility bill has skyrocketed from all my extended bubble baths?

Well, that's between me and the water heater.

Miraculously, no articles about my drunken island shenanigans made it to print. And even though our filming location's been compromised and there's been an endless parade of photographers at security, I'm tasting something that feels suspiciously like freedom. The kind I haven't experienced since before I knew what a call time was or that green juice could be considered breakfast. Before every moment of my life was scheduled, filtered, and approved by a committee.

"This feels illicit."

"I agree." Ramsey's voice comes from behind me.

"Come now, kids, where's your sense of adventure?" Dante puts on his showman smile and pushes through an ornate metal door at the bottom of the stairs, revealing a sight that takes my breath away.

The hidden space can only be described as an intimate jewelry gallery. Crystal chandeliers cast rainbow prisms across gleaming glass cases filled with the most exquisite gems I've ever seen. Emeralds, tanzanite, black opals, diamonds, and rubies sparkle beneath museum-quality lighting. The air down here feels different. It's a world away from anything I've ever seen.

"I fail to see how this place is going to help me prepare for my role," I say dryly, though my eyes can't help but linger on a particularly stunning sapphire.

"Robyn's a master thief, isn't she?" Dante's voice drops to that rich, persuasive tone that makes my knees weak. "Shouldn't you know what real treasures look like? Not those plastic props they've got you working with on set. Consider this life imitating art."

"Hey, those props are very convincing under the right lighting," I protest with a laugh.

"Dante, my Adonis!" A figure in impeccable black couture emerges, gliding across the carpeted floors. They plant one dramatic kiss on each of Dante's cheeks, then do the same to me. "And *moi cher*, you are Aphrodite incarnate."

I tense immediately. Every new person is a potential leak. Dante notices immediately, his dark eyes flickering. "Relax. Paulie's under NDA. No cameras, no social media." He leans closer. "Just us. Changes the shop location every month. Keeps the riffraff out."

I swallow. "If you say so."

"This month we're doing business beneath a dog store with dusty toys and moth-eaten kibble." Paulie laughs. "But what else can you do when you have a jewelry vault that would make the royal family blush?"

Dante taps the nearest display case. "Show us what's new."

"Straight to business," Paulie hums, adjusting their oversized tortoiseshell glasses with bejeweled fingers. "For this lovely creature? I have just the thing." They reveal an array of delicate chains. Some meant for thighs, others for waists and ankles. One particular piece catches my eye. A gossamer-thin emerald-studded chain that captures light like dewdrops.

"These are stunning," I murmur, my fingers hovering over the emerald piece. "But not really for me…"

"The thigh chain would look exquisite on you," Dante says, pointing out the exact one that caught my eye.

"I'll leave it here for you to consider, darling." Paulie winks.

"Now, Dante, my favorite customer, what are we looking for today?"

"Got any interesting rings? She made quite a point of telling me how much she loves mine." He nudges my arm. "Thought you could help me pick out a new one."

My mouth opens. Closes. That night floods back to me. Drunk on absinthe, doing things with his rings that in no world can be considered proper. Kissing them. Rubbing them against my skin. Oh my. I definitely hallucinated that whole interaction, right? But Dante's expression is pure smug satisfaction, the kind that says he's been waiting to bring this up at the most mortifying possible moment. Then I steal a glance at his forearm. My signature is still there, although it's nearly faded.

Not my finest night.

"Lucky for me you chose a permanent marker to tattoo me with," he chuckles.

"I don't know what you're talking about," I scold and pull off my baseball cap and sunglasses, tucking them into my hoodie pocket.

"For someone who acts for a living, you're remarkably unconvincing."

I can't help the snort that exhales through me. I don't know why it feels like we're old friends. We've known each other for such a short time, and we hardly got off on the right foot, but I feel close to him. Can someone feel close to someone like Dante?

"Darling souls, the tension is simply unbearable!" Paulie exclaims and guides us to a velvet-lined tray. "Though who could resist him? Now then, precious, let me show you what I've curated."

"Tell me what you think," Dante purrs. The rings sparkle as he roams through the display case. He picks up the first ring, and I'm hyperaware of his proximity. The gaudy diamond feels all wrong.

"It's…" I search for the right word. "A bit flashy for my taste."

Dante doesn't flinch, just smoothly slides another ring across the velvet. "Next."

"Now this," Paulie swoops in with theatrical flair, "is a gold signet ring for the pinky finger."

"Too…" I try to mask my nervousness with humor. "Corleone." The heavy gold would look clunky on his elegant fingers. His hands are made for something more refined.

"Ah, my dear, I can read you like a rare gem. You'd rather see these beauties on him, wouldn't you?" They gesture to Dante, who's leaning against the counter with infuriating grace. "I'll give you two some privacy."

Before I can stammer out a protest, Paulie glides away in a cloud of expensive perfume, leaving me alone with Dante and his knowing smirk.

"Maybe you're not a fan of these because you don't wear much jewelry yourself," he observes.

"I do for awards shows. At the Golden Globes this year, I wore earrings that came with their own bodyguard. This guy in a black suit followed me everywhere—even waited outside the bathroom like I was planning a heist."

"And these?" Dante gestures to my pearls.

"These are actually mine. First piece I ever bought myself after winning my first Teen Choice Award. No bodyguards required."

"They're lovely."

"How did you get so confident with…" I gesture vaguely at his whole…everything, from the artfully layered chains to the chipped nail polish catching the light. "All of this. Was it like a switch flipped one day?"

The corner of his mouth quirks up. "Yeah, I emerged from my mother in a leather jacket, obviously." When I shoot him a look, he leans back, considering. "It was gradual. Aesthetics are a language, aren't they? A way to write your own story before anyone else can."

"No baby photos of you brooding in chains then?" I laugh, trying to picture him as anything other than this curated image before me.

"God no. Went through every phase imaginable. Preppy. Sporty. Brief California surfer period—puka shells around my neck and everything. I wanted to fit in but never quite found my people." He absently touches one of his rings. "Then I started fencing. Something about holding a sword, being good at it, changes how you carry yourself."

"Fencing always seemed more buttoned-up to me," I say, watching his fingers trace the silver band.

"It is. But that's what made it interesting, bringing something different to it. The sponsors liked that, actually. This whole thing"—he gestures to himself —"it made the sport feel more accessible somehow."

"Meanwhile, I've been basically the same since I was on *The Sweet Life* with Cleo," I admit, fidgeting with my necklace.

His eyes follow the movement, lingering. "We all wear armor. Yours happens to be pearls instead of silver."

I blush, and my eyes flick to one of his silver rings. I'm pretty sure it's the one I decided to kiss last weekend. "What's the story behind this one? You always have it on."

"Got it after winning my first tournament," he says. "Nothing special. Sterling silver from some pawn shop when I was fifteen. But I keep it on." His voice is flat, matter-of-fact, though something in the way he touches the ring suggests there's emotion there.

"It may be one of my favorites," I admit and look back down at the velvet box. "Although…"

I spot a delicate piece and lift it up. It's titanium, with a lustrous pearl shell like a precious accent. "This is beautiful too."

He gives me his hand, palm facing down, and only the middle finger remains empty. "Let's try it on."

The ring shimmers. My fingers tremble as I take his hand in mine, steadying it at the wrist.

I trace the collection of rings already adorning his fingers. When I finally slide the new ring onto his middle finger, the moment stretches, sweet and thick like the summer twilight back in NOLA. His entire body goes still, and suddenly this hidden jewelry vault feels far too small to hold all the things we're not saying.

"There," I say, pulling away.

"I'll take it. What can I get for you." It isn't a question.

"No." I wave my hand dismissively. "I have a vault full of stuff that just sits there, gathering very expensive dust." Besides, accepting jewelry from a man like him feels dangerous. It would be red flag number…well, I've lost count, and that says all I need to know.

"Look at you, pretending you don't want anything when I saw you eyeing those chains earlier. The one with the emeralds is quite beautiful, no?"

"It's not really me."

"Says who? Come on, tell me what you want."

You to push me against these counters and run your pretty fingers across my skin until I forget my own name.

"I don't know…"

"You deserve to let someone treat you to something nice, don't you think? Besides, Felix has been a prick all week. A beautiful thing can brighten up a day." He says the last words with a weight I try not to read into.

"Don't remind me of him." I bristle, the moment shattered. "He's been even more impossible this week, and I didn't think that was possible."

"Heard him threatening another stunt double."

"Some of the studio execs are visiting set next week, and

Felix has gone full helicopter parent, convinced they'll yank our funding faster than he can say action." The words taste bitter in my mouth. "He's hovering over my every move, but he won't actually tell me what I'm doing wrong anymore. Just hits me with disappointed sighs and groans like some frustrated bulldog."

"Whatever that prick says, this film works because of you." Dante's dark eyes hold mine. "Trust me. Your control is perfect. Every mark precise. Trust your body. Trust your instincts. You're not acting the part. What were your words? You are the leading lady." My heart expands in my chest. "Felix wants you weak," he says bluntly. "I've noticed that he's barely shooting your corrected scenes. You okay with that?"

I hate how he sees me so clearly. "Obviously not. But what am I supposed to do? I'm *only the actress, darling*." I imitate Felix's nasal voice. "I'm not codirecting, not producing. This whole production, this director—I'm drowning in pretense." I exhale sharply, the sound echoing off gleaming display cases. "After so many years of being Hollywood's perfect little porcelain doll, I'm exhausted from being sculpted by some other man's vision, like clay in hands that don't understand what they're molding."

"Have you never worked with a female director?"

"Sadly, no. But what a dream it would be to work with someone like Amara Bellamy—"

"Amara?"

"Her work is revolutionary," I press on.

"Mari's actually staying on my yacht. Old friend from Princeton theater days."

My mind conjures images of them lounging on deck, sharing inside jokes and creative visions. The surge of possessiveness catches me off guard. I have no right to feel territorial.

"If I'd known you were a fan…I could have arranged something weeks ago. Called in a favor," he says.

"Don't tease me," I warn. "Her vision, what she did with Saoirse Ronan and Florence Pugh, even Margot Robbie—it's everything I dream of."

Dante tilts his head, eyeing me. "Who says I'm teasing?"

"It's your default setting."

"Not wrong," he says, his voice flat. "But your answer disappoints me. The fact that working under a woman director is some rare, coveted thing is fucked up, especially when you're making films about women's lives. But that's obvious. I want to know what you want. Really want."

I let the question settle in my chest, where it mingles with all those late-night dreams I barely let myself acknowledge. The ones where I'm not reciting someone else's vision but crafting my own. Where I'm not the face on the poster but the force behind the lens.

"I want to own my own production company and direct movies," I say, the words tumbling out before I can catch them. It's the first time I've admitted it to anyone. Not even Heather. Or Cleo. "I've been dreaming about it since I was sixteen, spending more hours analyzing director's commentaries than actually watching the films. But there's this gap between knowing how something works and actually making it work yourself."

"All those years on set isn't only observation," he counters. "You see things others miss. Like on Thursday, you suggested changing the blocking in scene forty-three? Pure director's instinct."

He noticed? The tiny change I'd suggested, having the villager crumple inward with despair instead of lashing out in rage when Robyn delivers the stolen goods? It was such a small note, but he'd caught it.

"Though if we're talking actual directing experience," I add, feeling oddly exposed, "my crowning achievement was terrorizing the neighborhood children into performing *The Wizard of*

Oz when I was eight. Ten tiny actors, including an extremely unwilling infant we cast as a flying monkey. Their parents still bring it up at block parties, though I maintain that the baby's performance was Oscar-worthy."

"Fuck me," he says, letting out a low laugh that makes something twist in my stomach. "I did that same show. Let me guess, you were Dorothy."

"Guilty."

"I played the Tin Man," he says, and the air between us shifts, like tectonic plates grinding beneath the surface. "Typecasting, probably. All metal, no heart."

I recite the line before I can stop myself: "'Hearts will never be practical until they can be made unbreakable.'"

"'But I still want one.'" His words hang in the air, delicate and dangerous. I understand, suddenly and completely, that we're not talking about *The Wizard of Oz* anymore.

The emerald chain catches the light, and I think of all the times I've said no to the things I wanted, afraid of wanting them too much. My fingers trace the glass case, leaving crescents of condensation.

"Paulie?" I call out to the back, and they appear. "I'll take the chain."

Maybe sometimes the bravest thing isn't refusing to want but letting yourself want anyway, even when it might break you.

Chapter 20
Reese

"You'll never escape!" Dante crashes through the forest, shirtless and chasing after me. "The king's gold belongs in the royal treasury!"

I spin around, my heart racing from both the chase and the way his dark eyes lock onto mine. I'm enjoying this pursuit more than is rational for a living, breathing human woman being chased by a man with a weapon through the woods.

"Oh, but it belongs to the people, dear Sheriff!" I call back with a laugh. "Consider it wealth redistribution!"

Shadows dance across Dante's shoulders as he moves between the trees. We took our training outside today to rehearse for tomorrow's scene.

"When I catch you, you'll be hanged for this treachery!"

"*If* you catch me!" I tease. Pine needles crunch beneath my boots as I dart between trees. "And that's quite a big if, wouldn't you say? The forest is my home, Sheriff. You're just a visitor here!"

"Curse you and your tricks, Hood!" Even in character, there's something about the way he carries himself that's irresistible.

I weave between the towering redwoods, my pulse racing

with more than just exertion. "Come on, Sheriff. I thought you were supposed to be some big protector."

His footsteps grow closer, heavy boots thundering against the forest floor. He's catching up. I pivot, executing the choreographed fall we've practiced, letting my momentum carry me backward.

"I have you now!" His roar echoes through the forest as he tumbles with me. The world spins, and my back hits the ground with a soft thud.

His arm muscles ripple as he braces himself above me, his prop sword pressed to my throat. We're both breathless, huffing and puffing in sync.

If anyone saw us like this, they wouldn't think we were just running lines. They'd assume exactly what any person would assume seeing a shirtless man on top of a woman in the woods.

Goodness.

Heat pools low in my stomach as the weight of him hovers just above me. If I arched my back, I'd feel him against my thigh. If I leaned in just a little more, I'd finally know what he tastes like.

His hand steadies my shoulder, his fingers firm. The damp forest floor grows thick; my body feels like vines are going to pull me down into the earth. "By the saints..." he whispers, and shivers zoom down my spine. "You're a woman?"

"Your observational skills are remarkable, Sheriff."

Kiss him, that bad-girl voice in my head sings. *You know you want to.*

No! I can't. Because if I do...well, so many things could go wrong. What if he wants to stop training me? Though I doubt that. Dante would probably start giving me very different kinds of lessons if we kissed. The scarier fear blooms to mind—what if he leaks whatever this thing between us is to the press and tries to take over my moment like Ricky did?

And last, but certainly not least, what if I kiss him and like it? What if I want to do it again? And again?

I blink, pulling myself together, and say, "You didn't mess up any of your lines. I'm so proud of you."

"And your choreography and delivery are perfect," he huffs out, making his abs tense where his stomach meets mine. "We must be excellent teachers, Professor Sinclair."

"Maybe I won't need you for much longer."

"Ah, I take that back. Your footwork is a mess, and that fall? Never seen anything worse."

A laugh bubbles up before I can stop it, the sound turning into a shriek as his fingers find my sides and tickle mercilessly. My sports bra rides up; more of his skin rubs against me.

Then neither of us says anything.

I have over six feet of Olympic-trained muscle holding my five-foot-four body in place. His thigh shifts, nestling into my core, one hand cradling my head against soft pine needles. My core is hot, coiled, and tight. He can tell. I'm certain he can, because he's looking at me like *that*. I glance away.

"Love it when you resist what you want."

"Resist?"

"Maybe you like the pain as much as I do. My little masochist."

I swallow, my heart beating so loud I swear the earth is vibrating beneath me. "Is that what you are?"

"When it comes to you, I think so. But the way I like to play," he says, thumb ghosting across my jawline. A shiver runs through me at his touch. "The control. Release. The space between wanting and having."

"And what does that mean?"

"It means learning to trust. Ropes. Blindfolds. The kind of surrender that strips everything away until there's nothing left but pure sensation." I can't suppress the small gasp that escapes my lips. "The kind that changes you."

"I—" The last three years of my life have been a desert of

self-imposed celibacy and late-night dates with my trusty bedside companion. But something about Dante has awakened a creature inside me, one that purrs and stretches and demands attention.

"Imagination running wild?"

"Just a little bit." I laugh, feeling heat rise to my cheeks. "Though I'm about as far from a masochist as they come. I mean, I can barely handle a paper cut, let alone…" I trail off and let my finger trace one of the intricate designs on his neck, suddenly hyperaware that my acting lessons have abandoned me entirely, leaving me with nothing but my increasingly unhelpful hormones.

"My tattoos?" he asks, mercifully saving me from my awkward rambling. "You like them?"

"They're beautiful," I manage. "Must have hurt, though."

He rolls off me, and I immediately miss his warmth, a small frown tugging at my lips. But then he's reaching down, his strong hands gripping mine as he effortlessly pulls me to my feet.

He takes a moment to brush leaves from my hair and clothes with gentleness. Handing me my Berg bottle.

I throw back the cold water gratefully, watching as he does the same with his own bottle. A single drop escapes, trailing down that perfect neck and bobbing Adam's apple, and I have to remind myself to breathe.

May the Lord help me.

"Do any of them have any special meanings, like your rings?"

"No, everything's art. Love how my skin looks this way, apart from the one on my thigh." He props his knee on a nearby log, and his shorts ride up just so.

I want to scream.

Can we go back to the deliciously charged moment when he was talking about ropes and trust? That felt infinitely more natural than watching him maintain these maddening boundaries I set and now desperately want to cross.

"These are Olympic rings, for my first gold four years ago."

I can't help but bring my hand toward it, hesitating as I trace over the rings and the crest above it—a rampant lion, scrollwork framing it, with a Latin motto beneath that reads *"Fortis et Honorabilis."* "And this? 'Brave and Honorable'?"

"That's my family crest. Felt right to tie the two together."

"I like them a lot. This and the rest of them."

"Thank you, Reese. Maybe if your bad-girl method acting lasts, we'll get you one."

My eyes shoot wide open. "Oh gosh, I don't know about that." I laugh.

"I'm kidding." He gives me a nudge with his elbow. "Scene feeling good?" he asks, all professional now. Two days, and I'll be trading my bathtub practice for the actual lake. A month of preparation, and my stomach still flips.

"Still planning to play lifeguard for me?"

"A promise is a promise," he says.

"I expect the full fantasy—zinc oxide on the nose, whistle, tiny red float?"

"What about a Speedo?"

"That…" I swallow hard, my mind instantly providing high-definition imagery. "That would definitely make drowning a real possibility." He laughs, and I try to look annoyed instead of charmed.

"It's not the water that's making me nervous—it's having to multitask with both hands," I say, then immediately regret my phrasing as his eyebrows shoot up. "The sword! I meant handling the sword while trying not to drown *and* deliver my lines." His knowing smirk makes me stumble over my words. "You know what I mean! It's hard to keep everything in my mouth—I mean, memorized! Oh heavens, stop looking at me."

"But it's so fun."

Chapter 21
Reese

"Stop rolling!"

Felix again. I swear I've started to hear his screaming in my nightmares. The extras flinch in unison. We're all conditioned to his outbursts by now. But the executives lining the trees just nod, like a director having a fit is as normal as drinking tea.

We've been set up a few meters away from the lake, at a makeshift ship dock, since 5:00 this morning, running the same sequence until my muscles ache, trying to nail whatever impossible standard he's created in his head.

My temples throb.

Four weeks of constant criticism, of being told I'm inadequate, incorrect, or whatever arbitrary standard Felix has decided applies today.

"This is a hundred-fifty-million-dollar embarrassment!" he thunders. "I've crafted box office gold for fifteen years. All my movies have real action, real stakes. The studio wanted their female-led blockbuster, and now I'm stuck with...*this*." He gestures dismissively in my direction, like I'm merely a prop that's been misplaced.

I dig my fingernails into my palms, struggling to maintain

composure as fatigue and frustration build inside me. I've rehearsed this scene with Dante until I could perform it in our sleep.

But Felix would criticize a sunrise for being too predictable.

"Felix, if we could—"

"Save it." He steps toward me, invading my space. The crew falls silent. "Everything went sideways when Lawrence pulled out. I should have walked when they couldn't recast with someone who understands the physicality required." His finger jabs the air inches from my face. "Someone who can sell the action." Several crew members avert their eyes, uncomfortable with his aggressive stance.

"The sequence follows exactly what we've been practicing for weeks," I say, keeping my voice steady. "If you could give me specific direction on what's not working—"

"What exactly is your role here?" His words drip with condescension.

"Excuse me?"

"Your job title. What is it?"

"I'm the lead actress." Each word tastes bitter.

"Then start acting like one!" He yanks at his hair like a mad scientist. "I shouldn't have to spell it out. We have one shot at tomorrow's underwater sequence, and you can't even nail the setup."

Weeks of biting my tongue, of maintaining professionalism, of working within his vague parameters. My eyes burn with tears that I refuse to let fall. Not here. Not for him.

"I'm trying my best, but your feedback isn't actionable."

These ambiguous criticisms are infuriating.

All bluster, no substance.

What concrete direction am I supposed to extract from that? Does he communicate differently with his male leads, some unspoken shorthand I'm not privy to? The thought makes my jaw clench.

I want to throw something. Preferably at his head.

"Trying?" His sneer twists his face into something ugly and cruel. "Where's the raw sex appeal? The money shots?" Behind me, the wooden dock creaks beneath us as Dante shifts closer, his familiar presence solid at my back. "The studio pays for eye candy and explosions, sweetheart, not some PBS special!"

Each insult hits like a slap. So much worse than a wooden sword to the jaw.

This wasn't part of the dream. Not during that first audition, not during training, not during those late-night script readings where I discovered who Robyn Hood really was. This isn't how I imagined proving myself.

"I think we should take five," I say, keeping my voice level despite my racing heart. "Give everyone a chance to reset—"

"Oh, now you're directing too? These divas nowadays." His gaze sweeps the crew like a searchlight, hunting for allies, but he finds only averted eyes. "Tell me, Sinclair, who exactly did you have to sleep with to land this role?"

There it is—the ugly truth. A familiar burn spreads through my chest, radiating outward until it reaches my fingertips. No matter how much I prepare, how hard I work, how deeply I understand my craft, to men like Felix, I'll always be just a body to be desired or dismissed.

I taste blood where I've bitten the inside of my cheek.

"Watch your fucking mouth," Dante growls, and I've never heard that edge in his voice before, not even during that mess with Nick. The hair on my arms stands up as the rest of the stunt team silently forms ranks behind me.

Felix takes a step back, his shoe scuffing against the wooden dock. I watch as realization dawns on his face—he's alone against a wall of people who make their living taking controlled falls from buildings.

But wounded egos are dangerous things.

"Listen here, pretty boy," he snarls, compensating. "Go white knight on your own time, not the studio's dime. We all know you're just trying to get in her pants. She's nothing but another—"

"Finish that sentence," Dante says through gritted teeth. "I dare you." He draws himself up to his full height. The entire crew holds its breath, and the birds seem to go quiet.

My heart stops, then restarts with a vengeance. My hands start to shake as the frustration I've been suppressing all morning finally surfaces, burning in my throat.

"This isn't about the scene, is it?" I struggle with the clasps on my costume, the impractical metal breastplate and exposed midriff that make stealth scenes laughable. "This is about me refusing to film soft-core porn disguised as an action sequence. Because that's not in my contract, Mr. Langford."

"I was making blockbusters while you were still playing with dolls. Your artistic integrity means jack shit when you can't grasp what sells tickets. But please, enlighten me about how your little romance movies trump my Oscar wins."

"Enough." I finally wrench off the chest plate with a satisfying click, followed by the heavy chain mail belt—the physical embodiment of how he's trying to transform this character—and drop them at Felix's feet. I pull out the extensions that have been causing me a headache all day and wipe at the excessive makeup.

"We're done shooting today." My voice carries across the set. I stand taller, steadier now that I've made my decision. "Your crew has been working fourteen-hour days. They've missed birthdays, canceled plans, and pushed through exhaustion. I've given everything to this role. And your response is to belittle everyone's contributions?"

Around me, cases snap shut with deliberate force, equipment dismantling.

"You ungrateful little—" he starts, but I interrupt.

"Consider your next words carefully." I maintain eye contact, refusing to be intimidated. "This industry is smaller than you think, and I'm not without my own connections."

My body moves before my brain catches up, feet carrying me along the river, through the redwoods like muscle memory. Branches whip across my face, leaving stinging kisses as walking turns running turns sprinting deeper into the forest.

My lungs burn, but it's nothing compared to the inferno of rage in my chest. I run until I reach the waterfall on the far side of the lake. The same lake that had me hyperventilating during that panic attack weeks ago, when even the splash of water against my ankles sent me spiraling.

I should've seen this coming.

Felix finally revealed what's actually eating at him—that he, Hollywood's favorite purveyor of testosterone-soaked explosions, has to acknowledge that women can do more than ask *What do we do now?* or die prettily to motivate the male lead.

"I put everything into this!" I strain. "I trained until my muscles screamed. I memorized every word. I faced every fear. I fucking learned to hold my breath underwater. And what am I to them? Just another pretty face with an expiration date!"

My boots kick at loose rocks, sending them skittering into the rushing water. The waterfall looms ahead. I'm left in my leather skirt, leather boots, and leather vest. Yet, for the first time, I feel more like Robyn already.

Kick. Pace.

Four. Seven. Eight.

The mist hits my face in tiny needles of ice. Each step closer makes my heart slam against my ribs like it's trying to escape.

Heather was right.

Should've pulled out when she told me to. *Be strategic*, she said. Instead, I'm ruining my image, sneaking off set, risking everything I built to become the latest set diva who can't work with a visionary director.

The studio will bury this movie.

They'll blame me.

Why wouldn't they? They sure as hell won't blame their pal Felix.

I pick up a rock and hurl it at the falls. Then another. And another. Each splash disappears into the thundering white noise, but it feels good.

"After everything I've worked for!" I scream at the rushing water. They're going to fire me. "All because I couldn't shut up and smile!"

One step forward. My body screams retreat. Another step. The spray hits my bare stomach. Cold. Sharp. Real.

It makes me feel alive. *Screw it*. I step right into the water until it hits my skin like needles.

Good. Let it hurt.

The falls pound against my shoulders. Like the sound in my head when I read reviews that Geraldine can't hide from me. When I hear the whispers. When I catch the crew's pitying glances. When I imagine tomorrow's headline: *Reese Sinclair Melts Down, Tanks Hundred-Million-Dollar Production*.

My feet slip on algae-slick rocks. I steady myself. These legs can hold a sword stance for hours. These arms can lift my body weight.

This strength is mine.

Not Felix's. Never his.

Water streams down my face. Or maybe it's tears. I can't tell anymore.

Nothing matters except the scraping in my chest. Everything I've worked for, sacrificed—gone in one defiant moment.

What is wrong with me?

I scream.

The sound tears from my throat—feral, dying. Everyone at the dock must hear me.

"I hate this!" It echoes until my voice melds with the falls.

Years of smiling, nodding, being good—bleeding out of me like an open wound.

Let them hear. I'm done.

I don't notice Dante until he's there at the edge. Watching. His gold eyes steady on mine.

He sees everything. Always seems to.

"Reese, you're in the water," he says, like he's commenting on the weather and not witnessing my breakdown.

The falls pound against me, soaking my hair and clothes. The cold brings clarity now, not panic. What remains of my costume clings like a second skin as the current pulls at my legs.

He walks through the downpour until he's before me.

His gaze isn't concerned or pitying—it's just my own reflection.

For the first time since landing this role, I'm not auditioning for my own life. That's how it feels with him.

He was right. Something wild in me begs for both release and control.

I look at him—steady, firm—nights of temptation and fantasies rushing all at once as my heart forgets its rhythm.

Not from fear. From something dangerous and inevitable.

I have nothing left to lose. Not even my hard-earned control.

No excuses. No job to protect. No directors to dodge.

Whoever catches us, it doesn't matter. Felix already spread his filth about me to the crew.

"I'm in the water," I repeat, the falls pounding against my back. What I hope he hears: *I'm not afraid.*

I'm done playing good.

Because being a good girl consumes you whole. It smothers and suffocates. Devours you from within until nothing remains but a hollow shell of pleasing smiles and careful words.

And right now? I want to tear my perfect life apart with my teeth.

Dante's eyes catch mine through the water's curtain. Dark.

Intent. Burning. He drags me into that liminal space between fury and freedom with his gaze.

The boundary I dance along whenever we're together.

I crave danger.

I need to ignite.

My body moves before my brain catches up. I clutch his shirt —fabric bunching between my fingers like salvation—and crash my mouth against his.

I kiss Dante Hastings.

Nothing gentle exists here. It's all teeth and tongue and weeks of raw wanting.

He answers instantly, violently. His hands brand my skin through soaked clothes, lifting me effortlessly, strong fingers digging into my thighs as my legs instinctively lock around his waist.

His mouth devastates mine, tasting of adrenaline, desire, and something uniquely him that makes my head spin.

The waterfall thunders around us, but only the heat of his skin against mine matters.

I bite his bottom lip, and he growls—actually growls—his fingers marking my thighs.

Good. I need evidence.

Proof I chose chaos over control.

A sound tears from my throat—desperate, wanting—as his hands slide up my spine.

"Fuck," he whimpers against me, one hand winding into my hair, pulling just enough to arch my neck. "You're killing me, Reese."

I surrender to his hungry, desperate mouth, and for once I believe. Believe I'm as untamed as he sees me, that our inferno could reduce the world to ash.

That I want that smoke again.

I want it scorching my lungs.

His grip tightens—possessive, demanding. The world shrinks

to sensation. Muscles flex beneath my exploring hands. My teeth in his shoulder, tasting water, salt, him.

My existence has been restraint incarnate. Perfect posture, perfect smile, perfect sound bites served for mass consumption. Always responsible, reliable, the good girl failing at the impossible game of being woman enough but never too much.

I'm sick of her.

Sick in my marrow, between heartbeats, in every swallowed rage that poisons me like arsenic.

I choose mess. Choose the unlidded fire within.

Dante's teeth graze my bottom lip, pulling a gasp from me. I welcome the pain. Crave it. His hands slide up my rib cage, thumbs brushing the undersides of my breasts through wet leather. I rake my nails down his back, feeling muscles ripple beneath.

He pulls back just enough to see me, his breath hot against my lips. Water streams down his face, catching in his lashes. For a moment, we stare, our chests heaving.

He's so beautiful—dark and certain of himself. Being with him makes me feel magnificent.

Then he kisses me again—slower, deeper, like he's memorizing my taste.

Dante's fingers tangle in my wet hair as the waterfall mists around us, the slight sting of pain delicious. The heat of his mouth ignites my nerve endings. I press myself against his chest, feeling how strong and solid he is.

He tastes sweet, and my lips tingle from the force of our kiss. My thighs shake around his torso, but he holds me up effortlessly, as if I weigh nothing.

I've been kissed before, but never like this. Never in a way that made me feel simultaneously unmade and completely myself.

I want that.

I want him to remind me that I can exist as pure instinct, desire, and freedom.

Time liquefies. Each kiss becomes rebellion. Here, under thundering waters, in Dante Hastings's arms, I shed my carefully constructed image.

There's vicious pleasure in murdering your curated self—the one packaged in acceptability and tied with desperation's ribbon.

I'm finally Reese Sinclair with a capital *Sin*.

Chapter 22
Reese

"Any update?" I ask Heather, pacing my trailer. The anxiety coils in my chest like a living thing.

The production-wide email arrived like a death sentence: shooting cancelled for today.

I spent years climbing Hollywood's ladder, and I've never had a director cancel shooting out of the blue, unless they came down with the flu. Even that's a rarity.

What if this isn't just for the day? What if this is a permanent termination of the project?

This is all my fault.

I messed up. I got a little too confident.

My mind races through the milestones, from that lucky break on *Clubhouse* to becoming America's sweetheart, churning out hit rom-coms like clockwork.

My career could be over. Who knows what Felix will tell the media. I thought I was okay with this, but with the possibility of messing up my image so close, I want to run.

"His team says he's 'regrouping,'" Heather says. My stomach lurches, knowing the studio's gamble on me might have gone up in flames.

"Regrouping?" I grip the phone tighter, my other hand unconsciously touching where Dante's fingers gripped my thighs yesterday. "I know I shouldn't have lost it, but if you'd heard how he spoke to me—"

"Darling, that man's ego needed deflating. You don't snap without cause." Heather's tone softens. "Let me handle the suits. Meanwhile, those scripts I sent over…give them a look just in case."

"This has to work," I whisper, pressing cool fingers to my temples. All those hours of training, pushing my body to its limits, learning to be someone new—I can't let it slip away.

"The jet's fueled if you need an escape to LA."

"No. He might return. I need to be here."

After hanging up, I stare at my phone's dark screen. The weight of responsibility crushes my chest—my career and hundreds of jobs hanging by a thread because I couldn't swallow my pride.

Three sharp knocks break my spiral. Dante. My pulse jumps. My fingers absently trace my lips, which are still sore after yesterday's adrenaline-filled angry kiss. One reckless moment. I can't do it again. I got distracted, and that's exactly what I said would happen.

My moral compass has completely lost its true north.

Felix will be back tomorrow. My racing pulse betrays my doubt.

Yet when I see Dante, it's like coming up for air.

"Come with me?" He leans against the doorframe, all leonine grace.

"No. I should stay here, just in case—"

"Reese." My name comes out of his mouth like a verdict. "You're sitting here letting that prick's ego trip eat you alive. The agents can handle this shit." He looks at me then, and there's this raw honesty in his face that makes my stomach clench. "Back in elementary school, I broke some kid's nose. He'd been harassing my sister. I got suspended for it. Sometimes you do the right thing, and it costs you. That's how it works."

One month of working together, and he reads me like a well-worn script. Following him now feels like striking matches in a room full of dynamite.

"But what if he calls—"

"Phones stay on. But I'm not letting you spiral alone in here." He extends his hand. Rationality wages war with want. This is such a terrible idea.

"Come on, what would Rob—"

"Don't finish your sentence," I scold. As if he knows the thing that would get me out of this cabin better than I do. But, against my better judgment, I take his hand anyway.

The early autumn air hits my face as we step outside. The set thrums with nervous energy, crew members trading worried glances. They greet Dante with easy familiarity, inside jokes, and casual touches, while giving me a wide berth. Untouchable.

"Miss Sinclair." Marcus and two other stunt team members approach, their presence a welcome distraction.

"Marcus," I smile.

He turns to Dante, eyes lighting up mischievously. "Regardless of whether or not we have a job tomorrow, our offer for today's session still stands."

The weight of their livelihoods sits heavy on my shoulders.

"Not a chance in hell," Dante laughs.

"Come on! It's a day off, and your character sheet's getting dusty." I'm grateful for their playful banter. It pulls me from my guilt spiral. "We'll let you bore us with your historically accurate weapons rants…" Marcus grins.

Dante blows them a kiss. "Don't miss me too much."

As we walk away, I study his profile. "What's their mysterious offer about?"

"They run this whole D&D campaign between takes. Been trying to rope me in since day one."

"D&D?"

"Dungeons & Dragons. It's a role-playing game. And I love to dabble in that sort of thing, but they do it so earnestly, huddled around a table with their dice and their carefully constructed fantasies about dragons. It's all very wholesome." I catch the curl at the corner of his mouth, and something in my chest shifts imperceptibly.

"Sounds better than sitting alone overthinking everything," I admit, surprised by my own honesty. "At least they seem unfazed by yesterday's drama."

"Maybe take a page from their book," he suggests.

"Says their resident favorite," I tease, trying to lighten my own mood. "Your reputation does precede you."

"And what exactly have you heard about my reputation, Miss Sinclair?"

"That you like—" The words stick in my throat. "People?"

"And?"

"And doing stuff with people."

"Sex?" he asks flatly, examining my face. "I love to fuck, Reese. The way bodies find each other in darkness. The brief animal moments. How two people can occupy the same space and time and still feel utterly alone afterward." I swallow hard, knowing I'm in dangerous waters. His golden eyes find mine, darkening. "Though celibacy can be just as intoxicating."

As Dante's words coil around me like smoke, Felix's dramatic exit blurs into a fever dream. The production crisis gnawing at my insides dissolves into something hazier, less urgent. My mind, usually Olympic-level at catastrophizing, fixates instead on bodies finding each other in darkness.

I should be having a proper Hollywood meltdown in my cabin. Instead, I'm caught in Dante's gravity, my anxiety melting like cotton candy in rain. "Quite the celibacy expert, aren't you? What's it been, forty-eight hours?"

"Thirty-six days," he says.

The day of the table read. The day he met me. The number hits me like a confession, making my skin prickle with possibilities I have no business considering.

"Try three years," I blurt out, immediately wanting to swallow the words back.

"No wonder you're wound so tight during training."

"I cannot believe I just told you that." I press my palms to my burning cheeks. "The last twenty-four hours have already been a dumpster fire. Why am I adding kindling?"

"Don't." He towers over me like the ancient trees around us, all dangerous grace. "Your whole life's been about the work. Even on Mars, people would know your face. Most relationships crack under that kind of pressure. The real ones, anyway."

"Bold of you to assume I'm a relationship girl," I challenge.

"*Sweetheart.*" The word drips with knowing.

I want to complicate things until they're deliciously unsalvageable.

I'll just blame the lack of sleep for my dwindling resolve.

This isn't professional. I take a deliberate step back, though he radiates the kind of magnetic pull that makes my skin hum. I force myself to redirect.

Production. Focus on production!

"I was supposed to review the harness setup today. Nick promised me time with the heavier sword for tomorrow's shoot. If Felix waltzes back in like nothing happened, what then? Are we still doing the raft scene?"

"I could show you," he drawls, producing a key with the kind of casual confidence that makes my stomach flip. "I have access to the armory."

I arch an eyebrow. "Pretty sure that violates about twelve insurance policies."

"Probably thirteen," he says with that infuriating half smile that makes me want to bite his lower lip. "But the stunt team and props department have a flexible relationship. Consider it a contribution to the artistic integrity of your performance." He turns dramatically. "Promise not to touch anything off-limits?"

Like his forearms? Like the hollow of his throat?

"Promise," I lie through my teeth.

The walk to the armory feels endless, my mind replaying yesterday's indiscretions in vivid technicolor. The taste of him. The way he'd made me forget my own name. How easy it would be to let him wreck me again, for a little while.

"This feels illicit," I whisper, pulse quickening at the forbidden thrill of it all.

"Is it breaking and entering if I have a key? Sometimes the most dangerous moves are the ones that look perfectly innocent."

"Until they're not."

The door squeaks as he leads me inside. Rows of weapons line walls, racks, and wooden tables.

I inch forward, making sure we're alone. I don't want to get caught here.

"Stay right there." Dante stops me, his eyes darting around. "I'm gonna go turn off the cameras."

"Cameras? No, no, no," I whisper through clenched teeth as I press myself up against the door. But Dante's already down a hallway. A second later, he's back, looking way too pleased with himself.

"All better. Wouldn't want to get you in trouble."

I glance around, stepping toward him, suddenly way too aware of how very alone we are. "This feels like a lot of trouble! Millions of dollars' worth of insurance trouble."

"Don't worry! Now, look, here it is." He steps behind me, reaching around to retrieve a massive sword. His chest brushes my back—definitely not an accident—and I struggle to maintain composure. "This is tomorrow's weapon. It's heavier, but remember your form. Feet shoulder-width, core engaged." He hands the metal to me, and then his hands ghost over my hips, a touch that's pure muscle memory by now.

"So you want me to keep my feet shoulder-width apart, fight off some guards, remember my lines, jump into the water, and make men fall in love with me, all while wearing a metal bra? Easy," I joke.

"You got this." His breath is hot against my ear. "You always do, Miss Perfectly in Control."

I grip the hilt of the sword tighter, trying not to think about the fact that we are alone. "How do I look?"

Dante's eyes scream of hunger. "Lethal." His voice roughens like sandpaper on silk. "Your technique is flawless. Now we need to work on your…release."

"What's wrong with my release?"

"There's a distinct lack of one."

"Watch it, or I might test this blade's balance on you." I raise the sword overhead.

"But then you'd miss out on all my *expertise*," he murmurs, gently taking the sword from my hands and setting it carefully on a nearby rack. He advances until my thighs hit a wooden table. The solid press of him behind me sends electricity up my spine. His hands bracket me, caging me in. "Easy there, fighter. Don't let yourself get disarmed so easily. Or did you forget everything I taught you about maintaining position?"

No more pretending. I want this. Want him. And if this movie is over, if Felix has quit, at least I'll get to tell Cleo I ended my three-year celibacy. "Show me how you'd disarm me. The technique."

He doesn't hesitate. He hooks an arm around me and lifts me onto the table. With his other arm, he slides his fingers across my collarbones. "Sometimes surrender is the most powerful position you can take."

"Is this meant to be your disarming attempt? It's hardly working."

"No? Then why does your breath catch when I touch you?" His fingers snag on my bike shorts, and I curse myself for not wearing something easier to remove. My hips press closer, seeking friction. My core burns for him. "Yeah, just like that."

"Not fair." I drop my head near his neck, kissing him once, his salt mingling on my tongue. I drag him between my spread thighs. His heat makes me dizzy with need.

"Tell me to stop."

"I can't," I resolve.

"Can't what?"

"Can't say I don't want you."

"Why?"

"Because I do," I confess.

"Fucking finally, fighter." His soft lips find mine. His kisses start soft and then turn greedy. The taste of mint spreads across my tongue.

"I want you to teach me everything you can teach me."

"Such a needy little student." His hand wraps behind me, and he slides me closer to him. I can feel him get hard through his pants.

I surrender to him completely, letting him teach me a different kind of choreography.

His fingers tangle in my hair and tug—a sharp, sweet ache that sparks down my spine. I gasp.

He rocks against me. I wish we were already naked. "First lesson," he says with a heavy breath against my neck. "Your body betrays you."

I force myself to watch him, but as his hands inch up toward my jaw, my eyelids flutter open and closed. I swallow the moan at the edge of my throat, but as his thumb presses into the soft spot below my ear, I let it slip.

"The way you lean in—" He demonstrates by pulling back, making me chase his touch. "The dilation of your pupils—" His other hand skims my collarbone. "And all these breathy moans —" He presses harder against my throat. "Caught right here. Let go."

All the blood rushes to my head. I can't think or breathe; I'm just consumed by his touch.

He reaches for my waistband, his fingers brushing my bare skin. I nod, lifting my hips. He takes his time, sliding the fabric down inch by torturous inch. The air feels cool against my exposed skin. My sweatshirt follows, and I shiver—from the cold or anticipation, I'm not sure.

His eyes rake over me, drinking in every detail. "Fuck," he says through gritted teeth.

Through my thin cotton bra, his thumb traces slow circles.

I love the way he's staring at me. It makes me feel strong seeing him so consumed in me like this.

I buck toward him, inhaling his smoky skin, my new favorite scent. His chest is firm against mine, all solid muscle beneath his shirt. I ache for him to touch me. I want to scream at him too, but my voice is lost at the moment.

I reach for him, my palm pressing against his hard length through his sweats. Heat pools low in my belly at how thick he feels.

He grips my wrists hard, pinning them to the table.

A warning. A promise.

"What did I tell you about touching things you aren't supposed to?" He exhales, his arousal apparent. He's holding himself back, and I don't want him to.

I try to form words, but all that comes out is a small, needy sound. "But—"

"I'll give you what you want." He cups my waist. "I'll let you misbehave, since that's what you've been begging for." The words leave me raw, exposed. No one has ever seen me like this.

"I didn't beg."

"No?" A soft laugh, dangerous and low. His hand disappears below, ghosting along the elastic of my panties. My nipples harden, and his gaze skims down the length of me. I'm exposed.

"Here in the armory, where anyone with a key could walk in, when we probably shouldn't do this at all?"

We could be caught, but the thought intensifies my need for him. I've been good for too long.

"Or maybe we should see how much you want this," he says. I nod. The edge of the table digs into my palms as I brace myself, heart thundering. Fear and want tangle in my chest. "You like that, don't you? Being naughty with me?"

This isn't a role anymore. The realization hits me like a physical force.

"Maybe I do."

"Be a good girl and tell me how dirty you want me to make you." My fingers curl against the wood, knuckles white. Breathing becomes a conscious effort.

"Touch me."

"Where?"

"Anywhere, Dante. Anywhere you want."

"Now," he says, his practiced indifference cracking around the edges, his need bleeding through, "here's your second lesson. When you've got someone exactly where you need them, you take what you want. You make demands."

He's so hard. So willing. I love the power coursing through my veins.

"Then get on your knees," I command. "Show me what you've been thinking about doing to me."

He kneels before me. "You've been so bad denying your body what it needs, fighter." His breath is hot against my inner thigh as he works methodically. First one shoe, then the other. He spreads my legs wider, and I let him. The cold air hits my skin.

"Give it to me."

"I want to hear you," he challenges. "No holding back."

And I couldn't help it if I wanted to, because when his tongue presses against my clit through cotton, my spine curves involuntarily, and I let out a sound I don't recognize. The pressure feels so good. I jut my hips against him, seeking more pressure, more friction, more him.

For once, I'm not calculating my next move or worrying about how I look. My body knows what it wants. It wants this.

"Don't stop, Dante." My head falls back.

His tongue traces careful patterns that make my thighs shake. He pinches my nipples, and my limbs tighten under him. I tug at his hair, using it to anchor myself as pleasure builds and builds.

With two large fingers, he pulls my panties to the side, and his tongue finally makes contact with me. No barriers.

"You taste better than you did in my dreams," he says, lapping again. "This pretty cunt of yours is going to be stained with my touch."

With him below me, something primal fills my chest. He feels it too. Darkness envelops the gold of his irises. The sight should terrify me—we're surrounded by weapons, cloaked in shadows—but it only feeds the fire burning through my veins.

"I want more," I say, needing him inside of me.

His fingers press bruises into my thighs. "Fuck, Reese."

The words slip out before I can stop them, my face burning. "Give me more, Dante."

I rake my nails across his scalp, drawing out a sound that vibrates through me. His mouth is relentless, precise. Each movement of his tongue sends electricity through my nerves until I'm trembling.

I don't break eye contact as he slips a finger into me, curving it and pulsing it slowly at first.

Oh my.

He adds another finger, and the fullness is exquisite. My hips move of their own accord, chasing the pressure. His tongue finds my clit again and works in slow, deliberate circles that make my toes curl. I let out a throaty cry.

He understands my body. He's methodical in this like he is with everything, each stroke calculated, each curl of his fingers intentional. The thought flits through my head—all those hours watching him train, and this is how he applies that focus.

My thighs won't stop shaking. The table creaks beneath me. When he lifts my legs over his shoulders, the angle shifts and—*oh.*

"You're so perfect like this." His breath is hot against my inner thigh. "My dirty girl, coming apart for me."

The pressure builds until it shatters. I contract around him. When the pulsing stops, he pulls his fingers out. Without breaking eye contact, he slowly puts his fingers in his mouth, tasting me.

"I fucking love the taste of you undone, fighter."

It is the hottest thing I've ever seen. He kisses me, and I collapse my head against his chest, boneless.

Then, like a cruel joke, reality crashes back like a wave. My face burns. My chest rises and falls rapidly against the cool air. The enormity of what just happened settles over me like a heavy blanket.

Words fail me. "That was—"

His eyes catch mine, dark and knowing. "Careful now. Don't overthink it."

But I am overthinking it.

Every possible tabloid headline flashes through my mind: *On-Set Scandal. Costars' Steamy Affair Revealed. Reese Sinclair off the Rails.*

I've worked too hard to become another cliché. I've already crossed every professional boundary here—with Felix, with the movie, with everything I've built. Is this my quarter-life crisis catching up to me? Or am I making deliciously bad decisions and pretending not to love every second?

"Hey." His hand finds my chin, tilting my face up. His thumb traces my lower lip, still sensitive from his kisses. "Stay here with me. You're just a woman who knows what she wants. Simple."

Simple. Nothing about this is simple. But when he looks at me like that, everything else falls away. The critics. The cameras. The carefully constructed image.

"Thank you." I reach for him, my fingers curling into the fabric of his shirt.

"For what?"

"For making me forget myself."

Chapter 23
Dante

MAKING Reese Sinclair orgasm felt like a religious experience.

A deeply specific kind of power.

She lets me hold her hand on the way back to my cabin, her cheeks still a perfect shade of rosy against her soft skin.

"You're quiet," she says, glancing up at me.

"Just thinking."

"About?"

"The way you taste," I say, squeezing her hand.

She's nervous in a way that makes me want to protect her. On set, she's all sharp edges and certainty, but with me that armor slips. Just like mine does around her.

"That's mortifying." She swats my chest playfully.

"Don't say that," I say, voice low and matter-of-fact. "I loved making you feel good."

When we step into the cabin, I head straight for the bathroom. It still has the rustic charm of the old summer camp—wood-paneled walls, a sloped ceiling—but I've made it my own. A plush rug softens the plank floor, and a stack of thick white towels sits neatly on a reclaimed wood shelf. As I pull back the deep-green linen shower curtain, the brass rings glide smoothly along the rod. I turn on the shower, adjusting the temperature until the water is tepid.

At the bathroom door, Reese fidgets with her hands, biting her bottom lip. "I…are you okay that you didn't, um—" She gestures vaguely. "I mean, I've never had someone focus on just me," she continues, playing with the door handle now. "Usually it's more rushed, mutual. Or honestly, mostly about him—" Her rambling is delectable, and it makes me laugh. She stops. "What?"

"You're cute when you're flustered."

"Uh, I am not flustered," she protests. "I just wasn't raised to discuss these things."

"Be selfish, Reese." I kiss her softly, smoothing my thumb over her worried brow.

"But aren't you uncomfortable?"

I snort. "You mean blue balls?"

She shrinks in on herself. "My ex used to claim it was this huge deal. I've read conflicting things online, but most articles by men insist it's absolutely real. I don't exactly have a lot of guys I can fact-check with."

"Your ex was a manipulative ass," I say bluntly. "And blue balls isn't a fucking medical problem. There's an art to anticipation."

"Oh, is that what I should call my three-year dry spell?" She leans against the bathroom counter, arms crossed. "The art of anticipation?"

"After my Olympic win, I went fucking crazy. Parties, people, pleasures. You name it. Ended up so spiritually bankrupt I signed up for this intense silent retreat. Forty-five days. No talking, no pleasure. No *solo* adventures."

Her lips part, and the steam curls around us, making the space feel more intimate. "You went that long without…?" The way her words fade, her cheeks flushing, is unfairly adorable.

"I discovered I like the tease of waiting," I say quietly,

moving closer. I haven't touched myself in thirty-six days, haven't sought comfort in anyone else either. There's something perverse in this calculated restraint, but watching her process the implications makes every second of waiting worthwhile. When I get to share a release with her, as long as she'll have me, it'll be earth-shattering. My finger traces the curve of her arm. "Makes everything more…intense. When you finally let go after all the buildup? It's transcendent. Tantric, even."

"Tantric?" she squeaks.

"Ancient practice of prolonging pleasure. Building energy. Making every touch…" I let my voice trail off. "Here." I grab a fresh, fluffy towel from the shelf, setting it on the counter along with a new bar of lavender soap. "Take your time. Think about it."

She shyly closes the door, and I return to the living room.

In the armory, she'd looked at me with this raw vulnerability, pupils blown wide, lips parted. Like she was seeing something new.

She trusted me. Wanted me. Not the version I show at parties or competitions, but the real thing. When I'd touched her, she'd made these small sounds, arched up against my hand. She'd let me kiss her neck while her skin burned against mine.

Soon Reese joins me in the living room, wrapped in my towel, smelling like my soap. The domesticity of it hits somewhere deep and animal. I want to press her against the wall, but I don't. Every will in my body hates me for it.

"You know what sticks out most to me about your retreat?" she says, patting her hair dry.

"What?"

"That you didn't talk for forty-five days."

I laugh and pass her some clean clothes. She tugs my black Prada T-shirt over her head. It hangs loose off one shoulder, the fabric swallowing her frame. I love seeing her in my clothes.

She moves through my space like she belongs here, her

fingers brushing absentmindedly over the edge of my desk, pausing to glance at the row of books stacked haphazardly on the shelf. There's an ease to it—like she's been here a hundred times before. Like she could be here a hundred more.

"You don't want to go next?" she asks, pointing at the shower.

"No." The thought of washing her away makes my chest tight. I want to keep her on me, in me. The taste, the scent, all of it preserved. "I want to savor the moment. Including…" I press my tongue against my teeth, remembering. "Well. Some memories deserve to stay fresh."

I catalog the water sliding down her neck in clear rivulets, the suggestion of her perfect breasts beneath the cotton, her unconscious humming. She exists in a state of unaware performance.

There's something different about her. A softness that belies strength. She makes me want to be good, which is precisely why I shouldn't be allowed near her. But I don't listen to that voice.

We migrate to the kitchen, the worn wooden floor creaking softly under our steps. It's old and lived-in—sturdy pine cabinets, a stained farmhouse sink, and an oven that takes twenty minutes to preheat, but it's perfect for what I need today.

"Now, before we got sidetracked, I had something else planned," I say, lifting a towel from a silver bowl. Her face brightens with recognition.

"Is this what I think it is?" She peers in, inhaling deeply. The rich scent of vanilla and yeast fills the air between us.

"Authentic Cafe Du Monde beignets. Had the ingredients shipped here specially."

"Just for me?"

"I don't see anyone else here."

She looks around, a playful smile on her face. "I guess not."

The small cabin kitchen fills with her memories as she works the dough, her movements precise and practiced. "Haven't made these since Christmas with my grandma."

A soft dusting of powdered sugar drifts onto the butcher block counter as she dips a finger in the bag, sampling it with a pleased moan.

Her lips are sweet when she kisses me. Her laugh echoes off the walls when I make a mess. And I realize, with startling clarity, that this isn't just another night, another casual encounter. This is Reese Sinclair. In my clothes, beside me, under my hands, making my kitchen smell like beignets and possibility.

Reese, who doesn't know the darkest parts of me yet, the parts I'm terrified will send her running.

Reese, who I've wanted for so long I can't remember what it felt like not to want her.

Being with her is different than I imagined.

I've had her poster on my wall since I was thirteen—lying in a field of magnolias, hair spread out like liquid gold. I used to trace the curve of her smile with my finger, wondering what it would be like to kiss the lips those magazines always described as peach-perfect. They don't taste like peaches at all.

They taste like sugar and something darker, which makes my head swim with want.

The reality of her surpasses any imagined versions I've dreamt up.

"You've got flour everywhere," she says, brushing it from my nose. Her fingers are cool against my skin.

"Worth it."

"When did you get so sweet?"

"I'm not sure." The words come out flat, honest.

I fucking hope this film doesn't get cancelled now that she's opened up. It doesn't matter. I have her number saved. This thing between us has weight now, momentum.

I'm not going to lose that.

Chapter 24
Reese

Viggle Alert: Felix Quits *Robyn Hood* Amid On-Set Friction

HEATHER

We have a problem. Ramsey is picking you up, need you in LA stat.

Felix Langford quit Robyn Hood, paid back his director's fee, and now the movie status is unclear.

I hover outside the production company's conference room. Inside, it's like a beehive that's just been struck with a stick—a table full of people who could end my career with a single decision. Executive producers, a head screenwriter practically vibrating with anxiety, and the production team scrambling to maintain order.

Next to me, Ramsey shifts, the only sign he's just as uneasy as I am.

Twenty-four hours ago, I was barefoot in Dante's kitchen, licking powdered sugar off his fingertips. Delusionally letting myself believe that taking a day away from thinking about Felix would do me any good. Now, all my worries and fears have come to life.

I yelled at an Oscar winning director. I became a diva. Threw away the movie of my dreams.

I conceded to almost everything Felix wanted, but slandering me in front of the crew wasn't professional. He accused me of sleeping my way to my role. It wasn't right. I stood up for myself. I had every right to.

Maybe it isn't about you at all, the logical voice in my head suggests. I can't be the only one who had issues with him. Heather tried to warn me about this back in June. His toxic behavior was unbearable, the belittling comments, the public humiliation, the explosive temper that had the entire crew walking on eggshells. Maybe the executive producers learned about what happened at the lake and let him go.

Or maybe everyone here knows about what I did in the armory with Dante. We violated the insurance policy, for goodness' sake. That's such a liability. What was I thinking? All so I could touch his sword?

Someone surely saw us there before he turned off the cameras.

Or at the waterfall.

Or the late-night training sessions, which should be aboveboard but now feel illicit.

I search for him in the room and my eyes land on him fast.

He's here.

Seated at the table, face unreadable. Next to him, a man I assume is his manager sits pin straight.

I swallow hard, my mind swinging wildly between best- and worst-case scenarios as I push open the conference room door and step inside. The shouting escalates.

"We're hemorrhaging money by the minute!" someone yells.

"Has anyone spoken to Felix?"

"The press is already sniffing around—"

"Order! We need order in this meeting!" The head executive producer slams his fist on the table, making coffee cups rattle.

I press my palms together, grounding myself, and glance at the ice bucket in the center of the table. I'm tempted to place a cube in my palm, just as Dante showed me.

Four. Seven. Eight.

Ugh, this breathing is no use.

Dante finally looks up. And everything inside me unravels. Whatever happened between us yesterday feels like pretend. I need to focus. No matter how much I want to be next to him.

I settle into the chair next to Heather and Geraldine and whisper, "Status?"

"The studio's trying to keep the movie alive, but it's not looking good. Without a director, it's going to be hard to justify finishing this project," Heather explains. "Plus, whoever comes in will likely want to refilm, and that'll mean a month's worth of footage burnt up."

It's not my first project to be cut mid-production, but I'd rather take another dip in 'Gurt's vat of yogurt than see *Robyn Hood* die.

"The set's been a powder keg since the beginning," someone mutters. "Bringing Felix on was a mistake."

"We're in too deep to pull out now," the producer at the head of the table barks. "The budget we've burned through is astronomical. Three hundred crew members' families depend on this paycheck. Felix paid back his director's fee, but the sets alone cost an arm, a leg, and a whole fucking cadaver."

"Shutting down production would be catastrophic," another executive adds. "If we fail to deliver, no one will trust us with a budget of this size again."

Their voices swirl around me like a gathering storm. I sink deeper into my chair, feeling as miniscule as I did on my first red carpet, standing there in a thrift store prom dress because I didn't know any better and didn't have the right team around me yet.

I didn't know myself.

Do I know myself now? Do I know how to handle something like this?

Something inside me cracks open beneath the spinning torrent of doubt.

What would Robyn do?

That's an easy one. She wouldn't sit here frozen by fear. She'd take charge.

There's no point in denying it any longer—all the method acting, the bad-girl lessons with Dante, the freedom of yesterday, and the desire to burn, to fuel, to catch fire. I have to become Robyn if I want to save this movie. "Then we find another director." I project my voice into the room, pushing back my chair and standing.

Silence.

The same crew members who've been avoiding my eye on set are seeing me for the first time. I'm done playing small.

I continue, "I can call in favors." Even as I say it, I know how impossible it sounds. Most directors are booked in advance, but I refuse to give up. "Felix never understood this film. The heart of it, the original script, the true vision. It's all still here. We need someone who can see it through."

"Sure, let's say we find a director." An EP leans forward, his tone skeptical. "We don't have the budget to pay them."

"I do," I state, confidently. "I want to be a producer."

The room stills again. Worse this time.

I know the movie has a one-hundred-fifty-million-dollar budget. If the other executive producers don't pull their funding, I'll probably need to invest ten, maybe twenty million dollars. It can't be more than that. Doubts creep into my mind, but I push them away. I can panic later.

Heather adjusts her glasses. "Executive producer."

There's a big difference.

A producer handles logistics, and onset operations. An executive producer secures financing, negotiates contracts, and makes the high-level decisions that keep a film alive.

"Yes." I smile down at Heather, glad to see she has my back. Maybe her warning me back in June against taking this role was because she didn't want us to be sitting here in this exact position. "I'll pay the director's fee," I continue. "I'll forgo my salary, except for what's contractually required to go to my team, and I'll cover an extra month of filming."

A producer exhales sharply. "That's going to be a pretty penny."

"I stand by what I said."

And I do. The public assumes we actors are all living glamorous, expensive lives. But thanks to a few successful product launches in my early twenties—Reese's Peach lip gloss and perfume—and my own frugal nature, I've made money, and I've been smart with it. Aside from my house in LA, which I bought years ago, and a summer home in Italy, I keep my spending minimal. Most of my designer wardrobe comes from sponsorships, and my glam team's expenses are covered in my contracts.

It's time to invest in myself.

"And I want production profit shares as well." The studio execs, the investors, the all-male crew of executive producers all stare at me. "Or there's no movie."

"Reese, if you can fund this film and find a director to start filming immediately, I'd let you tattoo your own name on my fucking ass—pardon the language," the producer exclaims.

I feel so out of my element, but another idea strikes me—a little farfetched and impossible, but perfect. Dante watches me like I've turned into someone else. Maybe I have.

I hope our telepathic conversations work past the comfort of set.

I need a favor.

He raises a brow. *Anything.*

With that, I don't hesitate. "We have an in with Amara Bellamy."

"Miss Sinclair is right." Dante straightens in his chair. "She's a longtime friend who owes me a favor, and I have an inkling she'd love to work with Reese."

The Amara Bellamy. My heart soars with possibility as my nerves dance.

The executives practically pounce on him.

"Can you make it happen?"

"We need this, Dante."

"Whatever it takes."

His voice remains steady despite the weight of hundreds of careers hanging on his words. "No promises, but I'll try."

This could actually work, or it could all come crashing down around us. Either way, there's no turning back now.

"If we can get Amara on this project stat, we have a chance to finish filming by Christmas and keep the July release date. I'm willing to put in the hours and extra work to get this done," I say.

After discussing the logistics of Amara's potential involvement, the studio's marketing strategist clears his throat. "Everyone but media damage control, take thirty."

Dante and I move to leave, but Geraldine cuts in, "You two stay."

We sink back into our leather seats.

"Even if Amara agrees, we face a press problem. Headlines everywhere have declared the movie dead. Worse, Reese—" Geraldine exhales sharply. "The articles are blaming you because Felix is running his mouth to the press."

A publicist slides a manila folder toward me, grave-faced as she reveals printouts from entertainment sites.

"Reese Ruins Robyn: Director Felix Langford Says Star's Demands Sank Production," screams one headline. Another reads, "New Hollywood Diva Strikes: How Reese Sinclair

Torpedoed *Robyn Hood*." And perhaps worst of all: "Sources Confirm: Reese Sinclair 'Impossible to Work With.'"

My stomach plummets as I skim through the quotes. The weight of these accusations pressing down on me like a physical force.

"Do whatever needs to be done, Ger. Put me on the circuit. I can handle it. Interviews, whatever," I say. "We've got to be able to turn this around—"

"Reese, darling." Geraldine laments, adjusting the skinny scarf draped around her neck. "You know as well as anyone that the world is waiting to tear down a woman at the top. I'm afraid you speaking out will only make it worse."

My teeth grind together.

She's right. Men get labeled visionaries and misunderstood geniuses; women become "difficult," "emotional," "too much." If Felix's story sticks, I won't just lose this film—I'll become industry poison.

"But I've been up since two working with our data team, and I have a solution," Geraldine adds, and she tosses the *Stone Times* onto the table. On the cover: Dante and me laughing at the beach, his hand on my back. She slides a thick binder out of her bag and onto the wooden table. "This is our escape route."

The exec flips through it. All eyes shift between Dante and me.

"What is this?" My confidence crumbles.

Geraldine folds her arms. "You two are our way out of this mess." This cannot be going where I think it's going. "The public devours your chemistry," Geraldine says plainly.

"The numbers don't lie," an executive counters. I pull the binder toward me, staring at the charts that reduce the time I've spent with Dante to metrics. "Look at these numbers," she flips a few pages. "Viggle searches for *Robyn Hood* skyrocket after you're spotted together. Your lip gloss sales alone have doubled since that beach photo leaked."

"But there is no chemistry," I snap, the lie scorching my tongue. "None."

Dante flinches. I can't face him.

"It doesn't have to be real. You know that better than anyone," Geraldine concurs. "Felix has the media in his pocket. You and Dante as Hollywood's newest power couple? That's our counterstrike. This will drive ticket sales, and you know it."

"No." My voice fractures. "Absolutely not."

But with the weight of my money on the line, my career teetering, and this film nearly crumbling before my eyes, can principles alone survive this fall?

Chapter 25
Dante

I KNOW what Reese Sinclair's cunt tastes like, but there she sits, adamantly turning down the opportunity to date me, and it feels like a blade being sliced along my Achilles' heel.

I don't do relationships. Never have. The concept feels foreign, like trying to speak a language I never bothered to learn. Now here's Reese, and suddenly I'm thinking about possibilities I shouldn't be.

The nicotine craving hits hard. Quitting seemed smart at the time.

She's spelled it out enough times: her work is everything, and she won't let anyone—especially not some guy, even if that fucking guy is me—eclipse that. I get it. This movie was meant to be about her.

 Now they bring up this shit.

"My client deserves input," Todd, my agent, asserts. "His image is at stake; he has a disciplinary review looming."

Geraldine scoffs. "Image? The same image that's showcased in fencing brawls and yacht photos with cocaine and women?"

"I'm not doing any of that right now," I say, drumming my fingers against my slacks.

"For now." Her glare cuts deep. "What about next month?"

The truth stings—I wouldn't trust me either.

"You're not hearing me," Reese cuts in. "I won't sell another film through tabloid romances. I chose this role precisely because it transcends that!"

"But Miss Sinclair," a publicist condescends, "audiences crave your on-screen to off-screen romances. Data confirms it."

"Don't you want success?"

"Have you considered the investment others have made in this project?"

"You have to do whatever it takes."

"Of course I want this movie to succeed," Reese insists, leaning toward her agent in a failed attempt at privacy. "But there must be alternatives to tired publicity stunts. Thoughts?"

Heather angles toward her. "We're not just in the big leagues anymore—we *are* the league. Rewrite the rules."

"Everyone quiet." Determination flashes as she surveys the room. "I need to think."

She glances at me with a flicker of apology or a silent request for alliance. I nod, acknowledging whatever comes next. Then resolution takes over as she uncoils, commanding attention.

"I have a vested interest in this film's success. If we do this, we do it my way. Here's the deal. We leverage our reputations without manufacturing a relationship. We can be seen together and sure the media will speculate, but we won't confirm anything." She pauses, scanning the eyes of everyone in the room. "My mainstream appeal balances his bad boy image; his fencing reputation can give me action-movie credibility."

I nod. A calculated non-relationship. Enough visibility to spark gossip without confirmation.

"I'm in. Whatever you need," I say.

I'm so fucking proud of Reese. In a matter of minutes, she's meticulously mapped out everything. She's seizing the power of her life.

"But Reese," Geraldine interjects, "we've spent years building your image—"

"And now I'm evolving it," Reese cuts in. "Speculation generates more buzz than any staged romance. It's the art of the tease."

She steals a glance at me. *Naughty girl.*

"But a confirmed public relationship will benefit your reputation," Geraldine argues. "Love is at the center of your brand. 'Good girl falls for the bad boy' is a narrative audiences adore."

"Isn't that absurd?" Reese frowns. "You've saved me from countless PR disasters, Geraldine, but I'm done being reduced to these shallow romantic storylines that overshadow my work. I don't want to date Dante—but I get it. A few well-placed appearances with him will shift the conversation away from Felix. People will speculate about us, sure, but more importantly, they'll be talking about *Robyn Hood*." Reese stands and starts pacing. "Once we have their attention, I'll take it from there—interviews, talk shows, red carpets, press junkets, social media. The focus will be back where it belongs, and the rumors about Dante and me will fade into the background."

She's brilliant.

Heather nods approvingly. "*Robyn Hood* isn't a romance film, so hopefully the dating rumors will burn out fast. If anything, being seen with an Olympic fencer only adds to your credibility and dedication to this film. It'll make you look serious about embodying the role by being close friends with a master swordsman."

Geraldine sighs. "I can see I'm outnumbered here. Just promise me you'll let me know before you make any major moves?"

"Of course."

"Reese's plan makes sense." I look up at her, permitting myself the prolonged eye contact.

"Dante," Todd warns, "the USFA committee is watching. Any more press could jeopardize everything."

He's not wrong. I consider the stakes. Yes, a scandal could derail my fencing career. But the math feels simple: A single beach photo didn't end me. The occasional late night with Reese won't either. The media will spin it their way regardless. *Hollywood's good girl goes rogue.*

Plus, it's nice to have the media buzz around us shift the focus away from my suspension.

Through I don't think I can tell her that. She might think I'm using her spotlight—just like Ricky did.

And after everything Susan's been writing about us…Christ, if I hadn't invited her on the yacht this summer, maybe she never would've gone after Reese. She already knew about the filming location, but I didn't do anything to stop her. The least I can do now is make sure this movie is a success. My throat tightens, the buried guilt spreading like ink through water.

"We won't do anything that would compromise Dante's career," Reese says to Todd. The statement carries a protective edge.

"I agree. We can keep it PG-13. I'm mentoring a kid in fencing now, helping her land a scholarship. New leaf and all." I meet Todd's gaze steadily. "Running around the Hollywood circuit with Reese a few times is hardly front-page news in Colorado Springs."

"We'll need ground rules and an ironclad NDAs," Todd insists.

"Works for us." Gerladine's planner opens with a snap. "Jaxon's party next weekend—your first big appearance since the *Love and Loathing* premiere. Every major outlet will be there, along with half the industry."

"The perfect opportunity to announce my new executive producer credit," Reese smiles.

"And brag about your intensive combat training," I add.

Heather nods. "We'll outfit you in something sleeveless to show off your freshly toned arms."

Geraldine continues, "The Diamond Essence shampoo campaign is in a few weeks. We can arrange for some candid shots of you two practicing sword techniques in between takes, it'll look completely natural and unplanned. The media will love the narrative: a dedicated actress honing her combat skills even during commercial shoots."

Todd continues, "There's the Hastings Gala in December."

"The family fundraiser for athletic programs," I explain when Reese shoots me a curious glance.

"What kind of people will be there?" Geraldine jumps in.

"Our sports connections run deep—Formula 1 drivers to Olympic medalists regularly attend. Plus, there's an impressive lineup of team owners from every major sport you can think of," I say.

"Excellent." Geraldine nods. "Being seen with these elite athletes will show the industry you've evolved to take up space in these new circles."

I've brought people around my family before. Entourages, groups, the kind of crowd that makes everything feel like a performance. But bringing Reese feels different.

I'm getting ahead of myself.

Still.

The image of her among the only other people who know me as well as she does is starting to linger.

"And it'll highlight Dante's philanthropy and willingness to help," Todd adds pointedly.

The room dissolves into logistics—press coverage, costume leaks, and appearances.

Under the table, my foot finds Reese's. The contact ignites a galaxy along my vertebrae. When she softens, I silently speak to her.

Good work.

Thank you. She fights with a smile, and I catalog the subtle twitch at the corner of her mouth.

I don't know what this thing between us is, but I've bought myself time to figure it out.

"Are you going to be alright with this?" Reese asks, her fingers tracing the edge of the conference table. "The committee watching, the press…I know it's a lot. If you're uncomfortable, we can call it."

The sky outside grows dusky. We've been here for hours.

"It's fine, Reese."

"Are you sure?"

"I promise." I stand and sit beside her, something I've wanted to do for hours. "I like helping people I care about."

She smiles, but slumps forward. "I appreciate that, but none of this really matters if Amara doesn't sign on."

"Trust me, Mari wants to work with you. Your reputation precedes you."

"If you say so." She wraps her hair around her index finger, pursing her lips like she's figuring out how to ask another favor of me.

"There's something else, huh?" I ask.

"This is going to be really awkward to bring up, please forgive me, but I'd appreciate your discretion regarding any other…entanglements. I know it's not right of me to ask since we're not—"

"Dating," I finish, letting out a deep chuckle. I like that she gets nervous around me. The setting sun turns her hair a light shade of caramel.

"Exactly."

"And you don't want to be," I say, needing to make sure.

She straightens a stack of papers that's already perfectly aligned. "I don't want to overshadow *Robyn Hood*."

"I understand."

"So?" She fidgets with her pearls draped along her perfect collarbones.

"There's no one else," I say, the truth slipping out before I can dress it up in something more casual. Truth is, however difficult it is to admit, I want to stay with Reese for as long as she lets me. She's sort of invaded me, and I hate how easily—those cravings for other vices haven't sparked up like they have in the past. I try not to think about what that means.

As if being with her…well, it doesn't make me want to get lost. Escape myself. She makes me want to stay.

"Our media circuit won't be long," she says. "We'll front-load our appearances, sprinkle them here and there. I'm sure it'll only take a handful of outings to bury Felix's headlines under our narrative. And then I can handle the rest."

"I'm not worried, Reese. We're good at improvising."

"Very good," she agrees.

"And everything else between us." I place my hand on her dress under the table. "We can take it slow like we talked about?"

Her eyes drop to my hand on her leg. "You mean what happened in the armory?"

"Hollywood's newest wild child needs to get comfortable talking about these things," I tease.

"The…physical aspects?"

"Getting warmer," I say gruffly.

"Sex?" My mind flashes, remembering the way she felt against me in the armory. How sweet her cunt tasted. How I'd do anything to hear her angelic moans again.

"Yes, I'd like that. Maybe we can keep things…" She pauses, choosing her words with the precision I've come to expect.

"Casual. That's more your style anyway, isn't it? Simple, uncomplicated?"

I hate how correct her assumption is. "We can do casual," I promise. "But we need boundaries. Working together, training, this—it's a delicate balance."

"Since when do you care about boundaries?"

"Since you decided to start breaking all the rules."

"And you'll keep me in line?" She bites her plush bottom lip, as if knowing I want to do the exact the same.

"Someone has to." I grin, my fingers inch down the fabric of her dress. She sneaks a peak to the empty room behind us. "What are you comfortable with?"

"On set, can we go back to being 'Mr. Hastings' and 'Miss Sinclair'? Exactly how we were before?"

Being professional on set while being reportedly linked will be interesting. Let the world keep guessing.

"I do love when you're formal."

She rolls her eyes. "And when we're alone…"

"Just Reese and Dante?" I finish.

"Exactly." She drops her hand to mine just as I reach the hem of her cotton dress, her thumb gently stroking along the top. "I'll still send you recordings, of course. Especially if there are script updates. And I'll still need someone for choreography training."

"You could just admit you want more time with me." I squeeze her thigh, digging my fingers into her strong quads.

"Your ego is truly something else."

"I'm looking forward to our new arrangement."

"We seem to be making a habit of cutting deals." She scooches her chair closer to mine until our knees are touching.

"Hey," I reach forward, cupping her jaw. "Can we acknowledge your first executive producer credit? That's fucking incredible."

She exhales, leaning her face into my touch. "I know. It feels like a dream. I should tell my parents. Maybe I can fly out tomorrow. But first, we should definitely see if Amara will be on board."

"Let's call her now."

"Yes, please."

I stare at her brown eyes a second more before dropping my hand and retrieving my phone. Her fingers brush mine as she takes it, and I'm struck by how such a small touch can feel like a freefall, how I'm starting to crave these small touches constantly.

"Show them what you're made of, fighter."

Chapter 26
Reese

Langford Reveals All: The Real Story Behind *Robyn Hood* and Sinclair's Nightmare Behavior

THE LOUISIANA SUN beats down as I relax on Mama's wraparound porch, the humidity shimmering above the pool. The same pool that terrified me as a child now feels like another part of home, like the gardenias Mama tends to obsessively in her wide-brimmed hat.

My phone buzzes against the wrought iron table, making the mason jar of tea wobble, ice clinking against the glass.

It's an email with Amara's contract.

I open up my text thread with Dante.

REESE

OH MY GOODNESS

Amara's team sent over the contract! We start filming next week!

Thank you for making this happen.

DANTE

Don't sell yourself short. Mari practically
swooned for you.

REESE

Still processing this!

I find myself daydreaming about him here, sprawled across
Mama's precious white wicker furniture like some sort of beautiful catastrophe. His tattoos, rings shinning under the sunlight.
Those eyes of his, gold and knowing, would stir up the neighborhood ladies for the rest of the year. And oh, the way the scent of
his skin would drift through the humid Louisiana air, making
Mama reach for her smelling salts, sneaking glances over her
monogrammed fan like a schoolgirl with a secret.

He'd be like an ink stain on a pristine tablecloth. Deliciously
out of place.

"Baby," Mama says, easing into her rocking chair with a
glass of sweet tea. Her ice cubes dance against crystal like wind
chimes. "You've been making eyes at that phone like it's whispering sweet nothings. Your daddy's going to start to fret."

My parents have been playing the role of proud hosts,
feeding me until my sundress protests and parading me around
the neighborhood, sweetly bragging about their daughter, the
executive producer.

"Work stuff," I mumble. But my cheeks betray me, blooming
pink under Mama's knowing stare.

"Sugar, did you forget I raised you? That smile you're wearing? Ain't about no business deal."

"It absolutely is!"

"Mm-hmm," she hums, fanning herself. "I suppose those
magazine spreads I've been seeing are just business too? That
cover of the *Stone Times* at a certain beach?"

Her look reminds me of being fifteen, caught writing Tom
Hardy's name in loopy cursive across my diary after I watched a

Wuthering Heights miniseries. Some things are constant, it seems, like my weakness for complicated men with good hearts.

Maybe I should've seen my antihero thing coming a mile away.

"The tabloids love their drama," I say primly, smoothing imaginary wrinkles from my dress.

Right on cue, Aunt Mabel sweeps onto the porch like a floral-printed hurricane, fresh from helping Daddy with barbecue prep. "Are we finally discussing that fine specimen of a man? I saw a picture of y'all on set—those tattoos! Nearly baptized my phone with my potato salad!"

"We're colleagues," I explain. "The director quit, so we've got this whole PR plan coming up, to evolve my image in the press. And, yes, Dante is a part of that, but that's it!"

"That Felix was trouble walking. Thank the Lord he never met your daddy."

Mabel claims another rocker, leaning in like we're trading secrets at a church social. "Speaking of your daddy, isn't it time you thought about settling down? Building something real? Don't let this one slip away. Those arms alone are worth a marriage license!"

"Aunt Mabel!" I protest, but laughter bubbles up anyway.

Sometimes I catch myself daydreaming about Dante with Em, the way his sharp edges soften when he talks about her, even when he pretends she gets under his skin. It's disarming, really, how naturally tenderness comes to him. I let myself imagine our hypothetical babies—a little girl with his easy smile, a boy with my contemplative brown eyes. "Things move differently in Hollywood," I whisper. "No one's rushing to have babies over there. People take their time. Besides, Dante and I are not having—"

"Time!" Aunt Mabel waves her paper plate at me. "I had two babies by your age. Your biological clock isn't turning back any further, Miss Hollywood."

Daddy materializes in the doorway wearing his *Kiss the Cook* apron, burger patties balanced carefully on a plate. "Babies?" The word catches in his throat, but his stern expression melts when he sees my face.

"No babies!" I insist.

"Well," Daddy considers, "any man who puts a smile on my baby girl's face can't be all bad. Even with those *decorations*, as Auntie Heather calls them. At least he's not one of those Hollywood pretty boys afraid of honest work. A real athlete—that's something!"

I'll need to have a strong talk with Heather about not always keeping my parents in the loop.

Mama fans herself, feigning distress. "Yes, those swords! Though I must say, the *Esquire* spread…" She trails off, a hint of appreciation coloring her mock outrage. "It did give me heart palpitations. That mask!"

"Heaven help us." Aunt Mabel grins, settling deeper into her chair. "Tell me fighting isn't the only thing he's skilled at. Does he at least know how to peel crawfish properly?"

"He hasn't learned yet, but he's a quick study. You'd love teaching him."

"Well then, sugar, tell that man of yours he's welcome anytime," Daddy says, heading back to his grill. "Just leave the swords in California. And fair warning: I'll be grilling him harder than these burgers. Speaking of which, these patties won't cook themselves."

Mama rolls her eyes fondly as Aunt Mabel fusses over him. The oldest sister, always mothering. My phone chimes again, and I attempt a serious face so I don't give anything away.

DANTE

How's the family reunion going? Has your mother stuffed you with beignets yet?

> **REESE**
>
> She's been drowning me in gumbo with potato salad, cornbread, AND red beans and rice. We're prepping for a whole family barbecue now.

DANTE

How wholesome. Be sure to keep your protein intake up for all that muscle we're building.

> **REESE**
>
> Speaking of which, did your coach agree to a new training schedule for you this week?

DANTE

Yes, but I'm babysitting his youth program MWF in return. I thought Em was bad. The rest of these kids are the actual antichrist.

> **REESE**
>
> You're such a good boy.

DANTE

There you go with the praise again. The jet is fueled and ready. I could be in NOLA by dinner.

The ceiling fan whirs overhead, and I count the blades spinning, trying to ground myself against his tempting offer. These kinds of thoughts drift like magnolia petals in summer wind. Decidedly unprofessional, definitely not strategic. I've never brought a man home before, not even Ricky. When Mama visited California, she chaperoned us with the diligence of a Victorian governess.

Would they see what I see beneath his carefully cultivated danger—the gentle soul who anticipates my needs before I voice them, who drapes his hoodie over my shoulders against the evening chill without a word?

The thought of him here makes my heart flutter. Watching

him tackle his first crawfish with adorable determination, too proud to ask for help but yearning for approval all the same.

I let myself sink deeper into this daydream.

REESE

As much as I'd love to give my whole family enough gossip to last til next Christmas, my parents have my whole week planned out.

DANTE

Come on, I bet you never had a boy climb through your window. First time for everything?

Could be the perfect first article to welcome your image evolution.

REESE

Missing me that much?

DANTE

Desperately.

REESE

Weren't you the one preaching about the virtues of celibacy?

Six more days won't harm you.

DANTE

You're cruel, Miss Sinclair.

A few feet away, Aunt Mabel and Daddy are fussing over the grill placement Their voices carry across the yard as I look toward the pool, memories washing over me like waves.

"Maybe we could go for a swim later?" I suggest, watching the sunlight dance on the water.

"Here?" Mama asks, raising an eyebrow as she pauses her fan-waving. "The backyard pool's been off-limits since…well, you know."

"Lord, remember when she fell in?" Aunt Mabel calls over. "Nearly gave us all heart attacks!"

I lean over and kiss Mama on the cheek, noticing that I'm getting the same wrinkle she has right along her smile line. How lucky am I? "Yeah. Maybe we'll start with hanging our feet in the pool."

"I'd love that!" Mama bounces up, clapping with delight, her face glowing. "Let me find you a suitable swimsuit. And none of those California strings you call bikinis!"

Daddy mutters something about *dress codes* and *respectability* as Mama hurries inside. Aunt Mabel winks at me before turning back to critique my father's grilling technique.

While they're distracted, my phone buzzes with another article about Felix. I can't wait to get back to LA and change the narrative.

But even more, I can't wait to get back to Dante.

With everyone occupied, I pull up the camera app. It's golden hour and my skin is cast in a bronze glow. I let the ruffle strap of my sundress slip ever so slightly off my shoulder and capture the perfect angle where sunlight kisses skin. I send it to Dante.

DANTE

You're making it difficult to focus on these insufferable children and their swords.

REESE

It's a shoulder.

DANTE

Your shoulder has a freckle I've never noticed before. I'm getting hard looking at it.

REESE

Very naughty, Mr. Hastings.

Chapter 27
Reese

September 25th

Top Action Director Quits Mid-Filming After Clash with On-Set Diva!

My heart tap-dances at the sight of Dante. He's at the bottom of the front steps of my LA home, ready to pick me up for our first public outing—Jaxon Elio's birthday party.

The universe has a twisted sense of humor because he's even more unfairly gorgeous than he was a week ago. His velvet suit looks like it was plucked off the runway. His dark hair is pushed out of his face.

If I were a stick of butter, I'd melt right here on these steps.

He ascends toward me, extending his hand. His nails are freshly polished, and each finger is adorned with a silver ring.

I internally combust, every neuron in my body dialed up to ten thousand. I don't just want him; I need him with an aching pleasure.

My fingers interlace with his.

I hear the *click click click* of cameras. The paparazzi have multiplied like rabbits on fertility drugs, their lenses shoved through my wrought iron gates.

Each flash feels like a spotlight, and I silently rehearse my role. *Be bad, be bold, be like Robyn.*

My mind races with the potential headlines: *Good Girl Gone Robyn Hood Bad.* Or maybe just, *Good Girl Finally Living Her Life.*

"Three-quarter profile," he whispers against my ear, making it look like sweet nothings. "They love that angle on you." I'm starting to love him directing me. "Looking sharp," I say, running my finger down his jacket lapel.

"With you on my arm tonight, had to make sure I earned it," he drawls, opening the limo door for me. "Sorry, Dad—shotgun's calling your name," Dante says to Ramsey, who gives me his patented *Are you sure about this?* look.

"I'm good, Rams."

Cars were definitely not designed for women. Nothing kills the illusion of effortless glamour faster than an awkward slide across leather seats, fabric hitching in all the wrong places. Even with his steadying hand, I barely manage to maintain my dignity.

He runs his hand lightly up my arm, appraising the defined muscles with admiration. "The cameras will eat up all this strength. You've put in the work, and it shows."

I shift self-consciously. "It's not too manly?"

Dante catches my eye with a knowing look. "Where'd you get that nonsense? Strength isn't gendered." His words calm me as he helps me adjust my outfit, smoothing out the wrinkles. "You're going to look flawless for your big entrance."

"Thank you." I blush.

"Your home is beautiful, by the way," he says. ""I'd love to see more of it sometime. Get the full tour?"

"I rarely have people over." It's my sanctuary, one I don't want burdened with memories of people who don't stick around.

"Keeping your secrets close. I respect that," he says, hand

sliding over my thigh, bunching my pink maxi skirt. "Speaking of secrets…that photo of you in the sundress. I haven't been able to stop thinking about it."

The back of his hand moves up my neck, and I gasp at the contact.

Ramsey adjusts the rearview mirror, catching Dante's eye. In one solid motion, Dante slams the partition button, and the barrier slowly blocks Ramsey's view.

"Finally alone." He shifts his body toward me. "I've missed you," he confesses. He's too close. Not nearly close enough. Eight days shouldn't feel like an eternity.

"I missed you too."

He grips my thigh with his other hand, his eyes searching mine—not predatory, but questioning.

"May I kiss you?" He cups my jaw in his hand.

"Yes." I exhale, his mouth sweetly capturing mine, and I forget where I am.

I revel in the kind of silence that only exists when his fingers thread through my hair. I can't control everything, but it's powerful to know that Dante will do whatever I ask him to do.

No questions. No judgment.

Who knew dominating men would be such a turn on?

"Fuck, Reese." My hips press toward him as he pulls me into his kiss, and I nip at his lower lip. "You know I love the pain," he growls into my mouth, wetness already pooling in my panties. "But so do you."

The kiss deepens, transforms. No longer gentle, but hungry.

I am neither the good girl nor the rebel.

I am simply myself, longing for Dante Hastings to never take his hands off of me.

I'm more turned on than I thought possible. Maybe he had the right idea about celibacy, because without his touch I've become feral.

The party is a vague memory in the recesses of my mind. My eyes flutter, and I yank him closer, aching for him.

That is until I hear, "Ahem," and a throat clears in front of us. Ramsey. The partition is down, and my bodyguard stares at me like, *I can't believe you.* The limo has stopped moving.

"Tried to tell you a few times, Miss Sinclair, but we are here," he says.

I gulp, cheeks flaring red. Ramsey has never seen me nearly inhale a man, let alone one who's minutes away from devouring me in return. "Give us a minute, please."

The partition slides up slowly, Ramsey shooting daggers at Dante.

I clasp my hand over my mouth, suppressing a fit of laughter. "I need to give him a big bonus this year."

Dante and I slowly, reluctantly peel apart, both of us panting heavily.

"I've wanted to kiss you all week," I admit. "I thought about more than kissing you." He nestles his head in the crook of my neck and inhales. "Fuck the party," he whines. "Come back to my hotel."

The offer is too tempting to pass up, but this is work. I need to focus.

"We have to go," I remind him.

"You're right, but I think this is the first party I don't want to go to."

"Let me fix you up." His lips shine with my lipstick, smeared like watercolor across his mouth. He lets me gently swipe away at the color until it fades.

Through the tinted glass, the partygoers pass, women in dresses that seem to defy gravity, all plunging necklines and strategic slits. My outfit feels too much like the old Reese Sinclair in comparison: a boatneck pink shell top, arms exposed, and a matching maxi skirt with a layer of lining beneath a gorgeous see-through lace above it.

"What's wrong?" he asks, reading me like a book.

"I'm second-guessing my outfit. I wish I'd put on something more sexy."

"I think you look lovely."

That's the problem.

I scan my outfit, and it hits me. If I pull the lining out, it'll look a lot more daring. A set of lace over my exposed, toned legs. I work, pulling away the lace layer and grabbing the lining of my maxi skirt, bunching it between my hand. My attempt to tear it fails miserably. The second attempt manages to pull a slight hole into it.

Dante's hands cover mine. "Allow me." With one swift motion, he rips the skirt cleanly across my mid-thigh. The tear echoes through the limo.

"Well, I can't deny that looks quite seductive," he says, his eyes darkening as they sweep over my newly exposed legs.

I can already see tomorrow's headlines: *America's Sweetheart Shows Off Her Robyn Hood Muscles.* The thought makes me smile, especially knowing they have no idea what happened in this limo.

"But something's still missing." I spot Dante's rings and remember the conversation we had at Paulie's jewelry shop.

How something as simple as a few accessories could change people's perception of you.

"Give me one of your rings," I say, strategizing. I unclasp my pearl necklace.

"You want to wear a piece of me?"

"I want to wear a piece of your armor." He extends his hand. A ring glides off his finger, and I thread it onto my necklace.

"Can I?" he asks. I nod.

He clasps my necklace back on, the cool metal of his ring sliding against my throat. His touch lingers longer than necessary, sending a jolt down my spine.

"What do you think?"

"So fucking—" He adjusts my lipstick with his thumb, cleaning up the evidence of our kiss. "Perfect."

Okay. I can do this.

As if Dante can read the plume of nerves billowing in my head, he asks, "Want to do your breaths before we go out there? Four. Seven. Eight."

"But they're waiting."

"They can wait all night for all I care."

He's right. I inhale, and he mimics me, and we make our own little moment feel precious and ours before stepping out of the limo. The usual parade of lights and shouting comes, but when I place my hand in Dante's and he squeezes once—a quick, private thing—I know I can do this.

I gulp, tilt my chin up, let my lips curve into the kind of smile that will be dissected in tabloids by morning. Dante's hand slides to my waist, firm and possessive, leading me while Ramsey flanks us.

Let's make some headlines, bury Felix, and sell my movie.

THE GALLERY IS EXACTLY what it sounds like, a too-cool-for-school art space in an old bank vault where beautiful people come to pretend they're not desperate for attention. Tonight, it's been decorated for Jaxon's birthday, which means the pretense of sophistication has been replaced by straight-up debauchery. Inside the vault's massive circular door, which is very James Bond, if Bond shopped at Supreme, neon art installations throb in time with a string quartet that's doing weird things to Taylor Swift songs.

Dante and I step out of the private elevator, and the air seems to hold its breath as we emerge into the champagne-soaked atmosphere. We navigate through a sea of perfect cheekbones and Academy Award winners.

Dante offers me a glass of champagne with a hibiscus flower floating in it, and I take it. The event photographer swarms, and I freeze instinctively, but his hand rests on my lower back, steadying me. I flash my brightest smile for the camera.

"What's next on your rebellious agenda?"

"Causing trouble, obviously," I whisper.

"You're getting dangerously good at this," Dante hums, his fingers ghosting across my back like he's teaching me proper form again.

I spot Jaxon weaving through the crowd. His shirt's already half undone, drinks sloshing in both hands as he staggers toward us. Even drunk, he carries himself with that particular brand of invincibility, the kind that makes me want to roll my eyes and hide in the bathroom simultaneously.

Can't exactly ghost the birthday boy whose party we're crashing for our own agenda.

"*Sinclaaaair!*" The nickname feels like nails on a chalkboard.

"Happy birthday, Jaxon." I dodge his attempt at a hug with the grace of someone who's had plenty of practice. Before he can respond, Dante steps forward, his presence commanding immediate attention.

"Dante Hastings," he introduces himself, his handshake firm and purposeful. "Olympic fencer and combat coordinator for the film." His voice carries a quiet authority that makes Jaxon's previous posturing seem almost childish.

"A new…friend?" Jaxon's gaze slides over him like he's sizing up competition, though Dante's presence fills the room in a way Jaxon's never could. He turns back to me. "Quite the crew change-up. First a genre jump, now this."

"I'm taking my new role very seriously," I counter. A small part of me cringes at how eager I sound, but I can't help showing off a little. "You should see what an accomplished gold medalist can put you through. Proper swordplay is quite the workout."

Jaxon's smile tightens at the corners. "I didn't realize you were so serious about your new role."

"She's mastering it beautifully," Dante interjects. "Natural talent combined with dedication. It's rare to find both. Surely you understand."

Jaxon's jealousy practically radiates off him. "Rough break about Felix jumping ship. Word is he walked because of you."

Dante tenses beside me, but I brush my shoulder against his —our own private Morse code. "That's not why Felix left the project," I say, using my PR voice. "Creative differences, you know how it goes. As executive producer, I had to do what was best for the story. Bless your heart for keeping up with all the industry gossip, though."

Jaxon's chest puffs like a peacock's. "EP? Since when?"

"Since last week. It's a little overdue if you ask me." I straighten my spine. "Thanks for having us, darling. Save the date for *Robyn Hood's* premiere in July?"

He grunts. "Wouldn't miss it."

Dante's wink is pure mischief. "Nice meeting you, Jason."

"Jaxon."

We slip away, and I'm buzzing with the kind of giddy rebellion I haven't felt since sneaking out of my first Hollywood party at sixteen. Maybe it's rude to snub him at his own birthday, but after all the PR stunts he dragged me into during *Love and Loathing*, turnabout feels like fair play.

"How's that for sending Felix a message?" I grin up at Dante, feeling light as champagne bubbles. "Jaxon's the biggest gossip in town; this'll be everywhere by morning."

"He's quite…what's the word I'm looking for? A dick."

"That's a diplomatic way of putting it," I laugh. "I've never been so bold with him before."

"And?"

"It feels like…" I pause, savoring the moment. "Like I'm finally writing my own lines. Oh look, liquid courage!" I snag two shots from a passing tray, the amber liquid glinting in the low light. "Care to join me?"

Dante shakes his head. "Sorry, fighter. New training program means I'm sticking to water tonight."

"Such discipline," I tease, but secretly, his restraint makes my pulse quicken. "Well then, more trouble for me." I raise both shots in a mock toast. "To making headlines!" The liquor burns sweet and dangerous down my throat.

"To the real Reese." His words carry more weight than he probably realizes.

The second shot blazes down my throat, making the party lights swim and dance. The crowd vibrates around us. Designer clothes and perfect faces, camera flashes popping like stars. There are snippets of whispers and curious stares.

"I never actually dance at these things," I admit to Dante.

"That's a shame. We could change that."

If tonight's about erasing Felix's slander and shifting the focus to my evolution, it's time to give them something to talk about.

"You're right, come with me," I say, tugging Dante toward the writhing mass of bodies.

Knowing every eye follows our movement, we slip between the people until we're safely hidden in plain sight. The music wraps around us, and I let my body sway with the same freeness I felt at Wizard Island.

A group in the corner turns their attention toward us, whispers rising over the clink of their cocktails. Their stares prick against my skin, sharp and uninvited.

I straighten, chin lifted—the practiced stance of someone who's always been told how to present herself. It makes me seem taller, more confident than I feel. But inside, I shrink with every glance.

Dante sees it instantly. His gaze locks onto mine, and I relax. "Hey," he says, loud enough for me to hear over the music. "Look at me. Just me. Ignore them."

"Okay."

"Like we do in training," he adds, his expression softening in a way he reserves for only when nobody else is looking. "Focus on your partner."

Something in me loosens, remembers how to breathe. I relax into the rhythm of us, into the careful space he creates, the one where I don't have to be anyone but myself.

I'm caught between worlds—powerful under his gaze yet vulnerable under everyone else's. Half of me wants to shrink away while the other half wants to shine brighter.

"I'm out of my realm here," I say, letting the confession fall between us like a small, fragile thing.

"Then pretend, Reese," he says. "Act the part. Act the volition."

He's right. I can play a part. I've been playing parts my whole life.

So I let my arms go up in the air, moving my body with a new freedom, keeping my eyes on Dante. There's something holy in the way he looks at me—like I'm both completely seen and completely safe. Every accidental brush of his fingers sends quiet lightning through me, threatening to pull me right into his gravity.

We maintain my PR-approved bubble of space between us, enough to look casual to the people watching. But the space grows smaller with each beat of the music.

He grazes my arm. Totally innocent, except the touch lingers longer than necessary, and I find myself leaning into it, wanting more pressure.

My hip bumps against his. A coincidence, I tell myself, though I know better.

Oh goodness.

It feels so good. To be here with him. So good that I let the room fade away completely until we're the only two people left in it.

"I feel like I'm getting away with something terrible in the best possible way," I blurt out, immediately wanting to slap my own forehead.

"You danced at a party. Revolutionary." His mouth quirks up at one corner, but his eyes stay soft. "But it looks good on you, being yourself."

A camera flash ignites his profile, and I notice—again—what I always do. The curve where his jaw meets his neck, the mess of dark curls, untamed from dancing. He moves through spaces like this with effortless confidence, never imposing, always aware.

His shirt clings to his shoulders, hinting at the quiet strength beneath. He smells like damp wood and something unmistakably him. It's a scent I've searched for in rooms he's already left.

The memory of his lips on mine in the limo crashes back— how gentle he was at first, until he wasn't. My skin burns hotter than studio lights. Every shift of his body, every twitch of his hands against my waist, pulses with restraint. And I want to be the one to break it.

The crowd surges, pressing us together. His body is solid and too familiar. My fingers brush damp cotton, catching on the heat beneath.

"Careful, Reese," he says. "Keep looking at me like that, and I might forget we're supposed to be keeping our distance."

I should step back. Instead, my gaze catches on the hollow of his throat, the constellation of beauty marks beneath his jaw— ones nobody else gets close enough to see. Sweat glistens there, and something dangerous unfurls inside me.

I imagine tracing that line.

He spins me, his hand a whisper at the small of my back and pulls me back in with just enough force to steal my breath. It's the same precision he wields in the training room—

measured, intentional, but with something wilder simmering underneath.

I want to drown in him.

It terrifies me how much I want him when I've spent years training myself not to want anything off-script. I calculate the distance between us, not to maintain it but to erase it.

His grip tightens on my hips, lingering a beat too long. And I smile—real and reckless—as another flash goes off to our left.

"Think we've given them enough?" My eyes hold his, asking a different question entirely.

"What, are you bored of me already?" he asks.

"Of you, never. But maybe, if we got what we needed, we could go…somewhere else. Somewhere private." The boldness in my suggestion surprises me but I keep playing the part.

Dante leads the way as I trail behind him. He moves with the same fluid grace he shows in everything—effortless but purposeful, creating a path where there seems to be none. We reach a secluded corner in the VIP section, hidden from view. I press against the wall.

"All I did was brag a little and have a shot in public. But why does it feel so good?" I say.

"Technically, you shared your achievements, and you should be fucking proud of them," he teases, and I swat at his muscled chest. "And if feels good because you're showing everyone Reese Sinclair can cut loose."

He moves closer, measuring the space between us—not touching but radiating heat. His arm plants beside my head. I catalog everything about him: the callus on his thumb from years of fencing, those absurdly long eyelashes, and the way he holds something back, like he's saving himself.

"The cameras won't see us here," I acknowledge. Even in the dim light, his eyes hold a comfort I've never found anywhere else. The careful restraint in them makes me want to tip forward into the space between us, to see what happens when his control breaks.

"That means we're just Reese and Dante now," he says, and something in me shatters quietly.

I don't wait to kiss him. I've waited too long already.

I don't overthink it—everything else in my life has been overthought.

The kiss starts as a question before it turns into a statement, a paragraph, a full essay. His jaw rakes against my skin as I press closer, clutching his velvet suit jacket like it's tethering me to reality. When he deepens the kiss, a small, embarrassing sound escapes me—half surprise, half relief, like scratching an itch I've been pretending doesn't exist.

His hands move with the precision he brings to everything, mapping my body like territory he intends to claim. And in that moment, I realize I've never felt more myself than I do when I'm with him.

"Dante," I whisper, his name catching in my throat as my body ignites.

"Yeah?" He makes a half-hearted attempt to create distance between us, though his palms still press gently into my waist.

"We want them to speculate, not confirm," I remind him quietly, trying to summon responsibility. But my fingertips betray me, already tracing the hard lines of his chest beneath velvet.

"Right," he says, scanning the room with practiced discretion, but my eyes have already found our salvation—the VIP bathroom door standing ajar, an invitation I know I should decline.

The old Reese would never consider pulling a man into a bathroom at a party. The old Reese calculated outcomes, measured risks, avoided headlines.

But something changed in that boardroom.

Something in me woke up.

The door clicks shut behind us with a finality that sends a tantalizing shiver down my spine. Dante lifts me onto the cool marble vanity with an effortlessness that makes my stomach flip.

Am I really doing this?

A knock at the door startles me, but Dante smirks against my neck, finding that spot below my ear that makes me forget how to breathe. The forbidden nature of it all—the risk, the secrecy—only intensifies everything, reminding me of the armory when nobody was watching.

"Excuse me?" a voice says from outside. The handle jiggles. "Is someone in there?"

"Last chance to be sensible," Dante says softly. His hands continue their careful exploration, gentle but insistent. I've never known that safety could feel like freedom, like falling.

"Sensible is overrated," I whisper, drawing him into me as my thighs encircle his hips. Something primal awakens beneath my skin, a version of myself I've kept caged until now. The risk of discovery sends lightning through my veins.

I unravel against him, my consciousness narrowing to each point where his fingertips claim me.

"Then I'm going to make you forget there's a world outside this door," he promises, teeth grazing my throat, tugging at his ring around my pearls.

His lips brush my pulse point as his hands slide higher. His warmth moves through me like a current, and I surrender completely.

"You make me feel so good," I gasp, my palm sliding over the impressive length straining against his slacks. My boldness surprises me, but there's a raw, thrilling freedom in it.

"It's so natural with you."

More knocks come, but I shut them out. My blood rushes in my ears, drowning out everything but the sensation of his skin against mine. I'm burning up, fever-hot, each point of contact between us sending tiny earthquakes through my body.

"I want to be selfish again," I say. My hands tangle in his hair, directing his mouth down my body.

"Fuck, that makes me so hard, Reese."

He parts my thighs with deliberate slowness, pushing up my skirt.

"Please do what you did to me last time," I beg. A blush spreads across my chest, up my neck, painting me in shades of want.

I buck toward him as he yanks down my panties, my behind pressed against the counter. The cool marble sends a shock through me, contrasting with the heat of his touch. I'm caught between embarrassment and desire, the thrill of doing something so forbidden making me dizzy.

He cups my breasts, squeezing my hardened nipples, then he's trailing up my throat. He spins the pearl necklace around his pointer finger before bringing his polished index finger to my lips.

"Spit."

"What?" My eyes widen.

"You heard me."

I do as he says, dampening his fingers.

"Look at you," he says. "Always so perfectly put together. Now I get to make it all come undone."

His hand disappears beneath my ripped skirt, and I gasp as two of his fingers find my sensitive spot. My back arches involuntarily against the faucet. "Oh my god," I breathe as he circles my clit. The tension in my body is already begging to be set free, like I'm simultaneously expanding and contracting, my whole world reduced to his touch.

"You're…" He pauses, watching my reaction. "There's nothing like you. Nothing comes close."

I barely recognize the sounds coming from my own throat. My usual overthinking dissolves into pure sensation. "Dante, I —" But I can't finish, can't find words for this feeling.

I'm too lost in my pleasure.

Too lost at how he knows my body like the back of his hand.

"That's it, stay with me," he instructs. "Just like that." His authoritative tone commands my full surrender, and I trust him to guide me through this.

Euphoria consumes me. I'm so close.

"I'm gonna—"

"Yes, you are," he demands. "Come all over my fingers. Come for me, Reese."

His touch is everywhere at once, featherlight kisses trailing fire down my neck while his fingers work their magic.

The pressure builds exquisitely, intensifying until it breaks over me in waves. Everything else disappears—the persistent knocking, the party beyond the door, my carefully constructed public persona—leaving only this brilliant pleasure.

My head falls back against the mirror as he finds that perfect spot, and I have to bite my lip to keep from announcing to the whole party how amazing this feels. The orgasm crashes over me with stunning intensity.

His movements soften as I come down, and he places more tender kisses along my neck, each one sending tiny aftershocks through my still-trembling body.

The banging on the door seems distant now, comical in its irrelevance.

I rest my forehead against his shoulder, inhaling him in as my heartbeat gradually slows. "Wow…" I lift my gaze to his and find something unexpectedly tender there. "I may become addicted to how good you are at that."

"Please do."

Chapter 28
Dante

THE FLUORESCENT BATHROOM light casts everything in a surreal glow. I drag my fingers across my tongue, chasing her taste. Her eyes meet mine in the mirror, dark and bottomless.

Fuck.

Ramsey's there when we stumble out, his disapproval a tangible thing. My hands shake with the need to touch her again, to make sure she's real.

"Boring party," I manage, the lie clumsy on my tongue.

She grabs my hand, and I follow like I'm tethered to her, like there was never any other choice. The need to have her is like a physical ache.

We make our way out of the club. The elevator doors open to chaos. Camera flashes explode, and each burst makes my muscles coil tighter. White spots dance across my vision, but my hand finds the small of her back instinctively. Ramsey parts the crowd with efficiency.

The questions hit fast.

"Reese, how's the *Robyn Hood* set without Felix?"

"How long have you been together?"

"Look here!"

"Did you make Felix Langford quit?"

They surge forward, hungry and vicious. My teeth grind together.

"Get back!" Ramsey roars, using both hands to push people out of the way.

The paps press closer, their cameras glinting like knives in the half-light. Every muscle in my body remembers the ring, remembers the dance of violence. A photographer drops low, his lens sliding up her torn skirt, and something inside me snaps clean in half.

"God," she whispers. "They've never—I've never seen them like this."

I knew she was famous, obviously, but this tabloid attack is different. I'm already moving, already stripping off my jacket. The fabric settles around her shoulders like armor.

"I've got you," I say into her hair, resisting the violent urge boiling under my skin. *Hold yourself together.* My somewhat violent protective instincts would destroy my chances at the disciplinary review. Keep her close.

"Give us some room!" Ramsey says again, but they're beyond hearing as he continues to swat them away.

They're animals now, pressing closer. A camera swings wildly, arcing toward Reese's face like a meteor.

My body moves before my brain can catch up. I extend my hand, protecting her face from the lens coming at her. The camera hits concrete instead of skin. Glass shatters.

"My goodness," she says against my neck. "Thank you."

When a photographer lunges too close, I move to extend another protective arm over her, but Reese pivots away from them, ducking fast, redirecting his momentum. Her reflexes are fucking impressive. The paparazzi hesitate, parting away from us.

I keep my focus on her and instinctively tighten my grip as

we slide back into my limo, drawing figure eights over her palm —a silent promise.

I've got you.

She looks up at me then, eyes fearful but trusting. Her fingers curl into my jacket, and I let my steady heartbeat become her anchor. I've never seen someone so fierce yet vulnerable—it makes me want to be worthy of that trust.

To be steady. Safe.

I want to make it clear she's mine to protect.

Our breath fogs the windows, creating a barrier between us and the predators outside.

"Hey," I whisper, searching her face in the limo's dim interior. Red shadows slice across her cheekbones. Her mouth parts, barely, and something inside me breaks. "Are you alright? Are you safe?"

"Yeah." She swallows hard. Her touch ghosts over my pecs. "God. That was—I can't believe—I can't believe I just did that. Did you see how I dodged that photographer?"

"I saw that."

She laughs. "That is going to be everywhere tomorrow. Me standing my ground? I feel invincible."

I smile. "Because you are."

"I want—this is going to sound crazy, and it's probably the adrenaline talking, but I want to finish what we started back there."

"Right now?"

"Right now."

"Tell me again." My voice comes out desperate.

"I want—" Her breath hitches. "I need you. All of you, Dante."

"Reese—"

"Just us. Please. You and me."

She punctuates each word with an open-mouthed kiss along my

jaw, and when she finally reaches my lips, everything else falls away. She tastes like liquor and bad decisions. My hands find her hair, her waist, desperate to memorize every curve of her. The way she melts against me only makes me harder, hungrier, more desperate.

"I've ached to savor you," I growl against her neck, my fingers digging possessively into her spine. Each touch is a claim, a mark of ownership. "Patiently waited through the torture of being so close to you.

"Really?" she challenges, pulling back with swollen lips and eyes dark with need.

"Watching you train day after day, those sweats hugging your ass, your pretty tits in your sweatshirt."

"Roll up the partition," she moans between kisses. A growl rumbles in my chest as I reach for the button, unwilling to break contact for a second.

My mind short-circuits at the realization—I'm about to fuck *the* Reese Sinclair. I haven't just wanted this for weeks; I've had a craving for her in the back of my mind for years. And I haven't just wanted. I've needed, craved, burned for. And now she's here, beneath my hands, surrendering to me, and I'm going to make damn sure she never forgets what it's like to be with Dante Hastings.

"You've turned me into someone I don't recognize," I pant. "Made me so obsessed with you since I had that first taste of your lips."

She gasps, arching against me, seeking more.

"I can't think straight when you're near me," I say. The words feel inadequate against the weight of what I'm trying to convey. "Can't think about anything but you."

My mouth crashes against hers with barely restrained violence. The streetlights flicker across her face.

"Me too," she moans.

"You drive me out of my mind, Reese. Then you go and put my ring around your pearls." I suck in my teeth.

She touches it with a deliberate slowness.

"Do you like it?"

"Fucking love it."

"Take me." She's begging now, her fingers digging into my shoulders.

"I've got what we need."

I pull out a condom from my wallet.

Nothing exists beyond us—just the leather seats creaking beneath us, her soft body molding perfectly to mine. I push aside the rest of her skirt. She slides down her panties while I roll the condom on.

"Here's what's going to happen, Reese. I'm going to fill this pussy up with my cock. And you." I exhale, not wanting to rush this. "You are going to take every last inch. Understand?"

She nods. Positioning myself at her entrance, her body splayed out before me, I slowly break my forty-four-day streak while staring into her beautiful brown eyes.

The sensation is overwhelming—tight, hot, enveloping me completely. Her body accepts me as if we were designed for this.

Her lips are my new addiction, sweet and pliant and perfect. The delicate scent of her perfume fills the confined space until I'm dizzy with want.

She moans, jutting her hips, and fuck, I'm about to come on the spot.

It's too good. Better than I imagined.

Fuck.

I've always prided myself on being in control, on keeping things casual. But with her, it's different. Every touch feels like coming home. The way her eyes flutter shut when pleasure overtakes her. The way she seems to always fight two parts of herself. Maybe that's the Gemini in her. Maybe that's the real Reese and Reese Sinclair.

Tonight, I get to have both. Tonight, I'm making all of her mine.

"More," she begs. I take a nipple between my lips. She rocks on my cock as I savor the salt on her skin. I've never felt this fucking turned on before. I'm trying so hard not to come. I want to make her feel good first.

"Fuck, wait—" I swallow the rush. "This feels so fucking good. I have to slow down."

She doesn't care. Her hands wrap around my waist, pulling me closer. The way she surrenders to me awakens something fiercer than desire, her inner muscles fluttering around me in a rhythm that makes my vision blur.

"Dante." She says my name like a prayer, and her pussy tenses around me.

Get it the fuck together, man.

"*Milaya,*" I whisper against her ear, and she shivers at the Russian endearment. "The things you do to me." My hands slide down to her hips, steadying her as she arches against me. "*Ty menya okoldovala.*" The foreign words roll off my tongue. "You bewitch me."

The way she envelops me is unlike anything I've ever known —as if she's wrapped herself around my very existence.

"I'm going to mess you up again and you're going to love it, aren't you?" I don't break my pace inside of her as I unclasp her pearl necklace and yank it off. I roll the gems between my fingertips.

"I am," she exhales.

I trail the pearls down her body, watching her shiver at their smooth touch. I keep slowly rocking into her. Her skin is a perfect shade of flushed. I wrap her necklace, with my ring still attached, around my fingers and place it on her clit, tortuously rolling the beads over her.

"Oh," she mewls. So fucking beautiful. "Oh my god. That—"

"Feels good, huh?" I groan, lost in the way she feels. "Your precious pearls rubbing up against your pussy." She parts her lips in this expression of pure pleasure that makes my chest tight. Then comes her smirk—that goddamn confident smirk that's haunted my dreams—and I drive deeper, claiming more of her, rolling the pearls faster.

Her eyes go wide, pupils blown with pleasure, and I know I'm moments from getting her there. But I don't want this to end too soon.

"Keep talking in Russian," she demands. She's close. Not hiding, not performing—just present, real, desperate.

"*Ty moya*," I growl. "Right now, wrapped around my hard cock, you're mine. Every. Damn. Part of you." My free hand digs into her hips, probably leaving marks. Good. "Aren't you, Reese? Getting fucked just how you like."

When she tightens around me, I have to stop moving entirely. Sweat trickles down my temple as I fight for control, wanting to make this last forever.

"You're making me—Dante—" She falters. The car fills with her scent—cedar and magnolias mixed with leather and sex.

"That's my girl." The words come out rough, primal. Her eyes lock with mine. "Come for me, baby. Come all over this cock and fucking mean it."

She tries to hold back the wave of pleasure, her teeth sinking into my shoulder as she conceals her gasping release. I come at the same time as her, wrapped in latex and the tight heat of her warmth.

Fuck. It's even better than I imagined. This release after forty-four days without any—I nearly pass out.

The windows are completely fogged now, like we're in our own private universe. But reality intrudes with a cleared throat.

"Mr. Hastings, we've arrived at Miss Sinclair's house," my driver announces through the intercom. My cock still throbbing inside her, I curse under my breath.

I pull out reluctantly, working off the condom and dropping it into the bin in the back of the limo before buttoning up my pants. "Come to my hotel. Let's not call it a night."

"Not tonight." The words carry a teasing lilt. The way she keeps me wanting more is maddening.

I help her smooth down her dress. She allows me to fix her lipstick, watching me with those eyes that seem to hold entire conversations we never speak aloud. When I tuck a stray curl behind her ear, my fingertips brush against her skin, and time stretches, thin and delicate.

I get out first, Ramsey's presence a dark outline in the window as I open her door. She steps out and turns to leave, and there's something devastating about watching her choose to walk away.

I find my voice. "Don't forget your pearls."

She looks over her shoulder, and I toss her the necklace, watching it trace a gentle arc through the air between us. She catches it, as if she knew exactly where it would be.

"See you back on set in a week, Mr. Hastings."

There goes Reese. She is both the woman I spar with, who lets me be myself, and Reese Sinclair, the untouchable star I've wanted since before I understood want. The distinction between these versions of her grows less clear each time we're together.

We'll return to set and maintain our arrangement—sex without complications, and by December we'll wrap up filming. Next year, the USFA committee will have me back, image sparkling clean, and she'll have drummed up sufficient publicity for *Robyn Hood*.

But then what?

This ache in my chest, persistent and unnamed, will fade. It has to.

Chapter 29
Dante

Reese Sinclair Living Her Best Life: Star Lets Loose After Creative Differences with Felix—And We're Here for It!

Breaking Free: Reese Sinclair Shows Her Wild Side, and Fans Are Loving This New Era!

America's Sweetheart Reese Sinclair Gets a New Knight in Shining Armor—Dante Hastings to the Rescue!

Robyn Hood Gets Fresh Blood: Can Academy-Award Winning Director Amara Bellamy and

Hollywood's New Favorite Bad Girl Reese
Create Magic Together?

FRANKIE

wait hold up…tabloids say u weren't drunk at the party last night???

Awwwww reese is changing u

DANTE

Need my wits about me when I'm with her. Can't risk fucking this up.

Besides, my liver's probably begging for mercy after a decade of champagne.

BROOKLYN

Is my baby brother actually growing up?

But seriously, you look…different. Good different.

DANTE

I am.

FRANKIE

btw Amara left your precious yacht in my possession darling brother

might have 2 use it as collateral in a teensy tiny bet

this absolute TWAT thinks his pathetic excuse for driving can beat my lap time LMAOOO

DANTE

…

If you lose my yacht, I want your Porsche 911 turbo.

FRANKIE

over my dead body x

The Bay Area fog creeps over the bay, blanketing the city

from view in my Nob Hill apartment. My phone's pressed to my ear as I survey my barely lived-in space, my sleek leather couch and carefully curated modern art collection. I've been home more in the last week than I have in years.

My laptop is open to two unread emails from Marcus going over Reese's new stunt choreography. The one I've just read, however, is from Coach, delivering news I have no interest in hearing.

He answers on the second ring.

"What? It's three in the morning here," he grumbles. He's at another tournament in Madrid this week.

"Just saw your email. What do you mean I can't go to watch Em?"

"Committee, they make things very clear—you cannot be anywhere near a USFA event." I imagine him rubbing that giant wrinkle on his forehead.

"It's a goddamn high school tournament, not the fucking Olympics. It's not even a big competition."

My Olympic gold medal is buried beneath a mess of old receipts and loose change, untouched since May.

Since my suspension. Since they took everything from me.

"*Da*, but if anyone see you there, committee will make suspension permanent, no going back."

This is stupid.

Em let it slip tonight that her parents aren't coming to her first tournament in three weeks. I asked Coach to ask the organizers if I could go.

Clearly, they're assholes. But I need to be there for Em.

Her voice echoes in my head. *They have my baby sister to take care of. She's five. Third attempt to get one of us right, I guess. My brother bolted before I hit middle school.*

The tournament allows kids in the audience, so it was a flimsy excuse, but I knew what she was trying to say. The middle child sandwiched between others.

She wants to get out of her situation, and I want to help her. She may not have the financial resources, but at least now she has me, and the right people can get you far.

"Her parents aren't coming. She needs someone there for her."

"I am flying back home that weekend. I will be there, and you say Sadie shows much promise for doing well too."

While Coach has been gone this week, he left me and the assistant manager in charge of the youth program. Most of the ten kids are hopeless, which is probably why he tapped me to train Em. She never would've improved if she'd stayed with the rest of them.

"Yes, but I want to be there. Besides, she only listens to me."

In the past week, I haven't seen any signs of her stealing, so maybe I'm getting through to her.

"And what do you think I have been doing for three months while you sail around on fancy boat, huh? Reading her bedtime stories like *babushka*?"

"You know what I mean. You're too old-school. She won't get you."

"Listen here," he says, voice dropping to a dangerous whisper. "Your reputation dangles like thread in wind. You cannot go."

My breath shudders.

"But Coach, it's her first competition." We've only had eight training sessions, but sparring together brings people close, fast. She's counting on me. I don't want to let her down.

"Ah, Dante." He clicks his tongue. "I knew this girl would mend something broken in you."

"Must you always be right?"

"Is like I tell you, you have soft heart for this one. Took her under your wing, exactly as I predicted."

"I'll work something out. The rules say I can't be *at* a

competition; they don't say anything about being *near* a competition."

I walk past my bedroom, and my eyes catch on the dagger resting on my dresser, untouched since I bought it weeks ago.

I've been waiting for the perfect moment to give it to Reese. Maybe once *Robyn Hood* hits number one at the box office. A blade for a true fighter.

"Whatever scheme is brewing in that thick skull of yours, *organizuyetsya po fekhtovaniyu* already breathing fire down my neck. Next season you must return to competition, or even my influence runs dry. Especially with media circus."

"I was saving her from a black eye. They're calling me a knight in shining armor." I rake my fingers through my hair, frustration mounting. "That's hardly something the committee will frown upon."

"Press always hungry for scandal like starving bear, Dante." My groan echoes against the windows. "Did you forget you have another *zoloto* to win?"

I flinch. Of course I have another gold in me.

"I've dedicated the past decade to my career. I wouldn't put it in jeopardy if I thought Reese could make me look bad. She's America's sweetheart, for fuck's sake." I settle on the end of my bed. "I know what I'm doing. If the committee is actually reading up on celebrity gossip, then they're going to see me as someone other than the guy who punched Quentin."

"I don't like this one bit."

"Trust me, every committee member will be begging for *Robyn Hood* premiere tickets in a month. They'll meet Reese and me, I'll sign some headshots, work my magic. Problem solved," I say, my chest constricting as I casually leverage Reese's fame without her permission.

"Life is not like Hollywood fairy tale, where everything bends to pretty smile and charm."

"And why the hell not?"

"Stay out of trouble, *pozhaluysta*."

"I will."

"And, Dante, you are watching little ones this week before running back to your big movie, *da*?"

"*Da*, old man, wouldn't miss it," I say. I know he sees right through me, down to the scared kid still trying to prove something.

Maybe he always has.

Chapter 30
Reese

REESE

Hypothetically speaking…after your training wraps and you're back filming, what if I acquired some craft services contraband and hosted an intimate soirée at my cabin? Strictly under the radar, of course

DANTE

Miss Sinclair, are you attempting to woo me with stolen snacks?

REESE

Only the finest day-old bread and questionable cheese for you, darling

DANTE

Perhaps I could upgrade our feast with some fresh-baked bread…

REESE

And maybe some artisanal cheese to match?

DANTE

You drive a hard bargain. Count me in.

AMARA BELLAMY IS ten minutes early to our one-on-one meeting.

I love her already.

We rush through the hellos, and I can't help it—five minutes in, I'm fangirling. She's the one person who can make me feel small and starstruck, even though I'm here, too, with my name on the poster. She exudes confidence in her red power suit and matching nails. She's nothing like other directors I've met.

The late afternoon sun filters through the director's tent, the cool breeze carrying the scent of sandalwood as she moves. The headlines have been perfect lately—*Sinclair Goes Rogue*—and with the reporters gone back to LA, the set has become quiet, turning back into a sanctuary.

We decided to keep our return to the redwoods under wraps, allowing us time to rebuild the movie in peace.

Amara's laptop clicks open, her Hobonichi Techo journal already marked with colorful tabs and notes.

"Before we bring in the producers," she says, her pen hovering over fresh paper, "I want to explore your interest in directing. This movie could be a sort of apprenticeship, if you want it, since you've been on set this entire time. On the call, you seemed to have a clear vision of where you want the movie to go. I thought we could help each other."

My throat tightens with unexpected emotion. Sure, I mentioned my interest in directing on our original call, but with the timeline being so tight, I didn't want to get my hopes up. But she's right here, offering to make it real.

"I would be honored," I say, pinching myself under the table.

"I've carefully reviewed Felix's footage." She taps on her laptop's mouse pad three times, bringing it to life. "The good news is we can keep a significant portion of the establishing shots, character introductions, and dialogue scenes. It's mainly the action sequences and character development scenes that need reshooting to properly capture Robyn's essence. With our current schedule, we can absolutely complete everything within the original timeline. What do you think about this approach?"

"Oh, thank the heavens!" I throw up my hands. "That sounds perfect."

Her shoulders slacken, like she was up all night figuring out how to tell me that she hated Felix's cut.

"I knew I liked you." She wiggles her manicured fingers together. "Also, I'm so sorry, but I can't stop staring at your arms. They look insane!"

"Thank you. It's great to be strong for a change." I rub a hand over my bicep.

"Robyn will need your strength, especially since I'm bringing on a female trainer for you since Nick left with Felix. Unless you'd rather have Dante train you?"

"I love training with Dante," I admit, "but having female trainers would be great too. Sometimes guys don't quite—"

"Understand how women's bodies work?

"Exactly!" Though Dante, my traitorous mind reminds me, seems to understand my body just fine. I clear my throat and my thoughts. "I'd love a female trainer, and it would be nice to run choreography with the crew and stunt team before we start filming. It'll give us a week to sync up before the other actors return to set."

"Wasn't that happening before?" Amara's brow furrows.

"Felix had different ideas about *authenticity*," I explain.

"Usually, I run all the choreography at the table read before we start filming. But since we won't be starting from square one, we'll do run-throughs in the gym on Sundays—to make sure everything looks good before we continue shooting on Mondays."

"That's excellent," I agree.

I lean back, calculating. "Barely two weeks after our original wrap date with Felix. Can we really do it?"

"Oh, we're doing it," she says. "My team's the best, and since you're backing this financially, we're giving you everything we've got."

I'll miss my weekly Sunday outings with Dante, but this movie is my first priority.

She snaps back into business mode as she opens up a file called "costume sketches." And goodness, they are beautiful.

My eyes widen. A structured green tunic that allows for movement, tactical pants with real pockets, and boots made for running and fighting. The leather armor suit for combat scenes looks powerful without being exploitative. Finally, clothing designed for action, not the male gaze.

Hours fly by as we plot action sequences, hair and makeup, and character arcs. The sexy, clumsy Robyn of Felix's vision dissolves, replaced by a fighter who knows her worth. Every training schedule, every choreography note, every minor script revision aligns with this new truth.

"Do you have any scenes you're concerned about?" she asks when she notices my lingering gaze on the underwater sequence storyboards. "What made you nervous about filming with Felix?"

I hesitate, then exhale. With her, I feel safe enough to be honest. "To be fully transparent, I'm afraid of diving underwater. But I've been working on it, and I want to do it myself—no stunt double. But wearing armor makes it more terrifying, especially the thought of struggling to breach the surface. And I don't want to do it the way Felix suggested, with that unnecessarily revealing costume."

Her pen is already marking changes. "We're scrapping that approach entirely. Light clothing, a dagger instead of that ridiculous sword. We'll take our time, do test runs. This scene should showcase your strength, not your vulnerability."

Relief crashes over me like a wave, bringing unexpected tears to my eyes. I blink them back, but she notices.

Having a director who listens, who adapts, who respects my boundaries. No more being pushed into uncomfortable situations or told to "just deal with it." She sees me as a collaborator.

"This is what directing should be," she says softly, pushing a box of tissues my way without making a fuss. "We find solutions together. And trust me, we're about to show those testosterone-fueled action films how it's really done."

"Thank you, Amara."

"I'm so glad Dante introduced us," she sighs. "I've known him since Princeton. And I don't know what's going on between you two—I don't need to know. But trust me, the bad-boy thing he puts on? It's exactly like Robyn's armor. Dante's got layers most people never see." She gives me a pointed look. "Just like someone else I know, who hides behind politeness."

I open my mouth to protest, then close it with a laugh. Caught.

Her grin turns devilish. "And hey, whenever you need extortion material on Dante, I'm your girl. Wait till you hear about his tweed newsboy cap."

"His what?"

"Oh yes," she cackles. "Princeton-era Dante wouldn't be caught dead without one. Thought he was channeling Cillian Murphy in *Peaky Blinders*."

"Well, now that you mention it"—I laugh —"he does have that same brooding intensity."

"Remind me later," she says, "and I'll show you enough photos to absolutely destroy him."

"I seriously love working with you," I beam.

"Good. Because we're about to change some narratives around here."

"Hell yes!"

The headlines flash through my mind—*Hollywood's New Power Player Takes Control*—no longer gossip, but prophecy. I'm not just starring anymore. I'm executive producing, profit sharing, learning to direct. I'm writing my own story.

Nothing can touch me now.

Nothing can go wrong.

REESE

Diamond Essence shoot got moved to tomorrow. We're still on for our impromptu training between takes?

DANTE

Perfect excuse to escape SF for a bit.

How's Mari treating you?

REESE

Barely coming up for air, but the script is
chef's kiss

She's everything

DANTE

Told you you'd fall for her.

REESE

Speaking of falling…maybe we could find
some trouble after the shoot?

Need one last adventure before nine weeks of
all work no play.

DANTE

I know just the place.

Chapter 31
Dante

THE STEERING WHEEL yields beneath my grip as I take another turn, the Porsche's tires creating the precise sound Frankie warned against. The black paparazzi SUV that's been following us finally concedes defeat.

It's a thrill driving a fast car with Reese in the passenger seat, pressing her nails into my thigh.

"I think we lost them."

"Your driving is atrocious, Mr. Hastings," Ramsey grumbles from the back seat. He's folded himself into what can only be described as security guard origami, his knees practically touching his ears.

Reese's laugh fills the car like sunshine. "Oh, come on, Ramsey! That was incredible!"

"Reckless."

"We could always make you walk," I offer, catching his glare in the rearview mirror. "Though watching you unfold might take us until next Tuesday."

"We might need a crane and a team of engineers to extract you," she teases.

"Or industrial lubricant," he deadpans, the vein in his neck twitching. "Perhaps some prayer."

"Look at you, making jokes!" Reese beams at him, and he smirks. The stoic bastard's warming up to me, I can tell.

"But I have to be the annoying voice of reason here," she says, scrunching her nose in that adorable way. "Why are we doing our best *Fast & Furious* impression?"

"The photographers already got what they needed at the beach—us running through that stunt routine in between shots. They ate it up. Why not get back to being just Reese and Dante?"

I've been mulling it over all day, staying away from the cameras. Coach made his point clear, and as much as I hate to admit it, he's right about the optics. Ten years of fencing, and though I enjoy being seen with Reese, I need to think long term. I want back on the piste, and bad coverage is a liability I can't afford. If Coach believes the press hurts my chances, then I need to stay as low-key as possible while still supporting Reese.

It's all about playing the game we've set. Me showing up to her shoot to fit in some extra training? Perfect. Total marketing gold.

And Reese? When she dropped everything to work on her choreography with me. That's the kind of thing that gets the committee excited—real wholesome, hero material.

But the committee's so obsessed with their image that even taking her to a bar could blow everything up. Especially with the stunt I'm pulling by showing up to Em's match. If they catch wind of that, it's game over for the disciplinary review.

But fuck it. I'm done letting them control everything. I want one night—just one—where it's us. No cameras, no bullshit. Is that too much to ask?

Reese gives me a skeptical look. "Mm-hmm, if you say so."

"I want you all to myself tonight, before filming starts on Monday, and the only time I get to see you is during training and our scenes together. Marcus has already been emailing me daily with updates."

"I'm sure we can sneak in some other training sessions too." She giggles, touching the pearls around her neck. "But honestly, I do not mind a little spin in this Porsche. Yours?"

"Frankie's. One of her babies. She treats them better than she treats me, honestly."

"How many does she have?"

"God, I've lost count. But don't worry, at the Hastings Gala, she'll give you a detailed PowerPoint presentation about each one, complete with their birthdays and favorite motor oil."

"I can't wait to meet everyone," she says quietly. Her fingers brush past the adorable headband she wore the first time I met her, searching for hair to twist.

She's nervous. I am too, if I'm being honest. I've brought women home before, sure—the usual entourage that orbits around me. But Reese is different.

"You'll love them, and they already love you. Brooklyn and Frankie haven't stopped talking about your gifts." I leave out how my sisters spent hours dissecting every detail of the package she sent: the autographed posters, *Robyn Hood* merchandise, even the signature Reese Sinclair cosmetics line. Their enthusiasm was endearing.

My gaze drifts to my forearm, where her signature from that night after Wizard Island has long since faded. I should have booked a tattoo appointment the next morning, should have made it permanent.

"Maybe that's why Frankie let you borrow her car?" She nudges me. "Because I earned you some coveted big brother brownie points?"

"It helped. That, and I kind of just took it." I laugh.

A week on set has turned her into something otherworldly, and it's not just the photoshoot glow. She's more at ease, wearing the same dress she wore in the picture she sent me from NOLA —I'm certain she wore it just to torment me.

"I've looked forward to seeing you," I say.

"I can tell." Her hand creeps up my thigh, thumb tracing the semi that's been in my trousers since she got into the car. I grit my teeth, eyes locked on where her sundress hits just above her knee. She shifts, revealing more of her thigh, sending a pulse straight through me.

Ramsey's grunt echoes from the back.

"We should invest in noise-cancelling headphones and a blindfold for our shadow," I say, catching his reflection in the rearview. His scowl has evolved into an expression of disapproval that's artistic.

So much for thinking he's coming around.

"Oh, speaking of just taking things, I grabbed you something." She rummages through her purse and pulls out a piece of fruit.

My eyebrows knit together. "An apple?"

"Not just any apple," she says, all proud of herself. "It's exactly like the one you had at the table read. Oh, wait." She sinks her teeth into the red flesh. "Much better. Wanna share it?" She does her best impression of me.

"Such darling manners." I laugh, snatch the apple from her hand, and take a loud, crisp bite—making a show of it—before handing it back to her.

She takes it, leaning in and taking another slow, deliberate bite. Her lips press along the apple.

Fucking hell. Add eating fruit to the list of things Reese can make erotic.

Silver Lake materializes before us, the streets alive with their usual nocturnal pulse. I slide to the front of the club, intent on getting inside before anyone notices us. I toss the keys to the valet.

The Velvet Mirage looms ahead, its imposing door wedged

between the mundane façades of a bookstore and a laundromat—a secret hiding in plain sight.

Another taste of my world for my girl.

"This is…interesting," she notes, taking in the black concrete block exterior. No windows, a silver reflective door that mirrors our figures standing together, and above it a marquee that glows with the words, *Temptation awaits*.

I don't bother explaining. Some things are better discovered than described.

"Let me guess—this is your Virgil act?" she teases, nudging my shoulder. "Leading me through the gates of Hell?"

I grin at the reference. Of course she'd make the connection to my namesake's *Inferno*. "Second circle. Lust," I say, pausing for effect. "Though I promise it's better than my predecessor's version."

"Well, Paolo and Francesca did get to spend eternity together. In some twisted, cruel way."

"You know your Dante," I say, impressed. "But I think we can do better than star-crossed lovers."

"Oh yeah?"

"In our canto, we'll make sure that breaking the rules leads to paradise instead of punishment," I say, holding the door.

Inside, we step into darkness. A single amber bulb dangles over the hostess stand, barely penetrating the thick shadows. Heavy velvet curtains drape the walls, their presence more sensed than seen.

Beyond them, jazz music whispers of what's to come, the main room still concealed behind another set of drapes. Reese takes in the mystery, her fingers trailing along the velvet rope that marks our path.

A hostess appears, graceful in a black dress. "Mr. Hastings, to what do we owe the pleasure?"

"Been a while. Wanted to check out how our lovely performers are getting on."

"Of course. Phones," she says, holding out a velvet pouch. "House rules." We drop our phones in. "Follow me."

She parts the long curtains, and Reese steps into a room made of dark cherry wood. Stained glass chandeliers from Morocco cast fractured colors across mirrored walls. Leather booths curve along the edges.

The jazz music thrums, *bum, bum, bum.*

Reese's pupils dilate, flashing from me to the stage, where dancers' heels clack.

Our booth sits at the edge of the stage, perfectly positioned, because that's what you can buy here—perfect positions. Ramsey maintains his professional distance while a bottle of champagne arrives unordered.

"Dante Hastings, are we…?" She shuffles closer to me in the booth, like she's scared of this place.

"Yes, Miss Sinclair?"

Her mouth stays open. "Are we at a sex club?"

"Not exactly." I drop my hand to her thigh. "Though desire lingers in every shadow here. It's more an exploration of what we deny ourselves."

Reese gawks at the women on stage, who are peeling off their gloves in controlled longing.

"Burlesque," I whisper into her hair.

The juxtaposition is exquisite. Her pristine sundress, innocent pink headband, the delicate pearl necklace against my ring. My cock stirs at the sight of her flushed.

"You like it?" I play with the edge of her dress, dying to touch her skin.

Reese peeks around the booth. "This is definitely on the list of things that might bring you bad press."

"This place breeds discretion." I pause. "I'm an investor, actually."

"Really?" Her eyes go wide as I pour a glass of champagne. "What other secrets are you keeping in that portfolio of yours?"

I can't explain it, but I'm eager to impress her.

"My money comes from the usual post-Olympic vanity projects—cologne campaigns, fashion lines—and my parents made sure each sibling received enough shares of Viggle that the returns alone mean none of us ever needs to work. But what really took off were some investments I made back in Princeton. Threw some money at a few brilliant nerds hunched over laptops. Turns out their caffeine-fueled coding sessions were worth something. I happened to have the cash and, let's say, a talent for recognizing potential."

"Oh, so that's how you got into D&D?" she chuckles.

"The Princeton D&D sessions had their own particular rules. The dice determined things beyond mere combat rolls." Another pause, deliberate this time. "Clothing was often the first casualty."

"Do you miss being at those kinds of parties?" she asks, her voice steady but her fingers fidgeting with the hem of her dress. "With people who enjoy those kinds of things?"

The question hangs between us. What she's really asking is clear: *Am I enough to hold someone like you?*

I look at her, considering lying.

I've always been good at that—saying what people want to hear. But with her, the thought of it makes my stomach turn. "That's a complex question."

"It's actually pretty simple," she counters, chin lifting. "I'm wondering what makes *this* different from your usual rotation."

"Because you're not in a rotation," I say, too quickly, too defensively. I rake a hand through my hair, frustrated by my inability to articulate something that feels so obvious to me. "Look, before, everything was transactional. Even when I didn't mean for it to be."

"And now?" Her eyes are bright, challenging, but there's vulnerability there too.

The real answer scares me. This isn't about fucking or escaping. It's about presence. When I'm with her, everything intensifies, expands. My feelings deepen with frightening clarity.

I need her. Not want—*need*.

The distinction matters.

There are parts of myself that never aligned properly before —fragments that existed without context, pieces I kept hidden. With her, these disjointed elements find coherence.

She sees me.

I recognize the banality of it. How utterly predictable it is for me to fall into the cliché I spent years avoiding. But perhaps clichés persist because they contain some essential truth, one that's impossible to articulate without sounding trite.

We sit together in the semidarkness, her question hanging between us. I could deflect with charm, but I don't. The truth is simpler and more complex than either of us is prepared to acknowledge.

"I used to accumulate things, experiences. People, sometimes. Now I want…what I'm trying to say is that it's a different kind of wanting." The words feel inadequate. "Because when you look at things, they become worth looking at again."

"That might be the smoothest thing you've ever said to me."

"Yeah, well. Smooth is what I do when I don't care." She lets me hold her hand under the table. "This is messier."

"Messy looks good on you," she says softly.

I kiss her, gently at first, then with more intent when she responds. When I pull back, the saxophone shifts to a more sensual tone. "Now, watch this part," I murmur, turning her toward the stage as the lights dim around us.

A spotlight blooms across parting curtains, illuminating a tableau of half-naked, glimmering bodies adorned in fishnets and corsets. A woman in crimson steps forward, rolling her hips, as a man follows, shirtless and dragging his hand across her torso.

"I've never…" She gulps. "Never let myself be so…"

"Comfortable with your sexuality?"

"That." Reese hides behind her champagne glass, her eyes shyly skittering across the dancers. She scoots forward, intrigued but terrified, like she's walking on the edge of a mountain. "I wish I could be. Connect with that part of myself, you know? That piece of my life has always been repackaged and sold. It's always been directed for an audience. I've never had control over it."

"What's stopping you from taking control right now?" I slowly move her hair aside, kissing along her neck. There's the smell of magnolia on her skin, which kills my self-control.

"Dante," she whispers, a warning and a desire.

"I'm serious. The only person who can dictate that part of you is you. In the private and public eye. Your sexuality is yours, Reese," I remind her. "And it's splendid."

"You think I can do what they're doing up there?"

"Why not? Tell me what you see," I command, wanting her to use her words. "Don't miss a detail."

"They're dancing," she quavers, and my cock strains against my trousers.

"I think you can do better than that." I move my hand up her thigh. "Who catches your eye?"

"They're all…" She pauses, biting her lip. "The redhead."

"Why?"

The woman slides down into a split, her nails trailing over her legs before she snaps her head back, looking directly at Reese.

"Because she's moving like she knows every eye is on her. She moves like she's the star."

"And the rest?"

She inhales sharply. I touch the strand of pearls at her throat. I drag my tongue along the cool gems until I reach my silver ring.

"Behind her—oh—" Her composure breaks, and mine threatens to follow. "They dance like something from a dream."

My hand finds her thigh and travels higher and higher until I reach the layer of silk beneath her cotton sundress. *Now what do we have here?* "The one in leather, feathers, a chrome mask—"

"Go on." The words come out strained. I'm achingly hard now, every nerve ending alive.

"The music…" She's struggling to focus, and I'm struggling to not take her right here. "It's like watching heartbeats." My fingers trace higher, searching for whatever other surprises she's keeping hidden. When my thumb finds its mark, I trace wet lace, not her regular cotton panties. "The dancer in black in those restraints, like you've said in the past, the control and surrender."

In the mirrored wall beside us, I watch the performance reflected behind Reese's silhouette.

"The m-music—" A dancer slowly peels away her corset, jeweled pasties catching the light. "It's like watching sin made beautiful. Dante, please…"

"Tell me what it makes you want to do."

"It's…" She turns. "Pure want." Her cheeks are flushed. "I want to be up there with them."

My breath is shallow as I attempt the careful façade of control. "Do it."

"I don't know." Her brown eyes contain multitudes—rebellion, desire, a hint of that competitive spirit I've grown to need like oxygen. "Is that even allowed?"

"It's my club. The choice is all yours, Reese."

Chapter 32
Reese

"Reese." Dante's mouth caresses my name like he's savoring it.

The piano quickens, each note tumbling through the red-stained club. My shoulders shimmy, feeling the music.

I'm transfixed by the dancers. I want to be up there.

I want to make Dante watch. I want to make everyone watch.

I don't want to be perfect, choreographed, or directed. I want instinct.

I'm done asking what Robyn would do.

Tonight is about me. *What does Reese want?*

My feet move before my mind can second-guess.

A dancer reaches for me—leather harness, exposed skin, body humming with invitation. I take her hand and let go.

The dancers spill around me like paint. Fluid, untethered— none of the control I've shaped my life around. Their hands brush my skin, and heat blooms. My pulse pounds at my throat, my wrists, behind my knees.

The air has gone thick like molasses, coating my lungs with each labored breath. My thoughts shatter like glass. I'm dissolving, becoming pure sensation—just nerve endings and wanting and the endless, endless ache. The music pulses through me until I can't tell where rhythm ends and my body begins.

The spotlight shifts, shining on me.

Everyone is looking at me.

He is looking at me.

I feel divine.

I keep moving. My sundress whispers against my thighs. My hair weighs heavy on my neck. A dancer's hands gently find my waist. I melt back into her touch.

"There you go, darling. Show them how you shine," comes a whispered encouragement.

Red light transforms me into something wicked, something wanting. My body burns with a hunger that feels like I've stepped into my own inferno.

Dante leans forward in his seat, watching me. It feels physical, like hands on my skin.

I can't look away. Won't look away. My hips move in slow circles, and I imagine his hands there instead.

The thought makes my thighs clench.

I want to undress, like the rest of the performers on stage.

I find the zipper at my side and drag it down so slowly I ache. Everyone watches as I reveal what's underneath my floral sundress: the crimson Agent Provocateur slip I ordered in secret.

One strap falls.

Then another.

My skin prickles with exposure, with desire. A dancer helps me out of the rest of my dress, her touch professional but still electric.

I spent hours choosing this lingerie. Clicking through endless pages of lace and silk until I found exactly what I needed. The way it sits against my skin makes me feel powerful. Like I could be devoured whole.

When I look at him again, his legs are spread wider. His hand rests heavy on his upper thigh, touching the obvious bulge in his pants. It makes my mouth water. It makes me think about dropping to my knees right here.

The dancers move around me, teaching me their secrets.

How to arch. How to bend. How to make every movement drip with sex.

In the mirrors, I am transformed. My neck is flushed. My nipples are hard against the silk. I look exactly like what I am—desperate to be touched.

I'm grateful for the club's strict no-phones policy. No cameras. No flashes.

Just this sacred space where I can exist as myself, not Reese Sinclair the actress, not anyone's daughter or project.

Just a woman. Just movement. Just desire.

For the first time, I'm not playing at sensuality. I'm embodying it. Each sway of my hips is a love letter to my own liberation.

No more scripts. No more handlers. No more directors.

My pearls rest heavy at my throat. I lift them, biting his ring. My tongue traces it slowly, tasting the silver. Between my legs, I'm embarrassingly wet. The kind of wet that makes thinking impossible.

And, as if we're on the same plane of the ether, he's losing control too. I can see it in the way his fingers clench and unclench, the way his throat works as he swallows. The violence of his restraint feeds something dark and hungry inside me.

I want to break him. I want him to break me.

Dante rises from his seat like a man possessed, and the sight of his very obvious erection straining against expensive wool makes my body buzz.

My hair is still held in place by the same headband I wore to our first table read. When he got close enough to smell the perfume on my skin and neither of us moved away. I take off the headband and throw it directly at him.

He snatches it out of the air, bringing it to his nose and

inhaling so deeply it's like I am his oxygen. His careful mask shatters. Raw hunger stares back at me, honest and unashamed.

My gaze asks what my lips won't. *Do you like what you see?*

Beautiful, he mouths.

He sees me—wild, wanting, finally free.

I close my eyes and give myself to the music completely, to the ache between my legs that pulses in time with the bass. After tonight, I can never go back to being anyone other than this version of myself. The thought makes me dizzy with possibility.

It makes me feel infinite.

I AM on top of the world.

"Fuck yeah." I giggle, thinking of the taste of Ivory soap, how Grandma would wash out my mouth if I uttered any curses.

I grab my hairbrush, staring at myself in the mirror as I attempt to tame my sweaty, hairspray-tangled mess. Dante should be here to help me undo this nightmare. Instead, he dropped me off at my cabin after my jet landed back in Crescent City with a forehead kiss and his responsible insistence that I get some rest.

So responsible.

The bristles catch in the back of my hair, refusing to budge. I tug hard at my scalp. *Ouch.*

Beauty is pain.

I've heard it at least five times a year since my earliest memory of my mama braiding my hair. But why does it have to hurt so damn much? Everything about being a woman is a pain. Our periods. Push-up bras. Brazilian waxes. Eyebrow threading.

Every decision about my appearance has felt out of my control. My body, my face, my career have been in the hands of someone else.

After tonight's dance, I've taken back a part of myself I never realized I lost.

My sexuality. The sensual, yearning parts of me that Dante has awakened. And it feels so fucking good.

Everything I've wanted. I acted like an empress. I took charge. I'm an EP now. I'm playing an active role in this film by working with Amara. I'm almost thirty and no longer headed to playing roles as someone's mother. The world's reaction, all the media attention—it's working in my favor.

Everyone loves this new era of me taking charge, and oh, so do I!

I try to work through the knot in my hair, but the bristles don't move. The brush is still stuck, caught at the nape of my neck. I tug at it again, but it's not moving.

I grab my brush again, yanking it and wincing. "Ow, ow, ow!" It won't budge, it just hangs awkwardly from the side of my head like a bizarre fashion accessory. My eyes land on the kitchen scissors sitting on the counter, the ones I used to cut the labels off my lingerie set before I packed for LA. I can surely cut around this. Can't exactly walk around with a hairbrush in my head.

I mean, it's only at the back of my neck, right? Like no one would notice.

I carefully position the blades around the brush handle, the metal cool against my fingers. *Snip*. A chunk of hair falls free, along with the brush, and oh—the feeling is new.

Liberating.

I hold up the severed strands, watching them shimmer under the light.

This isn't simply my hair—it's been my identity my whole life. Now, between the pads of my fingers, it's simply fragments of my past self.

The Sinclair.

My signature look since I was eleven on *Clubhouse*. The

hairstyle that made me millions in hair care commercials, that made me Diamond Essence's ambassador for over a decade.

But gosh, it was like wearing a crown made of chains. It's beautiful and suffocating. I've spent years taming it, styling it, forcing it into submission.

And now, one more cut couldn't hurt.

"Screw. This." I punctuate each word and snip at it again. Then I hesitate.

Maybe I'm making a massive mistake? Should I text Heather to let her know? And what would Amara think if she saw this? What about Dante?

No. I'm not a child who needs her agent's permission to get a haircut.

I have control in this film, and the haircut could be a marvelous addition to Robyn's character. If Amara doesn't see it that way, then there are incredible wigs out there.

And Dante? He'll love it because I'm going to love it.

Doubt tries to creep in; I push it away.

This is my hair. My choice. I get to do whatever I want to it.

I keep cutting, unevenly, definitely too short in places.

Snip.

Snip.

SNIP.

Blonde strands flutter to the floor.

The scissors feel like freedom in my unsteady hands as I make the final cuts, my bare feet dancing through the fallen strands on cold tile.

When I lower the scissors, my reflection shows a choppy, uneven pixie cut. My neck feels exposed. I run my fingers through the short strands, marveling at how different it feels.

I feel lighter.

So much lighter.

It's messy, amateur, absolutely nothing like the polished Sinclair—and I love it.

Chapter 33
Reese

THREE QUICK TAPS come at my door.

Dante's here.

Oh no.

My stomach launches itself into freakin' Jupiter as I stare down the massacre of my signature hairstyle. The Sinclair lies in defeated chunks on my bathroom tile, and suddenly I'm very, very awake.

Who decided it was a good idea to put scissors in my cabin?

"I'll be right there," I call out, grabbing the fluffiest towel from my rack, wrapping it around my head, and scurrying to the door. My bare feet slip on the hardwood as I crack it open enough to peek through.

"Good morning." I throw him a practiced smile and try to sound like someone who definitely didn't perform DIY hair surgery at 1:00 a.m.

"What's going on?" His eyebrow quirks up.

"I got a little carried away last night."

Dante, being Dante, uses his unfair advantage of pure muscle to easily push the door wider. I clutch at my towel fortress as he takes in the scene—the bathroom looking like a blonde piñata exploded, the scissors still lying accusingly on the counter, my guilty expression.

"I'm guessing you didn't go to sleep like I told you."

"Wasn't tired." I shrug casually.

"What a rebel."

I lean against the wall, missing the corner and having to catch myself. The towel slips precariously, and I grab at it like it's my last shred of dignity.

"So you gonna show me what's under there?"

I shake my head, feeling significantly lighter under the weight of my towel. "It's bad." A bubble of hysterical laughter escapes me, the kind that comes when you've surpassed anxiety and landed in a strange sort of acceptance. "Like, 'cutting hair is not a natural talent of mine' kind of bad."

"It can't be that bad." He steps forward, and I retreat until my thighs hit my small kitchen table and I'm trapped between solid wood and his amused gaze. "Let me see."

My cheeks burn as I slowly lower the towel, watching his expression like I'm revealing a particularly gruesome wound.

Dante takes one look at my choppy, uneven disaster of a haircut and immediately presses his lips together, his whole face twitching with the effort not to laugh.

"Get it out now," I huff. "Here, I'll make it worth your while." I strike an exaggerated pose, like I'm on the cover of

Vogue and not standing in my kitchen looking like I lost a fight with a weed whacker.

He moves closer, his mouth quirking up with a specific kind of suppressed amusement that makes me want to simultaneously kiss him and throw something at his head.

"Reese," he says, with the kind of devastating sincerity that feels like being hit by a meteor, "you could shave your entire body, tattoo the complete works of Shakespeare backward across your forehead, and exclusively communicate through interpretive puppet shows featuring socks with googly eyes, and I'd still think you were the most breathtaking thing I've ever seen in my catastrophically extraordinary life."

Ugh, isn't that the most romantic thing anyone's ever said to me?

And now he's over here freaking just—AHHHHH!

I run to the bathroom, hiding my blush and brushing my fingers through my choppy disaster. "I—I don't know what I was thinking, but I spent my whole life with someone else controlling every single strand. And I mean, it started innocently, when my hairbrush got stuck, and then…well, once I started, I couldn't stop."

Dante follows me into the bathroom, and his expression melts into that tender look that makes my insides turn to mush.

"Reese," he says softly, "you don't need anyone's permission to be yourself." He bends down and places a kiss on my forehead that feels like absolution.

"Yeah, well, being myself apparently means looking like Weird Barbie." I laugh shakily. "Heather's going to freak! I need to call her so she can send someone to salvage this mess."

"Let me do it," he says, eyes sparkling.

"You?" I blink. "Since when are you a hairdresser?"

"I cut my own hair," he says. "And I trim for my fencing team. There are skills I possess that might surprise you, though I hesitate to enumerate them."

I eye him suspiciously. "The last thing I need is to look like an eighth-grade boy who discovered online hair tutorials."

"Please," he smirks. "I'm about to create the next big thing. The Sinclair 2.0—edgy, bold, and completely yours. Let me grab my shears, clippers, and comb from my cabin."

"Are you sure?"

"Yes."

Dante jogs to his cabin, returning moments later with a small black case that looks far too professional for someone who claims to just trim for the team. He guides me to sit in front of my bathroom mirror, draping a towel around my shoulders.

"Ready?"

"As I'll ever be." I sit on my hands, pressing them into the wooden chair. "But I was thinking, instead of the Sinclair 2.0, I want this to be the Reese 1.0."

"Done." He pats my shoulder, looking at my reflection like he knows what it's like to be reduced to your last name.

"I didn't think I'd be doing this on my first day back on set," Dante chuckles, combing through what's left of my hair with expert fingers, each touch impossibly gentle. His brow furrows in concentration as he sections off pieces, measuring twice before each precise cut.

The soft snip of the scissors feels different now, careful, nothing like my hack job.

Right…filming!

We start tomorrow. "Oh no, I need to figure out how to tweak the script and tell Mari," I say, eyeing my laptop, a beat of hesitation stuck in my throat. I really hope she likes it.

My mind wanders to the script changes we'll need to make. Maybe I can swing this for Robyn's character arc, especially since we're tossing out most of the old footage of me anyway.

"I'm sure Mari will love this new look. She had short hair through most of college." He squints, a crease forming on the bridge of his nose. "Plus, it'll save time in hair and makeup."

True.

"Actually, now that I think about it, there's a strong case for Robyn chopping her hair. She's in the middle of a whole self-discovery arc. I could wear a wig for the first few scenes—it would make sense."

He smiles at me. "The most important thing is that you're happy."

"I am. The other great part is nobody knows we're back on set and filming this week. As long as the crew keeps things under wraps, I can probably hide my hair for a bit. They haven't leaked anything from last week, so I think they're trustworthy."

"We could just have you wear a beanie until Amara's intro speech tomorrow. Mornings are getting colder anyway."

I like the fact that he's looking for solutions.

"Oh my heavens, I can't wait to feel the cold air on my head. And this is going to take so little shampoo to wash." My heart drops. "What if Diamond Essence hates it? I've been with them for ten years." I pause, shaking my head. "That would be silly, right? Short-haired people wash their hair too. I'm sure Heather can handle it!"

Does he know how much he's helped me understand that I crave control? I'm calling the shots to make this movie successful—my idea, my choice, my rules.

"I like watching your mind at work," Dante says.

"I'm excited." Energy radiates from my body, making me feel like I could probably lift a car. "Everything feels like it makes sense."

"You know what else makes sense?" he says softly. "How right this feels."

My heart palpitates. "The haircut?"

"Everything about—" He clears his throat. "Everything about this new look. It suits you perfectly."

"Tilt your head forward," he murmurs, one hand cupping my chin to guide me. His thumb brushes against my jaw, and I let go. I close my eyes, surrendering to his steady hands grazing my scalp, the quiet brush of his shoulder against mine as he checks his work, the faint rasp of his voice that tickles my neck when he murmurs instructions.

The rest of the world fades away until there's only this—the quiet rhythm of his movements, the tender way he turns my head this way and that.

It feels like trust.

We've only known each other for two months. I've played every role in every rom-com script: slow burn, enemies to lovers, and the insta-love couple. The last was always the hardest heroine to play. I've spent countless hours wondering how anyone could feel so strongly about someone in an instant. But maybe it's not the amount of time that matters.

Maybe it's just the person.

"I don't regret it," I whisper. "Any of it."

"Good."

When he runs the clippers up the nape of my neck, the vibration tingles down my spine. I bite my lip to keep from making an embarrassing sound.

"Almost done," he says.

A few more careful snips, his fingers ghosting along my hairline, and then he's combing his hands through the finished cut, styling it. Each touch feels like he's rewiring something essential inside me. When his knuckles graze my cheek, I melt into the contact without meaning to, earning a low chuckle that makes my toes curl. My heart might burst from all the things we're not saying, but that makes it more perfect.

Dante steps back, and my stomach lurches with anticipation. His eyes meet mine in the mirror, holding something unspoken that makes my chest tight.

"There." He nods, voice low and measured in a way that makes me feel like I'm teetering on the edge of something vast. "You look..." He pauses, and his jaw works, like he's wrestling with words too heavy to say out loud. "Devastating, actually."

The once-chaotic mess is now a soft, tousled pixie cut that frames my face in ways I never knew hair could. It's shorter than I've ever worn, exposing the vulnerable curve of my neck.

I feel naked, seen, terrified, and thrilled all at once. My trembling fingers reach up to touch it. Dante watches me in the mirror with an intensity that makes it feel like I'm invincible.

Before I can process what's happening, he dips down, running the clippers along the side of his head.

"What are you doing?" I blurt.

He doesn't answer, just keeps methodically getting rid of those divine curls I've spent embarrassing amounts of time daydreaming about sifting my fingers through. The back of his head is clean now, deliberately reminiscent of my hair. The parallel makes my throat tight.

"Now…" He grins, putting our faces side by side in the mirror. "We match."

I glance at our reflection, at the way we fit together in the frame. It's so incredibly intimate. We look like we belong together.

"We look like the Beckhams," I say, trying to diffuse the intensity.

He kisses my cheek, his hands brushing loose strands off my shoulders. His touch seeps through my thin T-shirt like sunlight through water.

"Better, because we're Sinclair and Hastings."

There's something in the way he says our names—like they're meant to be paired, like it's inevitable—that makes my heart ache with a sweetness I can't quite contain.

Sinclair and Hastings.

But I don't want to only be our last names. Those names have so much power over us.

"I think I like just Reese and just Dante."

I stand, and Dante's gaze stays on me, full of that soft, tender look that leaves me feeling both seen and exposed. His eyes crinkle at the corners, a fondness so genuine it feels like something we've built together, intimate and earned.

"Why don't I stay, make you some breakfast while you work on your script notes?"

"You sure?"

"Of course."

Heat blooms in my chest, spreading outward like steeping tea. "Maybe after I'm done, you can give me my first training session now that you're back, and afterward we can come back here and have *dinner*?"

One more rendezvous before we start filming tomorrow will be good. Help us both relax for the weeks to come.

His eyebrows lift. "Yeah?"

I gather my courage, letting playfulness mask the vulnerability. "I remember something about you being at my beck and call?"

"I aim to serve and please."

"And maybe after *dinner*…you could make me an actual dinner." I widen my eyes dramatically, turning on my innocent doe-eyed act—though we both know there's nothing innocent about the way my pulse races when he looks at me like that. "I can ask Ramsey to get us some groceries."

"You realize that one of these days that look isn't going to work on me."

"Not today, though?"

He sighs, the sound caught somewhere between exasperation and adoration. "Not today."

Chapter 34
Reese

October 10th

HOLLYWOOD SHOCKER: America's Sweetheart Reese Sinclair Takes Dark Turn as Bad Boy Dante Hastings Goes Clean!

October 10th

EXCLUSIVE: America's Sweetheart Shocks Fans with Late-Night Burlesque Show: Is Former Role Model Leading Youth Astray?

October 10th

Filming Resumes for *Robyn Hood*—Will It Be the Next Blockbuster or a Major Flop?

October 10th

Sinclair's Private Jet Lifestyle: A Deep Dive Into Her Carbon Footprint

. . .

OCTOBER 10TH

TABLOID DRAMA: "Bad Girl" Reese Sinclair Spotted Partying While Reformed Bad Boy Dante Hastings Remains on the Sidelines—Sources Say She's "Desperate" to Derail His Olympic Comeback!

I TAKE a sip of my Berg water as I scroll through the headlines.

An uncomfortable feeling churns in my stomach. What is happening?

Photos from the burlesque club shouldn't even exist—they had a strict no-phones policy. It's a grainy picture taken from what looks to be under a table. What a way to spend your Saturday night, I guess. Being an absolute creep and sneaking in phones to places where phones shouldn't be.

I skim the headlines again and cringe. Calling my dance a "striptease" is a stretch. That slip had more fabric than half the gowns on red carpets these days.

How do I fix this?

I've seen this happen countless times, where the media turns on women overnight. But I had a plan.

The voice of doubt returns. Heather and Geraldine warned me about this. How I wouldn't be able to fix my reputation after diving headfirst into this new version of myself.

But maybe I can still handle it. I hope so.

Heather sends another message, and my pulse spikes as I open it.

HEATHER

Tell me you didn't?

> Article link: Did She Really Cut It? Sinclair's
> Shocking New Hairstyle Leaves Fans
> Questioning If It's for Robyn Hood or Her New
> Image by Susan Martin for the Stone Times

My eye twitches.

Is this day going to continue to get worse?

Twenty-four hours since my haircut, and the world already knows. The picture in the article looks like it was taken this morning—Dante walking me to the gym. His hood is up, but my new hair is on full display.

What on earth do these reporters have against me? From the snakes at *A!* to the journalists at *Sweet Southern* and these jerkfaces at the *Stone Times*. I read the byline. Susan Martin.

What on earth have I ever done to you, Susan?

Ever since that first leak, when Dante and I went to the beach, the *Stone Times* has had a permanent stakeout in my life. Ugh. I was silly to think I could keep it quiet for a little longer.

Panic bubbles in my system, and I hold the cold water bottle to my chest, focusing on the coolness against my skin.

Four. Seven. Eight.

Maybe I can still get control of the situation.

What's true?

I love my new hair. It's bold. It's mine.

Which means I won't let them twist it into something I regret.

"Reese, break's over! Got you all racked up for chest presses." Tori's voice snaps me out of my thoughts. She's already got the barbell ready, two twenty-pound weights on each side. A new record for me, but I'm too distracted to care.

I need to burn through some of this anger coursing through me.

I grunt, shoving my anger into the next two sets, each press harder than the last. Tori adds another five pounds on each side —ninety pounds total.

"Last rep! Make it count!" Tori shouts. "Push it, Reese! Channel your inner warrior!"

I grit my teeth. It's only our first day training together, but my new trainer's enthusiasm is exactly what I need—a refreshing change from Nick's gruff commands.

"How's that for warrior energy?" I wipe the sweat from my forehead with my towel. I'm already feeling better.

"Absolutely fierce! Now let's move to those weighted lunges. Want to know my favorite thing about training actresses?"

"Hit me. Actually, don't—I'm pretty sure a strong breeze could take me down right now."

"The raw intensity women bring to every session. It's about discovering your own capacity for strength. Every rep, every drop of sweat is you claiming your space, owning your power. That's what real transformation looks like."

"I never liked weight training before, but I have to say, in the last four months, it's grown on me." I grab a thirty-pound dumbbell for lunges. "Like I'm finally doing this for me, not just for the role. Though the role definitely appreciates these newfound abs." I lift up my shirt, glancing at the tiny bit of definition on my previously slim, line-free stomach.

Tori demonstrates the lunge with fluid precision. I mirror her movement, wobbling. My phone vibrates. *More headlines?*

"I saw you skimming articles over there." Tori catches my eye. "By the look on your face, I'm assuming it's bad?"

"Is it that obvious?"

"Look, I don't know what they're saying, and I don't care. You know who else was hung out to dry in the press? Portman when she gained twenty pounds of muscle for *Thor*. Sweeney, who transformed completely for that biopic about the boxer Christy Martin." Tori adjusts my form with a gentle touch. "The strength you're building? It's not just physical."

"But the press—"

"Will always have something to say," she cuts in, glancing pointedly at where the male actors are training. "You know what's funny? No one's telling them they're *too much* of anything. They're just right, aren't they? But every actress I've trained worried about getting t*oo bulky* at first. We're always told to be smaller, to fit in better, to slim down. But when women start taking up space unapologetically, whether in action films or weight rooms, we're changing more than our bodies. Hell, maybe we deserve to take up too much space."

I steady myself, finding my balance. "So what you're saying is…"

"Ten more," Tori encourages as the burn in my muscles intensifies.

She's right. No one gets to define me.

As I take a rest after my final lunge, the gym door swings open. In walks Amara—or glides, really, because that's what happens when you possess her kind of effortless cool. Her box braids are arranged in an intricate crown, and she's rocking overalls with a blue shirt and Docs. Script in one hand, clipboard in the other, headset perched above her head.

"Happy first day of filming, everyone!" she sings before locking her gaze on me. Her mouth drops open. "Darling, I simply had to see if the rumors were true. Had to witness this transformation firsthand."

"Amara!" I jump off the bench, my sweaty skin peeling from the leather. "Sorry, I meant to find you earlier but heard you were in meetings—"

But she's already appraising me. "This is absolutely divine. Reminiscent of our dear Posh Spice."

"You like it?"

"Um—I love it!"

A weight lifts off my chest. "It felt right for Robyn."

"Though I must confess, I'm rather disappointed." My heart

falters. "You should've called me right away! We could've gotten the whole hair transformation on camera—it would've been such a killer scene. The footage would've been—!" She puts her fingers to her lips and makes a chef's kiss.

"Actually, I was up half the night tweaking the script to make it work better," I add, shifting my weight and wiping my sweaty hands on my leggings. "I emailed my notes this morning. They're rough, but I think they could really work."

"Tell me." Amara taps her phone, bringing up my email.

"I was actually thinking that during that first sparring match, when my braid gets in the way, instead of it being this big dramatic thing, Robyn grabs a knife and cuts it off, because why keep something that's a liability in a fight?"

"Reese, this isn't gold—this is the kind of scene that will inspire thousands of re-creations and spawn at least three PhD dissertations on feminist cinema." Amara claps her hands together. "We are in perfect sync."

The energy between us crackles with creative possibilities. I haven't felt this kind of instant connection since Cleo—that rare spark when someone gets your vision completely.

"You're not simply stepping into the part," Amara declares, pacing the floor with infectious energy. "I'll have wigs here tomorrow. We'll restructure the opening to showcase this moment and spend the day making sure all the choreo is nailed. It's perfect."

"Even if the press is having a field day with it," I say, eyeing my phone. Has anything else surfaced?

"Oh, honey, those articles?" Amara waves her hand dismissively. "Free publicity. They're doing our marketing for us. Have you seen what they're writing about me? How I won't be able to direct an action movie?" She laughs. "If I stopped directing because some man said I can't do it, I'd never make a movie again. How stupid would that be? Ignore them."

She's right, of course. Time to channel my inner executive producer.

I could invite these critics to set, let them witness what it looks like when a woman claims her power without apology. Let them see how spectacularly wrong they are about everything. About me, about Dante, about what strength really means.

A slow smile spreads across my face as an idea forms. "Or what if we turned this around? Instead of doing a press conference to announce *Robyn Hood,* we could invite the press onto set? That way, they wouldn't leak pictures of us."

"Now you're thinking!"

The plan crystallizes in my mind, sharp and clear as a diamond. We could turn this into a whole circuit, bringing someone from every publication that wrote about the burlesque night. Especially the *Stone Times.* Let them all see what they think they understand so well.

"Let them watch me nail the three-person opening fight sequence we've been drilling." I straighten up. "And while we're at it…I can officially announce my new look, get ahead of the narrative. I'll have Heather and Geraldine coordinate everything."

Make them talk about my hair and *Robyn Hood,* not me dancing half-naked on stage.

"Look at you, playing chess while they're playing checkers. This is exactly why I wanted to work with you."

"This is going to change everything."

A tiny voice whispers, *Be careful what you wish for.* But I ignore it.

Amara gives my shoulder a squeeze before stepping back. "Come find me when you're done here. I want you to see how we're setting up the first shot. And I still owe you a camera placement walkthrough."

Then she turns to address the gym.

"Everyone else—" She claps once. "I know you all got your

welcome emails, and I love seeing you already putting in the work. I'll do formal introductions in two hours, but just know I am so excited to be working with you all. It's going to be an intense nine weeks, but we're going to make something amazing. And if you have any issues, come to me!"

Chapter 35
Dante

INDUSTRY BUZZ: *Robyn Hood* Controversy—Sinclair's Edgy Makeover Pushing Boundaries Too Far?

October 17th

Sinclair Bossy? Hastings Reduced to Personal Bag Boy?

October 17th

Dante Hastings Faces Setback After Rumored Girlfriend's Recent Press. Does the Olympic Team Really Need Him Anyway?

"Left, Em, your left!" I shout into my phone, gripping the steering wheel. "Christ, Coach, I'm getting an intimate view of your mustache here."

The FaceTime screen wobbles like a drunk person trying to walk a straight line.

"I am coach, not Scorsese," he grumbles, his accent thick as concrete. "You want fancy camera work, call your Hollywood friends."

"Just hand it to Sadie, for God's sake." Sadie's another one of Coach's misfit kids turned fencer.

I'm stuck outside the fucking high school gym, parked in the lot like some creep. I know how weird it looks—a grown man sitting outside a teenage fencing meet, staring at his phone—but there was no way I was missing her first competition.

Watching Em evolve from an angry kid into someone with real focus shifted something in me. Maybe if she does well, it'll help me too. I am the one making her great, after all. She could do what I did for fencing, but for the women's team.

My legacy.

I look back at the gift I bought her. Regardless of whether or not she wins, she'll need proper gear. No more hand-me-downs.

On screen, Em resets.

It's 12–13. Em's losing, and I'm developing an eye twitch.

Her stance is solid. Knees bent. Weight balanced—like I've hammered into her skull approximately ten thousand times. Her opponent mirrors her.

With Saber, there's no room for hesitation. Just pure speed and timing. One millisecond, and boom—everything changes.

The buzzer screams when you land a hit. But if both strike simultaneously, it's up to the refs to sort out who had right-of-way.

"She's getting sloppy with her bends!" I yell into my phone. "Her riposte's dragging like it's weighted down."

"Dante, *tishe!*" Coach barks, treating the phone camera like some alien technology he's encountering for the first time. "She is doing all she can. Just watch."

I grind my teeth.

12–14. One more point, and it's over.

"Get her over here," I demand. This is exactly why I needed to be in the fucking gym. She needs me.

"I cannot do that, Dante." Coach's voice crackles through the speaker.

I bellow for Em like a deranged sports dad who's had seventeen espressos. She materializes on screen, mask off, looking like she's run through a car wash. Her hair is stuck to her forehead in sweaty clumps, her face the color of a ripe tomato.

"Listen carefully—she's anticipating your riposte. Fake the parry, then catch her on the advance. Remember that drill we did last week? Quick wrist, light touch. You've got this."

"You're making me look mental," Em mutters, ducking her head. "The refs are going to punish me for all your yelling."

"Focus! Use the speed I know you have. Draw her in, then strike. Trust your instincts, and don't be hasty."

"Ma'am!" The tournament official appears like an avenging angel, clipboard clutched to chest. "No phone communication during matches. This is your only warning."

"Sorry!" Em laughs.

Coach Lev's bushy brows fill the screen. "Dante, you will get her disqualified!"

"Fine, Christ, make sure she—"

"No more back-seat coaching!" Coach's nostril looms into view, effectively ending the conversation.

Her grip resets, and she adds that cocky little twist she does as a signature. Silence descends over the gym.

The referee's hand rises. *"En garde."*

Like a coiled spring, Em drops into her stance. Her blade hovers. Under the harsh fluorescent lights, her mask gleams— and suddenly I'm up there with her, sixteen again and facing my own moment of truth.

Her opponent strikes first. Too eager. Too confident of victory. A rookie's mistake.

Em moves like lightning. When the other girl tries to counter, Em is faster, whipping her blade up like a striking cobra. Hit to the mask. Beautiful. The crowd gasps collectively.

13–14. The comeback starts now.

Coach mutters a prayer in Russian. Sadie's probably stopped breathing entirely. Am I breathing? My hands grip the phone tighter, pressing it closer to my face as if I could force myself through the screen.

Em is locked in. I know this look. I've worn it myself. Let them think they've won. Let them get sloppy. Then take everything.

"Fence!"

Her opponent lunges. Em dodges, stepping out of reach like we practiced a hundred times.

The other girl hesitates—too long. Too late. Em strikes. The blade moves so fast it's a silver blur in the air.

14–14.

Match point.

Reset. *One more, Em.*

Her opponent launches a desperate attack, lunging deep. But Em reads the movement perfectly. In one fluid motion, she side-steps, blade snapping down to catch her opponent's wrist.

The buzzer wails.

15–14.

I punch the roof of my Range Rover, raw adrenaline coursing through my veins. "FUCK YEAH, EM!"

The phone spins as Coach bellows, *"MOLODETS!"* and Sadie's screams pierce the mayhem. Through the chaos, Em turns toward the camera, raising her mask with a triumphant grin. I send a text to Reese.

DANTE

Em dominated her first tournament!

> I'm so damn proud right now I can barely contain myself.

LITTLE FIGHTER

> AHHH!! I KNEW she would! The way you've been mentoring her is incredible! Can't wait to hear every single detail during Sunday choreo.

DANTE

> Thank you for helping me pick out her gear.

LITTLE FIGHTER

> Send me pics of her reaction!

> Got to go, Mari is calling for us.

All the practices, the countless drills, and every hard-earned lesson come together. This determined student, who started as part of my community service, has grown into a true athlete.

She fucking did it. My very own champion.

Em's parents didn't show, like they said they wouldn't. Not even after she texted them to let them know she won.

They wouldn't even come to pick her up from the high school gym.

Assholes.

That's how we ended up at In-N-Out. The moment I suggested it, her whole face lit up.

A Double-Double Animal Style can do that to a person.

"What are my champions having today?" Coach rubs his hands together like he's plotting something.

"I'll have—" Em starts, but I cut her off with a grin.

"Let me guess, chocolate shake, Double-Double Animal Style, and fries drowning in sauce?" I tease. Em sticks her tongue out at me.

"And Mr. Fancy here wants his protein style," Coach chuckles, already pulling out his wallet. I reach for mine, but he waves me off with his signature scowl that's actually a smile. "Put it away before I make you do extra drills. You two will always be my kids, even if one of you is turning into a big-shot movie star. Now go find us a seat."

As Coach stands in line, Em slides into one of the plastic red booths.

"Hold on, I need to grab something from my car." I head outside and retrieve her gift from the back seat, opting to leave the saber back there. What is it they always say? *Don't bring a fencing sword to a fast-casual burger joint.*

When I return, I sit across from her, handing her the box. "Here. For dominating the tournament like the champion you are."

Em's eyes narrow suspiciously, but her lips twitch upward. "What did you do?"

"Just open it before I change my mind and keep it for myself."

She lifts out the competition uniform. Her face betrays nothing at first, maintaining that blankness that's particular to teenagers who've learned too early to guard their emotions. "New saber in my car too. Didn't want to get arrested for bringing a sword inside."

"I can't—this is too—" she stutters, shutting the box and letting her hair fall into her face.

"You can, and you will," I cut in. "Champions deserve champion-level gear, not hand-me-downs."

She runs her fingers over the collar. "Thanks, Coach."

She freezes, the word hanging between us.

Coach.

"Forget I said anything."

"You called me Coach."

"Stop it. Your face is getting all mushy." She rolls her eyes. "I can't be seen with you when you're being sentimental."

"Show some respect to your elders. Or I'll pull a page out of Lev's playbook and make you do footwork drills until your legs fall off."

Coach returns, sliding red trays filled with burgers and fries in front of us.

Delight settles in my chest—right before Em ruins it by grabbing a fry and chucking it at my head. Coach rolls his eyes and ignores us, too busy inhaling his 4x4.

"You know, you're a spitting image of my sister, Frankie. She's a pain in the ass, like you," I laugh, picking up my burger.

"I didn't think anyone actually ordered that." She eyes my lettuce-wrapped beef.

"You don't get muscles like mine without some vegetables." She snorts, already halfway through her burger. "You keep winning tournaments like this, you may have scouts looking at you next spring," I say.

"I'm leaning towards Princeton."

"Smart kid."

"Are you sure you'll have time to write me a letter of rec? Or are you and Hollywood gonna be too busy being all famous and stuff?"

That's what she calls Reese. *Hollywood.*

Being back on set feels different now than it did before Felix quit. Reese and I train together and sneak back and forth between each other's cabins after wrap.

Neither of us asks to stay the night. Probably safer that way.

The intimacy between us is new. Not only for me, but for her as well. I cook while she works the knots from my shoulders. It's domestic. Maybe pedestrian, but it's growing on me.

Knowing she's there. When my thoughts get dark, when I'd seek other vices in the past, I can just fucking be with her.

"She actually picked out the saber in my car for you. Wants a photo of you with it."

Em makes a gagging noise. "Gross, you two are disgustingly cute. But…tell her thanks, I guess."

Coach manages to take a breath from his burger and glare at me.

I'm thankful Em is here so I don't get another scolding.

Though I'm in a perfect fucking bubble on set, the press hasn't been doing me any favors recently. Old photos resurfacing. Painting Reese and me in a bad light. I thought I had it under control, but things are getting out of hand.

I can't deny it any longer.

I have more wins in me, and I want to get my sponsors back. Em's counting on me. The kids at the youth program too.

But now the media's fucking it up.

I agreed to help Reese because it was important to her—and fuck if that mess with Susan isn't still nagging at me, the mess with all of the reporters who are hounding us—but our appearances have evolved into something that could destroy everything I've built.

We claimed it would benefit us both. Now I'm not so sure.

I shake the thought away and look at Em.

"One win down. You ready for more?"

Her smile falters. "Yeah, I wish—"

She doesn't say it, but I know she wants her parents to be there for her. However complicated things are between them.

"That's not on you, Em."

"Yeah, whatever." She tries to play it off, but I see it—the way her eyes flicker, her shoulders tensing like a drawn bow.

I make a silent promise to be at every match, the way my parents were for me. The thought lands somewhere between gratitude and grief.

Is this what it means to inherit someone else's wounds and carry them like they're your own? Or maybe this is simply the fact that all the shit I thought was important—the image, the notoriety, the recognition—doesn't feel nearly as right as being there for the people who are counting on me?

Chapter 36
Dante

"COME HAVE LUNCH," Mari calls from outside the director's tent, ashing her cigarette. We used to share spliffs at Princeton, and now we're here together.

Life is funny.

"Can't, just got in!" I shout, not slowing down. The bag in my hand holds a carefully curated selection for Reese—a chilled Berg sparkling water, a prosciutto and burrata panini on freshly baked ciabatta, truffle-dusted Marcona almonds, and an apricot tart. "She's got five minutes. And I told her I'd bring her lunch."

"This is a good look on you," she says. It must be weird for Mari, seeing me do things for someone else. But I've always been generous. I've just never been generous in the way I am with Reese.

I find myself doing things for her without expecting anything in return, just wanting to make her world a fraction easier. It's terrifying how much I like it.

"Yeah, yeah." I wave her off.

I continue through the forest until the clearing in front of the makeshift press tent unfolds.

There she is.

I'm proud of her, taking control of her story.

My older brother, Cameron, had a similar situation last year after someone leaked photos of him. Cam, always so quiet with his football, retreated into himself when the media descended. But then he spoke out about his old team's misconduct and started an anti-bullying foundation. The first in the Premier League.

Funny how silence works—you carry it until you don't.

Reese is speaking with someone, fingers absently moving through her hair—a habit she hasn't lost despite the pixie cut. She's in her new costume. It's perfect on her. Not like that awful metal thing Felix had insisted upon.

Though I would be hard-pressed to admit that anything wouldn't be perfect on her.

When she laughs, her head tilting back, something inside me rearranges. The way it always does when she looks so pure. Her jaw, neck, the precise geometry of her face. Beautiful in a way that hurts to look at.

Her eyes find mine. *Hi.*

Hey.

I start toward her, smiling, but then the person speaking to her turns, and my body forgets how to move.

Fuck.

It's Susan Martin.

With Reese.

The world tilts sideways. *What the actual fuck is she doing here?*

I duck behind a tree, nearly dropping Reese's lunch.

Shit.

Maybe she hasn't said anything to Reese yet. Or maybe Reese will come over here and ask why I never mentioned knowing Susan.

Or worse—ask why I leaked the location of the set. The guilt that's been dormant for the last few weeks suddenly feels like it's choking me.

My mind spins. I need to get my story straight.

I only confirmed what she already knew. I never lied to Reese. Susan would have found us anyway, even if she hadn't been on my yacht. Even if I hadn't bragged about Reese over two months ago.

But the justification feels hollow.

Empty.

God, I'm such a fucking bigheaded idiot. I could lose everything—lose her—over one stupid fuckup.

A branch snags on my shirt, which only makes me realize I'm acting like a child hiding over here. I have to go tell her. I'm a fucking coward. I should have told her the moment the article appeared in the *Stone Times* with Susan's name on it.

"Dante?" Reese peeks around the tree. "There you are!" I spin around, nearly losing my balance. "What exactly are you doing?"

"I'm here with the tree," I say, touching the bark, aware of how absurd and transparent I must seem.

"In the dirt?" Her eyes narrow as she studies my face. "Are you okay?"

I shift my weight from one foot to the other, positioning myself at an angle that keeps Susan from seeing me.

There is a hollow space in my chest where my heart should be, though perhaps it is there and I simply cannot feel it through the thundering panic. Or perhaps I am actually the Tin Man from *The Wizard of Oz* and don't actually have a fucking heart of any kind.

"Yes," I say. "Fine. I brought you lunch."

I scan her face, asking myself if she can read the truth in mine, if she can see how my thoughts keep circling back to that day on the yacht, to words I can never take back.

But she's already reaching for the bag.

"Oh, you're a saint! I'm starved." The panini appears in her hand, and she bites into it immediately, her shoulders visibly relaxing for the first time today.

"How are the interviews going?"

"They're fantastic!" she says between bites, with a bright smile that doesn't quite reach her eyes. "I just had the most interesting chat with Susan Martin—you know, our dedicated stalker-journalist? I invited her myself. Figured I might as well give her something real to write about if she's going to keep trying to twist my story."

My stomach lurches. "How'd that go?"

Reese snorts, rolling her eyes. "Oh, you know, she said my haircut gave me an edge right before questioning my mental stability. Because heaven forbid a woman change her hair without first alerting the press that she's having a breakdown." She takes another defiant bite, her knuckles whitening around the sandwich. "And even if we are having breakdowns, we're still showing up, aren't we?"

"That's right. Think she'll write something decent this time?"

"She better," Reese says, then shrugs. "Though honestly? All this press probably doesn't matter anymore. We buried Felix's headlines after he quit, and that was the whole point of this. Now it's really about me taking back my own narrative."

It doesn't seem like Susan told her. The relief that floods into my lungs is cruel.

"The tabloids are always going to write shit and spin stories. I've seen it happen to my family and experienced it firsthand."

"You're right. I guess some of the press coverage is getting to me more than I want to admit." She runs a hand through her hair, that nervous habit she has when she's holding too much inside. "It's obviously not only Susan—it's all the journalists who are here today. Every single one of them has written something hurtful about me."

"Are you regretting your evolution?" I pull myself out of the dirt patch I was rooted to and step out of the tree clearing.

"No. Not regretting." She straightens her posture, putting on that media-ready smile. "I'm becoming someone new, and I'm not sure who that person is yet. I've always been this role model for young ladies, and I thought this transition would help that, show them that you can grow and be human and be bold!"

"But?"

"How do you know there's a but?" She raises a brow at me, her façade cracking just slightly.

"I know you."

"But." She exhales shakily. "I feel like they're all writing stories about a person I don't fully understand. Like they're turning this…whatever this self-discovery is into a spectacle." Her voice drops to nearly a whisper. "Between the interviews, the acting, learning with Amara, I just…I cannot have anything go wrong right now. Not one thing." Her eyes meet mine with an intensity that makes my chest ache. "This movie is everything to me. It has to be perfect. I can handle the press, the critics, all of that, but…" The parchment paper crinkles under her trembling hands. "I just can't handle any more surprises or bad news. Not until we wrap."

Fuck.

I can't tell her about Susan now. It would hurt her. No matter my intentions, she'll see me as another Ricky. Using her. And that's the last thing I want. She already has so much on her plate, and she just said it herself—she can't handle any more bad news.

Once the movie is over, I'll tell her. No matter what happens. Just not now. Not when we have months of filming left, when I feel closer to her than I ever have.

I hate this, this withholding information, this pretending. It's not who I'm supposed to be. Except it is, isn't it?

Or it was. I don't fucking know.

Maybe it's selfish. Maybe I'm just rationalizing this with

some bullshit protective instinct. Or maybe I'm just twenty-six years old and have never learned how to have a real relationship before.

"I don't mean to sound pretentious." I force the corner of my lip up. "But you're like a phoenix. When I first met you, Reese Sinclair was this contained thing. Becoming Robyn helped you burn it all down, and now you're becoming something else entirely."

"That's a very sweet way to think about it." She attempts a smile, but I can see how fragile it is, how close she is to breaking.

"It's okay to not know who you are right this second or how you want to show up in the world." A part of me has been trying to figure out the same thing since meeting her.

"Maybe I can continue trying to be just Reese?" She looks up at me hopefully, desperate for reassurance.

"Sounds like a good plan, if I do say so myself. Identity is fluid," I say softly, leaning in a little closer. "Questioning who you are shows how self-aware you've become."

"You always know the right thing to say," she sighs. My jaw tightens. "And you got me a fancy apricot tart—let's share it before I have to do another one of these." She smiles, and I forget everything else.

This is the best thing for Reese right now.

We settle onto a weathered log, the bark rough beneath us. I unfold a napkin across my lap, breaking the flaky apricot tart in half and passing her portion over.

The weight of what I actually needed to talk to her about today sits heavy in my chest. The timing feels wrong.

"Speaking of identity," I venture. "After Em's match, I want to keep training her. Even if my disciplinary review lifts. It's been fun." If *it lifts*, my mind whispers traitorously.

"I'm happy for you, but just remember that I was your first student." She winks.

"And my favorite." I rub the flaky crust between my fingers, feeling…scared? "That also means I need to be a little more buttoned-up in the press, and, well, you're right—the coverage has been vicious lately. Dragging up old skeletons, which isn't doing either of us any favors."

She nods, her expression softening with understanding. "We're so on the same page. I think we can both find some peace in staying out of the spotlight for a while. Yeah?"

"That would be perfect."

"Thank you so much for doing this for me, for helping me get this movie somewhere big in every way. I mean, not just in training me, but also dealing with the media circus." She swallows hard, guilt creeping into her voice. "I kind of feel responsible that the press is putting your review at risk."

"I agreed to this, fighter," I say, my pulse thundering in my ears like my own guilty drumbeat. "Plus, I figured with two more months of nonstop filming, we wouldn't have time to get into any more trouble."

"Maybe we could make some time for just Dante and Reese?"

"Now that," I say, a genuine smile tugging at my lips, "I think we can always make time for."

Chapter 37
Reese

October 22nd

Robyn Hood Stars SPILL THE TRUTH: "No Doubles Used—Sinclair's Stunts 100% REAL! Can She Pull It Off? Vote Here!

October 29th

SINCLAIR POWER PIXIE or Another Britney Breakdown?

November 2nd

Hastings Spotted Coaching After-School Youth Fencing Team

November 7th

NO Recent Sightings of SinHaste: Is This Couple Over Before They Even Started?

. . .

The Beginning of the End of America's Sweetheart

By Susan Martin

"Time to move!" Merrick shouts, gesturing urgently toward the getaway rafts bobbing on the dark water.

"Get out of here!" I clash blades with a guard, the impact sending vibrations through my arms. "I've got this covered!"

"But—"

"That's an order!"

A guard lunges. I spin, parry, and strike. The blood pack bursts perfectly, painting the deck crimson. One push sends him stumbling back into the water.

Behind me, Merrick crashes into a lantern. The prop ignites as planned, flames racing across the wooden deck. We've got one shot at this scene—no time for mistakes.

"This gold belongs to the people now!" I bite out.

Two more guards charge me. I deflect one blade, then strike. One guard staggers back with a convincing yelp, creating the perfect opening.

"You're dead, Hood!" the other snarls.

"Better dead than watching your king feast while children starve!" I retort, blocking a strike.

But Robyn celebrates too soon. A lucky hit sends my sword spinning away. In the water, the dagger waits for my descent. I make sure camera four catches me noticing it as I stare into the dark water below.

I've trained for this.

Those endless practice sessions in the tub, the swim in the pool with Mama back home, the fearlessness I've developed— they've all led to this scene.

A blade finds my leg—well, finds the blood pack on my leg.

I cry out dramatically. Moving fast, I roll away from an incoming hit and give myself some breathing room before the dive.

Ready. Set.

I plunge into the freezing lake. The water embraces me. Under my costume, Dante's ring is cold against my chest, like the ice was that day he helped me get through my panic attack.

Through the murk, I spot my target, the dagger nestled between the rocks. I kick down, grasp it, push off the stone lakebed, and burst from the water before I climb back onto the dock.

"Thought you could get rid of me?" I taunt, twirling my blade exactly how Dante taught me.

The rest of the fight choreography is like muscle memory in my skin.

Duck, spin, sweep—one guard down.

Dodge, step in, strike—another falls.

"Tell your king," I announce, "Northwood Forest has a defender now, and her name is Robyn Hood."

The last guard grabs for the gold. I'm faster, snatching the bag away. With a smirk and a wink, I dive back into the water and swim toward the getaway rafts.

"CUT! Fucking marvelous!" Amara's voice rings across the lake.

I stop swimming, gasping but grinning. The entire crew erupts in cheers and applause. Through the celebration, I spot Dante's face as I swim toward the dock.

"I did it!" I exclaim. "From panic attacks to freakin' perfect takes, and I called that last adjustment!"

Dante wraps a thick towel around my shoulders and pulls me into a tight embrace. "That dive was fucking perfect."

"The suit worked perfectly—not a single leak! And the ring…Dante, the ring helped so much. It was such a smart idea; it kept me so present." I swallow. "That fight sequence— did you see how smooth it was? I actually enjoyed being in the water! The angles I discussed with Amara have really worked.”

“Yes, baby, I saw all of that. I—” He stops, and something shifts in his expression.

Baby. Before I can stop myself, I rise onto my tiptoes and press my lips to his. In front of everyone, and I don’t care because there’s nothing I want more than to kiss Dante Hastings, dizzily and sweetly.

For one perfect second, there’s just us.

Then I remember we’re on set and pull away with an awkward laugh. “Oh, I’m sorry, I just got carried away there.”

“Reese.” I spot Heather at the dock’s edge, looking out of place among our medieval costumes in her crisp business suit and stilettos. Her expression is apologetic but urgent. “I hate to interrupt this moment,” she says carefully, “but I need to speak to you.”

My stomach tightens.

“You alright?” Dante asks.

“Yeah, totally fine,” I lie. “Just…Heather doesn’t do set visits unless there’s a five-alarm fire somewhere.” My fingers uncon-sciously trace Dante’s hands before I pull away.

I ache at the distance I create. This film, my vision, has to come first. Always first.

I give him an apologetic look before following Heather, who’s already clicking down the dock in her heels. My heart is still racing, but not just from the dive—it’s that familiar anxiety creeping in at the edges, the one that whispers I can’t afford any distractions.

My brain helpfully supplies worst-case scenarios. Is the movie cancelled? Did someone die? Are my parents okay?

“What’s going on?” I ask once we’re safely tucked away in a corner, forcing myself not to look back at Dante.

Heather’s weathered face softens. “Honey, I flew in from LA this morning. Didn’t feel right doing this over the phone, not after all these years." She straightens her Chanel jacket. "Diamond Essence is pulling your campaign."

The words hit me with a physical force I wasn't expecting. My throat constricts. "I'm sorry, what?"

"The pixie cut, darling." Her perfectly manicured hand gestures to my head. "Those shortsighted bastards are claiming 'brand dissonance' with their precious 'long, flowing hair' aesthetic."

A hysterical laugh escapes me, but inside something cracks. "Are you kidding?"

"Those people don't deserve you anymore. We had a damn good run with them, but honestly—" She leans in conspiratorially, like she did when I was an overwhelmed teenager at my first premiere. "You've outgrown them. You're heading into your thirties, starring in prestige pictures. This film? It's going to change everything. You had the right idea pushing for this, and now that Langford is gone, it's right."

My fingertips feel numb. The adrenaline from the stunt is crashing, leaving me hollow. "They really just want to drop me?"

"You need partnerships that reflect where you're going, not where you've been."

"But we've already shot everything—the commercial, the social media campaign," I protest.

"The coverage we ran from this set two weeks ago was a mixed bag. Good news is that the burlesque photo situation is dying down—yes, rather slowly, but Geraldine's working her usual magic there."

I shift uncomfortably, my wet clothes clinging to my skin. It's as if my body no longer belongs to me.

"Level with me, Heather. Is it just the haircut?"

"The image shift makes them nervous," Heather says carefully, her eyes flicking to Dante and the crew. "The edge, the evolution, the romance rumors…it's not their brand. Plus, that Susan article is getting a lot of traction."

I thought the *Stone Times* had dropped my story since all the other press that covered my on-set press release ran their articles last week. But no.

Susan Martin dug everything she could out of my closet, weaving rumors about relationships with costars, directors, everything. My movies pulled apart and dissected. Every interview I'd ever given put under a microscope.

Geraldine had warned me against speaking to the press directly, but I did it anyway. I figured I'd get to tell my truth. But Susan doesn't want my truth; she wants to make her career out of slandering mine. And I might've given her the ammo.

"Everything in her article was a lie," I say, the words tumbling out too quickly to be convincing. It hurts more than I thought it would. The weight of everything I've been holding back presses down on me.

I think of Dante's face after our kiss, the way he looked at me like I was both precious and strong. The vulnerability in his eyes was real, but it's the power I can't ignore. It's not just the Hollywood story. It's my story now.

As an executive producer, I have to keep moving forward strategically. My feelings for Dante are real, and maybe for now that's all that matters. I can stay out of the media for the next five weeks while we finish filming, and when I reemerge, the public will have moved on to someone else.

"Of course it was. I'm working on getting the article pulled," Heather says with diplomatic smoothness. "But Diamond Essence already signed on Summer Brown—nineteen, fresh from Tennessee, sweet as pie. Just like you used to be. Just like they wanted you to stay."

The words sting more than I expected. Diamond Essence was my first national campaign, the one that helped me buy my house in LA. Their shampoo's magnolia-peach scent still lingers in my master bath. I've become the woman I wanted to be, but saying goodbye to this chapter hurts more than I thought it would.

"They want that version of me back," I snap, combing my hand through my wet pixie cut. The cut is mine—even if it's costing me this campaign. Even if it might cost me more than that. "The sweetheart. But I can't go back to being led. I'm finally the one doing the leading."

"As you should be."

Heather grabs my shoulders with the fierce protectiveness that's guided my entire career. "Listen to me, kid. I've been in this town since Marilyn was doing test shots. You're not only changing your look, you're evolving. Making real moves. And some dinosaurs can't handle evolution. But trust me, after this film drops, they'll be begging to have you back. I'm already in talks with Starlight and Crown & Glory."

"Those aren't exactly Diamond Essence level…"

"The money's different, yes. But here's some wisdom from your ancient agent who's seen it all: sometimes you have to lose the tiara to find your crown. Like you said yourself, you can't stay America's sweetheart forever."

I nod, too stunned to think. Each change has brought me something amazing—the role, the confidence, the executive producer credit, Dante—but I'm losing things too, pieces of who I used to be, fragments I didn't know I'd miss. The price of ambition weighs heavy.

"Being Hollywood's new queen pays better than being America's sweetheart. Trust me on this one, kid."

"Right." My jaw clenches.

After all, I'm an actress. And as my hands flex and unflex against my sides, I realize I need to give the performance of my life. I need to be someone who isn't watching their world shift beneath their feet, someone who isn't mourning the ghost of who she used to be as she celebrates who she's becoming. Someone who knows exactly what she has to sacrifice to get where she's going.

I wanted this.

Chapter 38
Reese

I'VE SPENT the last half hour wandering the set processing the loss of my Diamond Essence campaign. These days, my emotions feel like waves. Sometimes gentle, sometimes overwhelming. Instead of texting Dante to come over so we can lose ourselves in our pattern of mutual distraction, I find myself drawn to his cabin.

I'm at his window now—yes, officially crossing into light stalking territory—watching him on his sofa. He's got his headphones on, lips moving silently to what I know must be next week's script revisions.

Something deep inside me aches watching him like this—so focused, so earnest. I love the way his hair falls into his eyes before he threads his fingers through it, how his entire face transforms when he smiles. And heavens, the things I once found insufferable—his cockiness and ego—I now see for what they are: a shield, hiding the soft, fierce, sexy, intelligent, funny man underneath.

I lift my fist to his door and knock.

Rap. Rap. Rap.

Our knock.

"Look what the night dragged in," he says softly, leaning against the doorframe. His sweats cling in all the right places, and his oversized sweatshirt looks like it could swallow me whole.

"Couldn't sleep," I say. The words feel heavy with everything I'm not saying: *I needed to see you. I needed to not be alone.*

He opens the door wider, a gentle "Come here" making my heart flutter.

Inside, a Diptyque candle flickers—the Pekin one he knows I love. The scent of magnolia, sandalwood, tea. It's so typically him, this love for the luxurious things in life, this need to make everything a little more special. I pretend to find it excessive, but really, I love how he turns ordinary moments into something worth remembering.

"What are you working on?" I ask, though I already know.

"Next week's scenes. Gotta be prepared for our three scenes together." His kiss is quick, tender, like it's the most natural thing in the world. Maybe it is.

"Lucky us."

"You know," he says, "you probably can't sleep because your bed is tragic."

"Oh, really?"

He abandons his script on the couch, leading me to his bedroom, where his ridiculous king-sized bed dominates the space. He claims it's because he's tall, but I'm certain it's because he sleeps like a starfish. Though I've never had the privilege of finding out.

The amber lighting makes everything feel dreamlike. The floorboards creak beneath my feet.

"Get in," he says, pulling back the duvet. I slide between his sheets, which are soft as clouds.

The mattress dips under his weight, and I instinctively curl into him. His arm tightens around me, pulling me closer, his lips pressing a quiet kiss to the top of my head. He's radiating like a furnace, and I melt into him.

We breathe in sync, his chest rising and falling against mine, as if he knows I don't have the words yet and isn't in any rush to hear them.

Four. Seven. Eight.

"What are you thinking about?" he asks softly.

"It's…" I trace the tattoos on his forearm. "This industry can be so isolating. You're constantly surrounded by people, but it's like being behind glass. Everyone's looking in, but no one's really seeing you." I pause, feeling silly. "Goodness, I sound ungrateful, don't I? Poor little actress with her perfect life."

"Hey," he says, fingers finding my chin. "Your feelings aren't less valid because other people might envy your life."

"Sometimes I feel like I'm playing a part even when the cameras aren't rolling."

"I get that," he says. "But not with me?"

"No," I whisper, surprised by how true it feels. "Not with you. You make everything feel real."

Dante makes me feel seen in a way that is both terrifying and exhilarating.

"Remember when you hated me?" he asks, amusement coloring his voice. "If someone had told me at that first table read we'd end up here…"

"I didn't hate you," I protest weakly. "I was…"

"Professionally skeptical?" His laugh rumbles through his chest, and I press my ear closer, wanting to memorize the sound. *When did I get so lucky?*

"You wouldn't share an apple with me," he reminds me.

"I made it up to you with the apple the day before I cut my hair."

"Can't believe that was over a month ago."

"But I am sorry for before. For all those walls I built and the assumptions I made without giving you a chance."

His touch is gossamer against my jaw. "Don't be. Can't exactly blame you, can I? We're like two different kinds of fire," he says softly. "You burn steady and deep, while I'm all flash and crackle. Sometimes we clash, but that doesn't mean we don't understand each other."

I nestle closer, drawn to him like a magnet finding metal. "Listen to you, being so poetic," I murmur into his chest and nudge my nose to the bookcase across the room. "And here I thought those books were props."

"They are, actually," he confesses with a laugh. "I mostly listen to audiobooks, especially when I'm on the road. Though nothing compares to when you read to me."

"I could, you know," I offer, feeling brave in the quiet of his room. "When we're away from set. Maybe start with Francesca and Paolo?"

"Or Dorothea and Will," he suggests, naming characters I don't recognize. "From *Middlemarch*."

"I'd like that." The silence between us feels comfortable, like a well-worn sweater. "You know, you always surprise me."

"Same here. When we met, I thought we would have nothing in common," he says, drawing lazy patterns on my back, and I melt. "But it's deeper than that, isn't it? It's how we see things, feel things. We don't need matching life stories to understand each other."

The truth of it hits me in waves.

"It's not like those romance movies I've done," I say, slipping into my Boston accent from *Heart in Boston*. "Where it's all, *Oh, my god, we both love blue and have dogs and eat lobster rolls! It must be fate!*"

"Missed my watchlist."

"Flopped spectacularly."

"Show me more accents?" he asks.

"Sugar," I drawl in my thickest southern belle, fighting sleep, "we both know which one makes you weak."

"Right you are, darlin'," he attempts, failing dramatically.

A familiar feeling floods into my veins. That dizzy, teenage feeling I thought I'd outgrown. After Ricky, I'd convinced myself closing off my heart was the mature choice. The professional choice. But lying here, I can't deny how desperately I've craved this kind of connection.

Maybe it's ironic that as a romance actress, I've acted out countless versions of love. But those were just scripts, carefully choreographed moments of perfection. This thing with Dante feels beautifully imperfect.

Being here with him, I let myself believe in the cliché that sometimes things do fall into place.

"You know, I like that we're so different. It's like we shouldn't make sense, but we do. My parents were high school sweethearts who grew up on the same street. Practically carbon copies of each other."

"When you meet my parents, you'll see a different kind of love story. Probably more similar to us," he says.

My stomach does this slow, pleasant flip at the casual way he says *when you meet my parents*, like it's inevitable. Like we have a future. "You think?"

"Tech geek meets basketball star? On paper, they're from different worlds."

"And they work?"

"Thirty years and counting." He yawns against my hair.

"What's their secret?"

He absentmindedly brushes over the short strands at my nape. "Well, besides the fact that my dad still looks at my mom like she's Morticia Addams."

"Every woman's dream, finding her Gomez," I sigh.

"Who wouldn't want their own Morticia? But really, I think it's their dedication. To each other, to their people—Mom to her team, Dad to everyone at Viggle. Our holidays were always full of this chosen family they built."

"I get that," I mumble, sleep starting to blur my words. "My family's the same way, close to our neighbors and friends."

"But there's something beautiful about how they fit together. They had this ritual of syncing their calendars every Sunday night. They always prioritized carving out time for each other like it was a game they were intent on winning. I personally think, and forget how this is going to sound"—he pauses dramatically—"it was like foreplay for them."

"Oh god! Like a love language made of Viggle Calendar invites?" I ask.

"Exactly. They built their life in the spaces between commitments. No phones on vacation, just presence. Just them. They're different in almost every way. Dad couldn't dribble a basketball if his life depended on it, Mom still prints out her emails, but they've created this beautiful thing together."

I draw patterns across his chest, quieting the restless stir inside of me. "What if your family thinks I'm too Hollywood?"

He takes hold of my hand. "The woman who spent three hours perfecting a single kick because it *didn't feel authentic enough*, who still tries to twirl her hair weeks after she cut it?"

"Promise to never stop teasing me like this? I think it keeps me grounded." I never thought I'd find someone who could see through my carefully constructed layers, who'd make me want to be seen. But here he is, making me laugh at myself, making me real.

"As long as you'll let me."

"They'll see what I see," he murmurs.

"Which is?"

"Someone who makes everything better. Brighter."

He kisses my head, and I burrow closer, feeling brave. "Come to New Orleans for Christmas?" I whisper. "My mama's gumbo will change your life, and I know this amazing chef at Hotel Monteleone who does private dinners overlooking the river. Plus," I add, "I need backup when Aunt Mabel starts her inevitable interrogation about my biological clock."

"Throwing me to the southern wolves already?"

"Only the ones who make transcendent pie crust."

"Then I'm yours," he mumbles, already half asleep.

We lie there a little while longer until his breathing deepens beneath my cheek. I should go back to my cabin, probably.

"Dante?" I whisper. No response.

Instead, I let myself sink deeper into his warmth.

Chapter 39
Dante

November 6th

BREAKING: Olympic Star Hastings Partners with Red Bull in Youth Training Initiative

November 10th

Diamond Essence Drops Celebrity Ambassador Sinclair After Hair Disaster

November 15th

EXCLUSIVE: On-Set Romance Sparks Controversy as Sinclair Caught in Passionate Kiss with Costar on Set

"Surprise!" my favorite voice fills the fencing gym.

"God, you're a sight," I rasp, drinking Reese in as she walks inside. Sweat still clings to my skin from Em's practice that ended a few minutes ago. "I thought your meeting in San Francisco wasn't over until later in the day?"

Heather arranged for Reese to meet with new hair care brands to replace her partnership with Diamond Essence. "Ended early. Besides, I couldn't resist seeing where Dante Hastings practices his art." Her gaze flickers over my stark training space. "Is that okay?"

"Of course. You just missed Em."

She frowns. "I'll have to catch her next time. I'm just happy to get away from the set. Three weeks of nonstop shooting has been exhausting. I figured it would be nice to be somewhere that's just us for a few hours."

At night, I've seen her scrolling, her phone's blue glow casting sharp shadows, every headline carving fresh wounds. It's intimate, witnessing her like this—all human, afraid even. I pull her close because it's the only thing that makes sense.

We've been sleeping together since she showed up at my cabin that night. Before that, sleep was utilitarian: six hours, precisely timed, alone. Or it was fleeting, bodies around me, release calming my pulse, waking up confused and lost. I had perfected the art of strategic exits from strangers' beds.

But Reese has systematically destroyed my careful rhythms. Now I find myself pathetically dependent on her presence, the sound of her breathing becoming some sort of essential white noise machine I can't sleep without.

Her fingers trace my jaw, reading tension I didn't know I was carrying. "Something's on your mind."

She sees right through me.

"Em's acting out. Caught her with stolen shoes. Kid's screaming for attention the only way she knows."

"Hey," she whispers, all soft understanding. "If anyone can reach her, it's you. You see her heart underneath all that tough exterior."

"Thanks, Reese." My voice comes rough with feeling. "Just want to be what she needs."

Her smile could melt steel. "You already are."

She sinks against me with a contented sigh, fitting perfectly.

I draw her closer, the pull of gravity undeniable. The silk of her blouse murmurs beneath my touch.

"I've missed you," she coos.

"Missed you more."

I spin her toward the mirror, my body so close I feel her lungs expand against my torso. I trace the delicate bow at her throat, and our gazes lock in the reflection, igniting something primal in me.

"Are you sure none of your teammates or anyone from the youth program is going to walk in on us?"

"Certain. We're safe here. Just us."

The silk tie of her blouse slips free, revealing black lace beneath. Each button I unfasten is a promise of things to come. Her nipples have hardened beneath the thin fabric.

"We look good together, don't we?"

My hands slide lower until they reach the button of her jeans.

"We do," she whispers, holding my gaze in the mirror. I expose the black lace of her bra, her pearls sliding against bare skin. "No wonder they can't keep their cameras off us."

"I'm so proud of you, Reese," I tell her. "You've been working so hard, pushing yourself to get this movie done. You're an EP, you're codirecting—it's so impressive."

"And yet I feel so out of control."

"I can help." She exhales as her free hand grips my thigh, my erection obvious against her ass. "If you want control, I'm here for you."

"I'd like that." She bites her lip like she's on the verge of revealing another side of herself. "I'd like to spend some time being..." She presses against my length deliberately, and I have to bite back a groan. "Whatever this honest, messy thing is."

"This honest, messy thing," I say softly, fighting the urge to bend her over right here, "is my favorite."

She places her hand on my uniform, and my cock jumps at her touch.

"And the more of you I learn…" I unbutton her jeans, and she nods frantically. "The more I want to catalog every part of you. Dig deeper." We're both pretending this moment can last forever, that the outside world won't eventually intrude. But in this quiet gym, where it's just us, maybe it can.

"Come here," she whispers. Her hands are on me, and coherent thought becomes impossible. "What would you do if you wanted some control? How would you take it?"

I want to give her everything.

"I'd find someone willing to show me how to tune into it. Control isn't about force, it's about trust," I say softly, watching the conflict play across her features.

"And do you trust me?" Her expression turns ravenous.

"I do."

"I trust you too, Dante." And it feels like she's saying something bigger, and maybe so am I. But right now, our bodies can speak for us.

I lift up her hand, bringing it to my throat. "How does that feel?"

"I can feel your heartbeat." She shivers, her hand sliding tentatively down my neck.

"Perfect," I breathe. "What do you want to do next?"

Her eyes are dark as she thinks, skimming my face as she pulls back the Velcro at my throat. "This uniform. What's underneath?"

"Find out."

She obliges, peeling back my white fencing jacket. The protective gear falls away piece by piece. First the plastron, then the chest protector.

"If denim is your kryptonite, these compression shirts are

mine." The grin on her face has turned wicked. God, this isn't just physical anymore. It hasn't been for a while. "So many layers, like a present." She pushes my shirt up slowly. I lift my hands, bending so she can take it off of me.

She traces old scars and fresh bruises from training. "Beautiful," she whispers, pressing her lips to a particularly dark mark near my collarbone. I shiver as she works her way down, mapping my skin with her mouth. "Mine."

Fuck. I am. I want to be.

She strips off my fencing knickers and kisses down my leg muscles, built and defined from years of lunges and footwork. My compression shorts do nothing to hide how hard I am.

"Last layer," she says, dragging them down until my cock springs free, precum waiting for her. It would be so easy to tell her how I feel, but maybe letting our bodies talk is safer. Maybe this is all she's ready for.

She sits back on her heels, drinking in the sight of me fully naked. Her pupils are blown wide with desire, her chest heaving beneath her open blouse. Whatever conversation we need to have can wait.

"I want…" Reese's eyes lock with mine as she picks up my fencing mask from the floor. With careful precision, she slides the mask over my face. "You to keep this on and show me how you…" She swallows. "Touch yourself."

"When I'm thinking about you?"

"Yes."

Easy.

Reese struts away from me, and I fist my cock. She bends down to slip her heels off and twists, turning away from me with a sultry smile as she slowly slides her jeans off.

She's stripping for me, my perfect Reese. The mesh of my mask distorts my view. I fucking want to tear it off and go rip the blouse she's slowly tossing to the floor. She puts her heels back on and stands before me, a fucking warrior in stilettos and lace.

"Get on the floor, please," she says with a shy smile.

I drop to my knees, feeling the cold against my skin. The piste is hard and unforgiving, but I find I don't mind.

"Now what, baby?" I beg.

"Crawl to me."

I do as I'm told, creeping toward her on my hands and knees.

"You know what this means to me. Giving you this power." I pause, letting the weight of the moment settle between us. "I trust you with it completely."

Her stiletto finds the top of my fencing mask, pressing down with a precise pressure that makes my breath catch in my throat. The gesture feels both tentative and bold, like she's testing the boundaries of her own desires.

"Touché," she purrs, and I've never been more turned on in my life.

My hands slide up her thighs, drawn to her heat like a moth to flame. As my fingers brush against her wetness, she snags my wrist in a vise grip.

"Did I say you could touch me there?"

"Please," I groan, straining against her hold. "I need to feel you."

"Beg harder."

"Please, Reese, let me touch you." I'm desperate. "I'll do anything you want."

She shifts her heel from my mask to my shoulder, her movements exact but tentative. There's a tremor in her leg, uncertainty rippling through her controlled façade. My hands find her hips.

"Such a good boy," she whispers, and through the mask I can see how affected she is. The pink lace of her underwear is damp beneath my fingers.

"You're already so wet," I admire, and she shudders. "This perfect cunt is missing me, isn't it?"

"Touch me, right there," she gasps as I push the lace aside.

Her legs spread wider, hips canting forward with a desperation that makes my cock throb. "Yes."

I circle her clit slowly, watching how she fights to maintain composure. Her hands grip my shoulders tighter, nails digging into skin.

I slip two fingers inside her. She's so tight around my fingers that I have to resist standing up and fucking her just like this.

She needs this. I need it too. To let go.

To be free under her.

"Don't stop," she manages, her voice breaking on the word. "Please."

"I won't," I promise and send my fingers deeper into her. Her thighs shake, and she throws her head back.

"I want—"

"Tell me."

"I want you…" She pauses, struggling with vulnerability, with letting go of control. It's endearing. "On the floor."

"Yes, ma'am."

She glances toward my gym bag. "Do you have…?"

"Yes." I nod, and she walks over to retrieve the condom.

When she returns, she kneels before me. I'm still wearing the fencing mask as she rolls the latex down my length. God, her hand on my cock is fucking gorgeous. Then she's straddling me, sinking down until I'm fully inside her. She pushes her hands into my chest and slams my back on the floor.

I want to give her everything.

"Fuck," I groan, overwhelmed by her wrapped around me.

What I would give to feel all of her without a fucking condom.

I've never wanted someone like that. But with Reese, I want to make her irreversibly mine in the most intimate way possible.

This isn't desire anymore. It's a physical need that consumes every cell in my body.

"I've never done it quite like this," she confesses. "With me on top, I mean. It's different."

"You're doing so good, baby." I guide her hips with gentle pressure, showing her how to roll them in a way that allows my length to hit deeper. "That's it," I encourage, watching her face contort with pleasure. "That makes me feel so good."

She bites her lip, fighting back moans, and it drives me wild. My hands slide up to cup her breasts, thumbs circling her hardened nipples.

"Look in the mirror," I urge. "Look at how you take control, how you take me. Can't you see how perfect you are? Don't you love this?"

"I do," she smiles, dragging her hips over me again and again. Reese finally lifts away the mask. The cool air hits my face before her lips crash into mine, hungry and desperate. She rests her hands on either side of my head. Her tongue slides against mine, and I punch my hips upward, filling her impossibly deeper.

How on earth did I get this fucking lucky?

Her pearl necklace gleams as she rocks over me. But it's the way my silver ring rests against her throat that holds me.

"You not taking off that ring, you know what that means?"

She shakes her head.

"You own me," I breathe against her neck.

With one hand, Reese reaches for the back of her neck and unclasps her necklace, sliding the silver ring off the strand and slipping it onto her right thumb finger. She drapes the pearls around my neck, the cool gems settling against my warm skin as our eyes lock.

"Now you own a piece of me," she whispers, fingers trailing along her necklace adorning my throat.

I manage to get harder, genuinely harder than I thought possible, and I'm afraid the moment is going to send me right over. I suck air through my teeth, a tight grip seconds away from causing me to lose myself inside her.

Reese's mouth attacks mine until I'm bruised by teeth and wet with her spit.

"Ride that dick, baby." My cock buries deeper into her, hitting where she ends while she cries out. "You have complete control over me. This cock? It's yours to do with as you please."

I've never felt this close to the edge before, every nerve ending on fire. Her pace starts to slow, and I can tell she's getting close.

"I want you to fuck me," she slurs with pleasure.

I yank myself up until I'm sitting. Her legs instinctively wrap around my waist as I guide her down hard. She presses her tits into my mouth. I lick and bite every inch of skin. The intimacy of it makes my head spin. She's so small in my grip, but *Christ*, the way she fights back. Thighs viselike around me, one hand fisted painfully in my hair.

"God." Her breath is coming in hot, desperate pants. She bites my lower lip hard enough to draw blood.

When she drops her head back, looking away, I leave one arm around her waist and grab her jaw roughly. "Look at me when I'm fucking you. Use me up," I growl, punctuating each word with a bruising thrust. "Use every fucking inch of me, Reese." She keens, her back arching. "It feels so good."

She retaliates by sinking her teeth into my palm, the sharp pain making me curse. "I want you to come," she groans. "With me."

"I'm right here. I'm right here for you." I thread my fingers into the short strands of her hair, drinking in her wicked grin before she bounces her hips onto me. The sound of slapping flesh fills the training gym.

"Fill me up with your cum, Dante," she begs, eyes rolled back. "I can take it."

My heart nearly stops. "I'm going to give you all of it, baby. Every last drop."

"Dante—ah—I—" Her words dissolve into broken moans as she grinds down harder, faster, chasing her release with animalistic desperation.

"That's it." She quivers violently, caught between surrender and defiance, but she holds my stare as she takes me impossibly deeper, claiming me as thoroughly as I'm claiming her.

Then she seizes around me, her whole body going rigid as the orgasm tears through her. Her teeth sink into my chest as she comes, marking me again. The pain pushes me over the edge, and I come violently, emptying myself into the condom with a guttural groan that sounds foreign to my own ears.

We collapse together, our bodies intertwined in the aftermath.

"I've never…" I start, then pause, struggling to articulate. "With you, it's like every nerve ending is alive. Like I'm finally awake."

She props herself up on an elbow, studying my face with that penetrating gaze. "Have you said that to anyone else?"

"No." I grip her chin, forcing her to meet my eyes. "Look at me. Really look. You…" I trace the curve of her jaw. "You have ruined me for anyone else."

She melts into me then, and I feel the moment she allows herself to believe it. The way she fits against me isn't just familiar anymore, it's necessary. As vital as breathing.

Like every meaningless encounter in my past was preparation for this, for her.

Chapter 40
Reese

NOVEMBER 29TH

Reese Sinclair's Career Is Over—What Happened to the *Heartland Heritage* Star?

DECEMBER 4TH

Sinclair's Silence: Is She Hiding from the Public Eye? Or in Rehab?

DECEMBER 10TH

Sinclair Was Once a Hollywood Darling, Now Just Troubled

"I CAN'T BELIEVE filming is over," I say as Dante and I step onto the narrow path, the one we've walked a hundred times over the past few months. The redwoods loom around us, branches creaking in the cool night breeze. The forest floor is squishy and soft under my boots.

In the distance, I hear the distant murmur of the crew, the last few stragglers breaking down the set and setting up the wrap party down by the lake.

Soon, they'll be gone too.

I inhale deeply, trying to etch this place into my memory. The thick fog ghosting through the trees each morning, the way the light filters through the branches in golden ribbons, the quiet hush of the woods.

And Dante.

"Come on, admit it," he teases, bumping his shoulder lightly against mine. "You'll miss our crack-of-dawn training sessions the most."

"And you'll miss me being your most well-behaved student," I shoot back, grinning.

My leather costume hugs my curves, my pearl necklace with his ring through it hanging exactly where it is supposed to be, while his sheriff's outfit makes him look unfairly handsome.

We did it.

Only two weeks after the original shoot with Felix was supposed to wrap. Mari was far more efficient than Felix ever was. After New Year's, I'm diving into postproduction with Amara. It'll be my first time seeing the editing magic happen so up close and personal.

"And is my star student going to give any indication about where we're going?"

"You've taken me on so many adventures; I thought it was only fair to finally take you on one." I wink at him. "Just keep your expectations low. Unlike you, my world isn't glamorous."

He side-eyes me. "Oh, sure. All you do is star in blockbuster movies, attend premieres in rented jewelry that requires body-guards, and have fans worshiping the ground you walk on. *How dull.*"

It hasn't quite felt that way lately.

"What you meant to say is all I do is memorize lines, go from set to set, shoot a minimum of two movies a year, and in between I visit my family or hang out with Cleo. In comparison to your adventures, I'm not that exciting." I roll my eyes, fidgeting with the sleeve of my leather Robyn Hood costume.

Dante stops walking. I glance back at him, but his gaze is fixed on me, unreadable in the dim light.

"I think you're very exciting," he says, and it lands deep in my chest.

I clear my throat. "Can you walk a little quicker? I want to get this done before the wrap party starts."

He slows his pace instead.

"I'm admiring the view," he says, grinning.

"Of my behind? Bad, bad boy."

"All those squats, Reese. Soon enough, you'll be able to bench me with all that muscle."

I throw my head back and laugh. Then, on impulse, I reach back and grab his hand. His palm is snug against mine, our fingers slotting together like they've done this a thousand times before.

The wardrobe and props tent looms ahead, its white canvas glowing softly in the twilight. A hush settles between us.

"This is a tradition I've been doing since I was eleven," I tell him, squeezing his hand once before letting go. "And I wanted to share it with you."

I undo the string on the tent flap, rushing us inside. The space is drenched in golden lighting and smells of worn leather and wood.

"The props tent? You know, the last time we were alone on set like this..." Dante's voice trails off, his hand gliding along my lower back. "Are we recreating the armory moment?"

My muscles tense at his suggestion. We could. Later.

Instead, I shoot him an exaggerated, scandalized look. "Dante! I said I've been doing this since I was eleven!"

"Right, sorry. All my brain is thinking about is green leather and your ass."

"Of course it is." I twist my hands together, suddenly feeling shy about sharing my secret tradition.

"Come on, tell me what we're doing here."

"After every wrap, I take something small from set. A memento."

His hands cup the sides of his face, feigning shock. "The pristine Reese Sinclair? A thief?"

"Not theft," I protest. "More like borrowed memories."

"So you return the items?"

"Absolutely not. They're mine."

He tsks, shaking his head. "And somehow this is not one of your biggest regrets? How does stealing rank below talking in class?"

"It's not stealing!" I insist, swatting at him.

"Forget what I said about not having anything in common." He laughs so casually I reach up to swat him again, but he grabs my wrist. Dang quick reflexes. "Hey, I don't judge! What loot have you *borrowed* and plan on never returning?" He reaches into a wooden crate, pulling out the doll Robyn's father gave her when she was a child.

I weave between the tables. "Let's see, a vintage brooch from *Heartland Heritage*. Remember the scene where Elizabeth finds her grandmother's jewelry box in the dusty attic? And an old brass key from *Strings of Time* that was supposed to unlock the mysterious music box. Oh, and my latest addition was this gorgeous cardigan from *Love and Loathing*."

"You're full of surprises."

My fingers trail over props as I search, but my attention keeps drifting to Dante behind me, the quiet weight of his presence, the way he's watching me. Then I spot it. The wooden dagger from when we ran through the forest, rehearsing until he was on top of me.

"This," I whisper, voice unsteady. "This is perfect."

"The dagger?" His fingers brush mine as he picks it up, sending a shiver down my spine.

I nod.

"Good choice," he murmurs, turning it over in his hands.

A beat passes. The tent feels smaller. The hum of the distant wrap party starting up barely registers.

"I got to see so much of your world," I say, forcing myself to sound normal. "I'm looking forward to coming to some of your fencing matches."

"You want to come?" he asks, like he doesn't quite believe it.

"If you want me there."

"Of course."

I swallow. "Okay, well, here you go," I say, pushing the wooden prop into his hands.

He takes it, eyebrows waggling. "Me?"

"I don't want to be the one to get caught."

A slow grin tugs at his lips as he tucks the dagger into his jacket. "This makes us partners in crime."

"Alright, partner. We should get to the wrap party," I manage, though I don't move. "Before someone comes."

His gaze lingers before he leans down to kiss me. We've spent every night for the past five weeks together, and I don't know how I'm going to go back to sleeping without him.

When he breaks the kiss, he says, "Now we can go. Before Mari comes and yells at us for stealing."

"*The* Dante Hastings, scared?"

"Around you? Terrified."

As we leave the tent, my lips still tingling, I know I'll be replaying this moment long after the night is over.

Everything I thought I wanted before this movie is still true —I want it to be successful. I want people to focus on my acting, to see me as more than a pretty face. I want to break out of the box they've shoved me into for years.

But the one thing I never predicted?

Falling for him.

And now, I don't know how to want anything else.

Breaking through the tree line, we're greeted by a massive bonfire that lights up the night sky. The lake stretches out beyond, its surface glittering with reflected flames and moonlight.

"Hey, it's our favorite duo!" Marcus calls out, rushing over to hug me. "That final fight sequence is going to look incredible thanks to you two."

The crew swarms around us, creating a comforting bubble of celebration. Tom from lighting reminisces about our early morning shoots, while Nina from props proudly recalls how we mastered her weapons.

When Dante's arm brushes against mine, his warmth seeps through my leather costume, and I close my eyes to savor this perfect moment. Looking around at these familiar faces, I realize this is exactly the kind of on-set family I've always dreamt of finding, especially after those tense days dealing with Felix.

I savor all of it because I don't want it to end.

Chapter 41
Reese

D‍ECEMBER 12TH

WHERE IS REESE SINCLAIR? Star Goes Dark Amid Rumors

D‍ECEMBER 17TH

BREAKING: *Robyn Hood* Destined for Box Office Disaster, Industry Insiders Say

"F‍AIR WARNING: the entire Hastings clan will descend upon us the moment we get inside." Dante laughs, pocketing his phone.

"Wait, let me do my family tree recitation one more time," I say, inhaling deeply in what I hope is a calming breath but feels more like preperformance hyperventilation. "Alec, Brooklyn, Cameron, Ezra, and Francesca. Parents are Selene and Leo. Cameron's with Daphne, Ezra's with Hazel, and I'm currently having an existential crisis." I tick off each name on my fingers like I'm counting down to launch. Luckily, his siblings are named in alphabetical order, from oldest to youngest, which makes them easy to remember.

"You know," he says, "most people just wing it and hope for the best."

"I just want them to like me," I confess, my voice small. What I don't add is that their approval feels like a life raft in an ocean of uncertainty—which is probably not the healthiest metaphor I've ever come up with, but hey, we're working with what we've got.

Dante opens the car door for me, and immediately we're bombarded by screaming paparazzi.

"Reese! Reese! Over here!" they shout, cameras flashing like strobe lights.

"Did you cut your hair during a breakdown?"

"How long have you two been dating?"

"When's the wedding?"

"Reese, are you checking into rehab?"

"Is it true you're taking a break from acting?"

The questions make my stomach turn. Not a single one about *Robyn Hood*. I push down the thought as Dante shields me from the chaos. The cameras continue their relentless assault as we make our way inside the elegant On Cloud Nine hotel overlooking the San Francisco coastline, where we're greeted by a luxurious space filled with fashion-forward guests and the subtle scent of expensive perfume.

The Hastings family is clustered together, and I have to steady myself. Even after years in Hollywood, where beautiful people are basically a currency, this family is different. They're unfairly, outrageously gorgeous, the kind of beauty that makes you want to check if there's spinach in your teeth or if your dress is on backward. Dante's father, Leo, is distinguished in sleek black, while his mother, Selene, shines in emerald green, her curls doing that perfect, caught-in-the-light thing that makes it look like she's glowing.

Together, with their children around them, they're startling.

"Everyone," Dante announces as we reach them, "she needs no introduction, but I'll do you all the honor anyway, my Reese."

His Reese.

My heart flutters at the words, but not for long, as a whirlwind of energy in a shimmering metallic silver suit with sparkling flames dancing up the sleeves practically ricochets into our space.

"Is that my scarf?" She points at Dante's neck, bouncing on the balls of her feet.

"You forgot it in your car, so I put it to good use," Dante drawls, tugging at the scarf with a cocky smirk. "Though I guess I can't complain about you raiding my closet, little sister."

"Ugh, he's impossible." The girl rolls her eyes dramatically before turning to me with practiced nonchalance. "I'm Frankie. Thanks for those signed posters, by the way. They look great in my trailer at the track."

"It was my pleasure."

"Hey, since we're here…" Frankie pulls out her phone with a mischievous grin.

"Don't you dare," Dante warns, swatting the phone away.

"Oh, stop! I'd love a photo." I laugh, earning an approving smile from Frankie. She bends down, and we take the photo, our cheeks pressed together.

"Oh my god, you are fucking ripped!" Frankie squeals, looking at my biceps, which are clearly visible in my gown. "Your arm muscles are nicer than Dante's."

I do feel strong tonight.

Another figure approaches, her movements graceful and precise. "Don't mind our youngest," she says with a gentle smile. "I'm Brooklyn. And can I say, we were obsessed with your movies growing up! We used to act them out in the backyard." I notice how conversations around us quiet, replaced by scrutinizing glances that dart away when caught.

"Oh my gosh, you never told me that!" I exclaim, poking at Dante's chest.

Frankie snorts. "Probably because he'd have to admit he dressed up as your character from *Heartland Heritage*."

"Complete with cowboy boots and belt buckle." Brooklyn's pink lips curl into a smirk.

"I have no recollection of such events." Dante puts his hands up, but the telltale redness climbing his neck betrays him.

"Oh, don't deny it; he's your biggest fan," Brooklyn insists. Like Dante, she radiates that magnetic Hastings DNA.

"Well, I'm his biggest fan as well." I laugh.

A tall, brooding man steps forward. "Cameron Hastings," he introduces himself, then turns to the vibrant woman with purple hair beside him, his eyes filled with unmistakable pride. "And this is Daphne." The way he says her name makes my heart squeeze—it's like watching someone describe their favorite constellation.

Daphne beams, adjusting the knitted bow tie at Cameron's neck. "Hi! I've heard so much about you!" Her enthusiasm is infectious. Cameron never stops staring at her, tracking her movements like she's the sun and he's caught in her orbit.

"Your dress is absolutely gorgeous," I say, admiring its intricate details.

"She made it herself," Cameron interjects before Daphne can respond. His voice is so rich with obvious adoration that I blush hearing it. Daphne twirls, the handmade dress flowing around her like liquid starlight.

"Let me get us something to drink," Dante murmurs, his thumb brushing over my knuckles. "Champagne for you?"

"That would be nice," I say, still unsettled by the scrutinizing glances that seem to follow our every move.

"Be back in a sec. You good here?"

"Of course."

As Dante weaves through the crowd, Leo and Selene approach, holding hands. "We're so glad you could make it tonight," Selene says, her voice carrying a maternal comfort that instantly puts me at ease. "Let's rescue you from this chaos. I'm Selene. Thank you for coming tonight and for your donation."

"It's my pleasure."

"Welcome to the madhouse," Leo adds with a bear hug. "Dante hasn't stopped talking about you."

"*So*, about those premiere tickets…?" Frankie springs forward, earning an exasperated "Francesca!" from Selene.

"What?" She shrugs. "He's being so cagey about it!"

"The whole family is welcome, and friends too. It would be my pleasure. This movie would not be what it is without your son. His help with my choreography was everything."

"Yes, he's mentioned," Selene smoothly redirects. "We can't wait to see you both on screen. And please, our home is always open to you. We'd love to have you."

Watching Selene and Leo with their children, it's hard to imagine them sending Dante away to boarding school. They seem so loving, so connected to each of their kids' big dreams and adventures.

But maybe that's exactly why Dante rebelled. Growing up in a family like this would be enough to make anyone feel like they needed to carve their own path and set themselves apart.

Before I can properly process the wave of belonging that crashes over me, the doors swing open to reveal four more figures.

I recognize Alec first; the entire room seems to shrink around him. Despite being the shortest of the brothers, he's monumental in his own right. With Leo's chiseled features and Selene's chestnut curls, he's the spitting image of both parents combined into something formidable. His tattooed arms fill out a crisp white shirt cuffed at the elbows, beaded bracelets and climbing ropes wrapped around his wrists like badges of honor. His eyes command attention. Dark, watchful.

"Before you ask, Mom—yes, we are still going on the K2 expedition," he announces.

Selene's groan is pure maternal concern. "I can't discuss this death-defying adventure of yours anymore. I've made my point clear."

"We'll be fine," Alec says with quiet confidence. He automatically positions himself between his family and the crowded room.

"Totally got this," a man beside Alec says. His shirt matches his friend's, his own wrists adorned with similar climbing tokens. "Hi, I'm Finn, by the way!"

Alec acknowledges me with a measured nod, his assessment palpable, checking to see if I'm worthy of his baby brother's attention.

"And I'm Ezra," says a striking figure with dirty blond hair that sets him apart from his siblings, though the sharp Hastings features are unmistakable. "This is my fiancée, Hazel."

The woman beside him is breathtaking. Intricate tattoos wind up her arms like living art, and her dark curls cascade past her shoulders.

"Oh gosh, congratulations!" I exclaim, spotting the ring.

Frankie groans dramatically. "Don't get too excited. These two are going to be engaged until we're all in retirement homes."

Hazel shifts, looking embarrassed. "Oh, you know, just taking our time. No rush," she says, waving her hand dismissively, as if trying to brush away the attention.

Dante returns with champagne flutes balanced expertly in his hands. "I see you've met the oldest and youngest of the Hastings clan," he says, passing me a glass. "And some of our adopted family members too."

Dante drapes an arm around me, and I nestle into his side, taking in the scene before us. Even now, he holds himself slightly apart. Sure, he shares Brooklyn's sharp steel edges, and his tattoos match Alec's intensity, the way Leo's chain echoes Dante's rings. You can see his fire doubled in Frankie's spirit.

Yet there's something different about him, something you wouldn't notice if you didn't know him well.

I understand how being part of such an extraordinary family could push someone to either shine brighter or burn out trying.

A group of well-dressed executives is approaching us. The crystal glasses in their hands reflect the light like warning signals.

"Incoming," I say to Dante and smooth my dress, mentally running through the talking points that Geraldine prepared for me.

Talk about *Robyn Hood*. Talk about working with Amara. Talk about all of the impressive stunt work I'm doing.

Focus on the important things.

"Dante!" A man in an impeccable suit completely ignores my presence. "The head of Red Bull wants a word about that charity initiative you brought up at our last meeting. Did you know he used to sit on the USFA committee? Could be a great connection for you to have with your review coming up."

My tight smile falters. "Reese, come with me," Dante says, his eyes bright with excitement. "There are some people I'd love you to meet."

"No, no, you go ahead," I say. "I think I saw some old friends from my last film."

Dante kisses my cheek before he's swept into a whirlwind of admirers. My stomach stirs with an emotion I'm actively filing under *Do not examine too closely*.

I should be happy for him. No, scratch that—I *am* happy for him. Getting to speak with someone who used to be on the USFA committee could be his chance to get his suspension lifted. His ticket back to the fencing world he loves and misses so much. The rational part of my brain is doing cartwheels of joy.

But there's another part of me that feels exposed and scrutinized as I stand here alone. And based on the sideways glances and hushed conversations around the room, I don't think my discomfort is just paranoia.

ACROSS THE BALLROOM, I spot a group from *Love and Loathing*, including Amrita Gupta, Kyna Wright, and Jaxon Elio, huddled near the bar with a few other A-list actors. I hesitate, my stomach churning at the thought of approaching them—especially after that weird interaction with Jaxon at his birthday. But as I scan the room, I realize I'm running out of options. The Hastings family has scattered to their own social circles, and I refuse to be the clingy outsider trailing after them all evening.

Besides, I reason with myself, these are my industry peers. If I want any chance at salvaging my reputation, I need to start somewhere. Even if that means facing the very people I've alienated. Taking a deep breath and squaring my shoulders, I make my way over.

"Hey, everyone," I say, my voice carrying a forced lightness I don't feel. The response is a chorus of mumbled acknowledgments and awkward nods.

Amrita's eyes meet mine for a fraction of a second before she deliberately turns away, angling her body to close their circle. Kyna, who last summer was begging me to consider a role in their upcoming project, suddenly becomes fascinated with their phone.

Jaxon, however, doesn't hide his disdain.

"Well, if it isn't Reese Sinclair," he says. "Shouldn't you be over there with Dante?"

"I—"

"We were just discussing the upcoming pilot season," Amrita adds, her tone clipped. She pauses, taking a calculated sip of her martini. "Though with all your recent...press, I imagine you might be taking a break?"

The implication hits like a slap. These people, who once clamored for my attention at every event, are now treating me like I'm radioactive.

Maybe I am?

"Actually, I'm attached to several promising projects," I lie, but Amrita's already engaging Kyna in an obviously forced conversation about their new beach house. Jaxon's eyes roll as he mutters something about reputation under his breath.

I stand there, the weight of their rejection settling heavy in my stomach. I've been in this industry long enough to recognize a subtle execution when I see one.

Gathering up what's left of my dignity, I make my way to a quiet corner of the ballroom.

The whispers, the averted gazes, the way bodies physically shift away. I snatch a champagne flute from a passing waiter. Fragments of *desperate* and *train wreck* float to my ears and make me want to sink through the floor.

Suddenly, I'm a pariah?

I cut my hair and stopped being their perfect girl, and I'm no longer acceptable?

This is so unfair, it hurts. It cuts deeper than Felix's rage-filled directing, deeper than stumbling through fight sequences until my feet bled, deeper than countless humiliating interviews where they tried to strip away my dignity one invasive question at a time.

I'm embarrassed.

An abandoned table stands by the windows, and I settle at it. I search for Dante, wanting to curl up under his big arm, but he's across the room, standing with the same executives who came by earlier, his easy laughter carrying over the crowd.

Things seem to be going too well for me to pull him away.

"Room for one more outcast?"

I startle, looking up to find Destiny Hope standing at my table. Her sleek black dress hugs her curves, strawberry blonde hair cascading in loose waves.

A year ago, her face graced magazine covers with headlines screaming about her latest scandal. Though now I can't recall what it was. Back then, I might have politely excused myself from her presence, not wanting to be associated with someone the industry had labeled as "difficult."

The irony makes me want to laugh and cry simultaneously.

"Please." I gesture to one of the many empty chairs surrounding me. "I seem to have plenty of space." My laugh comes out more bitter than intended.

"Destiny Hope," she says.

"Reese Sinclair," I reply, then cringe at my automatic need to introduce myself—as if anyone in this room doesn't know who I am, and for all the wrong reasons. "Loved your latest album," I add, trying to fill the awkward silence with something, anything.

"Thank you." She slides into the chair. "Couldn't help but notice you're getting the full freeze-out treatment tonight."

My shoulders cave inward. "Obvious, huh?"

"People can be so vicious."

"Oh no, they aren't—" I pause, swallowing hard. "There's no point in playing pretend here, is there?"

"They always love you," she says, each word falling like a stone into still water, "until they don't. You try to hide? They scream mental breakdown!" She jabs a finger into the air. "Show your face in public? Oh, you're just seeking attention. Stay quiet?" A harsh laugh. "They assume you're checked into The Meadows."

"It's brutal. I thought, maybe naively, that I was going to take control of my own narrative." I shred a napkin into tiny pieces, watching the white fragments scatter across the dark tablecloth like snow. The room suddenly feels too loud, too bright, too exposed. "I mean, I'm sure you understand, but all I wanted to do was live my life outside of the woman I've been for twenty-nine years. I wanted to be—"

"Normal?"

"Unconstrained."

"They always need someone to tear down. You're it. Last year it was me, the year before it was what's-her-face." Is that what this is? A full-blown teardown? "When I released *Disrepute* and entered my new era, I wrote songs about my career struggles, about female friendship, about my own growth." She rolls her eyes. "But since it was such a big shift away from my typical country love songs, they saw it as an opportunity to take my voice into their own hands."

There's a peculiar intimacy in shared exclusion—a sort of fellowship in falling from grace that feels both devastating and strangely freeing.

"I've never been on this side of it."

"That can't be true! What about that mess with Ricky way back when?"

I cringe. "You know about that?"

"Who doesn't, darling? You were assaulted on stage, an underage woman accepting her first award." She rolls her eyes. "I remember reading how his bombastic show of affection was *swoon-worthy*. No one dared to comment on how scared you looked after the kiss."

I was disgusted, violated, and afraid. The only thing I remember going through my mind was, *Smile, smile brighter, play it off, don't be problematic.*

Everything is different now. I don't want to be smaller.

"How did you get through it back then?"

"Back then, the media attention wasn't aimed at me. They saw Ricky as some lovestruck, committed boyfriend. But I guess if it wasn't for my family, my agent, my best friend…I don't know how I would've made it out alive. I felt so alone."

"As long as you have people around you that you can trust, you're going to get through this."

I have all those people around me still, and I know they'll stand by my side. I have Dante too—I scan the room to find him, and his eyes catch mine across the crowd. I love him, I know I do. The feeling blooms in my chest like wildflowers after rain, messy and inevitable and perfect.

Even though I can't map out where we're heading or if there's a destination worth reaching, even though I'm as new to relationships as a baby deer is to walking and Dante has *commitment issues* tattooed across his heart in invisible ink, I do know we trust each other in a bone-deep way that makes everything else feel like background noise.

Maybe that's enough of a starting point.

"How long did it take for everything to—?"

"Go back to normal? It never did," she says, each word a hammer strike. "But it was a year of hell before it started to simmer down. Every outfit criticized. Every performance torn apart. Every relationship dissected."

A year of this? The fake smiles, the whispers behind my back? How am I going to promote *Robyn Hood* in the face of all of this?

"To be honest with you, that just makes me want to hide in a hole." I laugh sardonically.

"That's exactly what you can't do. I tried it—pulled myself out of the public eye for a month, then two. But I missed the freedom I felt after letting my real voice out there, and once you get a taste of that, you can't let it go. Take it from me."

Destiny's hand finds mine, as if she can tell my mind is putting me through the wringer. "Honey, they've already decided what you are—too wild, too flawed, too real." She sweeps her hand across the room. "And why wouldn't they when they insist it's their right to decide, like we signed away our right to be human? Like all those journalists aren't turning our pain into their entertainment so the world can act shocked when we break."

There's something devastating in the way we've learned to internalize our own destruction, to mistake survival for weakness. "I don't want to break. I want to get through this," I say, determined now.

"You will. Everyone before you did." She counts off on her fingers. "Britney had a breakdown? They never asked why. Lindsay struggled? Turned it into a punchline. They can try to reduce us to our bodies, our relationships, our beauty secrets." Her laugh is bitter. "But that only works when we stay in their perfect little boxes. We can't let them pit us against each other, make us compete for a few seats at the table."

"We should be building longer tables together."

"Exactly."

"Look." She smiles. "Why don't I help you show up in a way that matters? The Women in Media gala is the day after Christmas, and I just so happen to be on the board. We need a speaker. Gloria Steinem had to cancel."

"Me? Are you sure?"

"Yes. Come use your voice. No one ever gave me a chance to speak up; no one cared. So, I'm giving it to you."

The invitation hangs. I take a slow sip of champagne, letting the bubbles dissolve on my tongue. Through the window, the city lights blink like distant stars, each one a story waiting to be told.

My story, perhaps.

Not the tabloid version, not the Reese-and-Dante version, but mine.

Chapter 42
Dante

My phone buzzes in my suit pocket. Across the room, Reese is laughing with a woman at a table by the window. I've been stuck here with these executives for an hour now, listening to them brag about their golf scores while trying to get an in with the USFA committee. The head of Red Bull is warming up to me, and his influence could help expedite my suspension review. But all I want is to walk over to my girl, wrap my arms around her waist, and—

My phone won't stop vibrating, the screen lighting up with an unknown number. Oakland area code. I reluctantly excuse myself.

Strange.

"Hello?" The word comes out like gravel.

"This call is coming from the Oakland Police Department Central Station on behalf of detainee Holly Hollywood. If you'd like to accept the charges, please press one."

Holly Hollywood. Who the fuck is that?

My stomach drops, acid rising in my throat as I realize. I slam the one button.

"Dante?" Em's familiar voice wavers, small and breakable.

"Em?" I retreat from the party's glow into the shadows, phone pressed against my ear like a lifeline.

"I'm in jail." Her fear mirrors my own at fourteen, when the cops arrested me for joyriding in my father's Rolls-Royce.

"Why the fuck are you calling me from there? You're not even eighteen!" The words crack like a whip. Christ, I sound like him.

"Wouldn't give the cops my info. No ID."

I dig my thumb and forefinger into my eye sockets, my jaw working. Of course she called me instead of her parents. Fucking hell. "Jesus Christ, Em." I exhale. "I'm coming. Oakland Central, yeah?"

"Yeah."

"Thirty minutes."

"Okay," she mumbles, fear bleeding through her tough-girl act.

"It'll be fine." I soften my tone, the same way I do when I'm walking her through a complex parry. The line clicks dead, and I pocket the phone, already mapping the quickest route.

"DIDN'T REALIZE you were into pearls and gold," I say, my grip tightening on the wheel. "Not your style."

"Fuck off," Em snarls, shoulders hunched.

The engine's low growl fills the space between us as we cut through Oakland's empty streets. I catch my reflection in the rearview—fuck, I see myself at her age, same cornered-animal look after my own brush with handcuffs.

The chief's words echo in my head. *Caught shoplifting, jewelry stuffed in pockets.*

Getting her out was easy enough once I dropped my father's name—same playbook as back then. Money talks, strings get pulled. But watching her shrink under the harsh station lights had stirred something visceral in my chest. What stings more is that she didn't come to me first. Didn't trust me enough to ask for help before it got to this point.

"Ugh, can you get the lecture over with already? I don't want to sit here in silence with you stewing."

"No lectures," I say, focusing on the road ahead. "But we're dealing with this."

"There's nothing to deal with."

"The theft ends tonight," I say. "And from now on, you come to me. No more hiding shit until it blows up."

Em shifts, staring out the window. "Whatever."

"Not whatever," I snap, then catch myself. I can't go off on her; she's a kid. A kid who's hurting, and I know what that's like.

I force my shoulders to drop and take one of Reese's deep breaths. In for four, hold for seven, out for eight. *Alright, fuck, this shit works pretty well.*

"Look, I know you don't want to hear it from me, but I know exactly how you feel, better than anyone. Wanting them to notice you. Trying anything, good or bad, just to make them pay attention. Feeling like you're screaming but they can't hear you. But stealing shit isn't going to make them see you. It's only going to make things worse. And lying to me isn't going to help either."

"Got a better idea?"

"Monday morning, we start over. Every day after school, you're mine. At the gym. No bullshit, no arguments, no secrets. I'll handle your parents."

She crosses her arms tight. "Don't need a savior."

"Good. Because I'm your coach," I say, catching her gaze in the mirror. "That's it."

These months with Reese have taught me something unexpected. There's a different kind of power in watching someone else find their strength. Maybe that's what Em needs, what I needed then. Purpose. Direction. Someone to be honest with.

"But I—"

"Listen to me, kid. This is not up for discussion," I cut in. "I don't care about your excuses. You're wasting your talent, and I won't stand for it." She shrinks beside me, and I adjust my tone. "You're not just decent at fencing. You could be fucking brilliant. Princeton brilliant, Olympic-level brilliant. But not if you're stealing shit and keeping secrets."

The words land between us with the weight of a blade striking true.

I'd kept these thoughts locked away, even from myself, in those dark hours when I pictured life beyond competing, beyond the metallic taste of victory.

But fuck it—the truth burns hot in my chest.

Em's got the talent, and I'm not about to let her fire die. Not when I could be the one to forge it into something lethal.

"Olympics?" Her laugh is brittle. "You're insane."

"Every competition that comes up, you're entering. Win, and there's something in it for you."

She rolls her eyes. "Like what?"

"Whatever the fuck you want, kid. You want jewelry? We'll get fucking jewelry. Want Princeton letters? I'll get my friends to write some for you too. Want new sneakers? Want to come to movie premieres? You got it. But you're going to be fencing."

She shifts. "Don't you have more important shit to do? Your stupid movie? Getting unsuspended? Hollywood?"

"Yeah, I do." I think of Reese's smile across the gala, my chance to get the Red Bull exec to put in a good word for me with the USFA committee. "But this matters more right now. I'll deal with your parents, and you're going to join Lev's academy full time, not as some fucking temporary youth program."

"I can't afford that."

"I can. But from now on, Em, you have to be honest with me."

The silence stretches taut between us, broken only by a

muffled sniffle. Em's shoulders shake, but she keeps her face turned toward the window. Without a word, I reach into my breast pocket and pull out my silk pocket square, holding it out to her without looking. She takes it, the fabric rustling softly.

"My parents…" she cries. "They fucked off to Reno for the weekend. Left me here on my own, and I don't know. I couldn't stand being on my own for another weekend in that stupid empty house, ordering pizza with the cash they left me."

Something raw and familiar twists in my gut. "What about your sister?"

"They took her with them, of course."

"And they're coming back? Are you sure?"

"Yeah, they always do. They just never bring me with them. I wanted—I thought if I took something big, that if they got a call, they'd come back. It was dumb. But then they didn't pick up, and, well, then I called you."

My heart aches so badly because I did have parents to pick me up. I had parents that were so panicked about me.

Em doesn't have that. But she will now.

"Then I'll find somewhere safe and comfortable for you to stay. All my siblings are in town—we're going to the family house for a few days. You can stay with us."

"I don't need your char—"

"Just say thank you, Em," I say.

She swallows. "Thank you."

My grip on the wheel loosens. I'm far from perfect, but I understand what it takes to claw your way out of the dark. I can't rescue Em from herself, but I can be what I never had—someone who sees the fire in her and refuses to let it die. Maybe that's why I had to walk through my own personal hell—to recognize that look in her eyes and know exactly how to break through those walls.

And watching Em be brave enough to trust me, to let me in despite everything—it rocks me.

Because I need to do the same with Reese.

I need to be honest with her, completely and totally honest.

Because in four months, Reese has become my everything. She's the person I want to be there for in every possible way, whatever that means.

Chapter 43
Dante

THE BACK ROOM of On Cloud Nine is all dark wood and leather, illuminated by sconces that cast a gentle glow across the space.

"Oh my god. Your sister is Frankie Hastings?" Em exclaims.

My parents are lounging on a plush leather couch, Mom's legs draped over Dad's, each with a crystal whisky tumbler in hand. They glance up when we enter, their expressions softening into affection, the kind Em probably hasn't seen much of lately.

"Where was this excitement when you met me?" I tease, raising an eyebrow.

"Nobody knows what fencing is," she responds. "But your sister is literally making waves in the racing world. One thing I actually have in common with Dad is we watch all the races together." Her voice catches on the word *Dad*.

"You're the girl Dante's coaching?" Frankie asks, walking over. "Ugh, I love you already! How old are you? You wanna drive my—"

"Don't finish that sentence," I warn her with a laugh, already shaking my head. "Can you keep an eye on her? Em's going to stay at the house with everyone tonight."

Frankie nods without hesitation and turns back to Em. "Wanna order takeout on his card?" she jokes.

"Okay!" Em responds eagerly. Her shoulders relax, like she's finally letting herself breathe.

She'll be fine for the night.

My mind drifts back to the gala, to Reese. I need to talk to her.

"Seen Reese?" I ask, hands shoved in my pockets, shoulders tight with an energy I can't quite place. The Red Bull exec and his friends are probably wondering where I disappeared to, but I couldn't care less.

"She was in here earlier," Mom says, readjusting on the couch with that casual grace she's always had. "Think she headed to the ballroom. Place is clearing out, though."

"The kid?"

"She'll be fine," I say. "Can she stay with us for a few nights? I need to talk to Reese."

"Of course, sweetheart."

I pivot toward the door, then stop. Memories of my own teenage years flood back: the nights I'd climb out my window, the fights, the constant feeling of being misunderstood. "Actually. Got a minute?"

Dad straightens, all attention. "Always, son."

I settle into the chair across from them. Mom watches me with that penetrating gaze that used to make me want to crawl out of my skin. Now I just let it land. "I need to say something," I start, throat tight. "About being such a fuckup when I was younger. Never properly apologized for it, I don't think."

Mom moves faster than I expect, perching beside me, her hand rubbing along my shoulder. "Don't you dare apologize."

"Why would you think you needed to?" Dad leans in, elbows on knees, face etched with concern.

"Picking Em up tonight. Made me think about all the shit I put you through. The reckless fucking choices. The selfishness.

Remember that time I took the Rolls for a joyride? Or when I got caught fighting behind the gym, bloody knuckles and a broken nose?"

"You were finding your way," Mom says softly, squeezing my shoulder. The memory of her tears that night at the hospital flashes through my mind.

"You shipped me off to boarding school." The words come out harder than intended.

Dad exhales slowly. "Son, we were losing you. You didn't want anything to do with us, with your siblings. Every night, you'd sneak out, run off, push us away. We saw how much potential you had buried underneath all that anger. Boarding school wasn't about forcing you to change, it was about giving you space to find yourself, to discover who you wanted to be, away from all the pressure of being a Hastings."

"And look what happened," Mom adds. Her touch is grounding. "Look who you became."

"Yeah, suspended athlete. Real success story."

Mom's scoff is pure indignation. "Princeton graduate. Olympic gold medalist. Elite athlete. And, more importantly, an incredible son, brother, and man."

Dad nods. "We're proud of you, Dante. Not for the medals or the headlines, but for who you are."

"I always felt like the fuckup, you know? Everyone else had their thing figured out so early. Like there was this mold of what a Hastings should be, and I couldn't fit it. Couldn't find my sport, couldn't be what you wanted."

"Christ, being a Hastings isn't about some fucking sport," Mom says.

"Look at me," Dad says. "I'm useless at all that athletic shit."

"Yeah, but I never…" I trail off, running a hand through my hair. "Never quite matched up to you either, Dad."

"Match up? You got into Princeton, while I dropped out of community college. Found my way by pure fucking luck. You're more like us than you think—stubborn bastards who figure it out in their own time.”

A tension I'd been carrying for years loosens in my chest.

“Thanks. These past months have stripped away all the bullshit I was chasing: the headlines, the attention, the fucking accolades. All shallow validation I thought meant something.” A harsh laugh escapes me, bitter and self-deprecating. “Christ, it sounds even more pathetic out loud. But seeing Em fence, watching her killer instinct take over when she nails a technique —for the first time, I'm not thinking about my own glory. I want to build something real with this sport. Something that actually matters.”

“We're here for you,” Mom says, her hand still steady on my shoulder. “What's on your mind?”

“Coaching. Been thinking about it.” My fingers drum against my leg, a restless rhythm. “Watching Em fight, seeing that raw talent, it's fucking different. Never felt anything like it.” The admission costs me something.

Mom's eyes dart to Dad, and she smirks. “Pay up.”

He mutters a curse, fishing out a hundred from his wallet.

I exhale sharply. “What's this about?”

“Had a bet going about which of you kids would end up coaching. My money was always on you.”

“Bullshit.” The word comes out hard.

Dad's wry smile confirms it. “I was betting on Brooklyn. Don't tell her, though; she'll lose her shit.”

“The Olympics aren't off the table. Next one, maybe after, if this disciplinary shit clears up. But...” The words stick in my throat. “I could use some pointers. On coaching. If you're offering, Mom.”

“I'd love nothing more. And Dante? Whatever path you choose—competing, coaching, anything—we're in your corner. Always have been.”

The silence settles heavy. Mom gets a look in her eye. The one that makes me want to bolt.

"So," she drawls, sharing a knowing glance with Dad, "are we going to talk about how you can't take your eyes off Reese whenever she's in the room?"

"Mom—"

"She's right. You've got the same dopey look I had when I first met your mom."

He pulls Mom to her feet, their hands finding each other with practiced ease. They've always been like this. Completely in sync.

"Sometimes," Dad continues, brushing a kiss against Mom's forehead, "you just know."

"Or you do what your father did and buy an entire basketball team to have an excuse to talk to me. God knows what kind of grand gesture you're planning."

I stare at my hands, suddenly finding the tweed armrest below me fascinating. "Mom, Dad…I need…fuck, I need your help with something."

"We're here," Mom says. I feel sixteen again.

"I think I'm in love with her." The confession tears out of me, raw and unpolished.

"When you think, you know," Dad says quietly.

I drag my fingers through my hair, messing up the styling. "That's the thing—I've kept something from her. Something important. And now that I've fallen for her, it's eating me up inside."

Mom cranes her neck against Dad's suit jacket. "Listen to me. You've learned to have better judgment, sweetheart. If you held something back, it wasn't out of malice. But now you need to be brave and face this head on."

"You're right," I agree.

"Besides, son, you're only twenty-six years old," he says gently. "And while that's not an excuse, I understand. Just this summer you were living it up on your yacht without a care in the world. You've never had a serious relationship, never let anyone outside the family get too close. We all make questionable decisions while we're figuring things out. It's part of growing up."

He's right. Four months ago, I was knee-deep in white powder and models.

"What if she hates me for it?"

Dad rubs Mom's back. "Relationships built on truth might get shaken, but they can weather the storm. It's the ones built on secrets that crumble. Tell her everything, give her time to process it, and then respect whatever she decides. That's all you can do."

Fuck, they're right. Of course they're right. My mind circles back through every moment with Reese—the late-night conversations, the way she calls me on my shit, how she makes me want to be better without making me feel worse. For the first time in my life, I'm not running from this feeling.

I'm running toward it.

"Okay," I say, standing. "I'm going to find her."

Dad grins, squeezing my shoulder. "Go get her."

I head toward the door.

Fuck. The thought of laying it all bare makes my throat tight. I've done this a thousand times before—the chase, the game, the carefully crafted lines. But this isn't that. This is real. This is Reese. And I'm terrified.

The weight of every headline I've generated, every scandal I've sparked, every heart I've carelessly handled—it all crashes down on me now. But with her…God, with her, I can see a different version of myself. One who watches fog roll in from a San Francisco balcony, who makes plans that stretch past tomorrow, who finally, finally stops running.

When I enter the ballroom, I spot her at a table by the window. The band has already packed up. My stomach lurches. Christ, I've never been this nervous about a relationship in my life. My palms are actually sweating.

"Reese?"

She turns, and fuck—even exhausted, even with her shoulders slumped, she's the most beautiful thing I've ever seen. Her smile, lazy and worn, makes my chest ache.

"Is Em okay?"

"Yeah, she is. My siblings are adopting her." I attempt a joke and sink into the chair beside her, trying to steady my racing pulse. "She's going to stay with my parents for the rest of the weekend."

Reese rests her head on my shoulder, and I have to close my eyes against the wave of guilt. "Does that mean I get you all to myself?"

I want to drown in that question, let myself believe I deserve the trust I hear in her voice. But I love her too much to keep lying. "Can we actually talk about something?"

She sits up, brown eyes searching mine. "Of course."

Chapter 44
Reese

"Over the past couple of months, you've made me want to be more than just the person the world thinks they know. No one's ever held all of me so gently in their hands, Reese," Dante says.

My breath catches in that delicate way it does when you realize you're living inside a moment you'll remember forever.

He's going to say it.

"You changed me too, Dante."

He runs a hand through his hair. "Which is why I need to come clean about something."

"Tell me anything, I'm here," I say tentatively, noticing his expression shift from nervous to a face I've never seen on him before. *Guilt? Pain?*

"Back in the summer, after my whole suspension mess, I did something stupid. I brought a reporter onto my yacht to spin the narrative." His jaw tightens with self-loathing. "Thought if I had them there, reporting on my whereabouts, it would pull the attention away from the fact that I wasn't at the Olympics this year.

"*Okay…*" This is not where I thought this was going. I rub my hands along the skirt of my silver gown.

"The reporter was Susan Martin from the *Stone Times*. The one who wrote the first piece about us at the beach."

The revelation hits me. The memory of our perfect beach day floats around in my mind.

"Did you plan on her finding us there?" My voice is suspiciously steady considering the pain that's climbing up my throat.

The smoky haze painting everything in dreamy watercolors, the sweet-tart burst of apricot jam on my tongue, the way his gaze had wrapped around me. The first time I felt like I could break free. All of it had been real to me.

"No, Reese." He frowns. His eyes look desperate. "Susan knew about the redwoods shoot location before I confirmed it. Yes, I confirmed it. Off the record, for what that was worth. And I did that before you walked into my life and turned everything upside down. Before I knew what it felt like to care about someone more than anything."

"Then why didn't you tell me before we started getting to know each other?"

The question I don't have a good answer to. Because I was immature? Because I was afraid? Because I'm just learning how this whole falling in love thing fucking works?

"I had no idea Susan would track us down, and I didn't give it a second thought until I saw the article."

My mind aches trying to piece together his words.

"She only knew about Redwood National Park?"

"That's all I knew about at the time, and after I got off my yacht, I had no other contact with any other reporters," he explains.

"But why hide it?" I wrap my arms around myself. "We watched her, and so many other reporters, tear apart everything I've worked for, and you didn't say anything," I explain. What would it have changed if he had? Goodness. "I invited her to the set." I feel so foolish now.

He hangs his head low. "I was a coward. At first, you

couldn't stand me—rightfully so. Then, when things started changing between us, when I started feeling things I'd never felt before, Felix quit, and you told me this movie was the most important thing. So I wanted to wait for the right time to bring it up."

"Okay," I say because I can't think of a better reply.

I recognize this as one of those rare moments where this level of vulnerability is both terrifying and necessary.

My past relationships, the ruthless media scrutiny, the calculated public appearances have left deep scars that still ache. And though I know with absolute certainty that Dante is different, that what we have transcends my past, there's still that quiet, irrational voice of fear that whispers doubts in the dark corners of my mind.

"The truth is, for the first time in my life, I had something real with you. Something that wasn't about me or public perception. It wasn't about fencing. You made me want to be better. The thought of losing that, losing you, terrified me into silence," he explains. "But I did my best to keep us out of the media after that article. Well, until you needed my help to take down the Felix headlines."

And even then, he risked his entire fencing career to help me with a PR plan that could've easily hurt him.

The bitter irony makes me want to laugh. Or cry. How something that started as mutually beneficial, him training me while I helped him with his lines, turned into a second arrangement to soften his image while simultaneously evolving mine, and grew into something that neither of us saw coming.

Something real.

Something that scared us both with its intensity, like a southern summer afternoon with no shade in sight.

These past four months have changed us in ways I never expected. We've pushed each other, challenged each other, forced each other to confront the faces and names we hide behind, like peeling away layers of old wallpaper to find the original walls underneath.

I fell in love with his walls.

"I think I need some time to wrap my head around this." I fiddle with my hands. "Not because I don't believe in us. God, that's the terrifying part. I believe in us so much it scares me. But right now…" The tears I've been holding back blur my vision. "I would like some space to process everything. Honestly, it's been a long evening. I feel confused and overwhelmed. And I don't know how to fix any of that right now."

Every cell in my body screams to close the distance between us, but I plant my feet firmly on the ground and get out of my chair.

We need space to understand where the headlines end and our real story begins.

"Reese, I l—"

I know exactly what word is about to skip off his lips.

Love.

"Please," I plead. "Don't say it." Tears stream down my face. "Because I do too. And I want nothing more than to fall into your arms and pretend none of this matters. But I'm done playing out my life like it's one of the movies I've spent my entire career shooting."

He reaches out to me, but I step back. "I understand."

"Give my best to your family and Em. Okay?" I roll my lips together. "I'll be in touch. I promise."

Dante's clenching his jaw, his hurt visible, and I hate that. "I'll be here, Reese."

The walk to the elevator feels like the longest journey of my life.

The polished doors reflect us both—two people who found something real in a world full of carefully crafted images. I don't look back. I can't.

Chapter 45
Dante

WHY AM I at a club the week of Christmas?

I should be in New Orleans with Reese, meeting her family. Or at least with my own family. Instead, I'm avoiding everyone who cares about me.

I collide with the bathroom counter. My stomach revolts at the absinthe's bite. Hours of hollow laughter and throwing back shots have scorched my throat raw.

The door slams shut behind me as I stumble into the VIP section. A light flashes. Someone thrusts a phone upward, recording, press badge partially concealed beneath leather, but I recognize predatory eyes.

"Mr. Hastings!" they shout, pushing forward. "Comment about Reese Sinclair?"

The vultures circle. Todd has been rejecting requests all week. *Vogue*, the *Stone Times*, *Vanity Fair*, and *Esquire* are all hungry for my relationship exposé.

Fuck them.

Security moves to eject the reporter, but I raise my hand and choose to nip their questioning in the bud. "No fucking comment."

I rejoin my table, swarmed with strangers. Someone—nameless in my memory—reaches for me. I recoil, nearly toppling a bottle of Dom.

Mei and Tiago are hunched over their phones. Mari shoots me a judgment-laden glance.

Whatever.

It's been two days since Reese asked for space. I understand why. I should've been upfront with her from the start. I know this distance is necessary, but missing out on being with her is a constant ache.

"Everyone having fun?" I pour myself a shot. "It's the holidays. Drink up."

Mari leans forward. "Maybe go easy? You seem—"

My laugh cuts sharp. "What, Mari? Am I not Party Dante enough?"

"Are you for real?" Mari stands, eyes steady with years of seeing through my bullshit.

"Why else are you all here, huh?"

"You act like we're only your friend because of who you are. Did you forget that I was there for your first Nike deal? When you vomited in my car before ESPN? When your suspension hit? I flew to you first." She catches herself, jaw tight, remembering my yacht summer that started this mess. "Don't pretend that you aren't reverting back to the old you because you're fucking hurt."

Was I always this transparent?

The club suffocates me now. "I am fucking hurt, okay? This is the only way I know how to deal with that."

"That's not true." Mari seizes my sleeve, fingers digging into expensive fabric. "Listen to me. Yes, things got messy with the media. But Reese fell for you—the real you. Not the tabloid version, not the highlight reel. She saw past all this shit you hide behind"—she gestures at the VIP section, the bottle service, the hovering paparazzi with their hungry lenses—"to the guy who forgot to perform when he was with her."

"I've never—Mari, I've never felt like this about anyone."

"Drowning in Dom Pérignon won't fix it." Mari squeezes my shoulder. "She needs time to redefine herself beyond the spotlight. Maybe you do too. To be just Dante."

I nod, not trusting myself to speak, feeling the room tilt dangerously. The truth is embarrassingly simple—I'd constructed a persona so meticulously that I'd forgotten how to exist without an audience.

Tiago and Mei chime in, phones ready. "Forget all that, darling," Mei says with a dismissive wave. "What you really need is a better party to get your mind off of all that heartache."

Mari glares at her. "Not now, Mei."

Tiago nods enthusiastically. "That new rooftop on Seventh? Everyone who matters will be there."

The familiar pattern beckons—another night of blurry excess, another headline. The easiest escape.

"No," I say, the word unfamiliar yet firm. "Not tonight." I turn toward Mari. "I'm getting out of here."

I push my way out of the club, nearly tripping over my own feet. Outside, the city pulses around me, indifferent to my small tragedy. The cold air hits my face like a slap, and somewhere in the distance, a camera flashes.

For the first time in years, I let myself be invisible.

It feels like coming up for air after drowning in my own reflection.

Chapter 46
Reese

THE SUN BEATS down beyond the wraparound porch of my family's home. Mama, Cleo, and I are sprawled across weathered rocking chairs, the sweet scent of pansies mingling with the left-over shrimp po' boys on the table.

My phone sits heavy in my lap, Dante's name glowing on the screen.

Cleo slides her lavender sunglasses down her nose, fixing me with a glance she's perfected since we were teens stealing peaches from old Mrs. Dubois's garden down the road when Cleo would visit. "Reese's Pieces, it's Christmas Eve, either text him or throw your phone in the pool, but this whole pretending-you're-not-missing him thing? I can't with you."

"I'm not—" My protest dies as the ancient rocker betrays me with a knowing creak. "Just checking the editing timeline with Amara, that's all."

"Baby girl," Mama says with her infinite patience, "your heart's sitting heavy. Let's talk about it."

I twist a loose thread on my sundress until it threatens to unravel, much like everything else these past few weeks. "What's there to say? Dante kept things from me when things between us were supposed to be simple. Then suddenly they weren't, and now…" I trail off.

Mama's nails tap a gentle rhythm against her glass. Her voice is soft but knowing, like Spanish moss in the breeze. "I saw how that boy looked at you in those photos. Like you were something he couldn't quite believe was real. Not just that, I saw how you were last time you visited. Bright and alive. You gonna let some scummy reporter steal it all away?"

"He knew her, Mama," I whisper. The words that have been echoing in my head all week finally spill out. "And he never told me."

"Never told you what, exactly?" Cleo shifts, arching an expertly threaded brow. Her bikini shows off her gym-sculpted abs. "That cameras might show up? Because, babe, that's literally your Monday through Sunday."

The truth of her words settles over me like the afternoon heat. Dante hadn't called the paparazzi or tipped them off about the beach. Amara confirmed it all after I'd walked away from him that night at the gala. Susan had known about us already.

I'd been discovered the way I always was, the way I probably always will be.

"I know, but some small, insecure part of me is afraid he may have used me," I say, but as the words leave my mouth, they feel wrong. "Like Ricky did. That's definitely my old wounds talking, I know it is, but it was my only other relationship, so I don't have much else to refer to."

"That bastard manipulated you when you were just a child. Lord, don't get me started on him." Mama shakes her head.

I grip my hands tighter in my lap. "I know. I opened up to Dante about Ricky, about all my fears of history repeating itself. And I know that Dante is nothing like him, but it still hurts."

"That's the thing you'll have to forgive, doll," Mama says gently. "When I met your daddy, I lied and told him your Grandpa Fern approved of him. Truth was, Fern didn't like your daddy much—never did tell me why. But then again, my daddy didn't like many people. Our little love story started with a lie too."

"See? Everyone's got their secrets; that's how you figure out who to trust," Cleo drawls, propping herself up. "Show me someone who claims they've never lied, and I'll show you a liar."

"Please. You're, like, pathologically honest," I say with a playful nudge to Cleo's shoulder.

"Oh, honey," Cleo drawls, a familiar mischievous glint in her eye, "there's plenty I don't tell you."

"Like what?" I challenge, leaning forward.

Cleo taps her chin thoughtfully before breaking into a grin. "Like the fact that you were the world's most adorable mess of a first kiss."

"CLEO!" I squeal, throwing a napkin at her. "I had braces! I was fifteen!"

"Just teasing, sweetie pie," she says with a wink. "You've clearly mastered the art since then."

"You are absolutely impossible," I say, but I'm already dissolving into giggles.

"Made you forget about your boy problems for a minute though, didn't I?" She reaches over to squeeze my hand, and I'm reminded why she's been my best friend since forever.

"Sugar," Mama says, "you both did your own wrongs, didn't you? With Felix gone and all that PR you wanted swirling around?"

The weight of truth settles in my bones. Yes, I used Dante. We used each other, really.

"You're right, but that's not exactly the start of a great love story."

"Could be yours." Mama's voice is gentle as she reaches for a chip, the bowl balanced precariously between her knees.

Could be. If I called him right now, he'd drive through the night to be here. And if he called, I'd catch the first flight back to California.

The truth is, after I left the Hastings gala and flew my jet to New Orleans, I saw why Dante did what he did—yes, he messed up. But it wasn't some calculated deception or strategic manipulation, it was a fundamentally human error. Just a man who made the kind of mistake people make when they're trying to protect something they care about.

I've spent years portraying artificial love stories—where romance follows a pristine trajectory, where leading men arrive fully formed and flawless, their histories conveniently blank. I played the girl who gets swept off her feet by Mr. Right, who never does a thing wrong, from the words he says to the job he works.

But they were always just that—roles.

Reality is messier. Nobody wants their heart rattled, their trust tested, their communication messed up, but perhaps that's unrealistic. True intimacy requires this constant negotiation between two imperfect people.

With Dante, everything had felt so natural that I'd forgotten a fundamental truth: even the easiest love needs trials and tending.

"Can you really commit to being with someone when you're still trying to figure out who you are?"

Cleo's laugh is knowing. "Reese's Pieces, none of us know who we are. We're all making it up as we go along."

Mama's eyes hold mine with that steady love that's always felt like home. "I know exactly who you are. Not the Hollywood version—I mean the one who cried at her first movie premiere because she wanted to share it with the whole neighborhood. The one who's never learned how to slow down since she was eleven." Her hand finds mine, squeezing gently. "And I know the woman you've become—kind, determined, fierce in all the right ways."

Something tightens in my throat.

"Life doesn't wait for perfect timing," Mama continues. "Your daddy was fixing cars when I met him. Now he's got people trusting him with their smiles. That's the beauty of finding your person—you get to witness who they become."

I let myself imagine it: cheering for Dante at his next competition, watching him coach young fencers with the patience he gave me. Celebrating another gold medal. Being there for his big moments like he has been there for mine.

And I want him beside me at the premiere, want to tell him about the production company Mari and I have been casually texting about starting all week, want to share Heather's excitement about investing in it. Fighter Films. I want to keep growing together like we have for the past four whirlwind months.

"Has he seen all of you?" Mama asks. "The temper, the scowl, all those pieces you try to hide?"

"Yes."

"Even the stubborn streak?" Cleo arches an eyebrow again.

"He's seen it all," I admit.

What happens if we do decide to be together? Will every shared glance, every casual touch, become fodder for speculation?

Destiny was practically exiled for a year after her scandal. The thought of dragging Dante down with me, of compromising his career, feels like too heavy a burden.

Realization dawns on me. This protective instinct coursing through my veins, this desire to shield him—isn't it exactly what Dante felt when he held back about Susan?

"Then it's for him to decide if you're who he wants to be with, sweet girl. For both of you to figure out together."

Cleo sits up. "Ask yourself one simple question: does he make you feel safe?"

Safe.

The word echoes through me.

"He does," I admit.

Dante never tried to pull me into the spotlight—I was already there. He just stood beside me, steady and sure, letting me shine in my own way.

Before Felix left, Dante would shield me from the cameras. The masquerade, the beach—they were meant to be just for us. He never dominated conversations on set or tried to steal focus like so many of my costars had in the past.

Unlike those who saw me as their chance at image redemption, he wanted to elevate me, support me. Even when the media storm hit, he only did what I asked, never feeding the frenzy.

"You're both right—it's okay to fall in love, be human, and make mistakes and figure things out along the way."

"Yes, darling," Mama says.

"You know," I say, "my Women in Media speech is in two days, and I think I just figured out how I'm going to end it."

Cleo's grin turns mischievous. "Sounds like we need to get our notebooks and pencils out." She bounces up. "That bottle of Sazerac rye still in the kitchen, Mama Sinclair? If we're having any more emotional revelations on my vacation, we're definitely spiking this tea."

Mama's laugh ripples through the humid air. "Now that's the first sensible suggestion I've heard all day."

Chapter 47
Reese

THE LOS ANGELES Convention Center's grand ballroom is all twinkling lights and strategically placed flowers.

The room is packed.

With my hands shaking so much, I've resorted to what can only be described as obsessive dress-smoothing. When Destiny finishes her introduction, I manage to put one foot in front of the other and walk into the spotlight.

Four. Seven. Eight.

I adjust the microphone at the podium and look out toward the sea of gorgeous people.

"Hi, everyone." I keep my back straight. "Heavens, it's surreal being here with all of you incredible women. Our roles in media…" The words stick in my throat like peanut butter. *Come on, get it together.* "They're…they're changing." I force myself to take a breath so deep my ribs protest. "Actually, no—they're not just changing, they're exploding into something entirely new. And no, that wasn't a line fed to me by my publicist, though, Geraldine, you can totally take credit for it."

I wink at my agent and publicist, who are sitting in the audience, dressed in their best winter gowns. Finally, I start to feel myself be more at ease.

"Full disclosure?" I say with a laugh, "I'm really nervous. The nagging voice in my head keeps whispering, *You shouldn't be up here*—which, by the way, is absolutely ridiculous, since we're all talented women who deserve to be in this room. But sometimes I still feel like that ten-year-old girl from New Orleans, wide-eyed and believing that sound stages were made of actual stardust.

"Back then," I say with a wistful smile, "I was so certain about who Reese Sinclair was supposed to be. Or at least, I thought I was. I wanted to be *that* girl. You know the one. The best. The brightest. The one whose name would make people smile and nod knowingly at dinner parties."

The agreeable girl. The one who followed orders. The one who didn't question things, didn't question herself.

"Every time I tried to color outside the lines," I continue, "I felt myself shrinking. It was subtle at first, then suddenly I was practically invisible. I didn't know my womanhood; I was too scared to even dream about producing my own projects or having actual conversations with writers that didn't start with, *I know this might sound crazy, but...*

"And I know I'm not alone in this," I say, scanning the room. "Look around this room with me. Really look. We've all self-censored in one way or another.

"This year, I realized there's no price, no amount of press, and certainly no amount of pleasing people that can make up for losing yourself. And trust me, I lost myself spectacularly in trying to become who everyone expected Reese Sinclair to be.

"But, to no one's surprise, I quickly learned that not only was I already a leading lady but that what I really craved was to lead and eventually give myself a chance to figure out who I am when the cameras stop rolling and there isn't a director in the room.

"So tonight, I want to leave you with this. Taking a chance

on yourself is one of the bravest things you can do. It might not always be easy, and not everyone will understand your journey. Even you might doubt yourself at times. But if there's one thing I've learned, it's that the people worth keeping in your life will never dim your light—they'll help you shine brighter. So be brave enough to embrace what truly matters to you, even when it feels messy or uncertain."

The room takes a collective inhale before erupting. The standing ovation feels less like applause and more like a rebellion, hundreds of women rising up against every *sweetie, good girl,* and *honey* they've ever endured, every creative note that began with *I'm not sure you understand,* every meeting where their voices got lost in the undertow of male confidence. For a moment, we're in every writer's room, every production meeting, every casting call where we learned to make ourselves smaller.

"And oh, one last thing. Please forgive me for my language here, but…" I pause, standing taller and readying myself to say the one thing I've never said out loud: "I'm proud to be Reese fucking Sinclair."

Chapter 48
Dante

The jet landed in Denver last night, the bitter December cold hitting us like a wall as we stepped off the plane. The drive to Colorado Springs was treacherous.

Since that night with Amara at the club eleven days ago, I've cleaned up my act. Stopped drinking, stopped partying, getting back into that competitive mentality. Staying offline, focusing on what matters. Today's hearing with the USFA committee will determine whether I can attend Em's upcoming matches despite my suspension. The stack of proof of my coaching and clean drug tests feels heavy in my briefcase.

Back in California, I'd have known exactly how to play this. The ghost of everything that's left back there—Reese, what we could've had—haunts the edges of my thoughts, but I push it aside. Focus.

My suit feels like a costume, and I'm sweating despite the freezing temperature outside. The committee members sit opposite me, Coach, Todd, and Em—whose absent parents gave her their permission to join us for this hearing—arranging laptops and papers with methodical precision. The USFA headquarters is all glass and concrete against snowcapped peaks.

I'd told the family to stay away; their particular brand of wealthy influence would only complicate things here.

With Em's tournament schedule getting busier and more intense, coaching her through FaceTime calls is no longer enough, especially with college scouts attending upcoming tournaments. She needs in-person guidance and support at her matches.

They're all positioned around me like some protective geometry.

Everything rides on this. Em's shot at something real, and my chance to prove I'm not just another trust fund kid who's pissed it all away.

"Well, well. Mr. Hastings." Committee Head Richard Thompson leans forward, his chair protesting beneath him. Light glints off his wire-rimmed glasses like warning signals. "Five months left of your suspension, and you're pushing boundaries?"

The panel stirs, exchanging meaningful glances.

He continues, "A year, Hastings. That was the deal. Not whenever you feel like staging a dramatic return."

"With respect, sir," I say, "I'm not here to contest the review timeline. I understand those terms stand. But I have a different proposition entirely."

Anna Rusu, legendary Moldavian women's Saber champion, sits to Thompson's left. "We're midseason and two days before New Year's, Mr. Hastings," she says. "And some of us had to reschedule actual training sessions to be here. What exactly are you hoping to achieve?"

I bite back the sarcastic retort dancing on my tongue.

"Look," I explain. "I'm not here asking for forgiveness or trying to score points for my review. These kids—Em, the whole crew from Lev's program—are important to me. All I want is to be there, on the sidelines, watching them grow into the champions I know they can be. The champions I've been training them to become."

Coach surges forward. "Bah! This boy, he practically lives at my gym now. Three, four days a week, sometimes more. The way he coaches these kids…" His weathered hands paint pictures in the air. "Is something special."

Anna's face hardens like steel. "We're not here to do more favors for your pet project, Lev."

Thompson's stare could freeze Hell itself. "Red Bull might sing your praises, but corporate gold won't buy you redemption here. We don't take bribes, Mr. Hastings."

"Of course not," I say, a hint of my old smirk playing at my lips. "Though honestly, you might want to reconsider that policy."

"Mr. Hastings. Since your suspension, your actions tell a clear story—and it's not one of redemption. Instead of showing reform, you've been living it up in Hollywood, grabbing headlines with celebrities and keeping yourself in the spotlight. Sure, there are the clean drug tests and records of your training, but it's not enough to clean up your public image."

The headlines flash through my mind, each one a fresh wound. But I think about what Reese would do now. Her Women in Media speech from four days ago is fresh on my mind.

Just be yourself, be honest.

Be Dante. *Just* Dante.

"You're right," I admit. "After the suspension, I spiraled. Wanted to stay relevant. Keep myself visible. Make those headlines dominate the year's discourse. Classic self-destruction." I pause, running a hand through my hair. "I hurt people. People I gave a shit about. But that's not why we're here." I glance at Em, her presence a reminder of promises I can't break, of the kids in the youth program who need someone to prove that change is possible.

"Here's my offer," I continue, watching Thompson's expression carefully. "Extend my competition suspension for another season. But let me expand the youth program—full-time, pro bono. And let me attend their competitions as their coach."

"Coach, you can't—" Em interjects, but I silence her with a sharp look.

"The U.S. Fencing team proved themselves without me. Took gold, even. But let's be honest here: I'm still one of the best this country's got. If my reputation is too smeared to let me back on the piste, then let these kids benefit from my level of training."

Coach lurches to his feet, chair screeching against the floor. "Madness! You have more medals to take, not throw away your—"

I ignore him and look back at the committee. "You want proof of change? Here it is: my career, my reputation, everything on the line for the betterment of the sport. Besides, where else will you find someone as decorated as me who's willing to work for free?"

The silence weighs more than any medal I've ever worn. This time, I don't flinch.

Em's palm slams against the table. "Look, I'll be the first to admit Dante's an ass—"

"Not now, Em," I growl through gritted teeth.

"*Tiho!*" Coach barks at her.

"Let me finish," Em insists. "Sure, he's got a big ego, and he's insufferably pretentious. But he's also the best damn coach I've ever had. The only coach I've ever had. He doesn't just teach moves; he gets it. Gets what it's like when everyone's waiting for you to crash and burn. Gets what it means to care for someone."

She takes a breath, and I see that familiar fire in her eyes. "Five months ago, I was ready to quit. Now I'm winning competitions I couldn't imagine entering before, and it's all because of this idiot screaming at me over video call, helping me land touches. And it's not just me—there's kids at the gym who couldn't afford private lessons, who'd never held a saber before. Dante works with all of them. Stays late. Comes in early. He cares. Actually cares. Which, trust me, surprised me more than anyone."

The committee members exchange glances, their faces unreadable. Thompson's voice cuts through the tension: "We'll deliberate. Please wait outside."

We walk out of the conference room, and the door closes behind us. The hallway feels like a cage. Coach stalks back and forth, his boots clicking against the tile. Without warning, he whirls on me, face red with fury.

"Another season? Have you lost your mind?"

"Coach, I can explain—" The words die in my throat as he jabs a finger in my face.

"Explain? EXPLAIN? You throw away everything—your career, your future—like yesterday's garbage! For what?"

"We're talking millions in potential deals," Todd says. "You've already turned down the Versace campaign—"

"Because it was contingent on exploiting my relationship with Reese," I cut him off. "Either they want me for my talent, or they don't get me at all. I'm done playing that game."

"Who cares about Versace? Fancy clothes cannot hide empty soul."

Todd scowls at Coach.

I chime in, "They'll never extend my suspension. It's a desperate play, and we all know it."

"Guys, shut up!" Em hisses, pressing her ear to the door. "I can't hear anything!"

Coach swoops over, yanking Em away from her eavesdropping. "Emily!" he thunders. "This is not James Bond movie!"

"I was just—"

"*Nyet! Sit!*" He spins back to me, eyes blazing. "And you—if committee says yes, I will destroy you. Triple—no, quadruple conditioning. No mercy."

I can't help but smile. "Here's hoping I can still afford protein shakes without sponsors."

The joke falls flat, heavy with truth. We all know what's at stake.

My phone buzzes—messages from everyone except the one person I want to hear from. Reese. But how would she know I'm here? I open Mom's text instead.

> MOM
>
> Any news?

> DANTE
>
> Still in limbo.

> MOM
>
> We're proud of you, sweetheart.

After what feels like an eternity, the conference room door creaks open. Thompson's face gives nothing away as he beckons us back in. My stomach drops—I've never felt more aware of how one moment could destroy everything. Em's gnawing her nails raw, Coach's brow is furrowed deep enough to plant crops in, and Todd's worrying his tie.

Once we're seated, Thompson clears his throat. "Mr. Hastings, after careful consideration…" He pauses. The bastard actually pauses. "You will be permitted to coach through your suspension period."

The relief hits like a tidal wave. Em's eyes light up.

"Furthermore," Thompson continues, "we see no reason to extend your competition ban." He holds up a hand as Coach starts to speak. "Your abilities are…exceptional. The sport needs athletes like you. However"—his eyes narrow—"SafeSport protocols remain in effect until the prescribed date. Stay clean, stay quiet, and the disciplinary review should go smoothly."

Coach explodes with joy. "*SLAVA BOGU! MOLODETS!*"

Em launches herself across the room with a shriek of delight, nearly tackling Coach in a hug. "We did it! We actually did it!"

Anna Rusu's sharp voice cuts through the celebration. "Are we clear, Mr. Hastings?"

"Crystal."

Gratitude washes over me, but underneath there's a familiar pull that whispers about celebration. About losing myself in the artificial brightness of downtown Denver, chasing the chemical certainty that used to make everything make sense.

Thirteen days since I last saw Reese, and the urge to obliterate myself with something stronger than winning sits heavy in my chest. Her words loop in my head like a bad song: *I think you can do anything you want.*

I look at Em's face and watch Coach's expression. Something shifts, settles. This isn't about me anymore—or maybe it is, but in a way that matters.

For the first time, I've got something solid to grip onto. Not the hollow promises of bodies or PR or the next big win.

Something real. Something Reese saw in me before I could see it myself.

As we drive back to our hotel, Todd at the wheel, my new troupe singing along to the French house music blaring through our rental car, I take out my phone and start deleting numbers. The ones that represent everything I'm trying to leave behind. They disappear in quick succession: dealers, enablers, all those people who were never people to begin with, just avatars of my worst impulses.

Training starts at 6:00 a.m. tomorrow. Em and the rest of the kids deserve someone who shows up fully present.

LITTLE FIGHTER

Hey Mari told me you're going to be able to go
to Em's meets. Congratulations! Those kids
are so lucky to have you.

Thank you for giving me space. I'd love to talk
in a couple days. Are you free New Years Day?

DANTE

Thank you.

Give me a time and a place and I'll be there.

LITTLE FIGHTER

My house in LA at 1pm?

DANTE

See you then.

Chapter 49
Reese

*R*AP. *Rap. Rap.*

For seven minutes, I've stood in the entryway, fingers tracing absent patterns against my jeans. Two weeks feels like an unfamiliar distance after months of Dante and I orbiting each other daily.

When I open the door, his presence fills the space in that quiet, unshakable way it always does. My breath catches with the subtle hitch of muscle memory. The way a body remembers what it means to want.

Dante.

My Dante.

He stands framed against the golden sky. His dark hair curls at his temples in a way that makes my fingers itch to brush it back. He's wearing a fitted charcoal sweater, sleeves pushed up just enough to reveal the tattooed skin of his forearms. One hand is buried in his jeans pocket, and the fingers of the other are flexing around a small white box.

"Hey." He says it like he's been holding the word on his tongue for days. He hands me the box. "Happy New Year's. I got these for you."

I don't have to look to know what's inside. The scent reaches me first—butter, sugar, something golden-brown and warm. "Mama Jones'," I whisper.

For a second, I'm back up north in the redwoods, sitting on the hood of his car.

"Thank you. These are definitely a treat." I take the box and set it on the credenza in the entryway. "Please, come in." I step aside. "Happy New Year's to you too, by the way. Did you do anything last night?"

"I was with my family, failing at not counting down the hours until seeing you again."

"Me too," I admit.

He crosses the threshold like he belongs here. And maybe he does.

Then Dante Hastings is perched on my sofa, broad shoulders curved forward, hands clasped between his knees. He's staring around at my space while I stare at the pitcher full of iced tea on the coffee table between us. Mama's doilies rest beneath two glasses.

I pour us some tea, but neither of us goes to reach for it as I settle into my armchair across from him.

"How have you been?" I ask softly. "Amara told me that you were petitioning the committee."

"I did. Not to lift my suspension," he explains. "But I needed to be there for Em's matches. Made them an offer they couldn't refuse. I'm her official coach now."

The title suits him. "That makes me so happy to hear."

"Your Women in Media speech was spectacular, no surprise there." He shifts, ringed fingers drawing slow, absentminded circles on his knee.

This is too stiff. Too artificial.

I want to be over there, in his lap, holding him so close that words become unnecessary. I want him to feel how much I still care, how desperately I want us to try again. How much I need us to try.

Be brave, Reese. Say the vulnerable things out loud.

"Thank you for giving me space. I've sort of been able to start to understand where I end and the headlines begin." I pause. "You've helped me realize that I can be both versions of myself. Reese Sinclair and just Reese." The one everyone sees and this quieter, messier person who loves him. Who wants to be both versions. "And that I want my life to be real. I want to be real."

And I want just us, I almost say, but not yet.

"I've been thinking too," he says. "Had a lot of time to reflect on how I've been showing up in the world. When all that shit first happened with Susan, I panicked. Thought I could protect you—protect myself—by keeping everything locked down."

"I understand," I say softly. "I really do. I understand why you did it."

"I should've still given you the respect you deserved and been honest from the start. There were so many fucking opportunities, and yet I was still too afraid." He swallows hard, his Adam's apple bobbing. "Afraid because I've never…" He trails off, the usual confidence in his voice faltering. "I've never had someone worth being honest with. Weak excuse, but there it is."

We've both been guilty of projecting polished versions of ourselves, carefully controlling what others see. It's time to move past that defensiveness and be more authentic with each other.

"We can be honest with each other." I inch forward on the armchair.

"Complete transparency from now on. Magazines and media have been sniffing around for dirt on you, on us, but just know I've turned them all down." He nods. "Every article and press request that comes, you'll know everything first."

There's a path forward.

"We can't go back to using each other either," I say, thinking about how this all started—arrangements and agreements. "No more arrangements or deals."

"Fuck that." He laughs. "I want something real with you, Reese."

"Just us."

"Just Reese and Dante."

The sound of our names together feels like home.

"In the spirit of honesty, I'm a bit terrified," I admit. "I've never done this before—been completely myself with someone. Been in a real, true, adult relationship."

"Me neither, baby." He moves and comes to kneel beside my chair. "I've spent years keeping everyone at arm's length, playing at being some charming bastard because it was easier than letting anyone in. Then you came along and saw right through all my bullshit."

"I like your bullshit," I snort.

"I'm going to earn back every bit of your trust," he promises. "I love you," he says. His painted fingernails graze my thigh. "That's what I want, Reese. I want you."

"I love you too," I whisper.

"We'll probably make a fucking mess of it, but at least we'll be honest about it."

I nod and take his hands in my own. "I'm fucking tired of being flawless anyway."

When he kisses me, it's gentle. Tentative. I think about the strangeness of intimacy, how we've shared so many careful words, and now this. He holds my face between his hands like I'm made of morning light. I could cry from the sweetness of it.

His smell wraps around me. I map my palm up his firm pecs, feeling his heart write its own wild story beneath my fingers.

The kiss deepens, softens, deepens again.

This is what truth feels like in the body. This is what happens when someone sees all your hidden corners and decides to build a home there.

"Want to see what it looks like upstairs?" I ask against his mouth.

"I'd love to."

Each footstep feels like we're ascending into a different version of ourselves. His fingers find the exposed skin at my lower back where my jeans hang low. I wrap my hands around his neck and pull him close. Once we reach my bedroom, my hands move to his jacket, and it drops to the carpeted floor.

When I stumble toward the bed, his hands catch me. Without breaking away from each other, we undress. My sweater and jeans pool on the floor beside his jacket, his shirt abandoned by the bed.

I pull him down on the bed and break our kiss for a brief moment. My body feels pliant and happy to be with him again. Every inch of my skin simmering under his touch.

"You're here, in my room." I laugh, barely believing it. "I really like it."

"I'm not going anywhere," he says with a crooked grin.

His tattoos look softer in this light. I want to trace each one with my fingertips as if they were new to me. Maybe in some way they are new to me again. His hand brushes over my duvet—my favorite one, with the floral pattern—and his ring snags on a loose thread.

We both notice it at the same time and share an awkward laugh that somehow makes everything feel perfect.

"Sorry," he murmurs, fumbling with the sheet. "I'm a bit nervous, I think? I've never…"

"Made love?"

"That."

"Me neither," I say, and the admission feels like another kind of intimacy. "But I like that we can be kinda nervous together."

He touches my face gently, touching his lips to my forehead.

"God, I missed you. Not just…this. But the way you want to be careful about things. The way you make me want to be careful with you."

There's no rush now, no need to count minutes or listen for footsteps. Just us, learning each other again, slowly and completely. I wrap my thighs around him, and my body responds to his in ways as the weight of him nestles between my legs.

"Wait," he says softly. "Protection?"

I shake my head. "Not this time."

"Are you sure? I'm all clear, but—"

"I'm on the pill. It's okay."

He whispers my name against my skin, and I pull him closer, feeling the steady thrum of his heartbeat against mine.

When he pushes inside me, it's so agonizingly slow and gentle. My thighs quiver against his hips.

"Wow, Reese, that's—fucking hell." He shakes his head as if he can't believe how good I feel. I can't believe it either. We instinctively find our rhythm. Our foreheads touch in quiet communion.

His forearms rest on either side of my head, and I plant kisses along them. His arms tremble slightly, and this small human detail makes my heart flutter. Words feel inadequate now. My body speaks for me, arching into his touch, telling him everything I can't say.

When our eyes meet, his are soft with wonder. As if he too is amazed by how seamlessly we fit together. How natural this feels. This isn't like before—not the electric anticipation of first touches or the desperate hunger of reunion. It's quieter. More certain.

This is love.

Chapter 50
Dante

I'VE NEVER FELT anything like this—this overwhelming sense that all of me recognizes all of her so viscerally.

I keep waiting for the familiar disconnection, that sense of watching myself from the outside, but it doesn't come. It never does with her.

Now, I'm terrifyingly present.

I'm just here, with Reese, feeling everything, and it's simultaneously the most frightening and most honest thing I've ever done.

Her thighs tremble against my back as I work in and out of her, and I kiss her neck exactly where I know she likes it. Her sheets are smooth against my skin, and they smell like her— magnolia and cedar mixed together in a way that gets me high every time.

I've never done this. Ever.

Unprotected. Raw. It's always been a fucking risk.

But with Reese. *Fuck.*

This is trust.

Trust that makes her feel like she was made for me. I savor

each push and pull of my cock in her warm pussy. She runs her fingers through my hair, and I let myself look at her properly. Flushed cheeks, toned muscles, and that gorgeous pixie cut.

I could be with her forever, and it still wouldn't be enough time.

I want to be with her forever.

She isn't just part of my future; she *is* my future—complete, irreplaceable, essential.

"I love you." I mutter words I never thought would feel so right before. "I—" Thrust. "Love—" Thrust. "You—" Thrust. "So fucking much," I groan, picking up the pace despite myself. The sound of our bodies meeting fills the room as I take what's mine. She tightens her walls around me, and I have to grit my teeth to keep control.

"I love you too," she breathes, tugging my hair. I let her take control of the kiss, needing her to know how much I want this too.

I run my hands over her ribs, her hip. Fuck, I hope she notices how much she affects me, how each tremor betrays more than desire. It's fear, it's awe, it's knowing I've never felt this exposed before.

"I'm never going to get tired of hearing you say that." I chuckle. My hardness stretches into the deepest parts of her with each thrust. I keep driving into her, feeling her body yield to mine completely. *Fuck.*

"I love you," she whispers. "I love you, Dante Hastings. I love you."

It feels like I'm about to explode, and from the way she's gasping, she's right there with me. The last threads of my control are unraveling, and I don't care anymore.

"Fuck—Reese—" I can barely get the words out. My carefully maintained walls are crumbling, and I'm letting them fall.

My sweat drips onto her skin. I can't think straight anymore

—just need, want, mine. The sounds she's making are driving me crazy, and when I see that same desperate hunger reflecting back in her eyes, I know I'm crossing a line I can never return from.

"I can't wait to feel you come, Dante," she moans. "I love you so much."

That does it. I'm finished.

Reese rides the wave of pleasure with me, her cries mixing with the sounds I'm making as I empty myself deep inside her, her body gripping me tight.

Everything else falls away, and there's just this. The perfect clarity of knowing exactly where I belong.

I collapse on top of her, pressing my lips to her cheek where it's damp with sweat.

We lie there. Neither of us speaks. How strange it is that two people can be this close, can share something so intimate, and still be separate beings with our own unknowable inner worlds. Maybe that's what makes moments like these so precious—their fundamental impossibility.

After a while, she shifts, turning her head to look at me.

I kiss her forehead, and she lets me.

I'm in love.

Steam billows as I emerge from the shower, water rolling down my neck. And there she is, looking at me like I'm the answer to a question she didn't know she was asking.

"What's got you looking so pleased?" I say, walking over like I'm not counting every step, memorizing how her floors feel beneath my feet.

She props herself up, the sheet sliding down to reveal the curve of her shoulder. "It's silly, but you're leaving wet footprints all over my cypress floors," she says. "And I love it. Love that you're here."

I understand completely. It's not about the damn footprints. It's about belonging. About finally letting ourselves have this, properly this time.

I lean down to kiss her shoulder. "Promise me I'm not going to wake up and find out this never happened."

"Not a dream," she whispers, fingers tracing my jaw like she's memorizing every angle.

"Good. Though God knows I've dreamt about this enough. About getting it right. We're doing this again?" The question lingers in my throat, loaded with all our past mistakes.

She sits up fully, letting the sheet pool around her waist. Her eyes meet mine. "We are."

"But better this time. No more hiding when things get scary," I agree, settling beside her. My heart pounds hard. Can she hear it? "No more trying to be what everyone else thinks we should be, either."

She laughs softly. "This is definitely a great way to start a new year."

"It is," I admit quietly. "We've come pretty far, haven't we?" She looks up at me with those brown eyes—full of everything we've built and everything we haven't said yet.

"I think so," she says. "I've actually been thinking that I'm going to start my own production company this year," she says. The words tumble out before she can second-guess herself, but I catch the flicker of doubt, the faintest shadow behind her confidence. "It'll be harder than anything I've done, and if *Robyn Hood* succeeds, I'll be terrified. But in a good way. Like how I feel about us."

"I fucking cannot wait to see what you accomplish." I kiss her. "We'll figure it out, together. Our own way."

"Our way," she whispers, her lips curling into a smile against my jaw.

I chuckle softly, gently stroking her short hair. "You know, you're never going to get rid of me, fighter."

"That's what I was sorta hoping for, Mr. Hastings."

Chapter 51
Dante

"Ramsey, my man," I say, watching him wrestle with the fencing dummy like it's got a personal vendetta against him. He's dragging it down to the gym downstairs as he helps me set up a gym at Reese's LA home, and he's not exactly thrilled about it.

Though, to be fair, I suspect he's never thrilled.

"Why do you need two of these dummies? And for the last time, stop calling me *my man.*"

"If I only brought one, I wouldn't get to see you struggle carrying the second one in." I laugh.

He grumbles, but then I hear the front door open, and I leave him to it. "Thank you! Love you too, Rams!"

When I step into the living room, Reese is standing there like she owns the whole damn world, which she basically does. The phone is pressed to her ear, and she radiates energy that hits me in ways that are illegal in several states.

We've carved out the next three days together—Friday through Sunday are marked in stone. Her meticulous planning used to drive me crazy, but now watching her map everything out for us both gets me fucking hard.

Our lives have merged naturally over these past couple of weeks. My stuff is in her closet, and we both have keys to each other's places. Yet we still guard this time together—time to be just Reese and Dante.

"Frank," she barks, "that timeline is completely unacceptable. I need those contracts revised and on my desk tomorrow morning. Thank you."

The *thank you* comes out like a threat. She's so fucking attractive. I grin like the lovesick idiot I am.

She ends her call with a crisp "We're done here" that sends a tremble down my spine and leaves me yearning to be on the receiving end of her attitude. She sighs, stepping out of her new heels. A crash comes from where I left Ramsey, and a string of curses floats down the hallway.

"Dante, you need to stop terrorizing my security team," Reese says, eyeing Ramsey still battling the fencing dummy in the hallway, but there's this little quirk to her lips that says she loves it.

"But he finds it so fun." I shrug, and we gravitate toward each other. "Come here, fighter."

Her pixie cut is a couple inches longer, grown out in this perfectly rebellious way that makes me itch to comb my fingers through it. She's wearing her pearls, my ring among the gems right where they belong.

"The way you walk should come with a warning label," I say.

"I doubt you've read a warning label in your life." Her eyes dance with mischief.

"Very true." I lean down to kiss her, taking a generous handful of her ass when I do. "I've missed you," I whisper in her mouth, yanking her closer to me. She lets go of CEO mode and melts with a sigh. I kiss her again, deeper this time.

Since we decided to make this thing real on New Year's Day, everything's changed.

Sure, it's only been a month, but we picked up exactly where we left off. What we've figured out is that relationships aren't about control; they're about showing up. Sometimes I catch her typing emails at 3:00 a.m., her face bathed in the cold glow of her laptop screen, and I'm hit with this quiet realization. It reminds me of my parents, passing each other in the kitchen in the mornings, swapping shifts like it was some delicate dance while they juggled their careers.

There's something more meaningful than just being together —it's in those small, unspoken moments of coordination when I know that being with her is the only thing in my life I'll never second guess.

We orbit each other like planets in sync, our paths crossing exactly when they need to. Breakfast meetings that work around my training schedule with the youth program and late-night calls while she's handling events. When she's buried in scripts with Amara, I'm out on the road, watching Em compete in tournaments, moving through life on autopilot while my mind drifts back to her.

But we make it work.

We text constantly.

Inane shit, really.

What I ate. *Protein shake, again.*

Whether the sky's doing that thing where it looks like we're in heaven. *It usually is.*

If a PA finally got her tea order right. *They never do*, and she never complains about it.

Dating someone as driven as me means accepting that sometimes she needs to choose herself more often than she can choose me. The game demands everything too.

So we steal moments where we can.

It works because we both know that the love we have for each other is monumental. Sometimes it means knowing when to push—I'm good at pushing—and when to back off. Still learning that one.

Reluctantly, we break the kiss, and I plant one on her forehead, just because.

"How's my favorite media empress?" I ask.

"Fighter Films is real." Her face lights up. "All signed. All official."

My throat gets tight, which is ridiculous because I'm supposed to be the composed one. "I'm so proud of you it hurts."

"And our prodigy?"

"Destroyed them all." I laugh. "A scout from Columbia tried their New York City bullshit, but she's Princeton material through and through."

Em crushed it in LA with the rest of the youth women's Saber team. They're headed back to San Francisco while I'm here, overnight bag ready, our new normal since Reese and I traded keys last month.

Seventy-two hours, just us. I've started to appreciate her obsessive scheduling, especially since tonight's blocked off for *sword appreciation time*…which sounds both ridiculous and incredibly hot.

"Like coach, like student." When she kisses me, it's all silk and steel and pure Reese. My brain short-circuits. Then she spots the TV, and her eyes narrow. "Is that—"

"Oh, it absolutely fucking is. *Heartland Heritage: Extended Cut*. Baby Reese in rhinestone cowboy boots is better than finding out about Ramsey's secret passion for ballroom dancing." On screen, she's trying so hard to be country, it's physically painful not to laugh.

"Changing all my door codes," she threatens, but she's trying not to smile. "And I'm burning every copy."

"Too late, got my contraband." I grip her hips like they belong in my hands, which they do. "Actually, speaking of contraband…I got you something."

"For me?"

"Anybody else here?" I wink, grabbing the box from my duffel bag by the couch and settling next to her on her couch.

"What is this?" She stares at me, calculating the weight of the box. "Is it a brick?"

"For Fighter Films."

She kisses my nose before placing the box on her lap and undoing the ribbon on it.

Reese gasps when she pulls out the dagger. She unsheathes it with perfect form, and my mouth goes dry.

She tests its weight with this casual authority that makes me want to drop to my knees. "Dante…"

"Found it at an auction back in September. The previous owner was some Greek warrior princess, which I thought was perfect for you."

"You've had this since then?" "It's the most patient I've been about anything in my entire life."

The look she gives me could level cities. Has leveled me, repeatedly. "We have to display it properly."

"Way ahead of you. Got something set up in the bedroom. For protection. And *other* things." The implications make my skin buzz.

Her laugh hits me in the gut. "I love it."

"Yeah?" I'm desperate for her approval. Always will be.

"Yeah. Not only do I love it, but I love you."

"I love you too, baby."

She laughs. "We must be in sync because I also got you something." She walks over to her purse and pulls out a velvet box. My heart actually skips several beats. "Here you go."

Inside is a pearl necklace that matches hers. "For me?"

"Ran into Paulie the other day."

She fastens it around my neck, and the brush of her fingers against my skin sends electricity straight down my spine. The pearls settle tightly against my throat like a collar.

"I think it looks perfect," she breathes, and the heat in her eyes makes me forget my own name, forget everything except the way she's looking at me. "Very Sinclair Hastings."

"Wouldn't want to be anything else." Then she's kissing me, and the world narrows to just this: her mouth on mine, the soft press of her body, the way my hands find her waist like muscle memory. She fits against me with a certainty that feels inevitable.

Our phones chime in unison. The Viggle notification on our screens. Seventy-two hours, blocked off in both our calendars.

No calls, no meetings, no fencing, no scripts.

No world beyond this.

She pulls back just enough to meet my eyes. "You know what that means?"

"Our time begins now," I say, and the smile she gives me is everything I never knew I needed.

"Exactly." The word hangs between us like a benediction. "Lead the way, my lady."

Epilogue
Reese

MAY 31ST

Dante Hastings Back in Action! After Controversial Suspension, Hastings Is Ready to Dominate the International Fencing Stage Next Season

JUNE 28TH

LOVE IN THE AIR: Reese Sinclair Stuns as She Joins Dante Hastings' Big Comeback at the Summer Nationals

JULY 15TH

Robyn Hood Premiere Turns Heads! Reese Sinclair to Grace the Red Carpet, as Early Reviews Hail the Film as "Revolutionary"

. . .

DANTE EXTENDS his arms as I slide the tailored jacket over his shoulders, my hands lingering. We move in tandem, helping each other dress in the hotel suite we booked near the *Robyn Hood* premiere.

Our matching suits are going to look so hot when we walk the red carpet together.

It's been three months since Dante moved his things into my place—boxes of fencing gear and trophies stacked beside designer shoes and scripts. The decision came naturally after his suspension was lifted in May, our schedules suddenly were parallel lines instead of intersecting ones. No more late-night FaceTimes from hotel rooms or weekends spent half-asleep on planes.

We get more time together now. More opportunities to be just us.

Living together means witnessing the small moments—him waking up at 5:00 a.m. for training, the unconscious way he stretches his shoulder when it rains, how he listens to me read through new scripts that have been submitted to Fighter Films for production. I leave notes on the kitchen island for him to read; he leaves apples in my purse. Domesticity that once seemed impossible now feels inevitable.

"Turn," I command playfully, reaching for his cufflinks. "Let me make you presentable."

"So demanding," he murmurs, a smirk playing at his lips as he offers his wrists. My fingers brush against his pulse point as I work with the onyx cufflinks, and his breath catches. "Careful now, or we'll be late."

"Now you," he commands. I spin obediently, and his fingers find the delicate buttons trailing down my corset.

"These buttons are impossible," he grumbles affectionately, though his touch remains sure and steady.

"Says the man who picked this outfit," I tease, glancing over my shoulder.

"Because you're exquisite in it." He slides the matching blazer over my shoulders. "Though you're exquisite in anything."

"Even in your fencing jacket?"

"God, especially that." His lips brush my neck. "But tonight, you have a premiere to grace."

I let out an exaggerated sigh. "Must we?"

I wonder if anyone would actually notice if I didn't show up to my own film premiere. The thought makes me smile.

But of course I have to go. Early reviews are already calling *Robyn Hood* timeless, praising my nuanced portrayal and Amara's masterful direction. Critics are even whispering about award season potential.

The world is about to see just how incredible this film turned out to be.

"Heather, Geraldine, and Ramsey will have my head if I don't deliver you to this premiere on time." He laughs softly. "Now let me see those hands. These rings complete the look."

I turn to face him, watching as he slides each ring onto my fingers with reverent care.

"Beautiful," I whisper, admiring how the silver bands catch the light.

"You always are." His eyes meet mine. "I do know how to showcase my girl."

My heart swells at the possessiveness in his tone.

Dante moves through the world with a quiet understanding of my needs that I find both comforting and unnerving. Sometimes I think about how he knows exactly when to let silence fill the space between us and when to break it. The way he challenges me feels inevitable.

After his suspension concluded, I've had the privilege of seeing him in his prime. At his return match, I watched him reclaim his place on the piste. He moved like he'd never left the sport at all. He demolished his opponent's defenses one by one. When he scored that final point, that defining moment that silenced every critic who'd doubted his return. I had to grip my seat to keep from running onto the piste.

There was something embarrassingly earnest about rearranging my filming schedule to accommodate his next matches, but I did it anyway. We both perform better when we're together.

Dante faces the mirror, and I can't take my eyes off of him. From his perfectly styled dark hair to his immaculate shoes, he's devastating.

We both pretend to hate when people call us a power couple, but maybe we're just afraid of how accurate it feels.

"Like what you see?" He catches me staring.

"Perhaps," I demur. "You do clean up rather well, Mr. Hastings."

"Just well?" His eyebrow arches as he turns to face me.

"You know exactly what you do to me," I say, heat coloring my cheeks.

I tilt my head up, and he kisses me, his mouth gentle against mine. My pulse flutters beneath my skin. Everything about this feels precious. The soft press of his lips, the way we fit together without effort.

The human body remembers things, mine remembers him from that first kiss and how now each touch feels both familiar and thrillingly new.

"God, Reese, I'm never going to tire of doing that," he says with a smile.

"Me neither."

We break apart, and I gather up my essentials before we head out.

Dante sits on the bed, checking his phone, his expression suddenly grave. "Finn's scan results came in."

I pause, anxiety creeping in. Finn, Alec's childhood best friend who's practically another brother to Dante, has been in Mercy General since a devastating climbing accident two weeks ago. "And?"

"The doctors want to try a more aggressive treatment plan to help him recover."

"When we get back to LA, why don't we drive up to Mercy General again?" I offer, remembering how Dante's eldest brother, Alec, had been a shell of himself during our first visit. "I hate seeing your family hurting like this."

"I would love that," he says softly, and I notice the way his voice wavers slightly, though he's trying to stay strong. "Alec needs all of us right now."

"I'll always be here for you," I promise, reaching for his hand. The simple gesture speaks volumes.

"Things might get messy. Got that Nike campaign in Italy. Exhibition match too."

"Funny you mention Italy." I try to hide my smile. "Amara and I were just talking about scouting for the *Thelma & Louise* piece there."

"The one with that writer you keep gushing about?" His smile turns playful, lightening the mood.

"Perhaps," I reply with a coy grin, my heart warming at how well he knows me.

He pulls out his phone, already working through our shared Viggle calendar with those capable hands. "We'll make it happen." The certainty in his voice makes me shiver.

"Private jets and stolen moments?"

"Something like that." He tugs me forward until I'm standing between his legs. When he presses his face against my stomach, I run my fingers through his hair. "Weekend rendezvous in Paris. Midnight walks in Vienna."

"Sounds exhausting," I tease. We both know I'm already planning which weekends I can escape.

"Worth every second, though."

I nod, allowing vulnerability to surface briefly. "Always."

The phone interrupts—our car is waiting.

The truth of the matter is that this is home now—not just our things together, our suitcases carrying both of our possessions, but this space between us. The careful understanding that we're a home together.

"I love you," I say simply.

"I love you," he replies. "Come on, let's show the world why *Robyn Hood* is amazing."

<hr>

THE SCREAMING fans shake the car windows. I trace our initials on the fogged glass, watching the letters disappear. Premiere night always hollows me out. So many films in, and I still feel this way—simultaneously too big and too small for my skin, like I'm wearing someone else's life.

"Four," Dante says quietly, his eyes finding mine. His hand reaches for mine without looking, our fingers finding each other in a way that feels inevitable. We inhale together.

"Seven," I whisper, holding my breath until my lungs ache, counting silently.

"Eight," we exhale as one. It's our private ritual, perfected over the year—something small and ours in this public life where we belong to everyone but ourselves.

He squeezes my fingers once, twice. "Ready?"

"As I'll ever be."

The limo stops. Through tinted windows, camera flashes pulse like lightning across the crimson carpet. My heart beats unreasonably fast.

"One last chance to change your mind," Dante says suddenly. His eyes meet mine, sincere without ornament. "You mentioned wanting your own moment. You can walk this alone."

Of course he remembered that comment from months ago. Dante collects everything I say, stores it away like it matters. Like I matter.

"Are you kidding?" I adjust his tie needlessly, wanting to

touch him, to feel his tattooed skin beneath expensive fabric. "We're doing this together."

His smile breaks across his face, brief but real. "Whatever you want." The words sound simple, but we both know they contain multitudes.

"What I want," I say, barely audible, "is you. Always you. Red carpets are optional."

His golden eyes darken. "Reese—"

Ramsey opens the door before he can finish. We emerge together, a fortress of two. The crowd's volume swells instantly, hungry for us in our suited glory.

"Reese! This way!"

"Dante! Over here!"

His hand finds the small of my back.

"They're losing their minds for you," he murmurs against my neck. "But who could blame them? You're starlight in human form."

"Sometimes I still can't believe this is real," I whisper back.

"Of course it's real. You're the most real thing I know," he admits, and there's something unguarded in his smile that makes my chest ache with tenderness.

We reach the reporters. Questions come at me fast.

"Reese, who are you wearing tonight?"

"Reese, what's your fitness routine?"

"Reese, how do you balance love and work these days?"

Before I can answer, Dante interrupts, his tone conversational but firm. "Maybe ask her about the stunt sequence she performed herself. Or her executive producer credit. Or the film Fighter Films is producing next summer."

The reporters blink, recalibrating.

I smile sweetly. "What he said. Also, Haider Ackermann, I eat whatever I want, and I don't 'balance' anything—I excel in every aspect of my life."

Dante's eyes crinkle at the corners. "She's being modest," he tells the reporter. "She excels because she's extraordinary."

"Stop," I say, feeling heat rise to my cheeks. "You'll ruin my reputation as a hard-ass."

"Never," he promises, and that single word carries years within it—fights and reconciliations, late-night script readings and early morning coffees.

We move through interviews. At the step and repeat, Dante suddenly shuffles back.

"All yours, fighter," he announces, kneeling dramatically. He gestures to the empty space before me. "The world awaits."

I laugh at his display. The photographers capture his devotion and my surprised delight. "You're insane," I whisper, loving him for it.

The crowd cheers as I pose in my suit. His devoted gaze is on me the whole time.

"Insane for you," he smiles back.

As we enter the theater, his fingers lace through mine. He stops walking suddenly and pulls me into a small alcove just before the entrance.

His forehead rests against mine for one euphoric moment before we rejoin the world, our private universe temporarily closed. But it's there, always there, a sanctuary we've built heartbeat by heartbeat.

"I love you, Reese Sinclair," he whispers.

"I love you."

When the lights dim and the film begins, his hand will find mine in the dark. And that will feel better than all the applause in the world.

Acknowledgments

When we started writing On Guard toward the end of last year, our world felt...suspended. As always, we intended to write our signature lighthearted romance, but fate had grander plans—as it usually does when we try to keep things simple.

All our stories pulse with themes that echo our deepest truths, and On Guard carries this tradition. Reese burst onto the page as a force of nature—fierce and unapologetic, yet harboring an achingly human desire to be truly seen. Not as a trophy case of achievements or a canvas for society's expectations, but as the wonderfully complex woman she is. We intimately understand this struggle, having walked the tightrope between professional personas and authentic selves in spaces where depth is often sacrificed for digestible labels. In a world where being a woman can feel like running an endless gauntlet, we've watched too many extraordinary souls get compressed into convenient stereotypes.

"Why are you being so emotional about this?" "You should smile more in meetings." "Sadly, she's no longer a 10." "Are you on your period or something?" "Maybe you should let one of the guys handle the technical stuff." "Such a nasty woman." "Who's watching your kids while you're here?" "You're too aggressive." "Isn't your husband worried about you traveling so much for work?" "You'd be so much prettier if you dressed more feminine." "She was out of her mind."

These aren't just fictional scenarios we pulled from thin air—they're real comments that have made us (and probably you) want to either cry in the bathroom or flip a table. Sometimes both.

Showing up as your authentic self can feel like trying to navigate a maze while everyone's shouting different directions at you. The constant pressure to prove yourself? Exhausting. But you know what's amazing about us women? We keep going. We persist. We thrive.

We love being women. We respect women. We champion women. We absolutely stan women. And we embrace all who identify as women. Full stop.

For too long, we've been told to make ourselves smaller—physically, emotionally, professionally—to fit into spaces that weren't designed for us. But here's my radical suggestion: What if we didn't? What if instead of shrinking, we expanded? What if we took up all the space we deserve? Because let's be real—whether you're "too much" or "not enough," someone's always going to have an opinion. So why not be gloriously, unapologetically yourself?

This is why we created Reese and matched her with Dante—a supportive partner who sees her in all her fierce glory. He steps back when she needs space and steps up when she needs support, letting her navigate life on her own terms. Watching their story unfold has been pure magic. And yes, we need to thank Miles Chamley-Watson for being our fencing muse—thank you for not blocking us despite our slightly enthusiastic social media appreciation!

As always, our entire writing career is held together by the incredible women who stand beside us.

To our editor, Caroline A., your ability to carve our characters out of the clay and make them better people (and, in turn, make us better writers) is something we'll always be grateful for.

Caroline K., working with you has been such a gift. Your patience, thoroughness, and expertise mean the world.

To our wonderful proofreader, Christine Yates, and our

amazing beta team Brooke, Isabella F., Juliette Sanpere Godard, Kelly Caroline, Logan, Kathy Hutchinson, Nicole McCrane and Tabitha, we adore you more than we could ever express.

To the Stone Romantics over on Patreon, your enthusiasm for our characters and our stories and your overall support, fuel us more than you know.

And to our readers, Thank you. Every post, share, message, and purchase keeps this dream alive. We started as two corporate gals with a big idea, and because of you, that idea has become our everyday reality. Your love for these stories lets us do what we love most, and for that, we are endlessly grateful.

Playlist

"End Game" by Taylor Swift, Ed Sheeran, Future
"Bubblin" by Anderson.Paak
"That Don't Impress Me Much" by Shania Twain
"Carolina" by Harry Styles
"man at the garden" by Kendrick Lamar
"AMOUR PLASTIQUE - TECHNO" by BASSTON, STROBE
"I Bet You Look Good On The Dance Floor" by Arctic Monkeys
"Long Way 2 Go" by Cassie
"What It Is (Block Boy)" by Doechii, Kodak Black
"The Hills" by The Weeknd
"Partition" by Beyonce
"Toxic Pony" by ALTEGO, Britney Spears, Ginuwine
"Bleed (feat. Omar Apollo) " by Malcolm Todd, Omar Apollo
"Not My Responsibility" by Billie Eilish
"Delicate" by Taylor Swift
"Nobody" by Hozier

About the Authors

Kels & Denise are authors, best friends, and the definition of the found family trope. The pair bonded over their love for romance and turned all their late-night chats into writing together. Their enjoyment for storytelling morphed into writing impactful love stories.

Stay in touch!
@authorkelsdenisestone
kelsdenisestone.com

Join our newsletter *The Sticky Note*
kelsdenisestone.com/the-sticky-note
Join our Patreon for exclusive content

Also By Kels & Denise Stone

<u>**The Hastings Series:**</u>

A collection of interconnected standalone sports romances about the Hastings siblings, scions of sports royalty.

Close Knit

Grumpy x Sunshine Romance

On Guard

Bad Boy X Good Girl Romance

Highest Point

A Sports Romance

<u>**Perks & Benefits Series:**</u>

A collection of interconnected standalone romances about people navigating their careers and falling in love.

Water Under the Bridge

Workplace Romance

Our Scorching Summer

Friends to Lovers Romance

On Cloud Nine

Fake Dating Romance

Falling for Meadow

Small Town Romance